HURT RUNS WITHIN

ZOLTAN VINCZE

The Book Guild Ltd

First published in Great Britain in 2024 by
The Book Guild Ltd
Unit E2 Airfield Business Park,
Harrison Road, Market Harborough,
Leicestershire. LE16 7UL
Tel: 0116 2792299
www.bookguild.co.uk
Email: info@bookguild.co.uk
Twitter: @bookguild

Copyright © 2024 Zoltan Vincze

The right of Zoltan Vincze to be identified as the author of this
work has been asserted by them in accordance with the
Copyright, Design and Patents Act 1988.

All rights reserved. No part of this publication may be
reproduced, transmitted, or stored in a retrieval system, in any form or by any means,
without permission in writing from the publisher, nor be otherwise circulated in
any form of binding or cover other than that in which it is published and without
a similar condition being imposed on the subsequent purchaser.

This work is entirely fictitious and bears no resemblance to any persons living or dead.

Typeset in 11pt Minion Pro

Printed on FSC accredited paper
Printed and bound in Great Britain by 4edge Limited

ISBN 978 1915853 967

British Library Cataloguing in Publication Data.
A catalogue record for this book is available from the British Library.

To any soldier who has fought for their country. For their families who have somehow been affected. For those who returned home and have struggled. For those who got back on their feet, and for those, who behind personal barriers, couldn't.

ONE

ORIGIN

> 0845hrs
> Tuesday May 15, 2012
> Mirabad Valley, Afghanistan. AKA The Badlands

Dying by a roadside bomb is a pretty savage way to go. If the blast doesn't take you, the metal inside the device will maggot your limbs, face and organs leaving you either maimed, disabled or disfigured. It's a deadly, awful trait left in the wake of a frustrated enemy. Why wouldn't they set them up and lay them across their homeland? Surprises are good for the enemy. Keeps them up at night. Keeps them guessing and cautious, and hopefully, afraid.

As a corporal in the transport arm of the British military, Mackay usually got priority of music selection on operations. Being Irish, Mackay was biased for a pub ballad. Celtic and folky. Harmonising violins, a quick tempo and a strong beat. He also favoured the Stones and old school rhythm and blues. Mackay can't recall exactly which song by which artist was playing when the IED went off, and none of his team were left alive to confirm either. It wasn't the noise of the blast he remembers when his patrol vehicle was hit. Rather, it was the distinct twang of a blues guitar humming through the speakers. A memory often played loudly on a loop. He would much prefer to remember the song than see the repeated images of his lifeless mates inside his head. That's the problem with traumatic experiences. Some parts of the brain shut down and filter things out, while other parts retain certain elements you would rather forget.

Dealing with an IED while stuck in a combat zone is nobody's idea of fun. Not knowing whether you're going to bleed out sends mixed emotions through your system. The adrenal gland regulators shoot rocketing levels of cortisol through the body, flooding it as it tries to maintain optimal blood flow to your major organs. Best thing to do is to not think about it and focus on staying awake. Once the medevac helicopter arrives and hauls you out of the hole you're in, your life is in the medic's hands. The more you think about it, the more cortisol gets dumped. Even if the body is maggotted, all it has to do is try and survive. It's the mind that hurts the most. The regret of losing friends. The guilt. The mind always takes on the greater suffering.

On that particular day, with that particular playlist, the operation was a convoy-escort-task. The packet of five vehicles included two Bushmasters and three Unimogs, spread out to transport two Danish diplomatic personnel. Military officials moving from Kandahar to Uruzgan through the Mirabad Valley. The "Badlands". Typically, through this route, the "Badlands" got its name because of the extreme temperatures, rugged terrain, lack of water and regularity of insurgent attacks. Not to mention the dozens of IEDs dug into the road. The diplomats were both seated inside the Bushmaster in fourth position. Second last in the packet. The task was simple: deliver the Danish diplomatic assets from Kandahar to Uruzgan. Maintain speed, maintain a staggered line, maintain surveillance points, and don't stop for locals. Apply warfare training in real-time should enemy contact occur, and report observation checks every ten minutes.

En route back to Uruzgan, communication chatter was quiet. All battle management systems came up clear with nil perceived insurgent threats. There was no motion or movement detected anywhere in the area. Whether the enemy is known to be within a designated area or not didn't really matter. Because some time prior, they had been there. Planting bombs into the ground just below the surface.

The two IEDs that hit Mackay's convoy took three lives: one soldier in the front vehicle, and two in Mackay's. Mackay was barely lucky enough to survive and wouldn't have had it not been for the tactical vest with its thick ballistics plate stashed under his seat. Plus, the swift actions of Hillan, an operator who jumped straight onto communications as soon as they were hit. Mackay simply reacted out of instinct. A balk effect. Although he was driving with an appropriate distance behind the front vehicle, his reaction to the blast was natural. He flinched and jolted. Any man would have done the same. Watching a blast that close and keeping your cool when everyone around you is tenser than a compact grenade, is tough going. Not knowing whether the enemy has fired a rocket or whether your friends are alive creates a cacophony of blood and adrenalin.

In his reaction to the initial blast, Mackay swerved his Unimog hard left. Careening the vehicle and diverting it onto the roadside, over the verge where his front tyre hit a second IED. Which hit bigger than the first, tearing shreds out of the vehicle and making it almost unrecognisable. Mackay's operator, Theckston, and his gunner, Freeman, were both taken out with scoring metal immediately. The fragments penetrating them through the glass windows, underneath the subframe and through the roof lining of the cupola. The Danish diplomats in the fourth vehicle were unaffected. At the front of the convoy, the armoured Bushmaster was still functioning, but the blast killed their gunner, Kirwan. The one standing up inside the cupola with an F89 machine gun. Two pieces of shrapnel claimed his life. The first piece took his left ear and the scalp surrounding it. The second piece – a rusted bolt – spat up and pierced the front of his neck through the trachea. Unsuspecting and brutal. The Taliban put all kinds of random metal fragments in their bombs, and if it didn't kill the poor soldier who copped it, it would maim them for life.

Because of two loose bolts from the driver's side suspension mounting, the blast from the IED fractured the entire assembly underneath Mackay's feet. The ferocity of the explosion cracked open the cylinder head inside, splitting the metal structure into two shards. One half of the shard penetrated the coilover, cut through the mounting bracket and shot up into the driver's firewall. Narrowly missing Mackay's left foot but piercing directly into his left ribcage. The other half did the same thing, only two feet to the right; cutting through the mounting bracket, up through the firewall, stabbing through his right ribcage. Trapping Mackay evenly into his seat like an insect on a pinboard.

Seven of the twelve paired cartilages on both sides of his ribcage ruptured completely. Front to back, bottom to top. Fourteen organ-protecting sections gone. The bottom three pairs of false-ribs and proceeding four pairs of true-ribs were crushed. Breached and replaced with the metal, separating like a block of Kit Kat. The fibres around his intercostals between each rib were also minced. A blend of bone, cartilage, and muscle. It was a miracle his lungs weren't pierced from either the shards of ribs themselves, or the metal from the cylinder. Luckily the extra fragments of exploded metal were caught in the tactical vest fitted under Mackay's seat. The ballistic plate housed inside was spattered with chunks of nuts, bolts and random steel, saving his life, leaving the rest of his body largely unaffected.

> 0930hrs
> Tuesday May 15, 2012
> Mirabad Valley, Afghanistan

At six-foot-one and eighty-eight kilos dry before being torn apart, the seven litres of blood expelled from Mackay's torso reduced him to a weak eighty-one. Mostly left pooled inside the Unimog and the medevac chopper. The Sikorsky HH60 Black Hawk took twenty minutes to arrive, then removing Mackay from the Unimog took a further ten minutes before he was on the ground on a stretcher. Fortunately, the two shards of metal spiked through his sides missed his lungs and major organs. Because it pinned him into his seat, the split cylinder basically held him together. The pressure of the compressed metal kept control of the blood that normally would have been lost. Still, he was trapped in the vehicle with the pain. Having to endure it. Unsure if he would bleed out slow and die or bleed out slow and live. Stabilising Mackay with the shard still in place was the hard part. Keeping the metal intact and supported so it didn't move around was crucial, otherwise blood loss would increase.

Inside the trauma bay, IV fluids were hung, equipment was checked, and body bags were prepped. The bodies of Kirwan, Theckston and Freeman would be sent home to RAF Brize Norton in Oxfordshire, while Mackay's body would be stripped back and worked on. The captain, and head surgeon, had called in the trauma and cardiothoracic unit for the mass mutilation that was Mackay's ribcage. He also called the burns and plastic surgery teams to manage what bits of muscle and skin they could take from one section, then move it to the torso to cover another. The captain's immediate concern, however, was

Mackay's pain. Using a stimulator delivering a weak electronic pulse, the captain was able to locate the nerves around Mackay's spinal column and eliminate it at the source. Blocking off the pain signals through his torso. Enough relief so the initial surgical procedures could begin. Fixing Mackay was going to be difficult. The surgeons had all seen their share of heavy trauma; severed limbs and appendages, sliced arteries, shattered skull plates and crushed organs, but this was different. His ribs from top to bottom were basically mush, with all the in-between fibres shredded like coleslaw.

The compound required to patch Mackay, however, was new. A synthetic compound which mimicked human bone and cartilage. A technologically advanced hardened gel capable of expanding with impact. Not unlike what they use in elite endurance running shoes, capable of moulding and setting firm into the bone it attached to. The nature of the substance was made specifically for trauma victims just like Mackay. Ideal for those requiring extensive bone, joint and cartilage replacements for limb mobility. This particular compound, a military-grade thermoplastic, had only ever been, and would only ever be used on defence personnel. For soldiers injured on the battlefield. If you were an unfortunate soul who'd been hit with heavy fire or struck with blast fragments, the surgical teams gave you preferential treatment. Patching you up with the thermoplastic. An organic 'super-fibre' incorporating a mixture of ballistic-grade Kevlar and spectra-shield commonly found in bulletproof vests. At its core, it was a pressurised polymer containing a number of different elements and properties: silicone, oxygen, carbon and hydrogen. Constructed inside British military labs, the groundbreaking process preserved and maintained human life. With its synthetic polymer combination, the super-fibre could absorb micro levels of gas through thin internal layers called bubble-walls which also filtered toxins and carbon dioxide. It was softer than human bone, could mould into any shape and had complete flexion in any direction. Harder than silicone, yet softer than most rubbers or polyurethane. In its fused state, it would never burst or weep and was able to bounce back and remould itself following any force or trauma. Its compression capabilities were elastic by design, and potentially, if bonded inside an infant or adolescent, it would stretch as their body grew with it. The body would never reject it, but it did need time to settle in, so immunosuppressants were required. It would never degrade or age, and by all current tests, would outlast its host like most metals. In any case, it offered the patient a comfortable, lifetime insert. Being a human 'aftermarket upgrade', it replaced exactly what the body once had and made it better. And Mackay was the first test subject to have it fused inside him.

> 1000hrs
> Tuesday May 15, 2012
> Kandahar Combat Hospital, Trauma Unit

Because of Mackay's low body fat percentage, the surgeons didn't need to cut into large amounts of fat. They didn't need to peel away excess layers of skin, or labour with adjusting any form of heft. Warfighters weren't made like that. Grafting the compound successfully to Mackay's damaged ribs, however, was not a straightforward operation. Normally it took two hours per pair of ribs. Broken end to broken end. Flushing away the shards of debris left inside his body was the hardest part, but it was easier than picking out specks of shrapnel. The med team needed to remove all the crushed bits first, then the thermoplastic compound went in, replacing all anterior and posterior ribs. Next, they sewed and reattached the intercostals and serratus, and lastly, both entrance and exit wounds needed to be closed – a further six hours. Which made it a twenty-hour operation in total.

Fusing the super-fibres onto the broken ends of Mackay's ribcage was the easiest part. The compound was malleable and sticky, and had been precisely engineered to bind to human bone like superglue. Once the end points of the thermoplastic have initial contact with bone, the process of fusion starts immediately – solidifying around the cartilage. And like osmosis, it merges oxygen, carbon and hydrogen within the existing structure. Post-fusion, it breaks down to a molecular level, into the marrow. Into the nitty gritty. Once it reaches the marrow, the compound's journey is complete. Becoming part of the host's genetic make-up. After twenty hours asleep on the table, Mackay had six months of rehab to look forward to.

Mackay was no Commando, Green Beret, or any other variation of the Special Forces. He was a corporal. A two-hook soldier. A senior member of the unit one rung down from sergeant. He'd seen some killing and had done some killing. He loved rugby and was a decent grease monkey under the hood of a car. His dream was always to play rugby for his home country of Ireland, but plan-B seemed to work out as a soldier. The silver lining; being picked for the British Army's 1st XV Rugby team. A combined-services team taking the best of the best from the Army, Navy and Air Force. As a right-wing, he was the fastest player on the team. An all-round athlete with a genetic edge in his legs. Mackay's quads were huge, overshadowing his upper body like the hinds of a gazelle. In the real world, he was just another fit grunt with a good work ethic. At least, that was until he was medically discharged. Since then, life became a chore. Everything felt unnatural. Living didn't excite him anymore and his anxiety from the onset of PTSD was through the roof. Sleep was never peaceful. His body may have stopped moving, but his mind was like a train without brakes. Often in some dark place behind the subconscious. A stormy mess of demons and false truths. Life didn't make sense anymore. In the shadowy recesses of his mind,

Mackay often thought about walking outside and getting run over by a bus. Or praying for a plane overhead to dive into the roof above him. Being stuck inside his brother's home in Guildford was the pits. It kept him angry. Aside from his fantasies of death, Mackay inherently preferred to have died along with his team inside his truck, or at the very least, wished he was back in the sandbox in Afghanistan, sucking in the dry brown air like a lizard.

> 1630hrs
> Saturday December 08, 2012
> Adelaide Terrace, Perth, Western Australia

On the other side of the world, Nicus Van Breeman stood in his high-rise apartment overlooking the swan river in Perth, Western Australia. He'd just shaken hands with his first client of the day. Likely his only client of the day. An older man with a briefcase full of cash. The apartment, which doubled as Van Breeman's office, was on the forty-seventh floor and had a beautiful, part wooden, part tinted-glass door built as its entry. The kind of tint that allowed you to see outside if you're standing in, but not inside if you're standing out. A custom job. It was heavy and thick, operated with a six-digit code from the outside and a traditional deadbolt from the inside.

Van Breeman ushered the man over to his executive desk. A magnificent antique item he had shipped over in a sea container from his hometown in Johannesburg. Stained to a dark cinnamon from before the great war. Van Breeman sat down in the big executive chair while the client sat opposite in a basic office swivel made of mesh and plastic. He faced an acetate plaque with Van Breeman's name engraved into it. Both men were dressed to the teeth. Thousand-dollar suits, thousand-dollar watches and shoes. The client crossed his legs close and tight, thigh over thigh. He was thin, so he could. It made his pants ride up from the ankle, exposing a pair of blue woollen socks in a chequered argyle pattern.

Van Breeman did not cross his legs. He couldn't do it comfortably. He was taller and broader than his client, but not in an overweight sense. His thicker thighs came from riding horses. All that galloping and straddling meant the extra muscle created too much congestion in the crotch. Built over time on his father's vineyard. The old wine country of Franschhoek on the outskirts of Johannesburg. Where he would oversee the mostly black staff who picked grapes at their peak for harvesting. Sometimes he rode with a whip, sometimes he rode with a shotgun. Sometimes both.

Van Breeman was a wine maker by trade, and now lived in Perth. He still specialised in wine exporting, and even considered himself a world-class connoisseur, but it was his side business where his self-made empire was built from. As an entrepreneur, he was proud of what he had achieved. Making it big all on his own without the backing or entitlements from his father. His offshoot business, away from the nine-to-five of managing wine exports, was very lucrative. The only downside was that his clients were rare, which made the business a tough venture. But the world was a strange place and even the most niche requirements for a niche clientele needed to be addressed. Needed to be met and resourced. These clients were 'one of a kind' types which made them hard to come by. There could be absolutely no evidence that might jeopardise either the client's, or Van Breeman's professional means. There were rules. All client names needed to be fake. During every initial phone conversation to set up the cash deal, Van Breeman required the client to state a bogus title. He gave the potential investor on the other end of the line ten seconds to think of one, otherwise the deal was off, and they'd never meet. Each hard-found, wealthy customer was also given assurances their false name would never accidentally slip through the wires. No gossip or chatter would ever be punched into any keypad on any kind of device, reaching any airwaves, cyberspace or digital cloud. These were the guarantees Van Breeman made in exchange for big money via the Dark Web – the underground smorgasbord of filth.

His little gold mine had had its ups and downs. It moved and shook like any first-time business trying to hustle amongst the big boys. Five years in, it was a well-oiled machine. For that to continue, he needed to pay top dollar for optimal anonymity and secrecy. Human resources cost, and to keep things secure, quiet, and intimidating, he paid top dollar for the best crew. All ex-cons, ex-military guys and heavy-hitting standover men. Top dogs under the head of the snake. All paid exceptionally well. And used often if a client decided not to show for an exchange. Which meant they'd backed out of a deal and had invalidated the set rules and parameters. Which also meant due processes needed to be followed up. Because in Van Breeman's eyes, nobody backed out of a deal. And if they tried, his well-paid top dogs made a visit. Usually with a Glock or a Magnum. Or piano wire, a couple of handsaws and maybe a woodchipper. Sometimes with a few barrels of hydrofluoric acid to remove all traces of flesh. Clothes can be burnt away, but burnt flesh still leaves DNA residue. All without sympathy and empathy, and no room for justification. Van Breeman's terms, his way.

TWO

ANGER

1630hrs
Saturday December 08, 2012.
Mackay's Unit. Guildford, United Kingdom

6 MONTHS POST-SURGERY

The dragging time sitting on the sofa inside Mackay's cookie-cutter home, in the cookie-cutter block of flats did nothing but sharpen his pain. Mackay gazed through the television, staring a hole in the wall behind it. Some run-of-the-mill, late afternoon cooking show was playing but his mind was vacant. Something else was in his head, moving like a cork in the surf. His hair stood in unruly tousled bunches and his upper lip gleamed with sweat. He found himself grinding his teeth and clenching his jaw – the small muscle mounds bunching at the sides. His anxiety was flaring but he couldn't pinpoint exactly why. He ran his fingernails through his hair. Hard. Over the skin of the scalp, opening the tiny little blood vessels beneath the surface, on the cusp of drawing blood. Back and forth like a grater releasing the tension. A quiet pleasure just enough to take his mind off his life, or lack thereof.

It had been at least four days since Mackay last showered and shaved. Which in effect made him look like a sullied inpatient at a care home. A week earlier he'd finally been given the okay to ditch the wheelchair he'd been using from his physiotherapist, which, for the most part was a huge relief. One step closer to independence. It meant he could now get around with just a single crutch braced under one arm, relieving the pressure from his ribcage. It was slower than the wheelchair but overall, it helped strengthen everything else. Readying his body for walking upright and unaided. Soon anyway. On the same day he ditched the chair, Malvin had bought him a homecoming present. An old-timer's gift. A cane. Finished in dark walnut with a cast handle crafted into a Viking's face. A Nordic god-like figure like Odin or Thor, complete with a metallic winged helmet. It was beautiful.

Not much of him felt right at all. Day or night the world outside seemed like it was caving in. Pressing down like gravity solidified. While half feeling sorry for himself, half wishing he was among the stars, he failed to notice his phone ringing. And ringing. Until it stopped. Only the chime notification from the voice message woke him from his dreariness. Picking up the phone, he listened. Out of boredom mostly. Hopeful something better than his planned dinner of blanched asparagus, steak and mash would lighten his evening. Two familiar voices crowed in his ear. Spritely and lathered with a hint of forced enthusiasm. Doing their best to try and liven things up. Mackay checked his watch; an old black analogue G-Shock. Military standard the world over. The familiar voices were coming over in five. Guildford locals. Warfighting brothers from way back.

'Alright then,' Mackay muttered. He grabbed his cane from against the sofa, braced himself to his feet and hobbled down the hall to unlock the door.

> 1700hrs
> Saturday December 08, 2012
> The Farmer's Arms Hotel, Guildford

Mackay really didn't feel like being there, but the Farmer's Arms was an old familiar hang with good beer. Plus, it was on doctor's orders to go out and meet people. Which admittedly, was a lie, and was actually just his brother's encouragement.

'Stay social,' Malvin had said. And more than once. 'Go out and meet people.'

The pub wasn't buzzing with life, but it wasn't dead either. It did its best to welcome families into a refurbished beer garden which doubled as a Mexican-themed family restaurant. Complete with a sombrero jumping castle and spring-coiled piñatas for the kids. It was approaching dinner time and Mackay sat in the back corner of the restaurant opposite the kids play area, staring at his half-empty pint. Chris and Luke held the conversation, catching up and drowning beers left and right. Extensively throughout the wider soldier community they were affectionately known as Cabbage and Bowser. Luke's family were farmers who grew cabbage, while Chris's name referred to his family business; a small number of gas-station franchises throughout southern England. Mackay also had a moniker, though his was a little more war related. To be fair, it was entirely war related. A whole different kettle of fish to the origin of Luke's and Chris's...

*

During his first week into deployment, Mackay's unit was sent on a task with the armoured corps: deliver rations and an armoured tank to allied Afghan soldiers camped in a compound for familiarisation training. Mackay's team ended up locked in enemy contact. Rounds were pelting down from a row of urban buildings raised across an intersection to their left. Mackay's Land Rover was flanked by a small, but well-supplied section of Taliban rebels. What the rebels couldn't see was their tank, hidden behind a shopfront, waiting to spring out like a jack-in-the-box. By the time the enemy identified the tank, it was too late. The tank operator had already locked onto their building and ripped it apart. Consequently, a suicide bomber was sent out. A lone Taliban on horseback, prepared for martyrdom and his seventy-two virgins. Allah's gift for those who die waging jihad. The horse beelined straight for Mackay's Rover with a hundred yards of distance diminishing quickly. Mackay had one option: put it down. In the heat of the moment, given it was his first week, Mackay was so flustered, he completely forgot about hitting the rider. His archaic brain took over. Instead of blowing the rider away, Mackay opted for the bigger target and lit up the steed. Automatic burst until the animal dropped. Both horse and rider exploded in sync, forty yards out. The heat of the blast was close enough to peel layers of paint off the Land Rover. Animal welfare groups would have been mortified – Mackay turned the horse into dog meat. A cloud of leather, hair, and flesh. Subsequently, Horse-Killer became Mackay's term of endearment, and stuck for all three of his deployments.

*

The Mexican-themed beer garden was scattered with people young and old. Varied wealth and class. The Saturday afternoon flock of trendy humans letting their hair down had started to swell, slowly building into a babbling pit of sweat, salsa, perfume, and tattoo ink. Some were dressed up, some dressed down. Mackay was tucked into a square table near the back, next to the playpen for kids. Which was empty aside from a small Asian toddler left crawling around a blow-up sombrero. Mackay sat to the left of Luke, while Chris sat opposite, chatting away over a tiny partition of salt and pepper shakers, a fake cactus and a bottle of token hot sauce. The fourth chair at the table was empty, which had Mackay's Viking cane propped up against it. He made a conscious effort to sip the fermented yeast and hops, thankful that the alcohol helped loosen the invisible reigns bearing over him. The numbing effect allowed his neck and shoulders to ease and slowed his thought processes down just a little. Even when his mind meandered off, the flashbacks stayed away. He contemplated whether he should have another pint. Or whether he should start on spirits next.

Mackay's eyes shot from Chris to Luke, then back again. Like a rally at Wimbledon. They'd been out of the military for three years now and it was a strange concept trying to understand how they were able to fit back into mainstream society so easily. He wished he could be like them and unbury himself, he just didn't know how.

'Wouldn't have mattered if Luke was Mother Teresa,' said Chris. 'He interrupted a woman trying to get laid. Her reaction was a given.'

'She called me everything under the sun,' said Luke. 'She sounded just like Sergeant Cross from the boxing gym. Way too much influence.'

Chris said, 'Mackay, you'd know Sergeant Cross, yea? The redhead from Aldershot?'

Mackay focused. The various sections of cognitive synapses searched the name.

'From the Army rehab centre at the base?' said Chris. 'She runs the boxing classes there. Pretty amazing if you ask me. No legs and all. They let her do her own thing, like a form of gratitude for her service to the country. She's not a serving member now of course, finished her rank at sergeant after the IED took her legs. A good boxer in her prime. Won both the Women's British Lightweight and European Lightweight Championships around four or five years ago.'

Mackay's mind finally completed the search and joined the party. 'Sorry, I don't know Sergeant Cross. I walk with a stick. What would I be doing taking a boxing class?'

'I'm not saying you'd be participating in the class,' said Chris, 'I'm just asking if you've seen her about. You should check her out, have a chat about your similar experiences. Both being hit with IEDs before being medically discharged and all. Foulest mouth I've ever heard on a human.'

Luke said, 'You do go to Aldershot Garrison for rehab, yea?'

'Yes.'

'Cross runs her boxing classes right there. It's part of the gym next to the rehab clinic. She also runs her old engineering unit's fitness classes as an acting physical training instructor, but it's easier to find her at the main gym.'

'Never seen her,' said Mackay.

'Never?' said Luke. 'Shame. Good-looking redhead in a wheelchair with a voice like a fucking drill sergeant.'

Chris said, 'Can hear it echo through the entire gym's corridors. Like a white Aretha Franklin on crack cocaine.'

'She'd have to be diagnosed borderline crazy,' said Chris.

'We're all crazy,' said Mackay.

'I like her version of crazy,' said Luke. 'She says it as it comes naturally. Totally unfiltered. Sometimes it's a breath of fresh air, sometimes it's outright nasty. She can get away with it too, nobody's going to come down on an ex-sergeant boxing instructor with no legs.'

'And she's fit,' said Chris. 'I'd shag her as is without the legs. You should seriously have a chat with her, Mackay, next time you're there for physio.'

'You two would definitely have a lot in common,' said Luke. 'A lot of your deep and meaningful shit could be opened up, bounced back and forth. You could listen to someone else's perspective. Another person's wisdom and experience with… can I say it?'

Mackay's back stiffened. 'With what?' he said.

'You know,' said Luke, 'all that PTSD stuff. Would be a good idea to…'

'To shag her? For shits and giggles?' spat Mackay. 'To say I've had me a veteran with no legs? Fuck off. I don't need to be matched up with another cripple just to get some release.'

'No man, ease up,' said Chris. 'To go talk to her. Proper talking like. To share stories, get things off your chest. Would do you good.'

'A worthwhile option at least,' said Luke. 'You've been stuck in your brother's apartment for months now, doing fuck all. I understand it must be hard. Really. But being a sad loner isn't you. I know you know this. You're stuck in a rut, but the whole post-traumatic stress thing…'

'What about it?' said Mackay.

'There's help out there,' said Luke. 'And Cross is a good start. She works close to your rehab. You've both been medically discharged and have lost mates in the desert.'

'And if not her, then go and see the Four Armoured Medical Regiment,' said Chris. 'I know for a fact they have PTSD groups for Veterans.'

'Not going there,' said Mackay.

Mackay stayed quiet, staring at his glass.

'I don't know how much help we can be,' said Luke. 'I mean, we were all out there sucking dirt, but I didn't see any real action like you, Horse-Killer.'

Luke smacked a reassuring hand against Mackay's shoulder. 'I held my weapon, the steering wheel and my dick,' he said. 'Only time I squeezed the trigger was during safety checks after unloading the magazine. The only bodies I ever saw were our guys being choppered into base in bags. How about you, Bowser?'

Chris said, 'I did maybe forty tasks and patrols, transporting food and then sticking around the locals, maintaining peace and security. Saw one air strike, which was amazing, and was there when that Afghan friendly had a change of heart and killed two Italians and an American. Other than that, I mostly talked to kids, gave them books and stickers, water bottles, hats, and toys.'

'Look,' said Mackay, 'the rehab clinic at Aldershot is the regional rehab unit for ex-serving personnel like me. I go there for the physiotherapy. I don't go for any chit-chat. I don't need to talk to anybody right now, okay? Except maybe you guys. That's enough for a start.'

'To be fair, mate,' said Luke, 'when we do get together, you don't exactly open up.'

Mackay continued. 'They've already given me a thousand contact numbers, pamphlets, email addresses, group therapy providers, all that shit. They've provided the referrals and I just need to show up to the group sessions. But right now, right this minute, I'm not ready.'

Mackay stayed silent for most of the conversation. He finished his beer and ran his fingernails through his hair. Once. Twice.

'I honestly don't feel up to talking to anyone about anything, okay?' he said. 'At least not yet. And don't ask me when. All I'm feeling now is hunger. So, let's order some food already.'

'Sure thing', said Luke. 'I'm starving too. This one's on me. What you all having?'

Luke memorised their orders. He went for the chicken fajita, Mackay the spicy salsa burger and Chris the beef nachos. They agreed on chipotle-smothered corncobs as sides, and a large serving of guacamole corn chips for the table. He stood, then sashayed through the growing crowd to order at the counter.

> 1700hrs
> Saturday December 08, 2012
> Adelaide Terrace, Perth, Western Australia

The client, who gave his name as Kristan, also savoured the concept of anonymity and was on time with ten minutes to spare. A good first impression. The way he sat, however, bothered Van Breeman: cross-legged, thigh over thigh, socks peaking from the ankle. He always thought it awkward for a man to cross their legs in that particular way. Figured it was more or less a sign of femininity. A cynicism passed down from his father. And almost certainly from his father's father. However, if a man or woman was sitting in front of him with a big chunk of cash, that was all that mattered.

Van Breeman opened one of two laptops lying on the oak desk. He was a pragmatic man and operated on two standard forms of personal computer tech. One old, one new. He opened the old one. The one that managed funds for his organised crime – not the new one that managed the wine exporting. It was a bulkier piece from the mid-2000s with a single program installed. An accounts table with an antique version of Microsoft Office from the XP generation. It had no email access, no Bluetooth, no airdrop or webcam. It was for the accounts of those rare breeds of clientele like the one sitting in front of him. It had never been updated and it never would. As a rare breed of human, he liked the obsolete hardware. He liked the set-up and flow of the old spreadsheet. He kept the accounts himself and managed the ebb and flow of each transaction meticulously. Each time a new client committed to a transaction, a new row was inserted, validating Van Breeman's hard work and adding to his self-worth. He wasn't a frequent consumer of recreational drugs, but seeing the numbers shuffle, change and rise, was as good as any hard hit from the street. Pill, powder or crystal. Punching in additional numbers gave Van Breeman that long-lasting high without the withdrawals or comedowns. The transaction itself was the stimulant. The ultimate drug was numbers and it was totally addictive.

Kristan leaned forward and placed his entire right arm with the attached briefcase onto the desk in front. With his other hand he reached inside his breast pocket and pulled out a key. A small Smith and Wesson item with a one-inch neck, a dinky tooth and a loop at the end. He undid the cuff from his wrist and swivelled the combination lock, rotating the numerals to a four-digit code before sliding the case across the table. Van Breeman flicked the fasteners. $1.2 million.

The bills were smooth, pressed, but dirty. Laundered through an unspecified business, which could have been anything. A coffee-roasting plantation, a franchise café, pizzeria or hardware store. Internally, Van Breeman was at fever pitch, yet he kept his gaze steady and his demeanour calm. There was no way he would express his elation through any form of body language or facial expression. Exuding confidence and self-control was paramount, otherwise he would never be taken seriously.

As a greedy sociopath, Van Breeman was still an honest businessman. Always true to his word for a clean exchange – if the client upheld their side of the set parameters. It was his turn to reciprocate.

'One moment,' he said, his South African accent coarse and textured. 'Let me collect your merchandise.'

Van Breman stood and moved towards the wall behind Kristan. Above a waist-high liquor cabinet filled with glass decanters of aged whiskey, was a safe. Concealed behind a hand-painted oil reproduction of Van Gogh's *The Night Café*. Twenty inches by twenty-four. Framed in reddish-brown mahogany with a satin finish. He liked having a frontal view of the painting. A pleasant sight at any angle, whether he was happy, frustrated, or exposing a client's throat. Van Breeman grasped the frame and slid the painting to the right. The safe behind it was equal in size to the Van Gough, necessary to keep the feel and allure of the room artistic, rather than corporate. He blocked the client's view of the spinlock with his body and twirled some numbers. The metal door released with a dull thunk and he opened it to its full width, which was necessary based on the dimensions of the package inside. He reached in with two hands and hauled out a large sports bag. A duffel: grey straps, black body. Thirty inches in length, sixteen inches wide. Good for sweat towels, water bottles, a change of clothes, a pair of shoes. Maybe two pairs. Maybe a suit and a selection of belts and ties if one was committed. It was filled to its maximal height which meant the zipper was firmly snug across the top. He slung it across his left shoulder, closed the safe and replaced the painting. He walked back to Kristan and shrugged the bag gently onto the floor next to him.

Kristan unzipped the bag and pried open what seemed to be a tightly closed lid. He stared back and forth for a solid ten seconds. Thirty inches up, sixteen inches across. He took a small piece of paper from his inside pocket. Same location as the handcuff key. Litmus paper. He reached back inside the bag for another healthy ten seconds, then smiled, happy with the secured contents. He closed the lid, double-checked it was pressed down firm, then zipped up the duffel and stood up.

Kristan said, 'Pleasure doing business.' He picked up the bag and hung it over his shoulder.

Van Breeman said, 'Most definitely. A future transaction would be beneficial for the both of us.'

'I've no doubt,' said Kristan.

Van Breeman downshifted to stern. 'However, you and I must never meet again,' he said. 'All future face-to-face contacts must be different. Same client, but a new face. All transactions must be unrelated and dissimilar every time. Agreed?'

'Agreed, Mr. Van Breeman. As long as you stay in business, my personal clients will be very happy.'

Kristan reached out his hand. Van Breeman thought it good character to offer the hand first, especially considering he was the client. Essentially a guest in Van Breeman's home. Good first impressions count. Van Breeman shook the hand and sent him on his way.

1800hrs
Saturday December 08, 2012
The Farmer's Arms Hotel, Guildford

Chris eyed their table of empty glasses and decided he wanted another.

'I got next round,' he said.

The main bar was much busier now than when they'd first arrived. The barmaid facing Chris delivered a courteous, *I'm ready for your order* smile. Chris doubted it was genuine or intended for him specifically, but it made ordering easier and certainly pleasant. The dark tones of her skin were creamy-smooth and tastefully on display with her low-cut top. He couldn't tell if she was Indian, Pakistani or Sri Lankan. Still, her smile was kind and professional. As good as you'd get in a place like this.

'Three pints of the pale ale please,' said Chris, pointing to the tap. She nodded and smiled back in an equally polite gesture. A social formality. The barmaid grabbed three clean glasses and got on with the order. As he waited, Chris prepped a crisp twenty-pound note between his index and middle finger, flat as a credit card. He traded beer for cash and placed the change in his pocket. He watched the foam coil its way down each glass like a snake as he triangulated the pints in front of him, spreading them carefully.

As Chris moved away with the pints, two inner-city Londoners in puffer jackets walked inside with a well-established vocal volume. Out for a wild night somewhere other than the usual big smoke. Aside from their voices drawing attention, the stud earrings, French-crop haircuts, neck tattoos and nylon jackets all helped. One wore it in red, the other in a mustard yellow. As they entered, they moved straight to the main bar. Chris had no other option but to pass them directly, losing two of the three pints' worth of liquid on the floor in the process. With no apology. In Chris's humble opinion, and in appreciation of the modern conception, he immediately classed the fine specimens as cut-price chavs. He also immediately noticed the words "Tamara" tattooed on the side of the red-puffer jacket's neck. Written in excessively large calligraphy script, appreciated by someone somewhere.

'Thanks for watching where you were going,' said Chris, balancing his hands and steadying the sloshing ale away from his shirt. He looked back at the two of them. The shorter one in mustard yellow turned first.

'What's that?' said Yellow-Puff.

At this point, Mackay had just returned from his slow walk to and from the bathrooms, back to their table. He placed his

Viking cane against the chair, sat and got comfortable. He looked out past the restaurant and through to the bar, which was when he saw Chris holding a tray with one full pint of beer and two half-pints. Which was unusual, and Chris wasn't one to skull another man's drink. Chris was also conversing with two men in colourful jackets. Chris looked heated. The guys in jackets looked mocking. Mackay's heart rate leapt instantly.

Yellow-Puff grabbed Red-Puff on the arm and pointed at Chris, trying to compute a response. Which, on all accounts, given the attire and ink, was going to lack a lot of social finesse. Chris on the other hand, struggled to decide if he should walk back into the restaurant, or stay and play.

'Alright, bruv?' said Red-Puff. 'Do we know him?'

'I fink we spilled the old man's beer,' said Yellow-Puff.

'Did we now?' said Red-Puff, louder, making sure Chris knew he was speaking to him. 'Maybe next time you only handle two beers instead of three, yea? Not our fault, bruv.'

Chris said, 'I wouldn't have spilled it if you and your mate were looking where you were walking. Bruv.'

'What the fuck?' said Red-Puff. 'Are you being cheeky, man?'

Yellow-Puff grinned ear to ear. From where Mackay was sitting, he could see that grin, and knew what it meant. It meant a) he was a common sidekick of an assumed alpha specimen, and b) it meant there was a fight brewing. Judging Red-Puff's body language – the straightened back and extended chest – Mackay could see he was drunk enough to want to fight in public. Ready to reinstate his dominance. Prove and assert his alpha specimen-ship to his smaller, Yellow-Puff sidekick. Although Mackay had just sat down and made himself comfortable, he shuffled his chair backwards, stood, picked up his cane in his left hand and the bottle of token hot sauce in his right.

'I spilled your beers did I, bruv?' said Red-Puff. The pitched sarcasm in his voice plus his use of 'bruv' bumped him up another level, confirming for Chris he was in fact a full-price chav. A social cancer.

Over a dozen sets of eyes from around the bar locked focus onto Chris and Red-Puff. Including the brazen-skinned barmaid. Like Mackay, Chris knew what was most likely to come. In many ways he wanted to stay and fight the wannabe alpha dog then and there, but the sensible part of him said it was better to walk away, drink his beer, polish off his nachos and support Mackay. After all, he and Luke had invited him out. Before he could say anything more, the barmaid piped in.

'It's alright, luv,' she called out across the bar, 'I'll pour you a couple fresh pints. No charge.'

'That would be lovely, thank you,' said Chris, the rush of his fight responses easing. Deep down he was thankful she spoke up, doing her bit to dissolve the situation.

She opened the taps and began pouring two more for Chris, but Red-Puff was having none of it. High on his chav-pride, his dumb, neanderthal ego hankered to prove his worth. Itching to show Yellow-Puff his alpha testosterone.

'I suppose that's for me then, yea?' said Red-Puff to the barmaid. 'There'll be a long, hard tip in it for you too if you can handle it.'

Yellow-Puff snorted. The barmaid ignored them, walked around the bar with the two fresh pints on a tray and made a swap, taking the spilled pints from Chris's hands.

'Thanks again,' said Chris, adjusting the tray.

'Isn't that some lovely service,' said Red-Puff. 'Now hurry up and bring those tits back here, leave the retard alone before he spills anyfink else.' Red-Puff was purposefully raising the situation. Egging for a response. Chris drew a breath, keeping his eyes firmly on the barmaid who was now showing initial signs of unravelling. She kept a brave face, but her hands were shaking as they held the empty pints. She glanced around the bar, looking for the hotel security who were nowhere to be seen.

Red-Puff raised the situation once again, 'Come on, I got money to spend. Or you going to stay there and polish him off?'

Chris didn't like that one. There were families with kids around.

'That's not a very polite thing to say for a little London boy,' said Chris. 'Considering you both look all coordinated for your little chav evening out, makes me think you two are a cozy little item. So how about you polish each other off outside instead, leave the grown-ups in here. I'll film it for you too, as I'm sure you're into that sort of thing.'

The barmaid pursed her lips and smiled cautiously.

'What'd you fucking say?' said Red-Puff.

Chris stood, breathing, contemplating. Staring at the three pints on the tray which were now unlikely to be drunk. All nearby voices around him dropped, and those closest to the bar began to leave. The music through the speakers changed. Another old-school RnB classic.

'Hey!' shouted Red-Puff. 'I'm fucking talking to you.'

'Let's start this from the beginning,' said Chris. 'If you weren't drunk and were looking where you were going, we wouldn't be here.'

'Is that a fact?' said Red-Puff, posturing, making himself taller as he took a step forward. 'I'll flip that. I say it's you who is drunk and should have watched where you was fucking going. So maybe you owe me an apology. Or how about you buy us a drink each and call it even.'

'How about neither,' said Chris. 'I was clearly out of the way, and you weren't looking at all. Plus, your comment toward the barmaid was uncalled for. I'm not buying anything.'

'Last option then,' said Red-Puff. 'Let's take it outside.'

The smile on his sidekick in yellow widened. Red-Puff slowly made for the exit, his fingers twitching and rolling in and out into fists. Chris liked the last option as much as Red-Puff wanted it. The only annoying aspect was he'd likely miss out on the beers and nachos. He too wondered where the security was, but it was still early. Perhaps they started an hour or so later when the crowd really kicked off. So, he resolved himself to Red-Puff's last option, almost gladly. He stepped towards the bar and for a split second, turned his back while he placed his tray of pints down on the table. Which was when Red-Puff doubled back and swung at Chris's head. A sucker-punch from behind. Early and without warning. Very ungentlemanly. Very chav.

Chris wasn't ready for the throw. Didn't see it coming. He fell sideways, over an empty table, two chairs and onto the sticky carpet. It was the last thing he remembered. The haymaker put him out cold. Luckily, the furniture was all he hit. And luckily nothing else happened to him. Because during the verbal back-and-forth between Chris and the Puffer-Boys, Mackay had quietly and slowly made it around the bar. Step by step, unnoticed with his crutch and bottle of hot sauce. Mackay had made a flanking manoeuvre. At the same time Chris placed his tray of pints onto the bar with Red-Puff doubling back for the swing, Mackay unscrewed the cap on the sauce, dousing the fiery red liquid over his right hand. It was rated three chillies out of four, which meant the heat was at a nice temperature for a burrito, enchilada or plate of nachos. Not so for someone's face. Especially the eyes. Mackay wasn't a great fighter, and even less capable with a cane, but he was angry. Angry at the situation, angry at himself, angry at the world. A quiet anger. The best kind. The kind that never surfaces in outbursts, it just simmers and seethes below the surface waiting for an imminent scrap to explode. And when it did, he always arrived with full enthusiasm. He'd seen his share of scraps both locally and on deployment. Pubs, streets, mess halls and garrison boozers. Usually against infantry grunts, sometimes against haughty Airforce crabs and Navy duckfuckers. Sometimes because it made for interesting recounts during beer-and-story-time with the lads, but then more often because there was a strong point to be made out of principle. This was one of those situations.

In the ascending heat between Chris and the Puffer-boys, Mackay decided that a release of anger might just do him some good. Relieve some of his pent-up frustrations for a cause. Out of principle for souring everyone's evening.

Edging himself close in behind Red-Puff's swaggering pride, Mackay reached around the front of him with his chilli-sauced hand and wiped it firmly across his face. Making sure his soppy fingers brushed hard into the crevices of the eye sockets. He knew Yellow-Puff would react first, but he was prepared, having thought out the entire process during his uneasy walk from the restaurant to the bar. He held the bottom end of his cane against the lower edge of the bar between the sticky carpet and the wooden skirting board, for leverage. Mackay knew his best defence wasn't upright bare-knuckle boxing given his healing ribcage, so he would have to use his legs. Although he had killed people on operations – including one unfortunate horse – fighting a couple of chavs in the civilian world was a totally different ball game.

Yellow-Puff reacted, just like Mackay knew he would. His hero mate was in trouble, and it was part of his duty to chip in. Which was a good thing, because Mackay was twice his size in width and twice the intellect in perception. He would easily go down first, cane or no cane.

With his hand steadied on the head of the Viking, Mackay waited for Yellow-Puff to turn back towards him. Then he let it go. A release, like a click of the thumb. A short breath of fresh air in the maddening world inside him. Mackay kicked out. Front kick straight into Yellow-Puff's pubic bone. He tried for the lolly bag, but it ended a little high. Still, a shot to the pubic bone can easily bring a man down. The kick landed brutally, pulling

Yellow-Puff's feet out from underneath him. Physics and kinetic energy hauled Yellow-Puff down onto his front, chin first onto the thin sticky flooring.

With one man down for the count, Red-Puff – all fuming and bleary-eyed – was now somewhat easier to handle. Wiping furiously and trying to assess who had juiced his eyeballs with the red-hot liquid, Red-Puff turned immediately, swinging and jabbing at the air. He could barely see, and Mackay knew the main heat of the sauce hadn't taken full effect yet, so he waited, counting down from three in his head.

'Holy fucking shit!' screamed Red-Puff.

And there it was. The alpha chav had found the pain. It wasn't just stinging his eyeballs, he was going to have a red-raw face in less than a minute. Red-Puff kept swinging. Right, left, right, rubbing maniacally at his eyes with his red sleeve at the same time. Which, given it was made of polyester, wasn't the best at absorbing the three-star fiery juice.

Mackay braced against his cane once more. At the same time, his peripherals saw a half-empty pint at the bar – left by one of the many patrons backing away from the ruckus. He picked it up in his right for backup. Red-Puff squinted, prying one fluttering eye open to calibrate his position for a connecting punch, but Mackay had the upper hand and kicked out a second time. Aiming even higher: the sternum. Something cracked underneath Red-Puff's jacket as he was flung backward into the wall, toppling into a heap on the floor next to Yellow-Puff. Then, for reasons that could only be related to his unchecked PTSD, Mackay didn't stop there. He flipped. From a calculated flanking manoeuvre, Mackay crossed over into the uncharted waters of animalistic madness.

With his cane in his left hand and the pint glass in his right, Mackay hobbled over to Yellow-Puff's lazy form and cracked the half-drunk glass across the side of his head. The smaller chav went out like a light, his head rocking weightless against the floor. Immediately after, Mackay threw himself onto Red-Puff, who was sucking air in partial gasps, trying to force his diaphragm to work. Mackay dropped a knee into the middle of Red-Puff's back and went to town. Right fist on repeat into the right ear. Left hand still gripping the cane, pressing down into the back of the man's neck.

'Mackay!' yelled Luke, back from the ordering counter.

Mackay didn't hear a word. He kept driving his knuckles into Red-Puff's ear. Pounding at the rubbery cartilage while the guy wriggled underneath him, trying but failing to cover the shots with his forearms.

'Say it!' growled Mackay. 'Apologise, you cheap shot motherfucker!'

Four, five, six drum-bursting whacks later, Mackay fidgeted his thumb to the front of Red-Puff's face and went for his eye. The ball moved like stress-foam as he pressed it into the socket. Red-Puff screamed and recoiled but was stuck under Mackay's thick, rugby-powered thighs. Before he could dip in past the knuckle, Luke had Mackay wrapped up in his arms and dragged him off. Which was when the police arrived in a wagon with an empty cage in back.

2000hrs
Saturday December 08, 2012
Guildford Police Station

The cops didn't really give Mackay a hard time. For visual purposes and the principle of the law they stuck to protocol and made the arrest look legitimate, and Mackay didn't argue. The police had Luke and Chris tag along to the station, for all round breath tests and statements which kept the chief inspector happy. The chavs were eventually brought in as well, although they were held back at the pub with a pair of paramedics, namely, to check over Red-Puff's head. A good thing, considering they didn't want the men crossing paths again on account of second-round shenanigans.

One of the two bobbies, Sergeant Mulder, an older guy blessed with an aged beer belly and sparse white hair, used to attend Mackay's brother's church. When Malvin preached in town at St Matthew's Anglican. His main concern was Mackay's ferocity. He'd never been involved with a Connolly. Never knew Mackay was the type to lash out like that. On the football field, Mackay was a machine. Perfectly built like it was genetically bestowed upon him from some divine Rugby-God. But nobody had seen Mackay throw himself into a violent rage before.

At the station, the bobbies were once again nice enough not to put Mackay in a cell. Chris and Luke had given their statements first while Mackay sat outside Sergeant Mulder's office. Watched by a fresh-faced lanky constable and an unimpressed older woman behind a monitor. An administrative assistant with fluffy chin-whiskers and a lined top lip. Classic smoker. A pack-a-day type for the last forty years. She punched away at the keyboard, her eyes occasionally darting up and down over the monitor making sure Mackay was still seated like a good boy.

Mackay's eyes wandered vaguely around the interior walls. The admin area had been thoughtfully decorated. British police hats from the late 1800s ran across a rack on the back wall, a list of officers killed in the line of duty were hung on the right, with landscape canvasses hung on the left. Mostly acrylics of tropical oceans, exotic birds, and palm trees. As Mackay slowly stiffened in the wooden chair, the good Sergeant Mulder poked his head out, waking him from his absorbed gaze.

'Mackay, I'd like your statement now please.'

'Aye,' Mackay said. 'I'll be honest, it's quite a basic recount to be sure.'

'That's all I want.'

'The short end of it, a pair of amadans walked in acting the maggot. Wasn't right, you know.'

Sergeant Mulder looked confused. Mackay was Irish.

'Right, I'll say it English-like. A pair of fools walked in the pub, began stirring trouble with complete disrespect. You follow?'

Mulder nodded.

'A maggot is a parasite. They ruined the mood.'

'I understand, Mackay, I know the type. I've been around and I'm inclined to agree with you. Anyway, your two friends have finished, and we have other matters to deal with this evening. Do you need a hand?'

Mackay drew a breath and a shook his head. He wobbled upright with his cane, shuffled into the room to an empty chair next to Chris and Luke and began laying out his version of events.

After everything was said and done, printed and signed, Mackay wanted a final word.

'If that crumb didn't sucker punch Chris, we wouldn't be here,' he said. 'That cheap shot in the back of his head could have killed him. I had to step in.'

'I think you did much more than just step in, Mackay,' said Mulder. 'As little as I think of those boys, one is now in hospital under observation. And you should be thankful he's not in intensive care. You almost took his eye.'

'Just being honest, Sergeant, I'd probably do it again if I saw a friend get hit in the head from behind. One eye isn't a bad exchange for a lowly fucker like that. Excuse the language. What if Chris wound up in hospital instead? Or died?'

'That's all relevant in hindsight,' said Mulder. 'All fair points. But you already had him. It was all over. If you did in fact mess up his eye, I'd have no choice but to put you in that cell in the room next door. That's grievous bodily harm which exceeds the grounds for defending your mate here for the cheap shot. I hope you understand.'

Sergeant Mulder looked across at Chris and Luke, projecting his quantified concern. A *this is serious* look on his face.

'Anyway,' continued Mulder, 'I doubt there will be any court proceedings, even if those two do wish to press any charges. It's unlikely though, given their criminal history, which we've just received from East London. Plus, your current physical ability, your past service to the country, your friend's witness statements, and the statement of the barmaid.'

'The barmaid gave a statement?' said Chris.

'Good as,' said Mulder. 'Notes were taken back at the bar. Her version aligns. That means right now, Mackay, it looks okay for you. But there is one thing we need to talk about, and that is getting help for your PTSD. Your friends here are very concerned.'

'I know,' said Mackay flatly.

'So, what's happening?' said Mulder

'What do you mean?'

'Inside your head.'

Mackay paused. He was borderline reticent, but the time and place to talk was now. He couldn't not say anything, especially after the evening's violence. He didn't want to reveal his thoughts, and he especially didn't want to burrow inside and bring up anything potentially horrid or unpleasant. Yet, looking at the piercing eyes around the room, he bit the bullet. The context and tension in the room was suffocating.

'Thanks for not putting me in the can, and thanks for the support,' said Mackay. He looked up at everyone in turn. 'I appreciate you all, really. As for the apparent PTSD, I'm sure a day will come when I do go to a meeting. But it won't be tomorrow. I hate seeing people. I'm just going through the daily motions, trying to fit into this place while everyone else has their eyes closed.'

'Closed to what?' asked Chris.

'To the *real* world. To the war still going on over there. Where I should be. Where *we* were.' Mackay eyed Luke, then Chris, then Mulder. 'Everyone just walks about oblivious, safe as houses. Thinking about their next booze-filled weekend, or what pair of shoes they're buying next while we're out there fighting for them. For them to live in this comfort. We went out there to represent this country while everyone else sits at home deciding on what brand they're going to wear or what video game they should buy. Slobs wondering what tattoo design they'll get because they want to express how much their fucking cat means to them.'

'There are thousands of ex-soldiers that feel the exact same way,' said Luke. 'But there are better things in the world that you could focus on. And as much as we've tried, it seems we can't really help you.'

'Your brother might be able to,' added Mulder. 'I know him well. He's a good pastor. But for now, son, you need to seek counselling support or therapy of some kind. Army therapy. With people you know. People you have a connection with.'

The sergeant paused a beat, then, 'My wife, my children and I attended your brother's church. You know this. Every Sunday when he ran St Matthews. Before his recent move to Bracknell. For the past five years we were regulars. I always wondered why I never saw you.'

'Church was never my thing,' said Mackay.

'Do you speak with him much?' said Mulder.

'Here and there. As much as brothers normally do I suppose. He knows when to leave me alone at least.'

Sergeant Mulder looked at Mackay serenely, then closed his eyes.

'Look, I don't want to preach to you. I'm not your brother, and I am not a psychologist, but what I am saying is, you need to be surrounded by good people. And you have two right here. But there are more people who are experienced with helping you with other specific needs. Part of my job is to try and steer you in the right direction.'

Mackay listened to the good sergeant with enough sincerity to pass as genuine. He maintained eye contact, agreed with a low murmur here and an occasional nod there. In the end, he agreed to two things: he would book in and attend counselling with one of the psychs at Aldershot's Garrison, and he would meet with Renee Cross the boxing coach. Chris and Luke even offered to drive the half-hour trip for him now that Malvin had moved to Bracknell. Talking it out with experienced battle-honed soldiers of similar ilk seemed an okay option, even if it was with a red-headed boxing instructor with no legs.

Overall, he felt good about how he'd reacted. He didn't feel it was irrational at all. In fact, the justice aspect of it felt right. The boys got what they deserved. And a slap on the wrist was better than spending the night at the station. Or quite possibly longer at Coldingley Prison.

> 0700hrs
> Monday December 10, 2012
> Mackay's Unit. Guildford, United Kingdom

At 0700 when Mackay eventually sat up in bed, he felt exhausted. Unrested. His overactive mind, the vividness of his dreams all added to feeling washed out, dry and hungover. He was scheduled for an 0830 appointment with the military counsellor at Aldershot, and Chris had offered to pick him up and drop him off, out of support and loyalty. Making good on his commitment. Mackay could probably have driven alone. The physio had given him the okay to drive since managing with the cane, which was a small step toward the light, as long as it was an automatic and not a three-pedal.

If Mackay didn't get moving, he'd be late. There was nothing on the wall except paint, and he needed to stop staring at it. He also needed to stop running his hands up and down his butchered, cheese-grater ribs, even though they itched like bollocks underneath the skin. Once he was on his feet (an achievement in itself), he moved to the kitchen, started the kettle, prepped an instant coffee and pressed two bits of bread into the toaster. At 0730, Chris entered Mackay's driveway to the complex of units in a blue dual-cab Toyota Hilux. It was too early to tap the horn on account of the neighbours, so instead he left the throaty hum of the diesel idling, hoping it was enough of a warble to signal his arrival. Which it was. Mackay limped outside within thirty seconds, threw his cane down into the footwell, then clambered in after it.

Chris followed the easy morning flow of traffic out onto the A31, then drove the half hour west from Guildford to Aldershot Garrison. The onset of trickling sleet reduced everybody down to stupid levels of slow, not to mention turning the tarmac to a greasy film spattering all over Chris's windscreen. The land either side of the motorway was an old familiar sight, but it made Mackay feel uneasy, invoking recent memories he didn't want circulating. Reminding him of surgery, which then reminded him of what he'd left behind: his career, his friends, and the friends that were no longer coming back. They arrived at Aldershot Garrison at 0815. At the security gates, the guard confirmed the appointments for both Mackay and Chris, as well as the correct registration quoted for the Hilux. He made a brief check through the vehicle's tray, glovebox and rear seats, then let them through. Chris dropped Mackay out the front of the medical wing, and the two agreed on meeting back there at 1000. An hour of psychotherapy fun, plus a quick look-see around the gym for the infamous boxing instructor.

The medical wing housed both the rehab centre and counselling clinic. Two single-story officers' residence buildings joined together. Old military housing built sometime after the Second World War. The two buildings were attached with modern interior renovations, new furnishings, and a reconditioned courtyard with a kept garden.

Mackay didn't need to sit down in the waiting room. As soon as he entered, the counsellor was standing at the front desk pointing here and there at a computer monitor over the shoulder of a skinny, middle-aged brunette. The receptionist. Probably reviewing the daily appointments. There was nobody else in the room. For the hour of the morning Mackay assumed he was first off the block. The counsellor was taller than most, somewhere around six foot two or three and likely a doctor with a PHD. Whether it was in psychology or psychiatry Mackay wasn't sure. He had a long face with thick spectacles and dark brown hair cut short and clean. *A mirror image of Postman Pat*, thought Mackay, the stop-motion children's television character. The receptionist also wore glasses, but her face was amped and edgy. Maybe from excess coffee or cigarettes. Probably both.

'Mackay Connolly,' said the counsellor.

'Aye, you said that like a statement, sir,' said Mackay. 'We've never met.'

'You're the first to walk through the door this morning, and your picture is right in front of me on our system. Only your haircut is shorter here. Your file was sent through from your surgeon in Kandahar. Captain Andersen. He works here now, at the hospital. Transferred not long after you were medically discharged. Honourably might I add.'

'Are you a psychologist or a psychiatrist?' asked Mackay.

The man stepped out from behind the reception desk and held out his hand. The closer proximity allowing Mackay to judge his age to a tighter ballpark of the mid-forties.

'I'm a psychologist,' he said. 'Dariusz Swibinski.'

Mackay braced with his cane and shook his hand. 'Nice to meet you,' he said. 'What's the main difference between your profession and a psychiatrist?'

'A psychiatrist is a medical doctor who usually makes specific diagnoses,' Swibinski said. 'I mostly focus on conversation. Verbal treatment for those suffering depression and anxiety. For deployed soldiers, a lot of that rolls off the back of PTSD. Does that sound like something you can relate to?'

Mackay downloaded the information, then analysed the question.

'You could say that,' he said.

'Honesty, that's good,' Swibinski said. 'Word of mouth says you were an excellent corporal, and so does your file.'

Swibinski gestured Mackay to the first door down the corridor. 'Don't stress,' he said. 'We'll just talk. Keep it simple. I won't diagnose you or prescribe you anything. I'm trained to assess problems in people's thinking and emotions.'

'Great. What I was hoping for,' said Mackay. 'So, Swibinski? Polish?'

'Bingo. And you grew up in Dublin.'

'Aye. Another statement. Good old military files.'

0845hrs
Monday December 10, 2012
Aldershot Military Support Centre

Inside his office, listening room, or whatever workspace the shrink community called it, there were two comfortable armchairs. No couches, sofas, or designer pieces. The army budget wouldn't allow for it. The chairs were quality enough, lined with soft cushioning, covered in leather and leaned to a slight recline. Doctor and patient both at eye level. Equal positioning. The room was relatively small, which worked to create a more personalised and focused approach without any major distractions. The carpets were cream, there was a short filing cabinet and a tawny-brown desk for writing scripts, reports and referrals. On one wall hung a wide frame of a serene waterfall, while on the opposite were two framed certificates: Swibinski's qualifications. A doctor in clinical psychology, and an accreditation with the British Psychological Society. What stood out most in the room was a bonsai tree. A ficus bonsai, with green oval leaves and a thick gnarled trunk. At least fifty years old if not more, and small enough to fit in the palms of two hands. Strategically placed at the corner of Swibinski's desk, closest to the patient's armchair. Either as a point of reference during reflections, or to spark discussion. Although dwarfish in features it looked like a thousand-year-old Major Oak from Nottinghamshire. Nestled in white pebbles inside a wood-fired clay pot it was meticulously cared for, as it should be, giving Swibinski a higher level of approval in Mackay's book.

'So, the bonsai,' began Mackay, sitting into the patient's armchair opposite the doc.

'Ah, the Zen question,' said Swibinski. 'Nice little addition, don't you think?'

'Is the tree part of my psych experience?' said Mackay.

'It doesn't need to be. Many seem to like it for what it is.'

'Which is? A small Japanese plant that looks like an old tree?'

'Sure. It looks nice though. Makes me look cultured as well, right?'

Mackay said, 'I'm assuming there's a concept where you use it as an analogy to paint a bigger picture for us, so we look deeper within ourselves.'

'All the above. Almost for every person that comes in here. Me included. You comfortable, Mackay? Is it okay if I call you Mackay?'

'Aye. That's my name.'

'Just checking. Being military, many prefer using their surnames.'

'First-name basis is fine, I'm not in the army anymore.'

'Okay,' said Swibinski. 'To be frank, Mackay, the tree visually represents harmony and balance. In this room I can physically control that harmony and balance by taking time to care for it. Giving it a snip here and there, giving it water. It's that control that is key for us as people too, but we often forget to take the time to care for ourselves. For me, my control in this room is to look after the tree, make sure it's thriving. Other things I have control over include having a place for everything. My books, the two chairs, my stationary, my keyboard. I keep things neat and tidy, placed in certain ways, in certain places. I keep things ordered, that's my control. Can you think of an example of what a control scenario looks like for you?'

Mackay sat and pondered, stretched his side and scratched involuntarily at his ribs.

'Not these days,' Mackay said. 'I couldn't be sure now. I guess I'm lucky if I get to my feet in the morning.'

'What about when you were still in the service? Corps of transport, right?'

Mackay chewed the inside of his lip. 'Well, it's the army, sir. There was an ordered way of doing things. For literally everything. Your bed, your uniform, the way you walked and cleaned your weapon. The army even tells you how to think. I went by that.'

'Of course. No need to call me sir either. Darryn is fine.'

'Not Dariusz?'

'A little uncommon around here. My mother calls me Dariusz. She likes to keep things traditional.'

'Control is associated with power,' Swibinski continued. 'We like having a personal power over our world, but sometimes we lose it. Without having our own space to control we can often start falling apart. It matters for the things we do day to day, as well as for the things that pop up unexpectedly. Like that IED explosion.'

Mackay closed his eyelids down tightly. The memory of the exploding flashes and dead bodies of Theckston, Freeman and Kirwan lit up his mind.

'When power and control are gone, when it goes up in smoke, the mind can change in an instant. How would you say your head feels right now, in your own terms?'

'I suppose I'm one big dark tunnel without any light at the end of it.'

'Mackay, I do need to ask you a serious question. Are you suicidal, or do you have any suicidal thoughts?'

Mackay paused. Searching his deeper recesses. Exploring the frenzied grey matter connecting dark memories. He paused maybe a fraction of a second too long.

'No,' Mackay said, as confidently as he could.

Swibinksi took the answer for what it was and nodded. 'Next hard question, are you drinking?'

Mackay knew where he was going with this one.

'A beer occasionally.'

'Heavily?'

'No.'

'Nothing excessive to numb the pain?'

'No. That was three questions.'

'Fair point, let's move on. I'd like you to open up on what's getting you edgy. What is it you're struggling most with? Take your time.'

Mackay put his hands to his face. Pressed his fingers into his eyes, his brow, then down the bridge of his nose. He scratched at his temples and ran his fingers through his hair.

'I'm always thinking about why I reacted the way I did.'

'React how?'

'Turning that fucking steering wheel and driving off the road. I'm constantly analysing and dissecting. Why did this happen? Why did that happen? Why didn't I just plant my foot into the brakes. My whole equilibrium feels shot.'

'Wallowing in your headspace after an incident like yours is part of the process. Like grieving. You're in an enhanced state of sensitivity. The mind is a strange, nonsensical, and magnificent mechanism. Even our own thoughts can hurt us immensely.'

The room stayed silent. The lack of sound felt comforting.

'Sometimes we forget to consider the positives we have in our lives,' said Swibinski. 'You're alive, your health is on the mend, you have your compensation, your family.'

'Fair,' Mackay agreed.

'It's no secret that everything in your file, everything we've uncovered, comes under PTSD. I'm sure you know this, right?'

'So people keep telling me.'

'Touching on the incident, had you ever seen or experienced an IED before?'

'I've seen claymores, grenades and mortars go off.'

'How close were they?'

'I should have braked hard and stopped. I should not have turned the wheel.'

'Your reaction could not, and cannot, be learned or practised. How did you know what to expect? It was down to an automatic response. How could you have known there were two IEDs planted in the ground?'

Mackay leaned back in his chair, the tears behind his eyes scratched at the surface.

'Here's my last perspective. If you knew there were IEDs in the ground at those exact points in the road, and you deliberately swung your vehicle over them causing those deaths, then that could potentially be considered murder. You'd be court martialled.'

'I suppose,' said Mackay.

'But you didn't know where either two IEDs were, because you were fighting for the British, and you're not an Islamic extremist.'

'Right.'

'So, what does that make it?'

Mackay didn't answer.

'An accident. Can you say that?'

'Say what?'

'The words. It was an accident.'

Mackay swallowed. His throat was dry. He couldn't answer. He wiped the corners of his eyes with his palms.

'We'll get there, Mackay,' said Swibinski. 'You had enough?'

'Aye.' Mackay tried to smile, it felt fake. He stared at the bonsai tree. As much as he thought the session to be okay, he still couldn't give a proper smile. The muscles in the corners of his mouth worked, but it wasn't real.

THREE

PROCESSING

0945hrs
Monday December 10, 2012
Boxing Gym, Aldershot Garrison

Mackay had fifteen minutes to spare before Chris was due to pick him up. So, he took the five-minute walk down to the gym. Which was normally a two-minute walk had he not been sauntering along with a cane. That then left him with ten minutes to find the red-headed instructor and see what she was all about. He pulled out his mobile phone and messaged Chris: *I'm at the main gym. See you there in 20.*

Mackay stood in a long foyer of rooms framed with glass and steel, built side by side across a vast slab of concrete. The rooms looked new or at least refreshed, scattered with soldiering motivation posters endorsing all the usual values of courage, teamwork and discipline. The first room he passed was a functional training room with open flooring filled with squat racks, pull-up bars, dip bars and kettle bells. The second room was bigger. A cardio room with treadmills, stationary bikes, stair climbers and cross trainers. The next room was the weights gym crammed with every kind of machine and vanity mirrors lined wall to wall. The last room at the end of the foyer was the busiest. The boxing hall. A replica of the weights room in size and dimensions, however the atmosphere was totally different. There were no vanity mirrors like the weights gym. Self-admiration was not required. The people inside were training hard and proper. There were no girls with make-up, straightened hair or fluro activewear. There were no guys flexing or wasting time in huddles staring at the opposite sex. Mackay stepped inside. The tangy draught of sweat slapped him in the face and then passed over him. Only three distinct sounds could be heard: the snick of skipping ropes hitting the floor, wrapped fists hitting bags, and a singular, exceptionally loud, roaring female voice.

The voice in the room belonged to a woman in a wheelchair. She sat tall, confident, and domineering as she bellowed instructions. Her hair was dark red, pulled back in a ponytail. At the base of the chair where her legs should have been, were two stubby limbs poking from the mid-thigh. A pair of black training shorts partially covered the rounded flesh which was white and pink and knitted with scarring. One stub was slightly longer than the other: the left ending just below the kneecap, the right ending just above. She worked her voice from the middle of the room, yelling at four people at once: two on the agility balls and two sparring in the ring. From one trainer to the next, she was at them, in her element…

'Robbie, move that fucking back foot, it's not made of lead.'

'Donna, keep your shit together, there's ten seconds left.'

'Don't you dare look down at me, Harry, eyes up, I'm not the one in the fucking ring.'

'Breathe, Pete, if you pass out again it's a hundred squats with me on your back.'

As her countdown reached zero, the corner of her eye detected Mackay's shape leaning awkwardly on his cane at the entrance like a tourist.

'You, get your thumb out of your arse and get changed. I don't give a fuck about your combat disability problems, you're late. We started ten minutes ago.'

Mackay blinked, taken aback. He hadn't been yelled at since Afghanistan. Mackay scoped the gym and looked for somewhere to sit or lean against. Wait out the right time for a quick word with the woman he was sure was Renee Cross. He gathered he had ten minutes to figure out how to approach her. He wasn't sure what he would say, and he didn't want to sound needy or desperate, but since he was there, he would do himself a favour and ask for advice on working through his PTSD.

At the opposite end of the gym was a walled shelf full of gym bags. It was isolated enough from the sweaty action, so he hobbled over. There were no chairs or benches, so he propped his cane against the shelving and leaned against the wall, easing the pressure off his sides. He leaned, he waited. After ten minutes, a drink break was called.

'We start back in two minutes!' yelled the red ant. 'Be ready, or you'll be training into overtime and sweating arse juice.'

The red ant wheeled herself in Mackay's direction, making firm eye contact.

'Obviously not here to box,' she said. 'What are you here for then, Tin Man?'

Her chin was high, her face sceptical and cold. She eyeballed him like a sniper on a fresh target. Her focus taking in a hundred pieces of information all at once.

'Haven't had Tin Man before,' said Mackay.

'Irish?'

'Aye.'

'You're stiff,' she said. 'And your frame looks awkward in those clothes. You wearing a brace or something?'

'No brace.'

'Then you either got shot up or blown up. So, take your shirt off. You show me yours, as I've clearly shown you mine.' She wiggled her stubs up and down.

Mackay noted the red ant's tone, the crassness of her voice, her face, her chair, her limbs. If she'd had her legs blown off, best guess, she was likely an ex-engineer. A landmine-sweeper. She had a lined face, not because she was old, but possibly from spending hours in the sun sweeping IEDs. Or maybe from all the yelling in the gym. To be fair, going through the trauma and stress of becoming an amputee may have aged her looks, but she was still pretty. Her refined jawline, adept eyes and lean torso from years of boxing had obviously helped.

'Show you what? My limbs?' said Mackay.

'Your scars, arse-hat.'

'Mine are still swollen.'

'Good. The bigger the better. You've seen mine as I sit before you, now show me yours. Soldier to soldier. Call it a rite of passage.'

'You're serious?'

'I want to see. My guys need to get back to it, so pull it out. Just as long as it's not your dick. Don't be a weirdo, unless it's missing, which would be interesting.'

Mackay took a defeated breath. 'Right here right now?'

'Right now.'

Mackay balanced himself without his cane, grabbed his shirt shrugged out of it. He wasn't ashamed but he still felt exposed and vulnerable. This was a first. In front of a strange woman basically in a public place. Aside from the surgeons at Kandahar, Malvin was the only person to have ever seen what his ribs really looked like. Because Cross had a certain authority, and because he was within her little part of the world, Mackay obliged. A few wandering eyes from the beat trainers looked over, their eyes lingering longer than Mackay found comfortable, but they observed with a recognition of respect. A war-dog's acknowledgement. Many made the classic double take, while some turned away with a faint shudder.

'Holy fucking shit that's fucked up,' the red ant exclaimed.

'You should talk.'

'I win by default, since I can't walk, but that…'

'Like a massive cheese grater, right?'

'Or a slab of beef cut with a blunt knife.'

'Thanks.'

'You said it was still swollen.'

The red ant wheeled herself closer and touched him down the side. Mackay watched her fingers against his skin. He couldn't feel a thing. She ran her hand down a second time. Open palm, top to bottom. It was cool to the touch. Not warm, like a normal body would be. She felt the ripples and bumps, the tiny undulations.

'I don't think it's swollen,' she said. 'Seems settled. Set like a crème brûlée. But this, this is not normal.'

'Feels mostly okay now,' Mackay said. 'Still itches sometimes. I can't feel your hand. Not even when I scratch at it.'

'You've got bragging rights, Tin Man. Good work, officially the biggest fucked-up thing I've ever seen. What's your name?'

'Mackay.'

'That a first or a last name?'

'First.'

'Sounds like a last. Should be a surname.'

'Parents didn't see it that way, so they put it at the front.'

'My name's Renee. Most call me Cross.'

'So I've heard.'

'Good things or bad?'

'Only that you've got a mouth on you.'

'I'll take it as a compliment.'

'Looks like you train your guys pretty hard.'

'Another compliment. Two's a bit much this early on. As easy as it might seem for a girl without legs, you're not getting into my pants.'

Mackay took half a step back. 'That wasn't what I…'

'I'm joking. At ease, soldier. You want to meet with me and talk war stories, yes?'

'Am I that predictable?'

'Last time this happened the situation was reversed. I was the one sitting in this chair looking to speak with another cripple. Wanting to ask how they got through it all. Guess it's my turn to pass the baton.'

'PTSD?'

'Happens to the best of us who come back wonky. We can meet tomorrow morning here, out the front of the gym. 0830. I live inside the garrison, but I'll scoot down. I can't drive, obviously,' Cross batted her limbs up and down, 'so chauffer duties will be on you. I prefer informal chats outside the wire, so we'll head off somewhere nicer. You got a ride big enough for this chair?'

'I'm sure I can get a hold of something.'

'We'll head to the Madam's Apprentice café. It's the cat's fucking pyjamas. You know the one?'

'Eastern end of the lakeside nature reserve.'

'Food's good, coffee's better. See you then. Now I have to fuck off, these soft foreskins have had too long a break.'

And that was it. She turned her wheelchair around and started up the yelling.

0900hrs
Tuesday December 11, 2012
The Madam's Apprentice café, Aldershot

Mackay woke at 0700, showered first, shaved second, then had a cup of English breakfast tea to warm his insides. Chris leant Mackay his blue Hilux for the day, making good to his commitment in seeing his old friend seek some social connection. Besides, it was with a member of the opposite sex, which could almost be considered a date. At 0855 Mackay pulled up to Aldershot Garrison's security gates, showed the guard his ID, then continued on to the gym. As sure as her word, Cross was out front waiting. He'd never helped a disabled person into a vehicle before, so he didn't know any of the steps or processes. Rather than assuming what to do and looking dumb while doing it, he figured his best option was to just ask. Mackay parked in line with her, leaned over the centre console and opened the door.

'Morning,' Cross said, rolling into view.

'What am I supposed to do?' said Mackay.

'I'll crawl in, then you can collapse my chair and put it in the back. Not in the tray. I don't want it slip-sliding around. Who knows how you drive.'

Mackay's brainwaves fired a number of blurry images into his head from the remark: explosion one, explosion two. The turn of the steering wheel. Kirwan, Theckston, Freeman. It was a throwaway line. There was no real connected reference to his driving – she didn't know his story. He clenched his jaw and blinked the comment away.

'Sure thing,' he said, and got out of the cab.

As Mackay walked around, Cross heaved herself up inside the passenger side.

'You know how to collapse a wheelchair?' she said.

'I'm not really sure,' Mackay said.

Cross watched and let him think on it for five seconds. She then watched Mackay remove the cushion, pull the seat inwards from its collapsing handle and place it in the back seat. Job done.

Ten minutes later, they pulled into the café parking lot which was huddled between a small car dealer and an independent computer repair store. Cross pulled a disabled card from her inside pocket and slid it onto the dashboard.

'We're good,' she said. 'We can be as close as we like.'

Mackay scouted the parking lot for the disabled spaces, of which there were two: one occupied with a sporty Mini Cooper, and one other which was free. Both up close to the café's front entrance. Mackay had been there once before. A hidden spot just out of town overlooking a small lake, or maybe it was a large pond, littered with moored boats mostly of the dinghy variety.

Mackay swung his legs out onto the blacktop then leaned over Cross's stubs to pull his Viking cane from the passenger well. He noted the altered fabric of the pinned denim cut short to fold neatly over her limbs. He walked around, removed the wheelchair from the back, then set it up alongside the passenger side.

'Do I help you get in?' said Mackay.

'No. Just watch and look interested.'

Mackay stood off to the side feeling like a moron. Helpless and special – and not in the neurotically brilliant sense. Cross moved fast. On autopilot, having done the in-and-out process a few hundred times at least. She grabbed the Jesus-bar near the roof lining, swung into the assembled chair, closed the door and rolled herself towards Mackay. Done and dusted in ten seconds. Bish bash bosh.

Inside, the café was stained wood all around. Maintaining an antique vibe that went with the lakeside location. It was busy but not crowded, or excessively loud. Mostly older folk in retirement age, aside from one table of four teens: two girls, two guys. Mackay took a long hard look. Judging. Making assumptions. They all wore various jackets matching the low temperature. No puffer styles though. The girls wore beanies, the guys wore caps turned backwards, but at least they were quiet. An overly friendly waitress, a frumpy girl somewhere in her late twenties, came out from the front reception and found them a table. She laid a couple of menus on the table and asked whether they'd like to order coffee straight away. *Good customer service*, thought Mackay. He was keen for the caffeine and needed something to help rejuvenate his conversation skills. Cross ordered a large double shot latte, Mackay a large double shot flat white. Neither requested sugar.

'How are they going for you?' asked Cross.

'Pardon?'

'The teens over there. Your attention was lost to them for the last ten seconds.'

'Yes. Sorry. I'm just settling into my surrounds. Predicting whether we'll have to deal with any obnoxious ferals.'

'Don't let them spoil our time, Tin Man, we're off to a good start.'

'I had nothing else to do. And you gave me no other choice really.'

'Good point.'

Mackay said, 'We haven't introduced ourselves properly. We should do the obligatory thing and shake hands.' Mackay stretched his hand across the table. 'Mackay Connolly.'

Cross clasped down on Mackay's hand like a vice. 'Renee Cross,' she said. 'So, you from the North or the South? Belfast or Dublin?'

'Born in Dublin. Moved over when I was fourteen.'

'I'm an Essex girl originally, though I grew up in Manchester. Then twelve years in the engineer corps. And now I'm here.' Cross looked down at her legs and smiled. Her first. Her eternally stern exterior completely vanished as her teeth, eyes, and cheeks all opened up to reveal someone warm, trusting and friendly. In the hazy daylight bouncing off the water from the lake, Mackay took her in entirely: a natural redhead highlighted to a deep ginger, scattered freckles over a fair complexion, and green oval eyes above that sharp jawline. She had perfect teeth on the top row, and slightly crooked ones on the bottom. She was older than Mackay by a few years, and overall, he pegged her as athletically sexy, rather than pretty or cute.

'Always happy to meet a fellow battle survivor,' Cross said. 'I do know who you are by the way.'

'I'm guessing there was a write-up in the *Defence* newspaper?'

'Everyone with a major surgery ends up knowing everyone with a major surgery. *Defence* news spreads like teen gossip. An IED explosion in the Badlands with three killed. One in the first blast, two in the second. Corporal Connolly pinned in his seat by two metal shafts from the blown suspension.'

'Good work. If I wore a hat, I'd take it off.'

'Shit. I'm sorry.'

'For what?'

'My comment before, when you picked me up.'

'I remember. About not knowing how good a driver I am?'

'Totally slipped my mind. I didn't mean it.'

'Under the bridge.'

Silence passed between them. Cross spoke first, relieving the tension.

'Captain Andersen did your work at Kandahar,' she said. 'Did mine as well. He's a good surgeon.'

'A better surgeon wouldn't have left me looking like a mauled wine barrel.'

'You're alive, aren't you?'

Mackay didn't reply.

'A better surgeon doesn't exist,' said Cross. 'Any other surgeon with half the quid of Andersen would still shit bricks if they came across a real combat surgery.'

'I'll take it back,' said Mackay. 'Andersen did a good job. My skin is still itchy, and looking at the scarring in the mirror makes me feel sick, but my ribs do feel pretty good. It's like there's a cool patch all around my torso. Colder than the rest of me, which I'm assuming is the thermo-compound.'

'Holy shit, you received the thermoplastic?'

'It replaced the old ribs along the attachment points damaged in the blast.'

'Lucky man. That's a whole new level, Mackay, some real fandangle shit. You really are a modern-day Tin Man, now let's order.'

Cross didn't bother waiting to catch the eye of the waitress, she simply yelled her name across the café. Numerous patron heads turned. Mackay's eyed widened, impressed at the display. Whether Cross actually knew her name because she was a regular or if she caught a glimpse of her name tag, Mackay wasn't sure. Either way, Katie came pronto. Cross ordered eggs benedict with a side of sourdough. Mackay went with avocado-smash with poached eggs. Katie wrote it all down, left, and then returned with their coffees.

Mackay turned to Cross. 'So, we're doing this, are we? The deep and meaningful?'

'That's what we're here for,' said Cross. 'I'll go first. Question and answer. My question, your answer.'

Mackay's cognition switches flickered. He needed more caffeine to engage in what was to come. He took a long sip of coffee, allowing the warm antioxidants to flood his cells and attune his brain to his mouth.

0915hrs
Tuesday December 11, 2012
International Airport, Perth, Western Australia

At the same time Mackay and Cross drank, ate, and unloaded war stories, Mackay's older brother Malvin and his family touched down at Perth's International Airport. They hit the tarmac a little after nine in the morning in one of the most isolated cities in the world – there for a family holiday where smoky orange sunsets fanned the Indian ocean. Malvin's wife, Neve, and their two sons, Lincoln and Angus, were glad to finally be on the ground. Twenty hours in the air is one long innings for any young family. As international guests with an appreciation for wine, Malvin and Neve booked their travels three hours' drive south of Perth city in Margaret River, the wine capital of the west. It was all about sampling and indulging. Aside from world-class wines, there were other assortments on offer, including cheese, chocolate, and wild game. But that was only half the menu. The other half involved surfing pristine beaches, fishing, snorkelling, and reading a good book or two.

They collected their luggage from the carousel and moved to the Hertz vehicle hire booth – the classic yellow-over-black font unmissable inside the terminal. They'd selected a late model Toyota Camry back in Bracknell, so they just needed their passport and credit card details to sign it out. The receptionist, a younger girl with straight blonde hair cut in a bob, confirmed their details then directed them outside, past the taxi rank and passenger drop-off points to the Hertz car yard.

With Perth being seven hours ahead of England, Malvin knew they'd need a day of recovery to freshen up before heading south to their main holiday retreat in the wine region. Namely to recover from the jet lag. Once the vehicle handover was complete with an exchange of paperwork for keys, the Connollys piled inside the Camry and drove to their pre-booked hotel. A ten-minute drive from the airport. A three-star, so nothing fancy considering it was only for one night. The next morning they'd drive the three hours south to

Margaret River where they'd hired a beach house for a whole week.

When booking the holiday, Malvin calculated he would need at least two weeks off from duties as head pastor of Somerville Baptist Church. Three days prior to departure to pack and get the house in order, and another three days post-holiday to unpack and settle back into the Connolly routine. Six days either side was as good as a week, so Malvin indulged and took the full two weeks off – delegating his responsibilities to the elders.

Malvin's wife, Neve, worked alongside Malvin at the church, helping out with the worship and music teams, but for the last six years since the birth of their youngest, Lincoln, she was mostly a stay-at-home mother. Lincoln was diagnosed with autism – somewhere in the middle range of the spectrum – and had numerous requirements that needed to be met for his support. Lincoln's autism, however, didn't make him entirely different or polarised from most children his age. Most other six-year-olds would never even know he was different. It was the social interaction, nonverbal communication, and repetitive behaviours which Neve needed to monitor and care for. She had opted to remain his full-time carer and homeschool teacher, as well as undertake every other mothering duty over the past six years. But this year was Neve's last with Lincoln in a full-time capacity. He was due to make the big leap to a special needs school in the new year, which also meant this overseas trip would be the family's last big holiday for a while. Lincoln was about to find out what the world was like on his own.

0930hrs
Tuesday December 11, 2012
The Madam's Apprentice café, Aldershot

'Here we go,' Katie said. 'Avocado-smash for you, sir, and eggs benedict with your usual side of sourdough, Renee. Can I get you two anything else?'

'No thanks, cheers, Katie,' said Cross.

Mackay watched Cross nod and smile with familiarity, confirming she was a regular. For the next twenty seconds, Cross watched Mackay hook into his food with amused awe. At it like a medieval butcher.

'Slow down, Tin Man, you won't shit for a week at that rate. Nothing will get digested.'

'Bad habits,' said Mackay. 'We always ate as fast as possible to get the better part of the desserts at the mess. What's your excuse?'

'I like tasting my food. It's not going anywhere, and even if it was, I can't chase eggs.' Cross dabbed the sourdough into some spilt yolk. 'So how is it you came to find me in particular?'

A loud burst of laughter erupted from the group of teens three tables over, wedging a pause between their conversation. Heads turned. The laughter died.

'Friends of mine want me to… get better,' said Mackay. 'I was recommended to meet with you, considering we were both hit with an IED. Aside from finishing your service at Sergeant, I don't know your story, I never really read the news.'

'If you don't read the news, then what? You must be a gamer? Xbox? PlayStation?'

'Neither.'

'Atari?'

'It was all rugby for me. Both for the Army and the Inter-service teams. Played wing. Number eleven, on the left.'

'Good fucking on you. Almost as tough as boxing. I like those shorts they wear, those beefcake rumps get me juicy.'

'Christ on a bike!' Mackay called out, almost choking on some hash brown. A few heads turned.

'Bloody hell, Tin Man, get your hand off it. Like you've never heard a female grunt talk dirt.'

'Sure, it's just… been a while. You've got some proper gobshite about you, no offence and all.'

'None taken. Calm your tits and get used to it. Yes, I've got a mouth. I'm a talker. I've heard it all. Look, I was an engineer, a Sapper. One of the first with a vagina sent on deployment for counter-IED. Checking for unexploded ordnance.'

Mackay listened intently, waiting for it all to be laid out. He picked up his coffee and drained it, as did Cross.

'In 2010, my team was working with the Americans,' Cross continued. 'They had upgraded equipment that we didn't, and we had the numbers, rank and morale they didn't. They wanted us to use and run their shit, which neither side was happy with, but whatever. Long story short, some official said we were going to work together, so we met, trained, and moved into the desert to clear mines. On a routine patrol the Yanks had us working with the upgraded Bobcat minotaur which they thought was the bee's fucking knees, but the wiring malfunctioned. The imaging systems weren't scanning. Fixing the fucker would have taken over an hour, so two of us volunteered to head out and do the last kilometre manually. Me and one other Yank.'

Mackay said, 'I heard the odds of a combat engineer being launched into the sky by a mine was one in six.'

'Shitty odds, right?' said Cross.

'That's World War One infantry odds. And was the American hit with the blast?'

'He was, but he didn't die immediately. The charge fragments fanned out left and right, not upwards, and the American was hit with a whole bunch of rusty nuts and screws. But it was the shock that killed him. Sent his heart rhythm into a meltdown. He died five minutes after our medevac chopper landed at the trauma hospital. His heart just stopped.

The discharge fizzled it like the wires on the minotaur. I have to live with that too.'

'You felt responsible,' said Mackay.

'For a long time. Blamed myself for months.'

'There's no way you could have known he had a bad heart. Or that it'd fry out.'

'Didn't matter. Either way my action contributed to his death. And that's how I saw it. Which I'm sure is how you've been looking at your own incident as well.'

'I guess. That's been hard to shake. Hard to see any different viewpoint.'

'Trust me, it was an accident. Call it the shithousery of life. By fate, or God, or the tree spirits, it's all an accident. It's not murder or manslaughter. It just occurred.'

Cross looked at Mackay with sincerity. She'd only known him for a few minutes but felt like she wanted to reach and touch his hand. Hold it, just for a moment. Like it was the natural thing to do. She knew how he felt. She'd been there. Instead, she let the thought go. No hand. She kept it at her side. Another loud burst of laughter erupted from the table of teens. This time from the two girls: one high pitch, the other long and warbled like a braying donkey.

'Noisy little fuckers,' Cross said, releasing a loud burp in protest. The two boys turned around and looked over. Cross looked right back.

'Suck my dick,' she said, audible enough for at least half the café to hear.

Cross raised her head and made eye contact with Katie, giving her the *what's up with this mob* expression. Katie sighed, rolled her eyes, and countered with a suggestive shrug: *teens these days, what can you do.*

Cross took a forkful of egg and ham.

'I was antsy and pissed off, so I moved quicker than normal. Hurried and unsafe. What threw me the most was the glare of the sun bouncing off chunks of scattered glass around my feet. Blown windscreens from trucks and cars. It was everywhere, like flickering beams inside my skull.'

'I know those routes,' said Mackay. 'Did plenty of kilometres on them myself.'

'The moment before the blast,' Cross continued, 'holding that fucking detector, I was so irritated from the glare I took a step in an uncleared direction and boom. Small mistake, big change. I forgot all about my training. I was in direct contact with the IED and got thrown into the air. Time completely slowed down in the moment. I distinctly remember looking up into the clearest blue sky you've ever seen. Still one of my clearest memories.'

'I know that blast sensation,' said Mackay. 'That first sound, the discharge so close to your body, I can still hear it. Petrifies me. Everything is silent afterwards.'

Cross nodded in agreeance. Neither spoke for ten long seconds.

'It took time, but I got through the toughest part of my PTSD,' said Cross. 'Not that I'm completely through all of it, I never will be. We want to point the finger at someone, and most of the time it's at ourselves.'

Mackay nodded. 'Guilt hurts,' he said. 'And there's no light at the end of the tunnel.'

Cross said, 'Blaming yourself, or finding someone to pin it on, is a total waste of mental energy. You need to let it go. Group therapy will help with that.'

'I get it, but it's...'

'Easier said than done,' said Cross. 'I know.'

Another ten long seconds of silence. Mackay changed course. 'So, your limbs. Did it hurt?'

'Some vets I've spoken to say they can't remember losing their limbs,' said Cross. 'I can still remember the rush of warmth in my legs. The heat. It wasn't instantly painful, but I felt lighter as I was thrown into the air, then I hit the ground ten metres up the road. Some days it's as if I can still feel my legs dangling in this chair. Warm, invisible.'

'The phantom limb,' said Mackay.

Suddenly, the four youths, the two girls and two boys, ran past their table, knocking Mackay's cane to the floor and almost barging him over. They fled through the front door, one of them hurriedly chanting *run*, another shouting *go*, as they hustled out to the parking lot.

'Hey!' yelled Katie, darting out from behind the kitchen. 'You haven't paid!' She moved her heft well for a larger girl, but in no way was she quick enough to catch them.

Mackay's jaw flexed. If he was his old self, he would have helped. Held the four of them under citizen's arrest. Arm-bars, wristlocks and headlocks. Whatever was needed. Stuff he'd learned in the corps for unruly locals getting edgy before a weapon was pulled.

Looking around the café, nobody else moved. No show of good social responsibility. Mackay bent down to pick up his cane and hobbled after them like an aged cripple, but he had no speed. At least it showed integrity. It was all too late though: the Mini Cooper had already started up before Katie got to the door.

'Fucking bollocks!' shouted Katie, puffing at Mackay's side. 'And they parked in the disabled park too, the little bastards.'

'I'm sorry,' said Mackay. 'I hope that doesn't happen often. That's a real dog act.'

'No, I'm sorry for swearing,' said Katie. 'I shouldn't be rude like that in front of customers. Thanks for helping.'

'Not much help I'm afraid. I didn't even catch their number plate.'

'Bollocks.'

Once back out in the car park, Mackay's pants caught Cross's eye. They were baggy and awkward around the hips. She hadn't noticed before as he'd mostly been walking next to her, not in front. She couldn't help but comment.

'Your pants are too big, Tin Man. They look ridiculous.'

'Yes and no. They are big, but I have big legs and a small waist. It's a rugby thing.'

'Where do you shop?'

'Normal places.'

'Normal for you or normal for fat people? They're fat people's pants. It's sagging at your waist and bunching around your hips. Once you can walk without looking like a spastic in a sleeping bag, I'll take you shopping.'

Mackay grinned back at her. Partly charmed, partly embarrassed. He straightened his back and threw a half salute.

ONE WEEK LATER

0650hrs
Monday December 17, 2012
Guildford, UK

Mackay lay with his arms behind his pillow. Not asleep, just resting. Staring at the back of his eyelids, thinking thoughts. Mostly worrisome, some self-doubting, a few pitiful. Cold blood pumped away in his chest. Thoughts on repeat: the sandbox, the convoy, the first IED, the second IED. The two dead in the truck lying next to him. His fault. His alarm went off at 0650, which meant he had ten minutes to work through the getting-up process. He promised Cross he'd be at her gym at 0800 for a session. His first ever boxing class, taught by a woman who couldn't even stand. He was interested all the same. She had the credentials, the experience, and the mouth to back herself. He showered and shaved, brushed his teeth, combed his hair. Microwaved a bowl of quick oats from a sachet and buried it down with an instant coffee.

Once Mackay arrived and saw the other trainers warming up, he felt borderline pathetic. He had adequate balance and poise, but everything else in his body felt different. The physio had said he was good to let go of the cane, but he almost felt naked without it. It'd been a full six months since surgery, but habits were hard to let go.

Cross blew a whistle and wheeled herself around, facing front and centre in the middle of the gym.

'Listen the fuck in,' she yelled. 'You're starting with a two-set repeat. Twenty push-ups, twenty double unders. Twelve minutes non-stop. If you don't know what double unders are, fuck off home, this is not a beginner's class.'

Mackay piped in, 'This is my first class, Sergeant, kind of makes me a beginner. Still want me to fuck off?'

Cross twitched her head and found Mackay near a bag in the corner.

'You're here as per request. And I'm not in service anymore so you can knock that sergeant shit off, there's no rank here. Can you skip with that mangled ribcage of yours?'

'It'll look shite, but I'll try my best.'

'East End prostitutes try their best. If you're not coping, you've got the water cooler or the door.'

Mackay hung in well enough for the twelve minutes. His upper body seemed to work as normal as he'd ever remembered, only that it felt looser and somewhat elastic. Like it was stretching as he breathed. His lungs felt capable, operating on-point, and the strenuous work felt fantastic. Like the good old days. The endorphins helping the flow of oxygen into his brain. Although the fibres around his new ribs were still adjusting to the movements, Mackay found a good balance between the pain. When it came to sparring,

Cross left Mackay out. Early days. Gloves and opponents could come later. When he partnered up for combination drills, Cross noted his footwork needed readjusting, which was clompy and leaden like a bison. She had him watch and follow the foot patterns of two trainers working a punch-and-shuffle: right foot, left foot, rotate and rip at the opponent's floating ribs. An offensive attack to the kidneys. Perfect for weakening the bladder, or the large intestine. At the end of the session Mackay took a drink from the water cooler, then sat and sucked the air calmly. Impressed he wasn't lying on the floor.

Cross was also impressed.

'I'm glad you showed,' she said, wheeling between the last of the leavers. 'For a beginner, you didn't look too bad. Most newbies vomit and cry. I've even had special forces in here keeled over holding their breakfast in.'

'I felt alright.'

'Good for you. Got plans?'

Mackay shook his head.

'I'd like to head into town, buy some necessities and what not. And you still need a new pair of pants. I was hoping you could do the pleasantries?'

'Not a problem,' said Mackay.

'You sure you don't mind driving?'

'Happy to oblige.'

'Just double-checking.'

'It's all good. You have no legs and I've nowhere else to be.'

'That Hilux isn't yours, is it?'

'It's a friend's.'

'Good friend.'

'He left it with me. At least until my army benefit scheme pays me enough to afford my own car. How could you tell?'

'You looked like a learner driver last time. Awkward and

unfamiliar. Either it wasn't your car, or you were scared because of… you know. No offence.'

'None taken. I get it. You're right both ways. PTSD comes in weird shapes and forms. I'd go with cautious or hesitant. Scared is a big word.'

'Fair call, I'll take it back. Anyway, let's get out of here. Refuel. Coffee and a snack. We'll go to the Sprocket Shot first. I like their ham and cheese toasties.'

'I'll go shower.'

'Good to hear. Wouldn't want your sweaty arse juice infusing in your friend's upholstery.'

0930hrs
Monday December 17, 2012
Sprocket Shot Café. Aldershot Town Centre

The Sprocket Shot was a franchise establishment, similar to most get-and-go places with its own custom colour scheme and staff uniform. Mackay and the red ant sat inside where it was warm. A two-seater where Cross could move her chair underneath the flat of the table. Mackay took out his credit card, left his wallet and phone on the table as a sign of territory, and joined the queue. He was fifth in line, which took roughly three and a half minutes to filter down to first in line where he ordered for the both of them: two ham and cheese toasties with two large double-shot flat whites. Easy to roll off the tongue. Keep the line moving.

The girl at the register asked Mackay for a name. He answered, not bothering with correcting any spelling confusion. He sat back with Cross, who glanced at a text message springing to life with a chime on her phone. She dabbed and scrolled then rapped at the screen with her thumbs. She pressed send and put her phone back down.

'This is going to be a short one, Tin Man,' she said. 'Might need to eat and drink on the move. We'll do my shopping first, get your pants, then get back to the garrison ASAP. The physical training instructors have fucked a booking. They need me back earlier.'

'Everything okay?'

'They've requested the boxing gym for an infantry unit's training session, only they're pushing it forward. Means I have to go back earlier. More money for me, but they haven't scheduled it through the proper channels, so someone's going to be on the other end of a one-way conversation.'

'Fucking Army,' said Mackay.

'Fucking Army,' said Cross.

A sharp voice called Mackay's name from behind the counter, then repeated what he ordered. The tone was all business, the subtext twofold: *come get your order now, we're running a tight ship here.*

Aldershot's main shopping hub was paved with rustic baggeridge pavers. Weathered in appearance, but smooth enough for the red ant's chair to roll along without jackhammering. Both sides were lined with high-end brand stores, independent shops, bric-á-brac, market stalls, cafés, bars and restaurants.

'I need new towels at the bed and bathroom store,' said Cross. 'I don't use fabric softener, so my current collection has gone to sandpaper. Might indulge and go luxury. Egyptian cotton. The skin on my arse is soft like tofu now and I want to keep it that way. Then we'll jump next door and look for some jeans for you. Head back to base after that. Happy to tag along?'

'I'm unemployed, where else am I going?'

'Good answer.'

Cross looked like she knew where she was going so Mackay followed. Cross wheeled and sipped, Mackay walked and sipped. Cross offered up Mackay's toasty from inside the paper bag. Cross wheeled and ate, Mackay walked and ate.

'How is it?' asked Cross.

'Toasty.'

After a florist, two independent cafés, a boutique French-Italian bakery and a tobacconist selling vaping tools and hippie flavoured tobacco, they came to the Bed and Bath. As they entered the glass sliding door, the creamy-blue walls made it feel more like a child's nursery, which Mackay thought worked in its favour. Namely because the floor was bustling with women; some pregnant, some weaving about looking for a sale, some comparing prices, some standing next to slack-jawed husbands scrolling through their phones. It was a female's domain, but it was a nice setting regardless. Calming. The fragrances potent but pleasant, and the daylight enough to offer a hint of warmth.

Cross searched through a few stacks of towels. Dark blues, light blues, dark greys, light greys. She kept away from the pinks and yellows which even Mackay thought were hideous and belonged to hippie singles or alternative vegans. Cross grabbed two towels: one dark blue and one light blue, which matched the same baby-blue coating the walls.

'These will do,' said Cross. 'Egyptian Cotton. Let's go. That vanilla or cinnamon or whatever incense in here is too much.'

Mackay liked the smell but said nothing. He followed her to the counter at the front where two middle-aged staff in black aprons and white turtlenecks scanned barcodes and took cards and cash. They lined up off to the side, waiting behind an elderly couple and a young pregnant woman in her mid-twenties. The wife of the two old timers was laying out the contents of her shopping basket onto the counter: hand sanitiser, smelly soaps and a plastic indoor plant probably for a porcelain bath corner or a windowsill. The pregnant woman had what seemed to be two bath robes – one his, one hers – as well as the exact same coloured towels Cross had, but in hand towel size.

The elderly couple paid with credit and the line moved on. Swift and efficient, which impressed Mackay as normally the old folk liked using cash. Long-time habits. Next was the pregnant lady. However, the robes and hand towels never made it to the counter. Instead, she was shoved violently in the back and thrown sideways into the elderly couple walking towards the entrance. Into the rear hip of the elder husband, who, through kinetic energy, then ploughed into the back of his wife, throwing her shopping bag and contents onto the floor. The purchased items sprawling out through the open sliding door onto the baggeridge pavers outside.

The pregnant lady went down, the old husband went down, the old wife went down. Tangled in a mess of arms and legs, hand towels, sanitiser, bath robes and soaps. Cross and Mackay were standing off to the side of the counter, so they missed being part of the action.

In the blurred explosion of bodies hitting the floor, Cross and Mackay first looked at the sprawled forms on the ground, then back up at each other. Like it was choreographed in a rehearsal for a play. They noticed two things at once: firstly, two young men wearing black backpacks were scrambled in amongst the tangled mess of limbs. Secondly, the same two men hustled furiously to their feet, headed for the exit, turned left and were gone. In the initial moments of brain activity that followed, Mackay struggled to piece everything together.

'Fuckin' shite,' he said, bewilderment, shock and irritation combined. Then confusion took place, why the hurry? Why was it necessary to knock a pregnant woman and two old-timers over? In the next wave of brain activity, recognition of the situation appeared, clearing said confusion. Which was immediately replaced with swarming anger. Partly at the injustice, partly at himself for not seeing it coming. Mackay's mental synapses quickly clarified the scenario: two tactless men had ripped the store off, bulldozing three hapless patrons over in the process. Zero respect. Poor form and uncalled for. Even thieves had the capacity to be mindful of the elderly, and the pregnant. Mackay's adrenalin pumped into his stomach, the hair on the back of his neck sat up. Reactively, his fists had clenched into a couple of meat tenderisers. Two seconds later, Cross turned and whacked Mackay against the thigh.

'You're on, Tin Man,' she said.

Mackay took it as scripture. Like a commandment given from God.

'Fuckin' aye,' he said.

For almost two weeks he'd been able to stand and walk and skip with a rope, which also likely meant he could run. Although he hadn't run in months – six to be precise – that old school muscle memory hadn't lapsed. That kind of thing was locked in forever.

Mackay bent down and took the pregnant woman under the arm, bringing her to a sitting position. He visually observed her general state, making sure she wasn't hurt, then noted the moving parts of the old couple who were already getting to their feet. He made a mental note they were all okay, then left the store.

Mackay exited the shopfront, turned left and began increasing speed. One foot after the other, like he'd known it all his life. His gait was steady. His balance perfect. Heel, toe, lift, stride. Faster, then faster again. His hamstrings felt right, his quads loose, his calves taught, the flexion in his ankles lubricated. Five seconds after shooting across the cobbled pavers, he caught site of the men: two distant figures, black backpacks, legging it a hundred and twenty yards ahead. Somewhere between a fruit and veg stall and the French-Italian bakery. The pedestrian streets weren't in their busiest period considering it was a Monday morning at a little after

1000, the beginning of the working week. Being mid-morning, the streets were mostly vacant aside from a lazy peppering of the usual local retail staff and career-driven suits looking for their mid-morning coffee break. Mackay calculated the crowd as he ran, his tunnel vision consistently re-evaluating the best line of sight to home in on the absconders. He dodged and danced between the scattered amblers until the pavers came to the end of the precinct, opening to a clear cement footpath and an opportunity to increase speed. Free of shoppers, back on the urban streets. Like reverse osmosis he'd moved from an area of high concentration to an area of low concentration. As he ran on, he noticed his sprint pace felt relaxed. His stride light and elastic. He was catching up easily. The hundred and twenty yards had dropped to fifty as the two men rounded a left bend with a pub on the corner, spitting them onto Aldershot's main street. For someone who hadn't run in six months, Mackay had gained seventy yards in less than twenty seconds, and he was still breathing through his nose. No panting, no puffing. The initial oxygen debt the body usually experiences from exertion didn't even arise. Like it never existed. He had stabilised to an optimal output faster than he could ever remember.

As he rounded the pub, Mackay gained a clearer view of the two men: skinny, average height, Caucasian. Both in jeans, sneakers, and beanies. One wore a hooded jumper, one a zip-up jacket. Two black backpacks. Big enough to fit towels, robes, and lotions. Small enough to wear comfortably for day trips, or for sprinting through pedestrian shopping precincts.

Mackay closed in with forty yards remaining. Problem was the two men had slowed to jump onto a motorbike. Parked kerbside at a forty-five-degree angle – facing the road for an optimal getaway. Planned ahead of time. Predetermined for ease of accessibility with minimum delay or setback. They'd done this kind of thing before.

The bike was a red and white Honda. Street bike, not dirt. No helmets. Easier to get on and get gone. Mackay didn't know his bikes, never spent much time on the two-wheeled variety. He was savvy with the four-wheel kind: trucks and cars. But he could tell the bike was quick by the size: big gas tank, big engine. A Japanese racing product built for speed, which also meant quick throttle response and instant acceleration.

With thirty yards left, the two men sat on the bike and flicked the kickstand. The one in the rear wrapped his arms around the one in front and pinned his feet over the passenger's foot pegs. The one in front inserted the key, which was when the man noticed Mackay from the corner of his eye – bounding beyond his left shoulder. Coming in hard and fast. Another man in jeans and a hoody. Arms pumping, legs pounding.

The man on the bike took a double take, watching the freight train coming in like a big rude shock. He hadn't noticed anything up until that point. No cops, no irate retail staff. Nothing. Not until an athletically built man with quad muscles like loaves of sourdough was pelting in his direction with twenty yards left. The man in the rear cottoned on and repeated the same motion. Double take. Big rude shock coming. The man in front went from top dog to trench rat in an instant, fumbling the key; once, twice. On his third attempt, the bike kicked into life. The engine engaged, he dropped the clutch and took off.

The bike lurched across the tarmac – first gear, shrieking like a scalded cat. With five yards out, Mackay was close, but he wasn't going to make it. The man wound the throttle and the bike shot off, hooking into the flow of traffic. The man in the rear let an arm go and flipped Mackay the bird – a skinny middle finger held long and hard. A token *fuck you*. The freight train had lost the round.

But today was different.

They didn't expect what the next three minutes had in store. They'd planned on a clean getaway, but they hadn't planned on

Mackay. An angry young man given a certain commandment by a certain red ant in a wheelchair. Sometimes, plans don't follow through as predicted.

> 1000hrs
> Monday December 17, 2012
> Sprocket Shot Café. Aldershot Town Centre

Aldershot isn't a big town, and being a mid-Monday morning, most people were at work or out on coffee breaks, so the traffic flow was light. Mackay's body felt aligned and purposeful. His breathing steady, his legs on point. His bones and cartilage gelled comfortably on the footpath, running parallel to the road as the bike headed north, away from the shopping hub. Mackay didn't slow. Even though the bike skirted off into traffic, there was plenty of room to hustle. Mackay kept up. He felt incredible. Like the warm-up had finished and he was ready for the hard stuff.

At the maximum urban road speed of thirty miles per hour, the men on the bike surged with the flow of traffic, then sat just under the legal limit. Nothing excessive, nothing frantic. No need to draw attention. With their pursuer lost as a fleeting afterthought, they rode on. Back on the high horse. Goods in tow. Making their way back to base to present the haul to the boss, evaluate the mission and take the rest of the afternoon off. Maybe sell their goods through some dodgy pawning business run by scungy immigrant gangs.

Mackay ran on. Trailing, but catching. Gaining speed steadily. Like riding a wave of torque, the blood and air inside him surged, pressurised, then liberated his muscles to project him forward. He strode off the footpath and ran parallel to the road, his feet skipping across the street. Fists clenched, arms pumping, one meaty leg in front of the other like pistons on over-boost. His body maintaining a slight lean forward for optimal trajectory.

Mackay lined himself up alongside a passing Mazda SUV. A family wagon with a mother hauling two kids. The closest child in the rear passenger seat – a young girl of about four years old – watched Mackay maintain pace as they drove along beside him. Them in the car, him on the road. At twenty-seven miles an hour. She waved. Her face blank with awe and confusion. Mackay didn't notice, all his tunnel vision could see was the red and white Honda fifty yards ahead.

After a quarter mile, the street came to an intersection. A crossroad with a stop sign. The bike didn't stop, it turned left, but Mackay was on his feet, which meant he was able to cut diagonally across the sidewalk. No need to stay on the road. It meant Mackay could maintain a straight line point to point over a kerb, past a real estate agent, down the kerb and back onto the road. He kept gaining pace and stride, cutting through the slipstream while it tugged furiously at his clothes. The two men still unaware a storming pair of legs were now forty yards at their seven o'clock.

Mackay didn't have a clue how fast he was going, the incivility of the two men barging into the pregnant woman and old-timers was still seething in his memory. It propelled him on, pushing him harder and faster. Unbeknownst to him, Mackay had hit and maintained twenty-seven miles an hour as he edged closer and closer to the Honda. At his maximal speed, Usain Bolt – the fastest human to have ever lived – had been clocked at just under twenty-eight miles per hour. His fastest hundred-metre run at the Berlin World Championships. Mackay was bordering on the same trap speed, and he was still accelerating. With twenty yards to go, he passed a Vespa scooter, an Audi sedan and an old Nazi-era Volkswagen Beetle, whose driver lurched in shock, swerving away and almost colliding into oncoming traffic in the opposite lane.

A fork in the road was encroaching at a roundabout fifty yards ahead. The front rider of the Honda flicked the indicator to turn right. Mackay was now down to ten yards behind. They had no idea he was still on the chase. For them, their job was done, complacency already set in hundreds of metres back. Before the fork merged into a dual lane, Mackay reduced his distance even further: five yards out. Basically, arm's reach. All forms of transport on the road started decelerating with the flow of traffic, bumper to bumper at the junction. The lead rider levered the brakes and the bike slowed along with everyone else. Bad for them, good for Mackay. Mackay reached out with both hands, aiming for fistfuls of jacket. He grabbed the man in front with his left, the man in back with his right, then tried easing off his pace. Which, at the speed he was moving, was extremely difficult.

With instinctive reaction, the lead rider slammed on the brakes. Reacting to preserve the alarm of the situation: big athletic form, about to collide. Mass times acceleration to create force. Newton's second Law. With Mackay's fists bunched firmly around the fabric of their jackets, their thirty-mile-an-hour momentum ripped both men off the bike at once: kinetic energy coupled with the bike's deceleration and braking traction. The brake pads bit the discs and launched the men over the handlebars onto the road, narrowly missing the Beetle in front. The locking tyres tossed the bike forward in an arc, sending it sliding across the tarmac and stopping dead underneath the Beetle's rear bumper.

With fists still clenched into the men's jackets, Mackay could not control the momentum and slow his stride. Decelerating from twenty-seven miles an hour took balance and eccentric muscle stabilisation which Mackay wasn't ready for. With the men in mid-air waiting for that raw taste of asphalt, Mackay hit the pavement along with them. Another tangled mess of three bodies. Tripping over the two men, Mackay fortunately landed with the weight of his torso on one of the backpacks. Lucky for Mackay, not so for the thief. It cushioned a large portion of Mackay's fall, and it helped that the contents inside the backpack were soft – likely towels or various thick cotton materials from the Bed and Bath. Mackay bounced off the man's backpack and tucked himself into a ball. An automatic reaction. Instinctive from years of playing rugby, withstanding all forms of scrums, tackles, and collisions. He landed on his side and, with the accumulated momentum, rolled over and over like a boulder until his rotating mass ran its course, coming to a stop against the sidewalk.

The three men were motionless. A disarray of slack limbs, but at least everyone was breathing. Seconds passed, then Mackay stirred first, slow and cautious. All chests rose and fell, though Mackay's rose slower, higher, and deeper than the other two. All three were grazed and bruised-up, which would soon raise its head in higher doses of pain. Within a minute, a generous crowd, including the man on the Vespa, the driver of the Beetle and the mother and daughter from the Mazda, had gathered around. Considering the event occurred outside on public roads, anyone who's anyone nearby wanted a look-in. Rubberneck the situation. Human nature. No less than twenty people had already gathered around the sidewalk, with the numbers quickly growing. Vehicles had pulled over, scooters, vans, all flashing their warning lights so they could gawk while the rest of the traffic moved around them. Mobile phones were out, and pictures were being taken. All witnesses to the drama, wanting to catch it live. An Aldershot traffic incident wasn't overly regular. Small town, minimal traffic. But this was news. Two men had just been ripped from their street bike doing almost thirty miles an hour. By a man on foot.

Mackay stirred some more. He was face down on the bitumen, curled in a ball. He opened his eyes and blinked, gathering clarity to his senses. Making conscious and subconscious calculations on his primaries: sustained injuries, genetic accoutrements, levels of movement and coordination. He rolled onto his front, staggered to his feet and stood up, exhilarated. The release of the running at those speeds felt indescribable. Like a consummate stimulant. A black-market drug easing all the amassed tension he'd ever had in his head.

All eyes turned towards the athletic man. Awkwardly wide in the chest, gulping in litres of air, taking in the commotion. You could almost hear the dry, wintery necks creak in unison as they turned to look. Their cold eyelids stretching wide in astonishment as he limped to the sidewalk. His jumper was torn across the right shoulder and his jeans were ripped through the lower thigh and calf. His head felt okay, as did his neck, back, hips and groin. Priorities assessed, no major alarms. His ribs were fine too, which was fortunate, as they copped a battering from rolling across the ground. He rotated his shoulders. Left, then right. Both a little painful from scuffing the tarmac but no issues there. His breathing was already back to normal, and he noticed he wasn't sweating, which was unusual. At the pace he was going, most people would have soaked through two layers of clothes and taken minutes to get heart rates back to level. Mackay had recovered in seconds. He looked around at the crowd – a little dizzy, a little weary. Then he looked at the men lying on the ground. No movement, still breathing, likely unconscious. Kneeling over them were two bystanders. Both women, who Mackay assumed were first-aiders, doing the noble civilian duty which was more than he would have given them.

A woman approached him slowly to his left. Late forties, a young girl holding her hand shyly behind her. The mother and daughter from the Mazda SUV.

'Are you okay, sir?' asked the mother.

Mackay blinked in recognition someone was speaking to him. He recouped his mental composure and processed the question.

'I guess I am,' he said.

'Are you sure?' she said, pressing carefully. 'You were just in a road accident.'

The young girl stared up at Mackay. Gorgeous brown oval eyes. Curious and awestruck. She wore a little white tracksuit with an embroidered logo of a banner flaunted above a pair of glittery shoes. A uniform of some type. For dance or cheerleading, or aerobic gymnastics. Her hips twisted subconsciously. Her brown peepers didn't blink once.

'Well, you were only sort of in a road accident,' she said matter-of-factly. 'You were running, and *they* were riding.' She pointed to the two with the backpacks lying roadside.

An older guy also approached. Heavy-set with a big unruly beard. The driver of the Beetle. The one who swerved into oncoming traffic as Mackay sprinted past. He joined the mother and daughter, then took another step forward, watchful, closing in. Mackay was unsure of his intention and demeanour, so he took half a step back.

'You passed me doing twenty-five miles an hour, man,' said the beard. Big rounded Scottish accent. 'Twenty-five bloomin' miles. I almost shat myself. Who are you?'

His tone was marginally irritated, probably because of the bike slamming into the rear of his car, yet he sounded wholly impressed at the same time.

'I'm just… just a guy,' said Mackay. 'You said I passed you at twenty-five miles an hour?'

'My word you did. On foot you were. Running like some wild African cat.'

Mackay didn't know how to respond. He didn't believe it. He was a good runner but reaching that level of speed was not possible.

A siren wailed in the background, pealing closer. Blue and red flashing lights rippled and bounced off the surrounding trees and business fronts. Someone had called an ambulance. Or the police. Or both. The crowd perked up and began to move and disperse as the wail dropped to a blurt with a firm *move out the way*. A silver Mitsubishi SUV with chequered blues and yellows navigated through the swell of the crowd. It rolled to a halt and parked kerbside. Two bobbies stepped out: male and female. An early twenties male, an early forties female. A young constable and an experienced sergeant, both with a spring in their step. Probably due to a recent intake of coffee, and because it was likely their biggest job of the week. Barked out of the office by the chief inspector.

Next, the rear driver's side door of the police vehicle opened. One of the Bed and Bath staff emerged: middle-aged lady, black apron, white turtleneck. The one from the payment register. The male officer led her to where the two unconscious lay. For visual identification, probably. At the same time, the female officer moved around to the rear of the SUV, opened the tailgate, removed a wheelchair and pushed it around to the rear passenger side. Cross swung out of the SUV like a gymnast and lowered herself down. She raised her neck like a periscope, scanning for Mackay. Mackay caught glimpse of her first and walked over before a second siren wailed. Marginally different tone to the first, marginally different tempo. An ambulance.

'What in the horse's cock have you been doing?' said Cross, pulling up next to him.

'I gave chase. Now here we are. What of it?' said Mackay, waiting for it.

'What of it? You look like you've been fucked by a walrus.'

'Aye, you're right there. Ended like shite in a bucket.'

The mother and daughter were standing within earshot. The mother pruned her face inward at the remarks while the little girl stared on. Still wide-eyed, still not blinking. The female officer, a Sergeant Rose according to her name badge and insignia on her epaulettes, pulled a pen and pad from an inside breast pocket ready to take notes. The male constable, a few feet over, was already at it, scribbling down information next to the Bed and Bath lady and first-aiders.

Cross continued, 'The radio in the car said a man had chased down two shoplifters heading towards this roundabout. On a fucking motorcycle. Explain that to me.'

'Ma'am,' the female sergeant said, interrupting. 'I need two minutes to take some notes. Then he's all yours. And I'll need a full statement back at the station as well. We can take both of you in our vehicle if you like.'

'Sounds marvellous,' said Cross.

> 1100hrs
> Monday December 17, 2012
> Hampshire Constabulary. Aldershot Police Station

Inside the station, Mackay gave his formal, extended version of events in a statement to Sergeant Rose. Cross sat next to him, listening, soaking in the details, running explanations through her mind. She weighed the reasonings and balanced the cause and effect with outcomes involving Mackay's IED explosion, followed with military-grade surgery. The good sergeant punched letters and words into a generation-old computer as she asked the basic line of questioning which repeatedly began with, *'to your best recollection'*, and *'what happened next?'*. In an adjacent room, the Bed and Bath employee with the white turtleneck gave her own extended version of events to the male constable. The keys on his board tapped away with refined rhythm as he created dates, times, and sentences. At the same time, the Vespa rider, driver of the Beetle and mother and daughter from the Mazda sat outside in the station foyer waiting to give their versions.

Once Mackay was finished, Rose logged out of the computer, swivelled her chair and gave Mackay the once-over – scanning him from head to toe. She was blonde, taller than most women, and a one-time glamour. On duty in the workplace however, she looked her age, her early forties seeping through in the artificial light of the office. Age plus motherhood had added to her classic pear shape, but she'd withheld good physical form with obvious attention to diet and exercise. Maybe she was a swimmer back in her day. Or a ball player. The type of physique that could hold her own in a raid or tussle. In a more personalised line of questioning, Rose asked the big fish, the main question on every lip in the station.

'Level with me, Mackay,' she started curiously, 'a lot of people are saying you maintained close to thirty miles an hour for over fifteen seconds. Do you think you were running that fast, or are they exaggerating? Because that's some proper speed. For all my athletic knowledge, that's world-record pace, if not better.'

'I've no idea, Sergeant,' said Mackay. 'I'm a rugby man. Played for years. Trained right here in Aldershot. Played all our neighbouring teams, as well as South Africa, Australia, New Zealand. We even played an American team once. My legs were always my best asset. I'm a fast runner.'

'That fast?'

'Maybe the traffic speed was wrong.'

'We have multiple witnesses saying the same thing. Same speed was mentioned.'

'Maybe science could explain it differently.'

'How so?'

'Were all the vehicles recorded in digital speed or analogue speed? Were the witnesses all looking at the speed at the same exact time? Because the traffic flow was slowing at various points.'

'I'm sure the difference in speed between analogue and digital is marginal.'

'But you couldn't be one hundred per cent.'

'I suppose we couldn't.'

'Suppose I was having a good day. The guys on the bike weren't. Like I said, my best weapon was always my speed. Tackling off the fly, hunting a getaway. Muscle memory just doing its thing. Either way, whatever pace I was doing, I couldn't have kept it up. I'm not an Olympian.'

Rose eyed him off again. Top to toe. Uncertainties playing ping-pong in her head.

'Well done for grabbing them anyway,' she said. 'Right good job however you managed. We've had them on our watch list for the last couple months. Plenty jobs they got done in that time too. Break-ins and shoplifting. Whoever's organising the snatch and grabs isn't going to be happy. An immigrant gang we think. We'll be pushing this one up the chain to the metro task force now, which is beyond my pay grade.'

'Now they're down two guys,' said Mackay.

'And hopefully they'll lead us to the top of the chain.'

'Can only hope.'

Cross chimed in. 'Will he be charged? For yanking them off the bike? They were out pretty cold.'

'They're awake now and cuffed to a bed at Hampshire Hospital,' said Rose. 'So I've been told. I highly doubt they'll make a case on your friend. They're being questioned about their gang affiliations as we speak.'

Cross said, 'I'm just considering how modern lawsuits have been evolving, justice systems rorts, cotton wool for the offenders. All that bullshit.'

Rose said, 'I see what you mean. Honestly, they have the option to charge him, sure. The way of the world says they can. But in our way of the world, in this part of England we're better than that, and so are our prosecutors. They'll have a snowball's chance in hell making a case given their history. We're on your side with this one.'

'How's the pregnant lady?' asked Mackay.

'Doing fine, as far as I heard from the staff at the Bed and Bath. We have her coming in soon for her statement. I'll pass on your concern. I'm sure she'd be very thankful for asking.'

Rose stood. Mackay took it as a sign that time was up, so he did the same. Cross made a one-eighty and began wheeling herself towards the door.

'Thanks for your civilian service,' said Rose. 'No reward unfortunately, but we're glad you've got an eye out for the town's better interest. Need more men like you. You Army?'

'Ex-Army,' said Mackay. 'Transport corps. Not entirely a local. Born and raised in Dublin, made it over to Guildford in my early teens. I know, I know, a West Brit.'

'I didn't say anything.'

'You were thinking it. I like both countries.'

'It's a big move.'

'There wasn't much work in my father's field. The market was saturated with his type.'

Rose stayed quiet and raised a brow, waiting for the follow-up answer.

'He was a mechanic,' said Mackay. 'Mostly diesel engines. Ran a shop. There was a hole in the industry for his expertise here, just not around Dublin. He's passed on now.'

'Condolences.'

'Thanks. Lung cancer. Long-time heavy smoker. Too stubborn to quit. Mum's still kicking on though. Lives near my brother in a care home in Bracknell, except he's on a holiday in Australia with his family. I should go see her.'

'I'm sure she would appreciate it,' said Rose. 'I like Bracknell. Nice part of the country. Generally quiet from what I hear.'

'True. The quiet can be good and bad,' said Mackay.

'Good for the police.'

'Noise usually makes things more interesting.'

'That's Army talk that is, if I've ever heard it.'

'The full battle-rattle.'

Cross rolled her eyes.

The good sergeant acknowledged with a smile. A brief awkward pause elapsed as both stood at a conversation stalemate. The mutual equivalent of knowing it was time to finish but struggling on how to part ways. There was nothing further to say from either party and Mackay wondered whether he should leave first or wait to be dismissed, like the good old days.

'So, we're all good then?' Mackay said, breaking the silence.

'All good,' said Rose. 'I've got nothing else for you. Don't be surprised if the local newspapers get in touch with you though. Apparently, you're fast. But from my end, if you hear nothing from us, then all's gone well and you're clear as mud. Hooroo.'

The stalemate broke and that was it. Mackay and Cross left the station just before midday. He was a little sore in the shoulders and the thick wing of muscle in his back, but the rest was fine. On the inside, Mackay still felt sky-high. Top of the world. He couldn't remember the last time he felt this good. Somewhere in his grey matter, his neurotransmitters were finally reprocessing a forgotten form of elation he'd been missing for months. Not since he went AWOL with Chris and Luke on their first tour. When they called in an air strike on some rebels whilst looking to buy some local sour hooch.

FOUR

SHOCK

1200hrs
Monday December 17, 2012
Hampshire Constabulary. Aldershot Police Station

A police escort, a young male probationary constable learning the ropes, was given the run-around duties. Tasked to drive Mackay and Cross in the same Mitsubishi SUV, back to Aldershot's paved pedestrian shopping hub. Back to the parked Toyota Hilux.

'So, you two are best friends now?' Cross said, sitting next to Mackay on the rear bench. She sat on the far right, he on the far left. The centre space a good two cold feet between them.

'What's that?' said Mackay.

'Getting deep and personal with the sergeant back there at the station.'

'She seemed decent. Bit of a gaffer, as they say.'

'You mean gammer. Gaffer is used for old men, Tin Man. You should know. Been in the country long enough.'

'We going there, are we? I'm sorry I'm not fully acquainted with the jargon. My new objective is to make friends, right? I'm doing my best. Those words might have even come from that wide mouth you got there.'

'With the bobby patrol?'

'Aye, with whoever. Let's just say I'm practising my social skills. Feels nice talking to people again. And people listening to me.'

Cross stared out the window. The probationary constable darted a glance in the rear-view mirror.

'Well, I admit you did pretty good then,' Cross said still facing the window. 'Opened up and answered all her questions. Full sentences too. Next step is to call her at home and schedule a dinner and a movie.'

'She was talking to me, not you.'

'Of course, you're the big shot now.'

'Why do you care anyway? Where's this going?'

'I don't care, just making a point of observation.'

'Cheers and thanks then, guv,' said Mackay, unsure if he'd done something wrong.

Neither spoke for the rest of the short drive back to the Hilux.

Once their escort parked, Mackay did the polite thing and hauled Cross from the passenger bench of the Mitsubishi, into the passenger seat of the Hilux. One arm under the backside, one arm around her waist, like they were just married, entering the bedroom. There wasn't much weight to her. Deceptively light for a double amputee. Amazing how much a solid set of legs weighed. Knees, shins, feet, litres of liquid, attached bone, cartilage and muscle all added up. Without it, Cross's body weighed like a child's. Mackay stepped around and grabbed her wheelchair from the SUV's load space, transferred it to the back of the Hilux, then sat in the driver's seat.

'So, the chase-down,' started Cross as Mackay slid and clicked the buckle. 'The speed.'

'I can't explain it,' Mackay said, turning the key. 'Never even realised what was happening. I was in a zone, gunning it, then I grabbed them, then I fell. Weirdest thing was that afterwards, aside from falling over and looking like a right twat, I felt totally fine. Wasn't puffing, wasn't sweating. Just sore was all.' Mackay rolled his shoulder back and forth. 'Everything feels okay.'

Cross said, 'Whatever happened, it's an anomaly. You're a fucking anomaly.'

'*Pog mo thoin.*'

'That's one Irish saying I do know. Don't get all salty on me.'

'I'm salty?'

'Can we move on?'

'I'm sure you will regardless.'

'Cheer up, Charlie. How in Christ you managed the speed and the take-down within five minutes is damn near impossible.'

Mackay pulled away from the kerb, mashed the throttle and shuttled into the traffic – the exhaust yelling in retort as he left. Aggressive and purposeful like he was biting back at Cross's remarks with noise rather than words. Mackay stared straight ahead, overtaking, merging, then overtaking and merging again. On repeat. All the way until all the traffic cleared away behind him.

A cold shot of anxiety began to split and emerge somewhere deep in the pit of Mackay's gut. Like a worm after a downpour, raising its head slowly and taking a peek at the world. Uncertain whether it continues to higher ground or nestles back into the mush. Cross was annoyed and upset over something, but Mackay couldn't put a finger on it. It was confusing. But this was Cross. A red ant with a big mouth. All talk, all military. He hoped it was just the nonsense from another Army brat who liked mouthing off. Heart on her sleeve, no shame, all confidence. Letting it go was the hard part. The whole water off a duck's back thing was difficult. There were always leftover uncertainties and zero clarification when it came to women. Running on the street had put him in a great mood, and he wished he were back out there. It felt good. Felt right. Then Cross cut him down. Maybe he was just thin-skinned or overly sensitive, but whatever her problem was, he was in the clear. He was sure of that. Neither spoke until they were on the main road leading to the garrison security gates.

Cross broke the ice.

'I don't mean you're weird or strange, or some sort of mutant,' she said, struggling to sound courteous.

Mackay kept quiet. Partly because he didn't know what to say, and partly because he was starting to feel tired. He pulled up at the security booth so they could both present their IDs, then drove on through. Mackay stared reticently at random passing buildings, observing the variations in colours and shapes. Making a point of ignoring Cross and keeping his mouth shut.

'Bloomin' hell,' said Cross. 'Grow up already, I hate it when there's silence. And don't take my words to heart either, you fucking panzy. This is some kind of phenomenon, we both know it. And we both know it has something to do with that new fucked-up cheese grater chest of yours. Guaranteed. It felt big when you carried me.'

'Carried you? When?' said Mackay, light-headed, struggling to focus on the streets and signs back to the gym. Extreme fatigue was pasting his brain, laying on stronger by the second. Working up from dull, to pointy, to razor sharp.

'Just now,' said Cross. 'From the police car into here, you goldfish. Your chest felt wide. Like it was… enlarged. Bigger than normal. I have felt other men's chests you know.'

'Okay.'

'Okay? That's it?' Cross turned and looked directly at him. His head and neck were sagged over, his chin almost resting on the horn in the middle of the steering wheel. He breathed in deep and sighed. Cross couldn't tell if he was annoyed or about to pass out.

'You okay?' she asked.

'I'm fine.'

'Quit cocking about, you look terrible.'

'I'm just tired.'

'Fine then. We can talk about this later after I've sorted out my bullshit with the booking swap. We're going to look for Captain Andersen to find more answers.'

'The surgeon?' said Mackay.

'What other Captain Andersen do you know who's a surgeon? You need some time to rest and reset, Tin Man. You look like shit and your brain is all over the place.'

Mackay took another long breath. His eyes were growing heavier by the second, petering just above the bottom of the sockets. He closed them, just for a second. His foot slipped off the accelerator.

'Where are you going? Mackay!' shouted Cross.

1300hrs
Monday December 17, 2012
Perth, Western Australia

Inside his high-rise apartment, Nicus Van Breeman closed his laptop then took the elevator to the basement parking garage. He sat inside his white Audi saloon and prepped the number for Bryson on the dash display, one of his top boys back at the winery. A ranked associate, smarter than most gym jocks but dumber than a cheap accountant. He needed to reply to a voice message Bryson had sent him. There was a major problem at the winery, and he needed to check back in immediately. Once he'd cleared the winding exit ramp and merged onto the main street, he hit dial and began the long drive down to Margaret River. The tighter side of a three-hour journey south of Perth.

Van Breeman hit dial. Bryson picked up.

'How big an issue is this?' asked Van Breeman, pairing onto the highway.

'Our biggest since, well, since Carice,' said Bryson.

Van Breeman was quiet for a moment, deciding on the best course of action.

'Sir?' said Bryson.

'Send all the staff home. Front gallery staff, and the others. Everyone except our main crew. Tell them it'll be a week of paid leave while we assess. You know the drill.'

Van Breeman ended the call.

Aside from fixing the problem, Van Breeman first needed to check in on his men. He needed a straight story. Following that, on the admin front, there was always work to do: check expenditure listings, observe the export spreadsheets, import deliveries and moderate the cash flow on all accounts. Most importantly, he needed to oversee his pet project – where the current problem had without a doubt initiated from. Especially if it had any similarity to what happened with his ex-girlfriend Carice, who'd caught him out and begun digging deeper into it behind his back. Asking questions that shouldn't have been asked. This annoyed him. He disliked problems, especially when it related to his off-chute pursuit. Considering it also kept the mainstream enterprise of the winery afloat, it therefore needed top priority. If issues arose, attention to detail was everything.

His winery still had the scent of his father spiritually rooted in the name, which Nicus hoped to change. But there was time for that later. Frans & Hoek was just that. A name. Based on the township of Franschhoek, outside of Cape Town where Nicus grew up. With Nicus's trust fund, old man Van Breeman bought out a retired dairy farm stationed over the land sometime in the late 1800s. Colonial times. Run by either French or English descendants. But that part of history didn't matter. What did matter was the land. Sprawled out across the skirts of the Jarrahwood State Forest. Prime real estate just outside the Margaret River valley. A haven with perfect soil for growing grapes and space enough to operate his activities undetected. Nicus's father set it up, but Nicus invested the time.

To help run the legal side of the winery, Van Breeman employed eight staff. For the other side, he had six. Lower numbers meant fewer mistakes, and a tighter affinity for trusted communication. The six men employed for the offshoot venture were heavy-hitters. Top dogs under Van Breeman's command and control. Two of the six were local cops happy to be on the take, while the other four were direct from the mother country: ex-soldiers and horse wranglers from South Africa. All self-absorbed, narcissistic, and money-hungry. Essentially, they were muscle. A security team overseeing the illegal operations. Much of it included shift work watching over the CCTV. Cameras were fitted to every building, set up at three-sixty-degree reference points throughout the entire property, even knocked into trees and wired into the main power. Internal. External. The whole nine yards. The front of house, wine press facility, underground cellar, maintenance cabin, the surrounding forest, and crucially, the strongbox. An extension built into the side of the main gallery where Van Breeman stored his precious goods. It was the first thing tourists saw as they drove inside the property. Dark web products hiding in plain sight inside a seemingly ordinary side office or supplies room. Illegal resources merely feet away as tourists tasted and tested the red and white range.

Overseeing the security system was a big job but the shift work was done on a rotation basis, easing up the workload. And most of it was done sitting down anyway, in front of a monitor. Seven days a week Van Breeman required a foot patrol around the bordering edge of the property – ensuring fence-line security. A three-kilometre check: front, back and sides of the property perimeter nestled deep into the surrounding Jarrahwood State Forest. Check for any gaps or slack in the line, check for leaning posts, eroding soil, and eliminate any wandering pesky wildlife. Sometimes, Van Breeman himself did the trip. Though his patrol was on horseback, involving a long-range weapon for sight practice.

Most people would think of a strongbox as some type of small, lockable box, made of metal for containing valuables. However, for Van Breeman's side project, he erected a complete supplementary structure. An entire room to protect and house his nest eggs. These special orders needed a cool, dry room, sanitised and sterilised, which was the one job in the wider operation Van Breeman would oversee personally. The strongbox housed a priceless network, and only Van Breeman could cast, mould and polish it to its optimal luster. Only he would count the numbers and protect its contents.

On this particular day, and with this particular issue, the information coming in from Bryson was moderately stressing. Nothing he couldn't deal with, but an issue existed where it shouldn't. One of his guys had made a mistake, and mistakes weren't part of Van Breeman's vocabulary. If one did pop up, amends were made, and if necessary, reprimands were served. How he would clear the issue on this occasion depended on a few things. Things he spent three hours driving to Frans & Hoek contemplating.

Once he arrived, he would require a full rerun of how the mistake went down. Then an examination as to how the issue arose in the first place. That would require a sit-down. A one-on-one with his crew. Nut out the right questions and get the right answers. How was it handled? Who was the inadequate cog in the machine? Was that cog a culprit of failure, or was there an accident that needed tighter parameters? In a nutshell, Van Breeman would eliminate that cog, then find a willing replacement.

> 1300hrs
> Monday December 17, 2012
> Aldershot Garrison, Medical Administration Wing

Mackay was lucky. The roads inside the garrison were quiet. There was no other traffic coming in from behind or in front. He'd hit the verge, taken the Hilux up the sidewalk, then taken out a waste bin before Cross grabbed the wheel. Lucky again Mackay's foot had slipped off the accelerator, Cross was able to hold the handbrake and steering wheel before shuddering the Hilux to a stop, parking it streetside tight against the kerb.

Mackay was sound asleep in the driver's seat. Unresponsive. Still breathing, but totally unconscious. Despite Cross's vocal attempts to shout him awake, shake him, even prodding her thumb inside his ear, Mackay was gone. And he didn't look good. Cross could raise the booking issue with the physical training instructors later, this needed to be squared away immediately.

Cross killed the engine, buzzed the window down and looked out for help. Which came in less than a minute. A soldier in uniform twenty metres ahead was walking from an administration block to her left, across the road towards a parking lot to her right. Male, tall and thin, moving slow and slouched. His rank wasn't visible from Cross's position, but from his stooped form and waif torso, she pegged him as a private. His physicality looked less than mature, almost childlike. Not lean in an athletic kind of way, just thin. Plain old skinny. Could have had two of him walking inside his uniform.

Cross stuck her head out the window.

'Soldier! Double in, I need your help.'

The kid bolted upright, straighter than the definition of vertical. He checked his peripherals for any danger, then seeing all was clear he looked over at the misplaced Hilux. Cross could see the mechanisms of thought flicker and spark, so she hurried him along.

'Yes you. March over here like fucking now. Left, right, left.'

The soldier moved. As best as his gamer-bod could, arriving at Cross's side of the vehicle breathless and wide-eyed. A private. She was right. Young, not even twenty years old. Red cheeks, earnest blue eyes. Innocent. Soft. Uncorrupted.

'I need you to get in the car and drive this vehicle up to the medical centre,' said Cross.

'I'm sorry, ma'am,' said the private, 'but my orders are to head back to our unit ASAP, we've got exams to prepare for.'

Cross leaned back in her chair, clearing the view of the driver's seat with Mackay slumped over, his forehead resting on the horn, the seatbelt catching the rest of his body from collapsing into the footwell.

'Step closer, Private,' said Cross.

The soldier moved up to the door and peered inside.

'Oh shit, he okay?' he said.

'No, and I need you to take over and drive. I don't know how bad he actually is. The medical centre is only two streets up ahead.'

'You want me to drive?'

'If I have to ask you a third time, we're going to have a real fucking problem.'

Cross hated making her disability an obvious point, but the kid didn't know, and right now he needed to, if they were going to get anywhere.

'Look down,' said Cross.

The kid seemed confused. Cross could see the uncertainties bouncing around in his head. His brow narrowed, his eyes focused in on Cross's expression, his own innate thought patterns processing her request.

'At my legs, Private, I'm an amputee. I can't drive. So, get the fuck in. Spit-spot.'

The kid finally looked down. He saw the denim jeans first, then the fold in the cloth with nothing protruding out of it.

'Shit. So sorry,' said the kid.

'Reef his chair back and sit on him to drive. Looks like he won't feel a thing.'

'I got you.'

'Thank fuck,' said Cross.

The kid bolted around the front of the Hilux, opened Mackay's door and found the handle to adjust the seat's sliding mechanism. He pulled it further back, then took a moment to consider how he was going to manage the driving part. Mackay's thighs were too big to sit between, so he figured he'd have to sit on top. Which he did, then closed the door and turned the key.

'You know the way to the medical centre?' asked Cross.

'It's basically my second home,' he said. 'Spend plenty hours in there.'

The private pulled away from the kerb and drove on down the narrow road.

'You got allergies? Always sick or something?' said Cross.

'No, I'm in the medical corps.'

'Well that makes sense. Was just considering how thin you are. Perhaps you get ordered there to take in extra supplements. Keep you alive or straighten that back of yours.'

'You should see my parents, ma'am. Both tall and thin. Mum's a dance instructor and Dad played basketball, but we prosper.'

The private turned left at a T-junction, maintaining balance on Mackay's legs as they rounded the bend. He then took another left a hundred metres further where the signage for the medical centre stood fixed in a grassy bed out front of a huge brick building.

'Park in the disabled. Close as you can,' said Cross.

The private obliged, slotting the Hilux into the closest disabled bay next to a zebra crossing, adjacent to the building's entrance.

'Now I'm going to need you to get my chair from the backseat.'

The private held his breath, contemplating what to respond with. Making sure whatever he was going to say next would come out the right way.

'If I may, ma'am, I want to help,' he said. 'I'm guessing you need someone from emergency, or one of the doctors or nurses. I can go in and call for help? I know plenty of the crew inside. Tell me who you need to see.'

'Good initiative, son,' said Cross. 'Do you know Captain Andersen?'

The private thought on it. 'No,' he said. 'That name is off my radar.'

'He is for most,' said Cross. 'Unless you've been deployed and come back missing stuff. He's a battlefield surgeon. Grab my chair, okay?'

The private got off Mackay and moved to the back of the Hilux. He pulled out Cross's wheelchair and pushed it towards the passenger door, holding it steady while she scaled down.

Cross said, 'Now you stay here with him and make sure he keeps breathing. This is a chin up, back straight kind of moment. You are not a duck's vagina. What's your name?'

'Stafford, ma'am.'

'Stafford. He's in a bad way, okay. If his head drops further, or you hear wheezy, raspy noises, tilt him up and open his airway, like I'm sure you've been taught. Just make sure he keeps breathing. I'll head inside and get the right person. Don't fuck this up.'

The private nodded. He walked around to the driver's door and watched over Mackay. On guard, eyes on, with good form, ready to impress.

Cross scooted herself over the zebra crossing, through the automated glass doors and into the front foyer. As a regular attendee over the last few years, she knew the halls, wards, and corridors well. She passed main reception, radiology, renal, oncology and headed straight for the orthopaedics nurse station. A regular face was on. Not regular in a way you're happy to see and chew the fat with, but regular for familiar communication only. A face with a voice. She was competent, but there was less than zero friendship between the two. Nurse Henry. Late twenties with an atypical, no-nonsense attitude. Brunette locks in a tidy bun, mild scowl, large in the chest.

'Is Captain Andersen in?' asked Cross.

Henry looked up from her keyboard and paused.

'Nice to see you too, Renee,' said the nurse.

'Well?'

'He is, but he's busy.' A reflex response. Automatic. The familiar Henry trait was in good form. Terse, flat, cold.

Cross clenched her jaw and breathed out. 'Busy with a patient, busy on a break having tea and scones, busy being a sex pest or whatever else "busy" means around here? Don't cock about, this is vital.'

'Pardon me?' Henry grew an inch in her posture. Her eyes widened, her cheeks flushed.

'Pardon you nothing,' said Cross. 'This isn't the time for back and forth. I need him now, Henry. So, calm your tits and listen the fuck in.'

A second and third nurse busy filing and typing at the station stopped mid-task and looked over. Noticing who Henry was talking to, they both rolled their eyes then turned back to whatever they were doing.

'I have an emergency in the car park,' said Cross. 'Sitting in a blue Hilux in the disabled bay. Mackay Connolly. He's unconscious but still breathing. There's zero response. I know you know him.'

Nurse Henry's scowl grew, then locked in place. The other two glanced back again at the mention of Mackay.

'Then why didn't you go to emergency, Renee?' Henry said through gritted teeth.

'Because, luv, I'm coming right to the source,' said Cross. 'Emergency don't know my boy out there, and if he dies in that car because you're stalling me with that face, it's going to be on you. Get Andersen now.'

Cross kept eyes on Henry and wrapped her fingernails along the desk. Henry closed her eyes for a long second, then picked up the phone and hit three buttons – presumably the intramedical line, direct to Andersen's office.

'Sir, I have a Renee Cross here stating there's an emergency with a Mackay Connolly,' said Henry. 'Apparently he's non-responsive in the car park.'

Cross raised an expressionless smile. Lips only, no eyes. Then she turned and began speed-wheeling her way back outside.

Captain Andersen arrived alongside Cross, just as she exited the automated doors. He wore a navy-blue sweater, tie, and dress pants. Formal. Professional. He slowed from quick jog to brisk walk. Behind the two of them, two male medics, one short, one average height, hustled a stretcher out the door and over the zebracrossing. They were Asian. Which was not unusual, considering Britain's multicultural society. Maybe Japanese, maybe Korean. Cross couldn't tell. She didn't catch their name badges. The stretcher made a crass racket as it bustled along, its little rubber stretcher-wheels chattering in protest as they danced unevenly across the tarmac to the Hilux. Cross wheeled in behind Stafford, still on guard, still at ease. His back had slouched a little more, but he couldn't be faulted for standing at the ready.

'He still alive, Private?' said Cross.

'Still breathing, ma'am. No change.'

'Good work. You're not made of soy after all. Now hang about, get into the back seat, and monitor his head and shoulders while these two get him onto the stretcher. It'll be a three-man job.'

Stafford moved.

The two medics replaced Stafford's position, easing the stretcher parallel to the driver's door. Captain Andersen stayed back with Cross. Even from her lower position in her chair she could smell coffee on his breath. She also saw tiny morsels of crumbs sitting just below the bud of his tie and the 'v' of his sweater. A cake or a biscuit. Maybe both. Cross gathered he'd been on his lunch break, then thought about Nurse Henry and her stalling. She made a mental note.

'Has he been taking his medication?' asked Andersen.

'No idea, sir,' said cross. 'Our chats never got that far.'

The taller medic undid Mackay's seat belt and eased him down first, working him like a contortionist. The shorter medic held Mackay's body as it leaned onto the stretcher while Stafford supported Mackay's head gingerly from behind. Once Mackay was sorted, Stafford jumped out of the cab and looked at Cross with a *what now* expression.

'You're done here, Oppo,' said Cross. 'Dismissed. Thanks for your help.'

'Oppo?'

'Means fellow soldier.'

'Thank you, ma'am.'

'If anyone has any issue with your tardiness, tell them you were with ex-Sergeant Cross and Captain Andersen, saving a life.'

'Ma'am,' said Stafford, and marched off in quick time.

> 1315hrs
> Monday December 17, 2012
> Aldershot Garrison, Medical Administration Wing

Cross and Andersen followed the two medics with Andersen grabbing Cross's rear push bars and stepping out in long strides behind them.

'Isolation ward, quarantine room four,' said Andersen.

'Sir,' replied the two medics as they moved the stretcher through the automated doors.

Andersen said, 'You still running those boxing classes, Cross? Here at the garrison?'

'What's that got to do with anything, sir?' said Cross.

'Mackay shouldn't be sparring. Not with his ribs. Not yet.'

'He's been boxing, but not sparring, thanks. I'm not a useless tit you know. I know about his surgery, and I know how to train my guys back from trauma. You remember my lack of legs? I instruct from experience.'

'Sorry, Cross, you're right,' said Andersen. 'I should give you more credit. You're a good trainer, but you only know half his story. I'll ask a better question. Has he exerted himself physically then? In the last hour or so?'

'Yes, he has. And it wasn't boxing. We were at the Bed and Bath in town. He just ran down a couple of getaway shoplifters on a fucking motorbike doing the town speed limit.'

Captain Andersen slowed his stride and shot a hard glance down at Cross. Part bewildered, part confused, part impressed.

'Okay,' said Andersen.

'Okay, what,' said Cross. 'What does that mean?'

'As in okay, that makes sense.'

'Makes sense to you only.'

'Correct. Me and about three others. He's had a special operation, which I'm sure you've heard about, but with a special thermoplastic not used before. He's our first-timer.'

Andersen strode out again, wheeling Cross faster, increasing pace to keep up behind the medics.

'If he's physically exerted himself to that extent,' said Andersen, 'maintaining a full sprint reaching… how fast? How many miles an hour?'

'They think it was thirty,' said Cross. 'It'll be on the news this evening no doubt, or at least tomorrow's paper.'

'Shit.'

'Shit? Like, bad news shit?'

'Didn't expect this level of accelerated response.'

'That's good in my book.'

'That's good in any book. World, Olympic, and Guinness. People will be asking questions.'

The two medics, the stretcher, Andersen and Cross passed radiology, turned and rounded oncology, then stood in front of a set of locked double doors. Isolation Ward. Andersen pulled a swipe card and let them all through.

'We're going to have to keep a tight lid on this,' said Andersen. 'And tight-lipped. How many people do you think actually watched him run?'

'Witnesses?'

'Yes.'

'No idea. Maybe four or five for certain. But I wasn't there. That's only from what I know when the police arrived and took witness statements. The roads weren't that busy initially, but afterwards, there was a crowd.'

'Shit.'

'You'll have to ask him when he wakes up. He will wake up, right?'

'He will, big time. Don't worry.'

The two medics moved Mackay from the stretcher to the hospital bed.

'Get a drip ready,' said Andersen. 'The morphine and the two bottles from the cabinet. He'll need the synthetic marrow assimilation solution. It's marked as the clear liquid, and the synthetic liquid-fibre polymer is marked as blue.'

Andersen took a thermometer, placing it inside Mackay's mouth under his tongue. He let it sit until it beeped. Forty-one degrees Celsius. High, but not alarmingly.

The medics removed their multi-patterned top jackets down to their olive drab T-shirts. Like a well-greased machine, they moved to the sink and washed their hands. Fingertips to elbow. First the shorter medic, then the taller, then Andersen following suit. Cross watched. Mackay drew air slowly.

'Aren't the nurses normally supposed to be helping with all of this?' said Cross.

'Normally, yes. But they don't know Mackay's trauma, and I don't want them to know. These two have been on deployment with me. They worked on Mackay in Kandahar. They're as good as any nurse in this garrison and know more about battlefield trauma than most.'

The shorter medic moved to a shelf with a pile of surgical gowns, pulled one, then walked in front of Andersen, threaded his arms through the front, then tied the lacing off at the back.

'How well do you know him?' Andersen asked Cross.

'Mackay? Only the last month. Made a connection because of our ordeals in the desert, plus our surgeries and life on tour. He needed a friend.'

'Okay.'

'Okay?'

'I guess he's found one. And you can be here and help him understand what I'm going to tell him when he wakes up.'

'Which is?'

'You can wait for that too. Take this whatever way you want, but his collapse was a possibility that we chanced happening.'

'What do you mean chanced happening?'

'It's not like it was life-threatening.'

Somewhere beneath the surface, Cross was starting to sense some bullshit. Her face perked from annoyed to pissed off.

'Don't you lie to me, sir,' said Cross. 'I've been on the other side of a life-threatening operation too. I know—'

Andersen cut her off. 'These patients, you, him and a multitude of others are in my hands too, Cross. I take on a tonne of responsibility, and I have to live with it no matter which way it goes.'

'You're a soldier first, so own it,' said Cross. 'It's your job. This could easily have been life-threatening, so you just waited it out? Does chancing it also mean chancing death? Just because you're good at your profession doesn't mean you're not going to completely fuck it up one day either.'

Andersen took a breath. Took a second. He pinched the bridge of his nose between his eyes and slowly released the air from his lungs.

'Hear me out, Cross,' he said. 'Mackay was given immunosuppressant medication so his body wouldn't reject the surgery. We reattached the fissures throughout most of his entire ribcage with pressurised thermoplastic. He is taking prednisolone for inflammation and cyclosporine for anti-rejection. Usual stuff you'd take for a transplanted organ.'

'But he didn't have a transplanted organ.'

'Not technically. We gave him completely new synthetic cartilages, which he needed.'

'Completely new ribs?'

'Yes. But there was one medication we didn't give him. A synthesiser for his bone marrow. For when the synthetic compound naturalised inside his body.'

Andersen moved to observe Mackay's slowed breathing while the two medics placed a heart rate monitor hooked up to an ECG machine. His chest ballooned as he breathed – expanding like a swelling wave wider and higher than any other human they'd ever seen. His breathing, however, had slowed in tempo, lulling to a pause of at least eight seconds after each exhale. Eight seconds with four heartbeats thrusting blood out towards his limbs and organs.

The medics prepped an IV bag full of saline solution and a morphine drip next to Mackay's bed. Cautious and professional. They also set up a surgical table with needles, syringes and two small liquid bottles: one clear, one blue.

Cross said, 'The military papers only wrote about the surgery realigning broken ribs and attaching intercostal muscle fibres. I thought they did a botched job too. Have you seen how raised his skin is? The barrelled chest? I thought it was just the post-surgery swelling taking an age to ease off.'

Andersen said, 'When he arrived at Kandahar military hospital, there was hardly anything left of his ribcage. The cartilage was in shards, completely shattered. He needed a full upgrade. We were testing a new organic super-fibre, integrated with an outside film of ballistic-grade Kevlar and spectra shield. It's flexible and expands as it sets into his existing ribs post-surgery. Hence the barrel-chest, like you said.'

Cross mulled on it, trying to pin her headspace around it all.

Andersen continued. 'The synthesiser for the bone marrow aids in combining the existing marrow with the new synthetic form. The thermoplastic consists of pressurised liquid polymer elements utilising silicone, oxygen, carbon and hydrogen. All of which are combined into a single unified form to match his marrow cells. This could only happen if we knew he would collapse from overexertion, if his internal body temperature passed forty degrees. The low end of dangerous. His running for that extended period was why he collapsed. His body was hot and exhausted, so it shut down. Like heatstroke. We needed to be certain his body needed it.'

'So, it'll hurt,' said Cross.

'Like a triple shot of adrenalin to the heart. It's a strong solution. It will hurt.'

'Great proactive measures you got going, sir. Good way to pre-empt the use of an essential drug.'

'Don't start, Cross. You know how many patients I see every day? How many soldiers like him are in a purgatory state, waiting for the right timing for the right drug? He was scheduled to see me for a follow-up at the end of the month for an assessment. How would I know he'd be up and about chasing shoplifters on a motorbike? Maybe someone encouraged him?' Andersen shot an accusatory glance at Cross. 'Besides, none of us had any idea his physical capability would be that good.'

Cross said nothing. She maintained eye contact for several long moments, then eventually diluted her resolve.

'Alright, sir, so you went along the conservative medical management route.'

'For all intents and purposes, military politics and soldier safety have to play their part. I'm sure you of all people can understand.'

The shorter medic inserted the IV needle into the vein halfway up Mackay's arm. Andersen prepped one syringe full of blue liquid and one full of clear liquid. He prepped a third filled with morphine then sat three hypodermic needles next to each, ready to go. The taller medic helped Andersen pull a pair of surgical gloves onto both hands, then placed a protective face mask over his mouth, strapping it behind his ears.

Anderson said, 'The pseudo-marrow compound is simply injected into the synthetic ribs. It will only have effect on a subject who contains the organic fibre. Now you know more than most. Even more than those in this field of practice.'

Cross said, 'I just hope the whole running incident in town falls on deaf ears. Or is made to look like a tall story from country folk wanting attention.'

'I guess we'll see,' said Andersen. 'We need to work now, Cross. Either hang around and endure his screams or go make yourself scarce.'

Andersen took the needle with the blue liquid while the two medics exposed Mackay's upper torso. The shorter medic took an iodine dab and wiped it across the skin. With his left gloved hand, Anderson dug his fingers across Mackay's thermoplastic ridges, pinched a solid mound and pulled it partially upwards. It moved about half an inch – stretching away from the ribcage itself. He then jammed the needle with the blue liquid into it. Immediately, he took the second needle with the clear liquid, dug into a second ridge and inserted it into the fibre. The shorter medic wiped another antiseptic film along Mackay's skin, then rolled his body back to neutral. At the same time, the taller medic started fastening Mackay's ankles and forearms with leather straps.

'Now we wait,' said Andersen.

1330hrs
Monday December 17, 2012
Aldershot Garrison, Medical Administration Wing

The two medics remained at the bedside: one near Mackay's legs, one near his chest, bracing like alligators ready for some unlucky source of food. At first, Mackay only twitched slightly. Curling at the ribs where Andersen injected the two liquid vials, collapsing inward like a Venus flytrap. In short order, like Andersen said, Mackay woke. Big time. His eyes bolted open, and he screamed.

At the same time, he was thrusting his whole body forward like he was trying to launch himself out of the bed. The taller medic planted his hands across Mackay's shoulders while he yelled out in a raw gurgle, way down deep in the back of his throat. Mackay whipped his body back onto the mattress then arched upwards, lifting his chest towards the ceiling like a possessed child during an exorcism. His eyes widened like a goldfish, veins, arteries, and muscle bulged and loomed beneath the skin of his neck. His legs tried kicking and his lower body rocked and bucked like a wild bronco, but the leather straps were strong. He hammered wildly on repeat: chest, legs, chest, legs. Beating up and down like a human engine block.

The shorter medic leaned what weight he had onto Mackay's upper legs, but his strength couldn't match Mackay's, so his body moved with the thrusts like a tornado ride at a carnival. He wasn't of much use. The ECG machine went haywire, the needle scribbling and jerking across the screen, beeping and zigzagging frantically in protest. The cardiograph line scrambling at random under an abnormal rhythm.

Mackay bellowed. Guttural and loud. The longest ten seconds Cross had ever heard another endure. Mackay convulsed and gasped air like a steam train. He rocked and shook for one last fit, then suddenly, it passed. His eyes rolled into view as he finally began to breathe normally, drawing full-bodied, steady litres of air.

Cross wheeled herself to the foot of the bed. Andersen stood next to her, observing. Mackay's eyes fluttered, opened, then blinked some more, clearing the glassy film. He was gaining clarity, dialling into the room and the people around him. He tried to speak, but his vocal cords were all burned out. He cleared his throat and attempted to ask the same question three times before a raspy, crackled sound eventually came through.

'Where am I?' Mackay asked. His eyes looked pleadingly at Cross as he tried to raise his arms and legs away from the leather straps. He then looked up at Andersen, the taller figure head and shoulders above the red ant, leaning over him. Andersen stared into Mackay's eyes with a medical penlight, watching his eyes move and pupils dilate to the correct level of light in the room.

'You're in the medical centre,' said Andersen.

'Aldershot?'

'Yes, Mackay. There are a few things I need to tell you.'

'Why am I tied down? What am I doing here?' Mackay said, again straining at the straps, pulling indignantly. The ECG machine fluttered, matching Mackay's heart rate in agitated effect.

'Relax, Mackay, we'll get those things removed,' said Anderson. He nodded at the two medics who began removing the leather. Mackay drew his hands and feet away in freedom and rubbed at his wrists, massaging blood back into the skin.

'Can you sit up?' asked Andersen. The taller medic helped Mackay slide back and upright against the headboard.

'What happened to me?' Mackay asked, flicking between the four pairs of staggered eyes staring back at him: Anderson, the two medics, and Cross low in her chair at the foot of the bed. He turned to Anderson. 'What's the story, horse?'

Anderson looked over at Cross, confused.

'It's an Irish thing,' said Cross. 'The man's out of sorts.'

Mackay lowered his gaze to Cross, searching her face for answers.

'You fell asleep in my car on the way back here,' she said, wheeling herself in closer. 'After giving your statement to the police.'

Anderson said, 'Your body collapsed on you. Luckily you were in a safe place with Renee in the car.'

'We drove you straight here,' Cross said. 'Well, me and the private I found wandering about.'

'A private drove me here?'

'He sat on your lap and used the pedals. I have no legs, remember. I thought you were asleep at first. But you weren't responding to anything I was saying. Or doing to you.'

'Doing to me?'

'Shaking and shouting at you,' Cross said, leaving out the finger-in-the-ear part. 'What was the last thing you remember?'

Mackay searched his memory bank.

'I put your chair in the back of the cab, after that police intern dropped us off. Then I put you in the front seat. Then I drove away. I think. It's fuzzy.'

'That far?' said Cross. 'You remember chasing down those two on the bike?'

'That I remember.' Mackay blinked more memories into the foreground. 'Hang on... actually, I remember driving off pretty quick, and you getting all stroppy about some shite. Like we had an argument. Did we?'

'Glad it's some shite, and not anything specific,' Cross said. 'Yes, maybe we did. Sort of. I was, well... feeling annoyed.'

Anderson cut in. 'You two can sort all of that out later. Mackay, I'm going to be straight with you.'

'Good. I'm listening.'

'Depending on what's being asked of our body, during a normal day its core temperature might rise to around thirty-eight degrees Celsius. Based on its surroundings and output. It's called thermoregulation.'

'The body's ability to regulate core temperature,' said Mackay. 'I know how it works. Been through about a million Army lectures on it.'

'When you arrived,' continued Anderson, 'your body was at forty-one degrees.'

'That's not too abnormal, is it?' said Mackay.

'No, not really. During your rugby training, or Army

operations in the heat, you may have reached the same number. However, it's not often a human body reaches over forty-five degrees. And I am willing to bet my entire career and qualifications that your body reached over forty-five degrees when you ran down those shoplifters.'

'I felt fine for a while,' Mackay said. 'Gave the police a statement, even had a chat to the good sergeant. Felt okay.'

Cross took a breath and looked away for a second. She composed herself, then chimed in for the big question.

'Sir, as you said, it's not often a human body reaches over forty-five degrees, but the same applies for a human running at urban traffic speeds. Aside from that being an anomaly of human capability, let's stop and answer that question for a moment.'

'Which is?' said Andersen.

'Let me simplify it then. How in the good fuck was he able to physically run at almost thirty miles an hour? Where's that explanation?'

Andersen turned to Mackay and set his explaining face.

'Mackay, two things make up your body now,' he said. 'New thermoplastic ribs which expand, allowing your lungs to suck in more air, and a new oxygen transport system. All synthetic, all military grade, which you already knew. It utilises groundbreaking properties to a mechanical effect never seen in biological chemistry before. We call it Phragazom. From the Greek word *sphragizo*, which means marked by a seal.'

Cross said, 'So he's *sealed* up with bigger lungs and more oxygen to inhale?'

'More than that,' said Anderson. 'Means he's marked with something special. Something specific and bespoke. Reserved for soldiers with heavy trauma who have no other way to stay alive.'

'Which is able to give me better stamina and speed out on the road?' said Mackay.

'Only partially,' said Anderson. 'It's half the equation. The incredible structure of your synthetic ribcage is an evolution of bone restructuring. They're not just new bones or cartilage per say, it's a completely re-engineered organ. An oxygen transport system and a filtration system. Simply inhaling larger quantities of air isn't enough to improve physical performance. The amount of oxygen the body delivers to the muscles, say, during running, is equally measured by how much carbon dioxide is also removed. When oxygen moves from the lungs into the blood by gas transfer, there is a pressure difference. High pressure in the lungs, lower pressure in the blood. With you, Mackay, your pressure difference is increased. There is a more efficient gas transfer effect from your synthetic ribs. They have the ability to absorb most of the oxygen and carbon dioxide your blood and muscles would normally expel. This transfer is what allows the expansion of your new ribcage. That's why it rises and falls so effectively. It is why you look like you have a large…'

'Barrel chest?' said Mackay.

'Sure,' said Andersen. 'But think of it as an advancement, rather than a disfigurement.'

'It's why you look like the Tin Man from *The Wizard of Oz*,' said Cross.

Mackay said, 'Because the synthetic ribs are full of oxygen and carbon dioxide?'

'Yes,' said Andersen. 'They're filling up, expanding, then filtering the clean oxygen back into your bloodstream and removing the carbon dioxide. Like an oil filter in a car. Fresh oxygen all day. Works even better when your body is under stress.'

'But an oil filter needs to be frequently replaced,' said Mackay.

'It's not the same with you,' said Andersen. 'The ribs will hold onto the carbon dioxide under stress, then eventually it flows back out through the bloodstream. Exhaled out through the top end, and your bottom end. Out your mouth, out your butt. Like most gases.'

'I end up breathing and farting out the excess carbon dioxide?'

'Exactly. While you were running, your synthetic system was doing its thing like it's supposed to. Expanding, filtering and moving oxygen at enhanced capacities. Coupled with your athletic abilities and musculature, you must have looked lethal sprinting through those streets.'

'I told you you're a phenomenon,' said Cross.

'I'm pretty sure you also used the words anomaly and mutant,' said Mackay.

'You do remember that conversation.'

Anderson said, 'Have you been taking your medication, Mackay? Your immunosuppressants from post-surgery?'

'Every day for the last six months.'

'The prednisolone and cyclosporine would have helped calm things down, keeping everything feeling normal, until it couldn't. Which was when your stress systems took over, but they were overwhelmed and needed to recover. So, you collapsed. Your body couldn't handle it. You basically had a form of heatstroke because of how fast you ran. You overloaded beyond what any elite athlete could cope with.'

'I remember feeling pretty tired,' said Mackay. 'Like now. I could fall asleep in five seconds.'

'That's because we just gave you an injection. Something we could only give you if you collapsed surrounding appropriate circumstances.'

'Like running at close to thirty miles an hour,' said Cross.

'To any other human, it's useless,' said Andersen. 'Basically, a poison.'

'What is it?' said Mackay.

'A synthetic bone marrow synthesiser,' said Andersen. 'Only useful to someone with your condition.'

'My condition?'

'The condition of the cells that make up the Phragazom. Your new rib structure. It's a chemical solution that unifies your existing bone marrow in its new synthetic form. The medication is now inside your marrow. It's part of you and should help during any overheating conditions that may come up in future, so you don't collapse. We could only give it to you while you were out. The stuff is painful.'

'Out?'

'Unconscious,' said Cross, not realising she was holding Mackay's hand.

Mackay looked at her, then down at their two hands, interlinked. He looked back into her face. Surprise and sincerity looked back at him. They held each other's gaze for another moment, then let go. Mutually. For Cross at least, their touch roused a deep feeling of connection she hadn't felt with anyone in years. She'd caught herself off-guard, a moment of vulnerability welling a warm sensation in her chest and stomach. Mackay was still barely with it, so he wasn't sure how he felt. The connection was merely friendship based. The hospital, the captain, the two medics, running at urban speed limits, the collapse. For him, it was all a bit much to comprehend.

'The injection is strong,' said Andersen. 'Part of it woke you from your unconscious state, part of it strengthened your recovery process.'

'This medication, this injection,' began Mackay. 'Is it tailor made? Like a bespoke drug for people like me?'

'For soldiers with the same density of organic thermoplastic inside them, yes.'

'And you went off like a frog in a fucking sock,' said Cross. 'You almost tore the bed apart, even with these two trying to hold you down.' She gestured at the two medics standing beside the ECG machine.

Andersen said, 'Your recovery systems, without having the bone marrow synthesiser, weakened your ability to recover.'

'On the street, I was feeling good,' said Mackay, letting it all sink in. 'I never even realised how fast I was running.'

'Fainting or passing out shouldn't be a problem now,' said Andersen. 'We've strengthened you back up again. But you'll have to start taking a bone marrow synthesiser for the Phragazom in pill form now. No big deal. Instead of taking two immunosuppressant meds, you'll have a third to throw in the mix. It's the way of your new world now, and it will prevent any further excessive fatigue or passing out.'

'Excellent. Can I go home now?' said Mackay.

'Yes,' Andersen said tentatively.

'What's wrong?'

'Here's the thing,' said Andersen. Both he and Cross turned to look at each other.

Cross said, 'You ran at an incredible speed. And maintained it.'

'And?' said Mackay.

'In public,' said Cross.

'With witnesses,' said Andersen.

'And?'

'And that's the fastest anyone has ever run before,' said Cross. 'Olympic or world record.'

'That information is going to get out,' said Andersen. 'People are going to come knocking on your door, calling your number. We have to keep a tight lid on this until we know how to deal with it.'

'We?'

'Us here in this room,' said Andersen. 'And my boss as well.'

'Sir, you're a captain,' said Cross. 'And the head surgeon for the entire British military. Who the fuck is your boss?'

'We all have a superior somewhere up the chain,' said Andersen.

Mackay looked at Cross. Uncertainty spilt adrenalin through his insides. He thought about journalists crowding his space, nosing around his business and asking questions he did not want to answer. Random people knocking at his door, making a fuss, and calling him day and night was too much. A small write-up in the paper for netting a pair of thieves was okay, but having camera crews and vans set up outside his unit? He wasn't sure he could handle that much attention.

'I don't know what to say, Tin Man,' said Cross. 'He's right. This will hit the news one way or another. Whether people believe it's fake news or not, someone is going to start asking questions.'

'Fuck,' said Mackay.

'Fuck is about right,' said Andersen.

1400hrs
Monday December 17, 2012
Frans & Hoek Winery, Margaret River Valley, Western Australia

On the legal front, Frans & Hoek Winery looked like an above-board establishment. There was internet marketing, billboards and shire community acceptance – the whole nine yards. Van Breeman had just driven three hours from Perth city to fix what shouldn't need fixing in the first place. Right now, he was stiff and thirsty, and he wanted answers.

'We messed up. We killed a kid,' said Bryson. His South African accent thick, his tone dry. Van Breeman's number two. A heavy hitter. Ex-army and a solid all-round fighter honed from years of rustling bulls on farms in Johannesburg. A straight up meat head.

'Who did?' said Van Breeman.

No one replied. Van Breeman stood still, waiting for a response. He stood front and centre in the visitor's foyer, the main wine-tasting gallery. With boots firmly planted on the polished floorboards, he eyed the six men scattered around the room: four goons from the old country, and two local bent detectives.

Bryson and Kimbala were calm. It wasn't their mistake, not directly. They'd screwed things up before but not like this. They leaned with arms folded against the wall, their forearms popping with dense, roped muscle. The door next to them had a small plaque with a discreet inscription that read, *Admin Room*. Although it contained a wall-mounted desk with a computer for administration tasks, the admin room also doubled as a supply room and break room. It was wide and long, built to the same width and length of the front of house only divided by a wall for privacy. It had the usual fittings with shelves full of paperwork and filing cabinets, as well as boxes of additional reds and whites when the front of house started drying up. It also contained a large, stained poplar cabinet filled with an arsenal of guns. Farm-standard weaponry for most country properties of similar size. Inside was an array of shotguns and rifles, namely for wild pests getting into the crops. Birds, foxes, snakes, dingos, or excessive numbers of kangaroos. Whether they were on the endangered species list or not, Van Breeman didn't care, they were shot and thrown back into the forest, or put through the woodchipper and used as fertiliser. The admin room was also fitted with tea and coffee facilities, pleather armchairs, a television, a fridge for keeping lunches and drinks cold, and along the rear wall, a wide flat-screen television for downtime.

The two cops, Taylor and Derek, were also at the top of Van Breeman's food chain. Principal operators with a law enforcement advantage. Dirty cops given big money to keep any scent of illegal activities far from courtrooms and the media. They sat in the small wicker armchairs in the corner – pleasant ornamental chairs reserved for visitors. The last two men,

Wynand and Snowy, were propped on their forearms across the edge of the wine-tasting bench. The immediate front counter. A polished granite bench with curls of white marbling that reached halfway across the room. The showpiece of the gallery. Snowy, whose real name was Petrus, stood out like dog's balls. The only one with bleached blond hair, hence the name. White as vanilla ice cream. Both Wynand and Snowy were young recruits from the old country, wedged in at the lowest rung of the food chain. Basically, low-level interns in the wider racket.

'It got complicated,' said Kimbala. Breeman's number one. A behemoth of a man with a dirty beard and skin as black as a moonless night. The pigment deep with centuries of African ancestry. Bigger and smarter than Bryson in every way with enormous heady eyes. A physical combination of cement block and sumo wrestler.

Van Breeman stepped between three wine display cabinets and walked behind the granite bench. He passed Wynand and Snowy, passed the wall with the signature series of whites and opened the visitor's fridge. Cool drinks lined top to bottom. Everything from colas, lemonades, ginger beers, and iced teas. At the bottom were bottles of water covered in plastic wrapping. Van Breeman pulled one and drained it straight from the neck.

Beneath the granite bench were three small cupboards. The one on the left housed a web of electrical leads and power points, the one on the right contained cleaning products, and the one in the middle contained the merchandise. Keyrings, drink coasters, pens and notepads. All printed with the Frans & Hoek logo: a caricature of a half-eaten fish with prickly bones riding a stallion. Van Breeman opened the centre cupboard, took out a notepad and pen and placed it on the bench. He then gripped his familiar, all-purpose six-shot revolver from the small of his back and placed the weighted piece next to the pad. A Smith and Wesson .38 Special. Fully loaded. He then picked up the pen and wrote down the words: *Time, Date, Place.*

'Start from the beginning', he said, raising his head to view the crew. Of the six sets of eyes, only four pairs stared back at him with surety. More often than not, the character of a person was in the eyes, and was usually all Van Breeman needed to see. Two of those pairs of eyes stared out the window into the late afternoon. Out to the visitor car park, which was empty. Only a couple of magpies were present, perched on the edge of a birdbath at the end of the lot, taking drinks in turns. An unsaid birds-of-a-feather rule: you drink, I watch your back, I drink, you watch mine. A mild afternoon breeze rustled their feathers and danced through the leaves and branches in the background.

Van Breeman looked at Kimbala who stared back, unflinching. He then gazed across at Bryson. Bryson panned his eyes across at Snowy – forearms still propped on the granite bench, staring out the window. Bryson kept his eyes on Snowy for a three-count, then nodded. It was all that was needed.

Van Breeman took a step and placed the pad and pen on the bench in front of Snowy. Snowy looked down at the pad, then up at Van Breeman. He held his tongue, which Van Breeman thought was either because he was acting tough, or because he was slowly working up the courage for an admission. Van Breeman gave him thirty seconds. Snowy maintained silence. The tough-guy act Van Breeman initially predicted. It was weak. Snowy was hiding something. It was in his face, his eyes, the edges of skin around his forehead, the tight contraction across his jaw. His breathing was much too controlled as well, as if he was labouring unnecessarily to keep a steady rhythm. All very awkward and unnatural.

Without warning, Van Breeman gripped his revolver, tracked his aim down to Snowy's left thigh and blew a slug through it. In through the front, out through the back. Clean. The .38 round leaving a dirty exit wound the size of a marble. Snowy's leg kicked out behind him from the force of the round, pulling him off the bench and onto the floor. His chin bounced off the edge of the granite as he fell, screaming. The noise drowning out the echo of the blast as he clutched at his leg. The man next to him, Wynand, backed away from the long slab, away from Snowy's howling. He tried joining Bryson and Kimbala along the wall, but Bryson pushed him away, back to the middle of the gallery. Where he stood on his own, arms raised at his sides. His breathing hurried, his hands trembling.

The two cops went for their sidearms. Glock 22s. Out of instinct and good training habits, but then let things be. The show was over. Van Breeman stepped up to Snowy and with the flat sole of his shoe, laid it over his throat, just enough to hear the slightest crackle of cartilage compressing into his windpipe. Snowy gurgled and fought for air. One hand clutching his thigh, the other clawing at Van Breeman's ankle.

Van Breeman looked up and raised the Smith and Wesson at Wynand.

'Go and take a seat,' he said. 'Swap places with Taylor.' He motioned the barrel where the two cops sat in the cane chairs. Taylor moved and gave up his seat. Wynand backed up to it and sat down like a good dog. Feet together, hands in his lap, back straight, eyes locked on the boss.

Van Breeman released his foot from Snowy's throat who was sucking air in quick sputtering gasps. He stepped over him and stood in the centre of the gallery.

'Kimbala, you mind getting him a bandage?' Van Breeman said. 'Should be plenty in the first aid box in the closet.'

Kimbala opened the admin room and moved inside. Snowy edged himself up off the floor and leaned his back against the wall underneath the signature selection of wines.

Kimbala returned with two bandages and threw them at Snowy.

'Wrap it yourself,' he said.

Snowy looked like a scared dog. Humiliated. He began taking the bandages from their plastic wrappers, extending them into long strips and pulling them tight around his thigh.

Van Breeman looked over to Wynand. 'Talk,' he said. 'From the beginning.'

Wynand swallowed. Air and saliva. A nervous reaction. Prepping carefully what he was about to say. He took a breath, held it, then exhaled slow.

'There were two kids,' he began. 'Mother and father. First tourists in for the morning. They were outside looking at all the coloured carp in the fishpond, throwing sticks and rocks. Normal kid stuff. We asked the parents if they were okay with us showing them where we press the grapes while they did all the wine-tasting. They were more than happy. Even said it'd be nice for them to take a look and appreciated the break. Normal procedure. Everyone friendly, everyone happy. I told them we would be back in ten minutes. Nothing different. Same as always.'

'So, where's the fuck-up?' said Van Breeman.

'We took them both down to the wine press,' continued Wynand. 'Showing them everything. I grabbed the first kid, the older one. Snowy grabbed the younger one, but as soon as he touched him, he went ballistic. Snowy struggled to hold him down. Couldn't place the rag over his mouth. Couldn't inject the ketamine shot. It was like he was loaded with meth freaking out. Never seen any kid react like that ever. It was like spasm after spasm, screaming relentlessly. Then he somehow slipped through Snowy's hands.'

'He ran off?' said Van Breeman.

'Screaming this obnoxious cry on repeat,' said Wynand. 'An intense shriek. Everyone heard it. Anyone within two kilometres would have heard it.'

Van Breeman looked around the room. Heads nodded. 'Continue,' he said.

'He shot out the front door and started running back towards the gallery. Snowy went after him. He still had the chloroform rag, syringe and ketamine vial in his hands. He caught the kid, but not fast enough to stop the screams out in the open. He got him back inside the wine press but then a second problem occurred.'

Snowy looked up at his boss. Ashamed. Van Breeman shrugged and motioned with a flick of his revolver at Wynand to keep going.

'The older kid, the one I had, was convulsing in my arms. Having a fit or something. He couldn't breathe. I'd given him the ketamine shot, and the rag had the normal amount of chloroform. Same as we'd done on every other kid. But it was like...'

'Like he was having an asthma attack,' said Taylor, pitching in. The leaner of the two cops. 'I've seen it before, on other jobs. People can have it whilst panicking, stressed out, or high. The kid's lungs couldn't take it.'

'He was choking,' said Wynand. 'Struggling to breathe, so I started CPR on him.'

'You useless dogs,' growled Van Breeman. 'Don't we have asthma ventilators, or a defibrillator with our first aid kits inside the press?'

He looked at his number one, Kimbala. The black mammoth shook his head. He turned to Bryson.

Bryson sighed and closed his eyes.

'I went and checked,' Bryson said. 'Short answer is no. We only have two first aid kits. One in here, and one in the main cellar.'

Van Breeman tried keeping his cool. Underneath, he was seething. His cheek muscles bulging at the sides as he grinded his teeth. Half his attention was on the revolver, the other half visualising, processing and piecing the story together.

> 1430hrs
> Monday December 17, 2012
> A31 Connection, Guildford, UK

The A31 Hog's Back streamed with the usual array of vehicles. Meanwhile, lukewarm anxiety festered inside Mackay's belly. The potential storm of reporters and journalists trying to catch a whiff of the road running story wasn't sitting well. The clammy hands and restlessness seeped a growing chaos in his head. Cross had no idea what he was thinking or feeling, and Mackay wasn't one for expressing them. Besides, Cross had her own reflections to work through: one third wondering how Mackay might be feeling, one third caught up in Mackay's infused thermo tech, one third confused at her own feelings towards him. Knowing she'd somehow clasped her hand around his inside the isolation ward was throwing a huge curveball. What did it mean? Had she attached herself somehow? Was there more than just friendship from her end? If it was more than that, did he feel the same? Had she started to care again… about a person other than herself? After years of self-isolation, was she beginning to open herself up to someone? She may have had a mouth, may have given up on caring what other people thought of her, but she still had feelings. Watching a fellow soldier go through intense, unimaginable pain, it was only natural for her to show compassion and hold the guy's hand, right? That's all it was, surely. He couldn't be more than a friend, they only recently met. It was too early, too fast. She tried throwing the thoughts into some deep recess of her mind she hoped would eventually disappear.

Mackay on the other hand, wanted out of the car. Away from Cross. Off the Hog's Back somewhere up into the greying, ragged clouds above. Or somewhere on an island with nothing but buttery sand and turquoise waters. He worked hard at keeping himself together, modulating the accelerator and breathing slow and deep. In through the nose, out through the mouth. Slowly, quietly, undetected. His inners felt like a pent-up malformed jack-in-a-box. He drove and thought. Thinking of the monstrosity of his inner human self. He was different now to who he was. What he was. Who he used to be. Physically and mentally. Why did his thoughts feed his insecurities? Why was he so feeble upstairs in the grey matter? Why was he so easily rattled and troubled at the unknown future that lay ahead? This was not the way he remembered himself. He was a rational guy. Or was he? The constant doubts played games with his mind, sucking him down into a pool of insecurity. What was wrong with him? He was technically faster than any living athlete that had ever come before him. But there was a fatigue issue. As long as he took the pills Andersen gave him, he should be okay. One a day. Marrow Maintenance Medication, as Andersen called it. Thousands of people take maintenance medication. Younger than him too. Some called them preservers or continuance meds. Look at all those children with type two diabetes. How hard could it be? And look at the bright side, he may be disfigured, but there was a silver lining. He had speed. How far he could push himself was anyone's guess. There were things to look forward to. Stay positive. He had friends. Chris, Luke, now Cross… hopefully. He had his brother and his family. Don't let the irrational demons take over. Don't be pushed to the edge where pills and alcohol, and ropes and guns, are within easy reach.

Time and space slipped by unknowingly. The sound of the traffic a mere echo. A subconscious hum somewhere in the background. A drone of nothingness until he found himself out front of his cookie cutter home back in Guildford with Cross at the front entrance in her chair, waiting for him to open the door.

Mackay spun the key in the door, let Cross in first, then followed in behind and turned on the kitchen lights. The air inside was still. A little cold, a little stale. Mackay hadn't had a visitor in months. His brother and his family didn't count.

Cross's peripherals took in the bearings of a small lounge room which, according to its size and scale, could have served as a small sitting room. It was half connected to the kitchen, which then connected to the two bedrooms and single bathroom. From her point of view, the minimalist decor, tidy kitchen and made bed peeking out from the hallway screamed military.

Cross soaked in the ordered interior. 'Holy shit, Tin Man. Don't tell me you can afford a housekeeper. Not on your veteran's pay. I must be doing something wrong.'

'What's that?'

'Clean as a sniper's rifle in here. Haven't let go of the past, have we.'

'Hard to, I guess. Good habits.'

'True,' Cross mused, flickers of her own career tinkling away. Somewhere in her buried consciousness where good, earnest times had come and gone. She felt totally out of her element. New place. No boxing bags. No trainers to yell at. The house was small with limited space and narrow walkthroughs. Not very wheelchair friendly. No railings or bars or platforms to help get her around, and guaranteed it was as tight as a sardine can in the bathroom.

As for Mackay, he was sombre and grey. Like a wet stick of timber refusing to light. He hadn't spoken the entire drive back home, and Cross wasn't about to pick at his head either. Not just yet anyway. With both parties' emotions fogging up the indoors, Cross was at least committed to putting her thoughts out of her mind. Leaving her feelings as they were, somewhere in a cloud of uncertainty and confusion.

'So then,' Mackay started, walking into the kitchen and opening the fridge. 'I'm supposed to offer you a drink, being a guest and all. I have water, juice, milk. The beer is in the cupboard at room temp, sorry. Can also do tea and coffee.'

Cross thought on it. 'Let's have some tea. And by *let's*, I mean you too. We both need something calming.'

Mackay nodded and began filling the kettle.

Cross said, 'This is going to be a day-by-day, take-it-as-it-comes kind of thing you know. It's the only way we're going to get through it all.'

'We?' said Mackay.

'Of course fucking *we*,' Cross said, rolling into Mackay's line of vision from the lounge room. This is not just on you. Don't be some selfish wannabe hero, bottling it in, dealing with it all on your own. That's what fucks people up. You're not taking this on by yourself. Hear me loud and clear, okay? This *we*, is you, me, Andersen. We're all in this together, Tin Man. Reporters and journalists or not. Your organic, super polymer, whatever bullshit is inside you, is a *we* story now. The whole of it.'

'Thanks, Cross,' Mackay said.

Mackay took two cups and two teabags and placed them on the bench next to the kettle. He locked eyes with Cross. She knew he really meant it. She held her eyes with his, searching for a clue to how he was feeling. Maybe to sense the feelings inside herself – testing her emotions through his expression like a conduit. Or maybe she was just being polite in the moment. Mackay maintained Cross's gaze a second longer, then looked for the sugar. He knew she couldn't drive herself home, and he certainly didn't want to drive back to Aldershot and drop her off at the garrison. Which meant she was staying the night. He wasn't sure if he wanted to be alone or not, but either way, he was also a gentleman, and knew how to be hospitable.

Mackay's phone vibrated in his pocket. He checked the screen. The number was long and scrambled. Not local, which meant it wasn't likely a reporter. A good thing. Hopefully just a scammer, which made it all the more irrelevant. A total non-issue. No point in dealing with anyone else for the rest of the night. He swiped on red and hung up.

'Some random long number,' said Mackay. 'Overseas probably.'

'Don't answer anything tonight. Just leave it. Turn it off.'

Mackay agreed. If someone really wanted him, they could leave a message and he'd deal with it later. Friends or strangers, he was done with conversation. In that moment, in that time and space, Mackay was a vacant lot and wanted to remain that way. At least until he'd slept off the synthetic drugs, the anxiety and the exhaustion.

Before he turned off his phone, it vibrated again. Same number. Long and scrambled. Mackay checked the screen and read out the area code.

'Sounds international,' Cross said, and had a look at the screen herself. 'Couldn't say where though. India, China, Russia maybe.'

Mackay swiped the red and poured the tea. 'Do scammers repeatedly ring back on the same number?'

'Who cares,' said Cross. 'Have a shower, watch some TV. I'm assuming I'm staying the night anyway.' Cross waited for a confirmation, which didn't take long.

'Yes, you're welcome to stay,' Mackay said.

'I'm obliged to look after you now,' Cross said. 'You know that, right? Doctor's orders. Otherwise, if you did ask me to leave, you'd be a right arsehole and I'd hate you forever.'

Mackay said, 'There is a spare room. Bed's made.'

Deep down, Mackay wanted Cross to stay. Not that he needed a woman in his life, or in his bed. Not that he needed looking after either, but because he needed *her*. He needed *her* specifically, and everything she had represented to him so far. As a friend, for the most part. A person who knew and understood who he was. Where he'd come from and where he'd been, both mentally and physically. There was a bond and connection between them few others would ever have, including between many of his mates still on deployment. Mackay hadn't had a woman present in his home since being back in civilian society. He couldn't even remember the last time he was with a woman that wasn't during deployment. Which made him feel a little uneasy. Unsure of himself. Unsure how to behave. He figured the best he could do was to bring back his basic social, hospitable skills. No awkwardness. They were just friends.

Cross said, 'I'll order takeaway. I'm sure there's Thai or Chinese somewhere nearby. You rest, okay? Go freshen up.'

Mackay took the cups of tea, handed one to Cross, then rolled her into the living room next to the lounge. A three-seater with a chaise. Mackay sat in the middle and hunched over his brew. For what seemed like minutes, he watched three stray leaves whirl around the top of the cup, circling and weaving aimlessly. Lost, like his thoughts.

Mackay's phone rang a third time. Same number.

Cross said, 'Leave it, Mackay. Turn it off already.'

'You said international, right?'

'So? Scammers are all over the place. Could be anywhere in the world.'

'I totally forgot,' said Mackay, clueing in. A lightbulb moment. 'My brother and his family are in Western Australia on holiday. Could be him. It's a repeat call. It has to be. No scammer is going to try three times in succession. Could be important.'

'It's important for scammers to scam money too,' said Cross. 'Or important for journalists to sensationalise a story.'

'Repeat calls happen for a reason,' said Mackay. 'If it's not my brother I'll hang up, promise.'

'Alright, I'll leave you to it,' said Cross. 'If it is your brother, I'd probably leave the whole organic fibre thing alone for now anyway. You can tell him about it another time.'

'Don't worry. I'm not telling anyone. Not even family. At this stage anyway. And I'm in no mood to talk much about anything. I'll keep it short.'

Mackay swiped the green. A short delay chirped through the receiver. Then two dull clicks, then another short dead space, then a soft, dreary voice spoke through.

'Mackay, it's me, Malvin.' His tone was quiet inside the speaker. Distant. Mackay couldn't tell if it was a connection issue, or if maybe Malvin had a cold with a croaky throat.

'Malvin,' answered Mackay. He looked up at Cross, Cross nodded, then worked on her own phone for dinner options. 'Good to hear from you. Sorry for hanging up, I thought it was a scammer. How's Perth? You end up doing any wine tours in… where is it, Margaret River?'

Cross danced her phone in front of Mackay, waited for his attention then mouthed the word *pizza*. Mackay looked up then mouthed the word, *whatever*, and turned his concentration back to his phone. Cross rolled into the hallway for a quiet space to order.

'Mackay,' said Malvin, thousands of miles away, 'I need you to listen to me very carefully. There's been an incident.' Malvin's voice was slow and pained. The connection was okay, but his tone was off. Dejected and sickly. 'My wife, Neve, she's been killed. Angus is dead, and Lincoln is missing.'

Malvin said it straight up. No ice. No chaser. No pussyfooting or beating around the bush. Mackay heard it, but didn't take it in. Couldn't, considering the space of time it was delivered. Mackay needed the information again. Needed a moment for a second round with more clarification.

'What? Malvin. Killed and missing? Who is?' Mackay's tone rose. His response fretful and quick. Before Cross hit the dial tab to order she'd heard the change. A night and day difference. She stopped and reverse-rolled herself back to the living room.

'Please, Mackay,' Malvin said. 'I don't have much time.' The phone at Malvin's end crackled and distorted as his lungs launched into a coughing fit.

'Malvin,' said Mackay. 'What happened?'

'Just listen, I can't talk for long… it hurts,' Malvin drawled, then heaved into his lungs again. 'I need you to come to Perth as soon as you can. Immediately if possible. Use the money from your veteran's account. The one I set up for you. Account details and password is in the vet savings folder on your desktop. Be on the first flight out if you can. I'll see you when you arrive and explain more when you get to the hospital.'

Malvin resumed another bout of thick, brutal coughing and heaving. Then he stammered quietly. Purposefully low and faint.

'And please, Mackay…' he said.

'I'm listening,' said Mackay.

'Do not speak to the police.'

Then it was nothing but dead air.

'Malvin! Hello? Hello?' Mackay's throat constricted. The phone fell lifeless from his hands. Ice-cold adrenalin exploded inside him, flooding every edifice of his body. He ran his fingernails through his hair, back and forth across the scalp, wondering what just happened. Cross sat opposite him, frozen and confused, confronted with just as many questions as Mackay had. She carefully inched herself forward and reached for his hand. Now for the second time.

'I only caught bits of it,' she said. 'What's going on?'

A darkness bled through Mackay's mind like a tumour.

'He said *not* to speak to the police.' Mackay looked down at his trembling left hand now held in Cross's palm.

1500hrs
Monday December 17, 2012
Guildford, UK

For an international traveller caught up in a serious incident, there weren't many hospitals in Perth which Malvin Connolly could have been admitted to. Struck with the abruptness of his brother's shocking phone call, Mackay tried returning the number immediately. After two attempts where nothing went through, he went for his laptop and got online. The Royal Perth Hospital was the only realistic option. Seemingly the only choice for any normal international traveller without any celebrity status. Cross moved herself next to Mackay's agitated form at the small dining table along the far wall. Mackay pulled up a search engine and checked the transnational code for Australia, then punched in the general enquiries number from the hospital's website. It was the best he was going to get. He gave Cross a quick glance, finger poised above the green dial tab on his phone. She affirmed with a nod. Mackay swiped and listened in. The signal bounced, clicked, rushed under the Celtic Sea, the North Atlantic, the floor of the South Pacific, and finally pinged into the main line of the hospital. After being passed between three reception nurses, he was finally linked to the correct line at the emergency admin desk.

'Emergency,' stated a sober voice, distant and delayed. Male.

'This is the emergency department?' said Mackay, Cross sitting in tightly next to him.

'Yes, please state the nature of your call,' replied the voice. All business.

'Good. Sorry if I sound like I'm freaking out, it's because I am. I'm looking for my brother. Malvin Connolly. English. Tall. Around forty. I'm his younger brother, Mackay. I'm calling from England. I was just speaking with him.'

'What was your name again?'

'Mackay Connolly.'

A delay followed. This time longer than expected.

'Hello?' Mackay said into the dead air.

More silence, then the same voice picked up again. 'Yes, sorry,' the man replied. 'I was checking through our records, confirming you're his next of kin. Glad you got through to us. I believe he called you not five minutes ago. There is a phone in his room. Sorry if you tried returning the call, it's wired for intra hospital calls only. Fat chance for international calls to come through.'

Mackay said, 'Yes, I was speaking with him just now, then the line went dead. What's going on?'

The man said, 'There's been a serious incident at one of the wineries in Margaret River. Your brother and his family were medically evacuated. An emergency rescue helicopter brought them in.'

'All of them?'

The absence of an immediate response said it all.

'Your brother was unstable for a time,' said the man, 'but then settled for a few hours, which is probably why he was able to call. I'm sorry but he's gone into ICU now.'

'And his wife? The kids?'

The distant voice avoided the question.

'I believe your brother suffered a gunshot wound, so was flown in with a couple of detectives who were first on the scene.'

'And... and his two kids? Angus and Lincoln. Where are they?'

'I'm sorry, sir. I don't have much more information at this point, but if you hold the line, I can try and find someone who knows more. I believe the police are here.'

Mackay lowered the phone and deliberated. *Do not speak to the police*, Malvin had whispered. *Two detectives were first on the scene,* the man had said. It all sounded off. Messy. Mackay's instincts knew it – deep in his gut where all the right answers were buried. Experience in the desert had taught him he should listen.

'Sir?' said Mackay back into the speaker.

'Yes?' replied the voice. Still distant, still delayed.

'I'll worry about those details later. Better if I'm there to hear it from him myself.'

'Sir, let me take your number just in case…'

'I'll be there soon. When you can, please tell him I'm on my way.'

Mackay swiped on red.

'Do you have a current passport?' asked Cross.

Mackay closed his eyes. 'Yes,' he said between a clenched jaw. Dark unshakeable images rose and looped around in his head. Manifesting within him like a plague, filling up space. He pressed the thick parts of his palms hard into his eyes and bellowed. Cross let his rage fill the room then waited for silence to take its place.

'I know you're hurting,' said Cross. 'But we need to think rationally before we make any plans.'

'I have to fly to Australia tonight, Cross,' Mackay said between gritted teeth. 'And there's no *we*.'

'I'm coming with you,' Cross said without hesitation. 'Whether you like it or not.'

'Like fuck you are.'

'My life here isn't that important, the gym will survive. And I've been to Perth. I can help. I know the city. I know people there.'

'What?'

'Pre-deployment training for Afghanistan, remember? I spoke about it at the coffee shop. Was there three years ago at the Campbell Barracks in Swanbourne.'

Mackay stayed silent. Head in his hands.

'We spent three months there,' said Cross. 'We weren't holed up at the barracks the whole time, we got out and about. I can help.'

'I heard you the first time. You're not coming. Not your concern.'

'Motherfucker,' said Cross, terse with disappointment. Heat and tension floated from her breath in resentment. 'Here is a moment now when you need to step up, step out of yourself and accept help when it's offered. Whatever happened to your brother and his family is fucked up, but if you're going to go, then you're going to need some help. And considering the state you're in, you won't be able to manage this on your own. Like it or not, you're fragile, Mackay, and like it or not, I'm the best help you have right now.'

'You're not coming, goddammit. This is a family matter, alright?'

'Don't care. You book a flight, I'll be on it too.'

'You do whatever you want.'

Cross raised her voice and posture. 'You're being a right arsehole, you know that?'

'Hate me then,' said Mackay. 'You're not coming.'

'So you want me to call a taxi now and go home? Back to the garrison? What are you going to do then?'

'I'll figure it out. Either way, that's a good idea. Call a taxi.'

'You don't have a clue what to do, Tin Man, because your head isn't on straight.'

'Maybe it isn't, so what. I'll go back to our local police department, see what they've got to say. I'm doing this alone. I can sort my own family matters myself.'

'How are you going to stop me?'

'You're not sodding well coming, Cross, for fuck's sake.'

Cross paused. She rolled her chair back a few inches and gave Mackay some breathing room.

'Mackay,' Cross continued, lowering her posture and easing

her tone, 'sometimes, doing a bit of your own investigation is exactly what you need to get to the truth. To get the right answers. Your brother, in confidence, said to come to Perth immediately. Said not to speak to the police, right? If you want to help him and his family, I'd toe that line. Honour his word.'

Mackay wiped his pulpy red eyes. He took a few breaths of the stale house air, then peered up slowly towards the red ant's face. There was an earnestness in the lines around her mouth, in the creases around her eyes.

Cross said, 'If you go down to the station and eventually convince them to make a few calls to Australia, what do you think they'll tell you?'

Mackay sat silently.

'They'll get transferred around a hundred times then, when finally they get to someone who knows something, critical time has gone by.'

Mackay sat silently.

'That's an entire day right there, just on phone calls. Then finally some relevant information comes back from Perth police, how do you know it's reliable? How do you know it's the truth? Or if it's part of some kind of bigger cover-up?'

Malvin's words rang inside Mackay's head again: *Do not speak to the police.*

'Sure, it could be nothing,' Cross continued. 'Could be a complete misunderstanding. Incorrect information is given all the time. Incorrect assumptions are made, all the time. But you don't want to take that risk. Wouldn't you want to know the truth first-hand? For your brother? For his family? Your family?'

Mackay watched Cross work. Watched and breathed it in.

'If the police are actually covering shit up because they think they have that power, wouldn't you want the opportunity to stop them? Do whatever you could to get to the truth and expose it?'

Mackay closed his eyes. He knew she was right.

Cross said, 'If you stay here in Guildford with your thumb up your arse, wouldn't you regret not making the better decision to get over to Australia and honour what your brother asked of you in the first place? When he was in his purest, pleading state, asking you not to contact the police?'

'I would,' Mackay said finally.

Cross nodded. 'The cops will just tell you to let the police handle it. They'll tell you to sit on it while you're getting nothing but purple hands in the process. Your brother asked *you* to come specifically. He made that pretty clear. He wouldn't have called otherwise.'

Cross watched Mackay retreat within himself. He didn't look good. Even for a white man in a British winter, the colour sapped from his cheeks. Sitting there, his body swooned and shuddered.

'This is all really bad timing,' Cross said. 'Everything you are going through right now is a mindfuck. Your physical changes, Malvin's phone call. But we can deal with one thing at a time. Together.'

Cross was right, Mackay thought. He was hurting, and he wasn't in the right mind to handle the moment at all. He clenched his fists deeper into the skin of his hands.

'We humans weren't meant to do life alone,' said Cross. 'You can't always fix life's problems by yourself.'

Mackay said nothing.

'This thing with your brother is a shitstorm. Like a wet pussy packed with STDs.'

'For fuck's sake,' said Mackay, his neck snapping back.

'There you go,' said Cross. 'Sorry, I just needed you to perk up a little. However you want to look at it, yes, this is something that needs immediate attention. And it needs to be done as a team. You're a soldier, right?'

'I know what you're getting at.'

'Great then. Soldiers work in teams. The only muppets that work alone are the SAS, but even commandos work in teams.'

'So, what do you propose?'

'We go. We hear what your brother has to say then work on it from there. But before anything, we need to book flights. Dinner is going to have to wait.'

Mackay nodded solemnly in commitment. Acceptance sinking in slow and worn. He put the fact Cross was partnering with him in his head and let it sit. His capacity to think clearly had drifted with the winter wind. He needed Cross in his corner now more than ever. Whether he knew it or not, and whether he liked it or not.

Mackay said, 'I need to get back online.' He went back to his laptop and found the vet savings account number and password. He then opened Google to search for the earliest flights out of Heathrow. Cross sat close, helping him punch the numbers and filter the best cross-continental flights, which at this point weren't cheap, especially being a week out from Christmas.

Cross said, 'We'd have to take the direct to Singapore with British Air. There's a three-hour layover before the next connecting flight to Perth, but it's the earliest there is. We'd still land three hours before the next fastest with Qatar.'

'It's scheduled to leave in four hours,' said Mackay.

'Book it.'

Mackay worked over the details in the booking system. On the page for ticking seating options, Cross took over.

'My special provisions will get us the best seats,' she said. 'At least for economy. And you're my help, so we won't need extra assistance from the airline staff.'

'We're both veterans.'

'Hopefully we'll get business class then.'

'Maybe. Depends how full the flight is.'

'We can query that at check-in.'

Mackay paid using his vet savings. A moment later he received a confirmation email in his inbox. He breathed in and held it, pushing his shirt to its limits as his barrel chest expanded. He let it out slow and long.

> **1500hrs**
> **Monday December 17, 2012**
> **Frans & Hoek Winery, Margaret River, Western Australia**

'That's not the end of the story, is it, Wynand?' said Bryson.

'No,' said Wynand.

'Go on,' said Van Breeman.

Wynand looked over at Snowy with a sharp nod. Flicking the rest of the story his way. A simple gesture; my turn's over, now your turn. Wynand had said all he needed to. The rest was out of his hands. He wasn't about to cover for things he wasn't agent to. Not at his lowly position. The price was too high, the consequences too extreme.

Snowy struggled to start. He was pale. His fingers pressed into his eyes and massaged the stress. The others looked on and waited. Snowy breathed in once, then leaned over and dry-retched.

'Talk,' said Van Breeman, waving the .38 Special.

'There was too much going on,' said Snowy, finally finding his voice. 'We were in the wine press. Me, Wynand, the two kids. Wynand was doing CPR on the older one, I was grappling with the younger who was screaming all kinds of hell. Then we heard the mother and father yelling for the boys outside. They were running towards the kid's screams. The mother opened the door first. I saw her face, she saw mine. At first, she just stood there, frozen. Then she wailed. Screaming and screaming for her son, repeating his name. Angus, Angus. The one lying on the ground with Wynand. Between her and the one I was dealing with, the noise was insane. Then the father came in behind her. Both saw their kids. Both saw me and Wynand. Saw the syringe and the rags, all there in plain sight. They saw everything. So, I let go of the kid, took the Glock from my jeans and put the parents down. Had to. You know I did. I shot the woman first, then the father. It was the only option.'

Nobody said a word. Van Breeman mulled on it all for a long, tense moment.

'Where did you hit the woman?' Van Breeman asked.

'In the chest,' said Snowy. 'Twice. Centre mass, like we're supposed to.'

'The husband?'

Snowy didn't reply.

'The husband,' Van Breeman said again, waiting him out.

'Couldn't be sure,' said Wynand cutting in. 'Couldn't see the wounds. It was clearer on the mother.'

'No one's talking to you so shut the fuck up,' said Van Breeman. 'The husband, Snowy.'

Van Breeman moved the revolver back to Snowy's face.

'I pulled twice, but I was out of sorts,' said Snowy. 'Shit was going on all over the place. I don't know if the first shot hit him. He fell after the second, but…'

'But what?'

'He was still moving and breathing,' said Snowy, sniffling back tears and snot.

'Why didn't you finish him off?' said Van Breeman.

'Because I'd already killed a fucking woman!' Snowy yelled. 'A mother! Because I've never shot anyone before!'

Snowy bellowed into his hands. Van Breeman waited.

'I didn't have time to think clearly enough,' Snowy said, blubbering. He choked back phlegm and cleared his throat. 'Wynand was doing CPR and I had just shot two fucking witnesses that happened to be the kids' parents! I was thinking about the other guests arriving in the car park and keeping things quiet. Last thing on my mind was to make sure the witnesses were executed. You weren't there. None of you were. If anyone else was in the same position, you all would have done the same. Or worse.'

'No, Snowy,' said Van Breeman. 'If you were doing your job like a professional, with the amount of money I pay you, then no. We're professionals here. Or so I'd like to think. Bryson, are you a paid professional?' Van Breeman turned his attention to Bryson.

'I am, sir,' said Bryson.

'You see?' said Van Breeman, turning back to Snowy. 'A confident immediate response. No hesitation. Professional. I like that. Sometimes though, I have been wrong. I have hired an oddball here and there. I can admit that.'

Van Breeman knelt down next to Snowy and calmly placed his left hand on his shoulder. His right hand still gripped the revolver, aimed loose and low at the floorboards.

Van Breeman continued. 'I don't need people who think in this job, Snowy. We simply have a role to play, that's why the money is so good. And for that money to keep being so good, going into your pocket, you don't need a conscience. You do your duty. The chain of command must always remain a constant. Otherwise, we fall short of the system, and then the system fails. And if the system fails, well, we don't get paid and we're all out of work. You follow me?'

Snowy said nothing.

'As for you,' Van Breeman said, turning back to Wynand, 'You should have known to have a functional first aid kit handy in the wine press facility.'

'How was I supposed to know the kid was asthmatic?' said Wynand. 'At least I could manage my kid. At least I tried with CPR.' Wynand eyed Snowy off, low on the floor, back against the wall still holding his leg.

'That is a true point,' piped Kimbala. 'None of us would have lost that kid in the first place. Ineptitude is a problem. It's bad karma.'

'Agreed,' said Bryson. 'They both fucked up. Now we're all in the shit and it won't be the end of it until we find that kid. He ran off into the forest, and the father is still alive in hospital.'

'Come again?' said Van Breeman.

'As Snowy mentioned,' said Bryson, 'he let go of the kid when he shot the mother and father. The kid ran away a second time. I didn't see the kid, but after I heard the two gunshots I came out and saw Snowy running around the grounds. I'm assuming to look for the kid, but the kid never returned with him.'

Van Breeman nodded. Kept his cool. In the moments that followed, he tossed up whether there was anything worthwhile or beneficial in the long-term keeping Snowy on the books. He mulled through a short conversation in his head, then made up his mind. The moment lasted briefly.

'All of this true?' Van Breeman said, looking back at Snowy.

'Yes,' said Snowy, refusing to make eye contact.

'I'm sorry, Snowy,' said Van Breeman. 'You left the father alive, and you lost the kid.'

Van Breeman shot off his second round for the afternoon. Through the front of Snowy's face. High on his cheek bone just below the right eye. Snowy didn't have time to flinch. His body position, seated upright against the wall, didn't move. His left hand, the one applying pressure over his thigh, slumped to the floor. His face did retain a brief look of surprise though, right before Van Breeman aimed his revolver in his direction. Mouth partially open. Eyes in the midst of widening. The wall behind him was now a mess of hair and skull fragments, splattered in a wonky halo of deep crimson. The bubble of frustration inside Van Breeman had burst, and Snowy's lifeless body was just enough to make him feel that little bit better. For now.

'Not really my place to say, sir,' said Bryson, 'but I know we're all thinking it. He needed to go and I'm glad he's gone. The balance of karma is back to neutral. This is good. For all of us.'

Van Breeman closed his eyes, then brushed the comment aside. He turned his attention back to Wynand.

'How long did your apparent CPR last?' he said. 'Before you realised the boy wasn't coming back?'

'He convulsed for about two minutes,' said Wynand. 'Then he stopped breathing and went limp. I tried CPR for maybe five minutes after that. There was no change.'

'Why didn't you go help Snowy look for the boy?'

Van Breeman pointed the weighted barrel at Wynand's chest. Centred. In line with the sternum.

'To be fair, sir, and no disrespect, but Snowy's a grown man. Was. If he couldn't find the kid, then that's on him. That shouldn't have needed more than one capable guy.'

'Convenient for you to say that now,' said Van Breman. He held the revolver steady for a long moment. Eyeballing the barrel's alignment with Wynand's mid torso.

Wynand said, 'Once I figured the kid wasn't coming back, I called Taylor immediately.'

Van Breeman looked across at Taylor and Derek. Taylor nodded. Van Breeman lowered the gun.

'So where do you two fit into all this?' Van Breeman said to the detectives.

Derek rose to the occasion. 'Wynand rang with the update of the shitstorm, so we turned up first,' he said. 'Standard procedure. The father was breathing, but only just. Tiny mouthfuls of air like a fish on land. As good as gone. We called our guy in the paramedics, but his partner was new. A ring-in. Didn't want to follow our guy's lead. He decided to call in the medivac air service. We figured nature would take its course and the father wouldn't make the ride back to Perth hospital, but he did. We were wrong.'

Taylor said, 'We won't use him again. You won't see him again, either.'

'The father is under full view of the doctors and nurses,' continued Derek. 'Plus, they have CCTV footage running throughout the wards. On top of that, he's an international. Apparently from the UK. Which means they'll have their national law enforcement agencies on the incident within forty-eight hours. Not much else we know at this point.'

'Only that he's breathing,' said Taylor. 'And that once he comes to, he'll talk. He's seen Wynand and Snowy's faces. He's seen mine and Derek's up close too.'

Van Breeman paced slowly around the room, paying no attention to Snowy's bloodied corpse getting colder against the wall. His black-hole mouth, drooped eyelids and cloudy pupils a constant reminder that failure and incompetence were not accepted in this line of work. His body had slumped lower, his hair painting the blood splatter behind him downwards in one long brush stroke. The thicker globules of red had now pooled around the bottom of the skirting board like molasses.

Van Breeman eyed the remaining five sets of eyes around the room. 'What else has to be done?' he said.

Taylor said, 'We'll pin the incident on Snowy. Cover it up to look like some lone-wolf terrorist event, then pay off any reporter who comes snooping around the place. If a woman named Lydia starts showing up, stay well clear. Derek and I know the people to see, so confirm with us. We know the reporters, we know the forensics team, and any other cops in the area. Including the rangers in the state forest, if the kid is spotted out there.'

Derek said, 'And we'll take care of the father in the hospital. Like Taylor said, he'll talk. If he talks, we're all fucked.'

Van Breeman soaked it all in. He took a few deep breaths, then walked over to the signature series of bottles above Wynand's grey matter and poured himself a glass.

'So, the kid,' said Van Breeman. 'We need to find him. How old is he?'

'Around five or six,' said Wynand.

> 1600hrs
> Monday December 17, 2012
> Mackay's Apartment, Guildford, England

Cross raided Mackay's bedroom cupboards for any clothing that fitted her, then removed a small number of essential toiletries from the bathroom. Mackay hadn't stayed in many hotels over the years because of deployment, so the options for mini accessories were limited. She found one of each of what was most important: shampoo, liquid body wash, a tube of toothpaste. There was only one toothbrush: Mackay's. Which wasn't a problem as most international flights had disposable minis she could request. Otherwise, some hot water to swish it through would have to do. She dumped them in a cooler bag she'd found in the pantry next to a bulk-buy of two-minute noodles and a few bottles of dried-up cooking sauces. Possibly only ever opened and used when Malvin and his family still lived there. Whatever she didn't have or couldn't find, she decided she'd make do and buy on the fly.

Mackay managed to throw some things together into an old Army-issued dive bag. He did his best to pack light for what he assumed would be a hot Australian summer, somewhere deep in the thirty-plus degrees. At least that's what he expected according to what he'd seen in various TV documentaries. He packed three of everything: tops, bottoms, socks, underwear. He grabbed his passport, synthetic bone marrow meds, immunosuppressants, and left his shoes on his feet. Lastly, he threw in a packet of sleeping pills he'd had since returning home from major surgery. Mild stuff Captain Anderson prescribed to help him get back into a normal sleeping routine. He figured it would help during the long flight.

'Time to go,' said Cross, wheeling herself to the front door with the cooler bag in her lap. Mackay gulped some water from the kitchen tap, turned off all the lights, wheeled Cross outside and locked up.

Once inside the car, Mackay blasted the heater while Cross typed Heathrow Airport into the navigation app in her phone. The drive was less than half an hour and got them to the Parking Express car yard at 1630hrs. How long they would end up staying in Perth was unclear at this point. Because of Malvin's sudden call, the express parking was their best all-round option. Allowing flexibility for any short- or long-term plans they wanted to make once they touched down.

Mackay took the ticket from the barrier and parked in the nearest available space. The shuttle bus to departures ran every ten minutes. They waited five. Once inside the terminal, Cross lathered on an unusually friendly demeanour, convincing the booking lady at check-in to approve a twin seater in business class. Veteran's benefits. Happy days. The crowds inside were thin. They found a quiet lounge opposite a duty-free store, basically a mini department store laid out with glass cabinets filled with exotic chocolates, high-end perfumes, boxed cigarettes and booze stands showcasing novelty spirits from all over the world. Most of them in tall, deluxe boxes. Being later in the afternoon, the overall bustle of the terminal was down to a mid-burble. The flights were less frequent, which meant that travellers were either up in the air en route back home, or they'd already made it and had started the unpacking. Easing the strains of the holiday journey. Maybe sitting down watching TV, or eating, or both. Or sleeping. Which Mackay wished he could be doing. Forget about life for a while. All of which was partly aided by the crooning Christmas music playing from the ceiling speakers, helping soften the overall mood. Mackay found it somewhat calming. Fewer people. Easy listening melodies.

Although mostly quiet, the duty-free store was alive. At least more than anywhere else. Like a street market coming to the end of peak hour. Taking in the last of the day's patrons for their pickings. Almost as if every traveller who'd passed through departure security had organised a group chat and agreed to meet there at 1800 sharp. Cross and Mackay hadn't bothered strolling about the terminal time-wasting before boarding, so they chose the lounge. Which at least had something pretty to look at and helped keep Mackay's mind off what was happening two continents over.

The store was decked out in premium Christmas attire with a distinct red, white and green motif. The pine trees were all fake but were spruced up to the nines with glittery tinsel, bulbs and candles. There were blow-up Santas, angels blowing trumpets strung up overhead, and dozens of tiny plastic snowflakes spread amongst the cabinets and stands. Which gave Cross an idea.

'Do you want to get booze?' asked Cross.

'You want to drink? Now?' said Mackay.

'Not for me. I shouldn't advise this, but tonight and tonight only, once we're on board, you may want to get yourself trolleyed and pass out. Help your thoughts stay off the radar for the next twenty hours. Cheaper than paying for whatever they're selling on board.'

'You're serious?'

'I know alcohol is usually bad news for anyone dealing with issues, but for the flight time, you don't want things preying on your mind. Sitting idle for that long could be a train wreck in waiting.'

'I brought sleeping pills,' said Mackay.

Cross thought on it. 'Let me see,' she said.

Mackay rifled through his bag and took out the box. Cross read it out.

'Triazolom. Captain Andersen had me take the same. Take both. One pill, plus the booze. Time should fly by. But I'll be keeping the box, and I'll give you the dose once we're on board.'

'Yes, ma'am.'

'Don't start.'

'Thanks for your permission and concern, but I'm not stupid.'

'Make a habit of this, and I'll fucking hurt you.'

Mackay stared back. 'Somehow I don't doubt that.'

Cross looked down at his crotch. 'I'll remove them,' she said. 'Now go over to the duty-free and buy a bottle of something. Whiskey preferably. Nothing too lavish, but make sure it's decent. I'll be having some too.'

Mackay wasn't a heavy drinker. He didn't mind beer, but never went for liquor, spirits or wine. He wasn't really sure which whiskey to go for from all the options on the stands, so he went for a common mid-range. One he'd seen numerous times before in his youth, standing proud in his friends' parents' liquor cabinets. A Chivas scotch. A twelve-year blended malt. Mackay had no idea how good or bad it might be. The striking shape of the bottle and grand design of the label made it look premium enough, and it was priced second down against a very expensive Japanese Hibiki. Surely Cross would approve. In any case, the forty per cent alcohol rating was enough to blend with the triazolom to keep his lids shut for a good while.

The flight was scheduled to leave on time at 1900. It was busy, but not full. And they got on without any carry-on checks, which was good news considering they'd boarded with almost a litre of scotch and a box of sleeping pills ready for a brain-wipe. For a long relax. After being seated up front in Business, Cross's chair was handled by a grounds staffer and packed with the rest of the luggage to go underneath. Before take-off, Mackay adjusted his watch eight hours forward to Australian Western Standard time, then managed to proposition a friendly stewardess for two cups of water. Namely for the cups. Before the water arrived, Mackay withdrew the scotch from his dive bag and placed the bag above in the overhead storage. He shoved the bottle low in the gap of the seats between his and Cross's hips, then once the water arrived, Cross handed over two sleeping pills. Mackay raised a brow. Cross shrugged, loose and carefree.

'You'll be fine,' she said.

'I get the feeling you've done this before.'

Cross shrugged again with a hint of a smile.

''Tis only a stepmother would blame you,' Mackay said. He downed the pills with the water first, then proceeded to crack the Chivas. Delicately. Low between their hips, away from any prying, judging eyes passing by. He poured his cup half full, knocked it back and held on as it passed from mouth to throat to stomach.

Cross did exactly the same. Two pills, half a cup of scotch. Mouth, throat, stomach. They let it sit for a couple of minutes until a hostess gave the call for all passengers to be seated, then both did a second half-cup. A third half-cup was administered as they taxied out to the straight, then finally a fourth half-cup once they climbed away into the ether.

Mackay passed out first, somewhere over the English Channel, while Cross lasted another ten minutes. Falling asleep somewhere over France, possibly right above the Eiffel Tower. Mackay slept the entire flight to Singapore. Just over thirteen hours. Happy days for him. Meant he didn't spend hours contemplating and pondering over thoughts. Ticking over the ominous unknown that was about to surface. It also meant no communication with Cross who was awake after eight hours. Which she didn't appreciate, but was happy for Mackay to slog it out in the land of dreams. For his sake anyway. In the bigger picture at least. It meant she had to occupy herself with movies,

TV shows, music and basic meals barely on par with a deployed catering company. Which she was okay with, but preferred conversation. Preferred interacting with verbal company. Even if it was managing Mackay's equilibrium and supporting his frame of mind. After all, she was a talker, and a self-confessed one at that.

> 2000hrs
> Monday December 17, 2012
> Frans & Hoek Winery, Margaret River Valley, Western Australia

Van Breeman spent the rest of the afternoon in the admin room. Making calls and wiring money. He used the time to wipe three things off his immediate to-do list. First, he called the local coroner and discussed appropriate sums of money to a considered value. A sum large enough to fudge an official statement. The transaction was a verbal agreement: money for paperwork declaring there was no foreign substance in the asthma attack victim's lungs when he died. That the young boy died of only that – an asthma attack. That he had a random episode and couldn't breathe, linked to some kind of pollen in the air someone from the United Kingdom hadn't been exposed to before. That he died before first aid could be administered. Second, he called his contact at St John's paramedics state office in Perth. Again, discussing appropriate sums of money to a considered value. Enough to have the unknown paramedic who decided to call in the medivac helicopter transferred to the state's far north. To keep things quiet. At least until things had settled down, or until other measures would be considered.

Third, he had his well-paid detectives, Taylor and Derek, knock up a quick, spurious statement. Van Breeman wanted to oversee it, so he made them write it then and there. Words in the statement were simple and to a basic effect, which kept everyone out of hot water by blurring the lines of the event's specific details. Which said that the two detectives arrived after the paramedics, and that once the medevac helicopter arrived, they followed it back to Royal Perth Hospital. To keep the victim safe from any second-wave attacks should there be a second lone-wolf shooter trying to finish the job. Which, in the bigger picture, basically meant keeping the victim completely quiet until death, or action an early termination if he started talking. Whichever came first. Which they all agreed was in the best interest for everyone. Employment-wise.

Once Van Breeman eventually cleared his immediate to-do list, which included a hefty loss of numbers in a discreet bank account, it was late. And there was still one major thorn in the day's proceedings: the lost boy. Around five or six years old. So, he joined the rest of the crew outside – scouring the winery surrounds. They went through the wine press facility, the visitor's gallery, in and around every structure and even leaned out into the bushland. A three-kilometre wire fence line on the southern edges of the Jarrahwood state forest. The night came up empty-handed.

With no kid in sight and nothing else doing, Van Breeman ordered a final clean-up. Snowy was wrapped and bagged and sent for the woodchipper parked out behind the old maintenance cabin near the bottom edge of the property. A massive brick construction, rough-hewn by early settlers as part of the old dairy farm's first accommodations. Erected by long-forgotten colonials who'd travelled by boat to take up the land, milk cows and create a thriving business before the turn of the century. It housed all the garden tools: one wall lined with star pickets, stakes, rakes and shovels, the other lined with wiring, rope, garden pots, gnomes and bird feeders. In the middle were two tractors and a ride-on lawnmower, while the back wall was full of empty, double-stacked wine barrels.

Later that evening, Van Breeman gave himself a buffer of time to think and make decisions. His men went back to normal operations monitoring the security feeds, the strongbox and making maintenance checks. Wynand was the only one ordered to stay out and continue to search for the kid, which was the only duty out of normal routine, but he'd messed up. So, he got the job. While all that was happening, Van Breeman went for a gallop. To clear his head.

The stable behind the maintenance cabin housed Van Breeman's three horses. Thoroughbreds. Ex-racehorses he'd purchased before being put down and turned into dog food. He used them to survey the crops with pace and height, and occasionally take out for a ride to think thoughts like tonight. He took out his thoroughbred, Rye. A chocolate-brown specimen with a sliver of white down the forehead. He rode up and back between the long strips of crop, Rye's drumming breath and pounding hooves the only sounds escaping over the vastness of the vines and leaves. He forgot about time and business as he rode late into the night – flushing the chaotic evening out of his system with clean air and the rhythmic hammering of the beast underneath. The isolation and purity of riding always helped him refocus and regroup his mind. As he returned and stowed Rye away, Van Breeman decided on three things: find the boy, eliminate the casualty in hospital, and cook up a sure-fire statement to the press. On his own terms delivered from his own mouth. A show of face and integrity. After all, he was an honest businessman, with at least an honest front. A public statement would place him above suspicion for the public opinion. And for Van Breeman, public opinion counted more than the truth.

Before his night ended, Van Breeman went to the strong box to check his goods. His babies. A personal necessity. The door was stout, made of treated mahogany with a keypad built into the handle. He punched in the access code and let himself in – a secret pin restricted only for him and his principal associates: Kimbala and Bryson. He turned off the alarm on the inner wall and closed the door behind him. The vague green light emitting from the ceiling lamps was comforting. Synonymous with ambience of the surrounding forest. Van Breeman knelt down and, with a small key kept inside the zipper compartment of his wallet, opened a small box. A stainless-steel item installed into the concrete flooring below the alarm unit. Inside the box was another key. Made of gold. For aesthetic reasons, and because it made it all the more special. Cut to unlock the four main storage units inside. Heavy rectangular prisms. Wide, long and deep. Positioned over a large set of digitised platform scales. The gold key unlocked the lids fixed to the main body of the unit. The room also had its own split system air-conditioning, keeping the room at a neat twenty degrees. All of which came from its own electricity source which was separate from the wine gallery. Isolating all the components and keeping a higher grade of reliability should a storm blow by.

Van Breeman opened each storage unit systematically and made his inspections, cross-checking everything with the paperwork itemised on a printed table attached to the front of each unit. The numbers on the scales looked good. Everything matched, which meant there was no change since the last inspection. Good news. Although, the numbers could have potentially been higher had the recent failures not taken place.

Van Breeman finished up, replaced the gold key back into the steel box, then moved out of the room, mostly satisfied. He ensured the front door was locked, then triple-checked it. As he stood outside in the warmth, he thought he heard an unfamiliar sound. Something new. Unidentifiable. He drew a breath, paused, exhaled, and listened. His rational mind said there was indeed a sound. Not one of his horses, not a roaming kangaroo, magpie, crow or kookaburra, but something else. He concentrated, forcing his ears to listen harder. Maybe it was just his subconscious making him think he'd heard something. Hoping it was a child's cry. Willing it to be a whimper. Or maybe it was a hum. An off-beat melodic tone. Something random. He stayed still. One minute. Two minutes. Nothing. No sounds came that mattered. No little boy crying in the dark. Nothing but the low thrum of electricity emanating from the refrigerators behind the door. The tiny whirr of the compressor constricting vapor, raising its pressure, and pushing it into the coils inside.

*

Lydia Ferreira was a good woman to know if you had information, and sometimes, if you wanted information. For the second time in as many years, the Margaret River local journalist caught a second gust of pulpy information relating to suspect activities in her region. Once again centred around the same winery as eighteen months earlier. Same region, same familiar names involved. In early April of 2011, Perth art dealer and socialite, Carice Hackforth, was disclosed as missing by friends and family. Carice was reportedly seeing millionaire Nicus Van Breeman, her then boyfriend. The news storm made it to local and national broadcast Australia-wide. Headline stuff. A big deal. The media put it in the oven and left the heat on it for weeks. Big money and big rewards were thrown out to the public from wealthy family ties. She was last seen by a small group of hikers walking through the Jarahwood state forest – six kilometres from the Frans & Hoek establishment. Prior to that, she was seen alive and well at a salsa dance class with Van Breeman the evening before in one of Margaret River's local community halls. They were observed to have been 'putting on a bit of a show', shaking hips and getting cosy while local photographers snapped away for the social spread. Four days later, police discovered a Mercedes SUV containing DNA samples of Carice's hair and skin, abandoned on a dirt track leading into the northern end of the forest perimeter. It was her vehicle, but no DNA evidence linking Van Breeman was found. That was the part Lydia followed. Doing her best to allude to police procedural mistakes. The cops did eventually follow a small trail of motor oil leading into the forest, but that was it. Just oil. Could have come from any number of sources – trucks, tractors, even woodchippers. There was no blood, no shoe prints, no signs of a struggle. No open graves or mounds of raised dirt. Nothing. Carice disappeared. Now it was a cold case. As time and tide carried on, the public eventually forgot and turned their attentions to the next swathe of daily horrors.

Van Breeman's supplementary earnings ultimately bought him an acquittal. Unanimously upheld by a court of appeal in May of that year. West Australia's attorney general and police commissioner both declined to acknowledge any existence of police procedural mistakes. They also refused to initiate a follow-up search for Carice's body. No evidence, no case, and no witnesses. Stalemate. Lydia Ferreira investigated for months. Doing the job no one else wanted because of the high-profile, criminal underpinnings of Van Breeman. Everyone else was scared. But Ferreira's journalistic efforts for Margaret River's online bulletin led to a small group of supporters, garnering enough momentum to push Carice's case to a federal investigation. Soon, that small group of supporters helped the online bulletin grow. Ferreira became a big fish in a small pond. Instead of accepting positions from larger newspapers and networks, she remained in her beloved region in the south. As good as she was, however, and as bold as her questions were, her report into the missing case of Carice Hackforth and the shady ties to Van Breeman was again quashed. Thanks to high-profile associates and big money from Dark Web transactions.

> 0630hrs
> Tuesday December 18, 2012
> Perth International Airport, Western Australia

After a three-hour layover in Singapore, allowing time for better food and restorative hydration, they eventually touched down in Perth. Mackay almost made it to sober but was still groggy-eyed and swaying as they stepped out of arrivals and onto Australian soil. The summer heat was stunning and immediate. Turned up to a mild roasting, which was a shock to both, and didn't help how either was feeling. A skinned pig left out in the open would have been edible in three or four hours untouched.

They made their way to the nearest foreign currency exchange and swapped out fifteen hundred pounds for a little under three thousand crisp Australian dollars. Next, they moved outside to the expanding taxi rank file and found themselves sandwiched between three interesting characters. A stooped middle-aged woman in front, and a loud-talking Australian couple behind. The stooped woman was way past her golden years, but despite her jelly triceps and pancake batter hips, her bent form inside a black and red polka dot dress made her look like a human ladybug. The couple behind them were young, somewhere in their early twenties, and were talking way too loud. They'd obviously been travelling abroad and doing whatever young Australian couples do when they go overseas – selfies, sex, drugs, booze, and purchasing cheap knock-off fashion. The girl of the pair had the kind of continuous blabber mouth with an everyone-listen-to-me volume, because what she had to say about her experience on the flight was a big deal. Apparently.

'Excuse me,' said Cross, wheeling her chair around and angling it towards the girl.

'Yes, darl?' said the girl. A skinny blonde with plenty of silicone and a mid-riff top exposing half her stomach. The guy standing next to her was a gym boy filled with tattoos. Sculpted up top but with chopsticks at the bottom. Shorter than Mackay by maybe half a foot.

'Do we know each other?' said Cross.

'What's that?' replied Lips.

Cross raised her voice, pronouncing each word with overt enunciation, 'Do... you... know... me?'

Lips didn't like Cross's tone. Something happened in her face. Stupidity trying its best to make out some kind of reply.

'Ah, I don't *think* so,' Lips replied.

Chopsticks rolled his eyes. Slow and languidly.

'So, why are you yelling in my ear then?'

'What's that?' said Lips again, the two flaps at the front of her face almost waved.

'We have a parrot, Tin Man,' said Cross. 'Likes repeating the same two words.'

Mackay raised a brow. He probably would have smiled if he was completely sober.

Cross said, 'Could you kindly piss and moan about the flight two steps back? Those lips of yours are so close they're almost touching my sphincter. Back up a little.'

Lips stood there. A dark hole gaping between the juicy plastic.

Cross went again, doing her best to look apologetic. 'Sorry, you must be unsure what a sphincter is.'

Lips' head turned to her boy like a bobble-head doll, gesturing for him to do something.

'Don't ask him,' said Cross. 'He doesn't know what it means either. Look at him.'

The corners of Mackay's lips eventually broke. He couldn't help it. The boyfriend stirred. Just a reflex. His spine adjusted, his chin lifted half an inch. He opened his mouth, thought about it, closed it, then opened it again.

'What's so funny, mate, you got a problem?' said Chopsticks.

'Aye, I have loads,' said Mackay.

'He does,' added Cross.

'I got no problem fixing it, right here right now,' said the guy.

'Neither do I,' said Mackay turning around completely. 'The line seems a little slow, so I'm happy to make the time. And my insurance is really good. How's yours?'

The dipped sockets around Mackay's eyes and bladdered face doubled for contempt and rage. The full width of his torso and barrel chest ousted Chopstick's entire men's-magazine image, which made the guy think. At least for once in his life. He didn't say another word.

'We don't want trouble,' said Cross, changing to sincere. 'We just landed. We're all tired. If your girl wasn't talking so much so close, I wouldn't have said anything. Maybe if you did your job and kept something long and hard in her mouth we wouldn't be in this position. My apologies.'

Chopsticks squinted and blinked, his mind slowly buffering the data. At least he took his hands out of his pockets – the minimum dutiful response for his girl. Lips did the goldfish thing but the rest of her remained idle.

Cross said, 'Sphincter is your arsehole, darl. A rectum. I'm sure he's explored it before. Now step back or I might react and bite those red bananas off your face.'

Chopstick's eyes widened. Lines began etching into his cheeks. Mackay swore he saw a wry smile. Like there was some level of agreement there. Then Lips took charge, grabbed Chopstick's hand and stormed out of the line. Hopefully to debrief over a coffee and a muffin.

The airport staffer in charge at the taxi rank designated Mackay and Cross a maxi-cab. A white Toyota Tarago with an ethnic driver. Dark skinned with hues of olive and red. He sported a black beard grown out to the top of his collar, and wore a white Kufi cap. A religious headdress. Essentially a Muslim turban. He remembered the name from a lecture way back at camp Shorabak during his first deployment. They were usually made of silk cloth and were wrapped in layers around a circular cap with a flat top.

The taxi was clean and neat. There was no burnt, smoky aroma imbedded into the fabric. Just a mild scent of cheap deodorant, which could also have been some kind of bathroom spray. Not entirely unpleasant but could have been used at half strength. The driver asked whether Cross wanted to be lifted into the rear by the hydraulic lifter, to which Cross declined. Politely. Mackay boosted Cross into the back of the cab then secured her wheelchair in the rear compartment. He sat in next to her and informed the driver of their destination: Royal Perth Hospital.

Sitting next to Cross inside the taxi, the first thing Mackay felt was apprehension. A learned reaction because of the driver: his skin, his Arabic background. It was, however, quickly followed by sadness, then respect. Apprehension because it reminded him of what his mates were still dealing with back in the desert, and sadness because he knew it was wrong to feel hate for a race of people. The man was just doing his job, making ends meet. The respect came from the fact the man had made it out of his war-torn country. Seeking out a better life for his family's future.

The radio in the cab streamed music from some easy-listening station. Mackay liked it. Early morning wake-up. At seven-thirty it changed to a news jingle, queuing the listener for the half-hour updates. Perth news, sport, weather. The husky female voice spoke for two minutes. The first thirty seconds related to local drama, which was totally irrelevant for their travelling purposes: riffraff being charged for drugs, a string of offences relating to petrol siphoning, and a head-on collision somewhere north of the city. The next thirty seconds was an update on a shooting in Margaret River: three dead, a boy missing, and a British male flown to Royal Perth Hospital. The second minute was all sport and weather. Once the husky voice finished, the driver did the polite thing and engaged in conversation.

'Bad news for Margaret River,' said the driver. 'Tourism might take a hit down there.'

Indian accent, not Arabic. He spoke quickly but fluently. A little muffled, but definitely educated. Mackay turned to Cross, unsure if he caught all the words as some of them melted into the next as they rolled off the tongue.

'Pardon, sir?' said Mackay.

'Sir? Thank you,' said the driver. 'I don't get much "sir" in this job. Mostly Australians say "mate". You are military, yes?'

'Yes,' said Mackay. 'That's quite an assumption.'

'If I'm honest, it is written all over your face. And your posture. It's very straight. Very broad. Are you planning on going to Margaret River?'

Mackay took a short pause, deciding on how relevant his answer would be to the guy. Cross shrugged, like it didn't matter the least, which was good enough for Mackay's hypothesis; the odds the driver was involved in his family's killings was less than one in a few billion.

'Yes,' said Mackay.

'Good. Don't let the news story stop you. Plenty of other wineries and things to do. There's a chocolate factory, dairy factory, sweets shop, plenty of restaurants. Beautiful part of the world.'

'Thanks.'

'Your accent is unusual. Not British.'

'Irish,' said Mackay. 'My friend here is British.'

'Ah, yes. I didn't want to be bold and guess incorrectly. Sometimes I confuse Irish for Scottish and vice versa. How many years in the Irish military?'

'I'm British military actually. Long story. Moved over to England when I was twelve.'

'That's good I suppose. I always thought it strange committing to the Irish military in the south when your northern neighbour merges with the UK.'

A well-reckoned statement, thought Mackay. The guy was educated.

'Good deductions,' said Cross.

'I was Indian military. Four years. It was the same custom for us to say "sir". "Sir" this. "Ma'am" that. Always respect. Even on civilian streets. Not like here. But, Australia has more freedom as a country, so I bring my family here. Now I drive. Things are okay.'

'Are murders common in Margaret River?' asked Cross, fishing. Which was in their best interest. The more information the better, so get what you can when you can.

'No, no, it's very safe,' said the driver, glancing into the rear-view mirror. 'This one is most interesting because two years ago there was a missing woman connected to the same winery. Same where the most recent murders occurred.'

'What happened in the most recent one?'

'A shooting. Some poor family. Also foreigners. British, like you two. You might even know the victim. The six degree of separation rule is real you know. Some say it's getting smaller with Facebook and social media and so forth.'

Cross moved the conversation along. Mackay sat quietly.

'Did they catch the shooter?' she said.

'They're saying it was a lone gunman. Some South African man working at the winery. Went crazy and demanded money.'

'Did the police catch the shooter?'

'Apparently they shot him. Shooter is dead, but so is the family. This is life, you know.'

Mackay sat quietly.

'Which winery was it again?' asked Cross. 'We just want to know which one to stay clear of.'

'Frans and Hoek. Everybody knows this one. Don't go there. Are you splitting up your time in Perth?'

'A few days.'

'Beautiful city. Beautiful food, coffee, parks, beaches, sunsets. Everything is here. You will enjoy.'

'You said everybody knows the winery. Why is that? Who was the missing woman?'

'Two years ago, a rich businessman was accused of being connected to a missing socialite. Pretty girl. Carice or some such. Her body was never found. The businessman owns Frans and Hoek. Everybody knows him.'

'What's his name?'

'Perth millionaire. I forget the first name. Something Van Breeman. Everyone suspected him of killing this woman. His wife or girlfriend, I can't remember. Was big, big news. All over Australia. They couldn't connect him though. Very unfortunate. But everyone knows.'

'Knows what?'

'Knows it was him.'

'Breeman?'

'Yes. They say they found her car near his winery.'

'Frans and Hoek?'

'Yes.'

'You like staying up to date with the news, don't you?'

'When there is no fair in the cab, I listen to the news. Always news.'

Mackay sat quietly.

Cross said, 'And this Breeman, is he still operating as normal?'

'Apparently. Police do nothing. Everybody knows. Nobody do anything. Too lazy.'

'Knows what?'

'The police work for Breeman. They must. Many of them corrupt. Like gangster. Crooked cops, like the movies. It's all rubbish. He has an office somewhere here in the city.'

'Here?'

'Yes.'

'Do you know where?'

'Probably in the CBD. In one of the two main streets. People see him from time to time. News peoples always trying to ask him questions.'

'What are the two main streets?'

'Hay Street and Adelaide Terrace. But you are going to the hospital on Wellington Street. So don't worry, all is safe. Rich people go to private hospitals. You won't see Breeman in there.'

The driver quietly chuckled to himself.

For the rest of the drive there was minimal generic chit-chat. Which both Mackay and Cross preferred. At least the questions they wanted to ask were asked, and the answers they hoped would be given, were given.

0745hrs
Tuesday December 18, 2012
Royal Perth Hospital, Western Australia

The driver pulled the maxi-cab into the drop-off zone of the hospital forecourt. He got out and started removing Cross's chair. Good service. Once outside the cab, the warmth stunned again like a slap in the face, the baking heat helping the two veterans back to sobriety. The first thing Mackay saw as he stepped out of the taxi was a large woman. This time shuffling out of the hospital's front entrance. Not that large women were such a novelty, not even in Britain. But this lady earned a triple take. The biggest point of reference that strained Mackay was the thick industrial belt clinched around her waist. A ratchet strap. Holding her pants up. Held mid-torso and pinched tight underneath all the folds front and back. Her stomach required a customisable implement and a ratchet strap looked like her best option. Mackay wasn't sure whether to smile or grimace. He did neither. Anxiety was taking hold. The anticipation of seeing his brother was increasing.

'What is that?' she said.

'It's a ratchet strap,' said Mackay.

'Blimey. She's wearing a tie-down for trucks and such?'

'Great first impressions.'

'Maybe she just came out of surgery for a stomach operation. What's it called when you get the stomach stapled?'

'Gastric bypass.'

'That's right. Maybe they just reattached whatever they took out back to her front. For sentimental reasons.'

Mackay pulled Cross into his arms and placed her in the wheelchair left on the path by the well-informed driver. Mackay paid the man, bid him a good day, then entered the front foyer of the hospital. Mackay and Cross quickly found the right desk, the right admin staffer and the right information which directed them to the ICU ward. Three minutes later, Mackay and Cross made it to the very reception desk where the male nurse answered Mackay's call two evenings prior. Opposite the desk was a waiting room, sanctioned away from the busy hustle of doctors and nurses, paramedics, visitors and security. There were important-looking men and women in coats, uniforms and scrubs. Some were in the middle of important conversations, some moved in and out of rooms, and back and forth through doorways. A tall, thin woman in a nurse's uniform stood at the desk with pursed lips, pushing pen to pad on some kind of diary or register. Her badge read, *Moffat*.

'One moment,' said Moffat, finishing up. She completed her last word, centred the pen in the middle of the page and panned down to greet Mackay with pinched eyes. She tried smiling, but it was hard sought. Must have been a hard start to the day. Or a long night.

'How can I help?' she said. 'You visiting family?' Her voice was soft and warm, but experienced. Maybe a little tense.

'I'm here for my brother, ma'am,' said Mackay. 'Malvin Connolly. I believe he was in surgery recently. Gunshot wound. We've just flown in.'

'Gosh, here already,' she said, genuinely taken aback. 'Well done. He only came in two days ago.'

Moffat went back to the register and leafed through the previous day's pages. She found a page, stopped and skimmed horizontally down the paper. Nothing matched. She turned two more pages, found a date, skimmed over another, found a time, then probably a doctor's name, a ward, then finally looked back up, this time at Cross.

'I can only give out information to the next of kin,' said Moffat.

Cross narrowed her eyes. Her expression both puzzled and irritated. Mostly it said *give me a break*. But Moffat was ready for it. She'd seen the same stare a thousand times over.

'I'm sorry,' said Moffat, 'but anyone can make up any story they like in here. Without proof of next of kin, I can't release any information. A driver's licence or a passport will do. We've had made-up stories come through over the years, and privacy is privacy. I'm sure you understand.'

Mackay pulled his driver's licence from the wallet in his pants, then his passport from his inside breast pocket. He slid the licence inside the passport and placed it on the bench, squaring it up neatly with the desk's wooden edge.

'This is me, Mackay Connolly,' he said, pointing to the blue covering. 'Brother to Malvin Connolly. I am his closest next of kin, ma'am. Our mother is back in England, and I believe his wife died in the same incident he was brought here for.'

Moffat breathed in and closed her eyes for a second.

'That's terrible,' she said. 'I know parts of the surrounding story. I'll just take a quick look at your documents if you don't mind.'

Moffat took the passport and license, checked Mackay's name on them both, then matched it with what had been written in the register. She nodded once then promptly handed both documents back.

'He is stable,' she said. 'Level three, ward one. Surgical ward. He's resting, but I'm sure he'll be happy to see you. I'll take you up myself, just give me a moment to make a call.'

Moffat dialled a number, told whoever picked up on the other end she was leaving the desk and needed a cover. She then led Mackay and Cross into the surgical ward, turned one corner, then another. She slowed down to a line of rooms spread left and right down a quiet hallway lit with fluorescent tubes running across the ceiling like a spine. Aside from a trio of nurses walking casually past them, the only others they saw were a gathering of six men. A congregation. A murder, if they were crows. All nodding on a point of conversation in vague assent. Four of them looked like hospital staff, two of them did not. All were standing and deliberating on hospital topics in an offshoot waiting room. There was one hospital security guard, two uniformed paramedics, and one wise old doctor. The two who didn't identify as hospital staff were men in suits. At first glance, Mackay couldn't determine who they were. And couldn't tell how expensive the suits were either. In passing, the materials however, came off as quality. Better than run-of-the-mill, but less than top-of-the-line. Something to wear for a full day's work, but not so elegant and refined that wearing it for a full day's work would seem over the top or undermine its purpose.

The two in suits held takeaway coffee cups and were directly speaking with the older, wiser-looking gentleman. The doctor. A stereotype with white hair, white moustache and white coat commonly seen in storybooks and children's movies. Most doctors had a field of specialty, which Mackay assumed was pulmonology for this guy. A physician who specialises in the respiratory system. Which was a fair assumption considering they were heading to the cardiac care unit, and the fact Malvin could hardly breathe and speak over the phone. Which drew one single conclusion in Mackay's mind; Malvin had been shot somewhere in the chest.

All men wore serious expressions as the white-coat doctor laid down his information. However, as Mackay, Moffat and Cross passed by, Mackay noted the two men in suits moved their attention specifically towards him. As if garnering immediate interest. Peas in a pod, moving in unison. Wondering who was seeing who, and why a legless woman in a wheelchair, a nurse, and an athletically built brick were walking through the cardiac care unit. The two suits eyeballed Mackay whilst he pushed Cross past their position. Their eyes lingering the whole length of the corridor. Which was enough time to make a tonne of assumptions. One of the men, the closest, had a flip-wallet clipped to the side of his belt with a shiny silver badge on it. Above it, jutting out from the inside of his jacket, was a worn leather pancake holster. If the other guy had one, which Mackay assumed he did, it was hidden by the cut of his jacket.

Mackay made note of the badge and the freshly shaved faces. He noted their size and features. The thinner one had a sheared widow's peak down to a number two, with a broad nose as Italian as they come. Handed down since Caesar ruled half the world. The other guy was sturdier. Fleshy with a textbook buzz cut. Short back and sides with a flat top. Old school. Both were around the six-foot mark, neither more than six-two. While they stared, Widow's Peak ran a hand through what remained of his once oily hair and turned to his partner and mouthed something. Buzz Cut nodded in response. From Mackay's perspective, they were smug gits with rank and a badge. Same-same in the military field. And often enough, for many an adult in any kind of uniform, rank and badges meant a whole lot of nothing. They both stepped away from the group and took a step forward.

*

'This is Malvin, here,' said Moffat, indicating to an open entrance reading 'Ward One' posted on the wall. There were six beds in the elongated room. Three per side. Four of them had drawn curtains while only two were open, exposing empty beds with neat drawsheets hanging evenly either side of the frame. The far wall looked out to an expansive lake with scattered trees and mansions on the hills around it. Below that, the city loomed with traffic, pedestrians, cyclists and neatly arranged bushes and palm trees.

'Malvin's bed is second on the left,' said Moffat, moving towards the second drawn curtain in the line of beds. Before she got there, a voice called out from behind.

'Nurse.' It was the heftier cop. Buzz Cut. Standing at the entrance to the ward. Moffat turned.

'Those two can't be in there,' he said, pointing to Mackay and Cross.

Mackay stopped. Cross eased on her brakes.

Moffat closed her eyes and mouthed, 'Oh my God.' Then she turned to Mackay. 'Really, these two need to bugger off. Been hanging around like a couple of blowflies since they brought your brother in.'

Moffat turned her attention to Buzz Cut. 'Can't they?' she said, condescension smothering her tone. 'Looks to me like they already are.'

The Italian with the nose sidled up next to Buzz Cut at the entrance.

'This is a police matter,' said Buzz Cut. 'That's why we're here. To secure the man for later questioning. You've seen us hanging around, I'm sure.'

'I have. Like two boiled eggs going off in the sun. And frankly, I don't care. This is not your ward.'

'We can't allow any visits from anybody,' said Widow's Peak. 'Not until we've completed our full investigation on the matter. You know the rules.'

'I do know the rules,' Moffat said, stepping forward, standing taller. 'The rules of the hospital. Where I work, not you. If you did, and if this was your ward, maybe you could throw your badge around and dictate what goes on. But I never saw your names on his visitation list. And I'm not denying the poor man the rights to see his family who've just flown in from Britain. My ward, my rules.'

Cross raised a brow and turned to Mackay.

'You can question him later,' said Moffat. 'Why don't you go have another cup of coffee. Or better yet, a shower. If you have a problem, you can go speak with Doctor Rowe. The same doctor you were speaking with before. This is his ship, and he likes his staff, because his staff run that ship tight.'

Moffat turned away. The two cops looked at each other for a long moment, then left. Moffat continued to Malvin's bed. The second drawn curtain.

'Sorry about that back there,' Moffat said. 'These police, sometimes they're real arrogant arseholes. Think they can run up and down this place doing whatever they like. Gets my goat.'

'You did great,' said Cross. 'Nice way to relieve some tension, telling the constabulary off.'

'Very true,' said Moffat.

Moffat pulled the curtain halfway back, enough to reveal Malvin head to toe.

Mackay couldn't look. He stared down at his feet, standing

there, unsure what to do. Trying his best to gather enough mental strength to raise his head. Cross looked up at him.

'It's all good, Tin Man, go speak with him,' said Cross.

Mackay stiffened. He slowly raised his eyes to Malvin lying there, a version of his brother Mackay hadn't met before. He was asleep, but he didn't look peaceful. A strained expression of pain and loss was drenched into the skin of his traumatised face. Ironed in. The fluorescent tubes weren't kind either – coating his grey face to a pasty sheen. Normally a healthy eighty-five kilos, Malvin looked drawn across the cheekbones and hollowed through the midsection. There was a shadow in his face. The brother he once knew was no longer there.

'He'll wake up in his own time,' said Moffat. 'The surgeons will likely be operating on him again tomorrow. Today is a recovery day. Not to sour the mood any further, but I'm always one to be honest and upfront. He has one collapsed lung which couldn't be reinflated, and the other keeps filling up with blood. The entrance wound from the bullet hit the left primary bronchus, and the exit wound was wide. About a ten-cent piece. A tradesman's thumb. It's allowing blood to spill over into the other lung. The surgery was difficult, enough to stop him drowning in his own blood for now, but he'll need another operation tomorrow. He needs rest, so best not to stir him awake. I'll need to head back to ER on level one. If you need anything, the nurses here can help. Just press the button on the console attached to the bedside.'

'Thanks for your help,' said Cross, blinking away jetlag. Staying clear and focused was trying.

Mackay took a step closer towards Malvin's pitiful shape, sucking air through tubes inserted into his nostrils. One tube was implanted in his side, through the ribs, taped and connected to a mechanical box. Hardware that Mackay assumed utilised a pump apparatus to help him breathe.

Mackay was tired and needed to sit. He turned and looked around for a spare chair to help ease the fatigue. He dragged one away from the opposite wall and placed it in front of Malvin's heaving chest. Cross rolled herself next to the foot of the bedframe. Mackay closed the curtain for privacy, then dumped himself into the chair. For what only felt like a matter of seconds, both Mackay and Cross fell asleep. Time was forgotten, as were dead nephews, dead wives and lost children. Their world stopped and time passed. Half an hour later, Malvin was awake.

FIVE

ACCEPTANCE

> 0830hrs
> Tuesday December 18, 2012
> Royal Perth Hospital, Perth, Western Australia

From Malvin's semi-upright position in the hospital bed, the first face he saw was the red ant's. She had woken only a minute or so before him and was stretching, yawning and blinking herself awake. She'd been looking at Malvin in the exact moment he opened his groggy eyes. The cardiograph on the heart rate monitor signalled a brief rise. He sucked air, flickered his eyelids and matched eye contact directly with Renee. Mackay hadn't stirred. He had dozed deep into purgatory where he didn't have to think about what was coming. But if Malvin was awake, then Mackay should be too, so Cross grabbed his upper arm and shook it gently. She felt its shape and form. Honed, hardened muscle from years of rugby and gym. Countless hours spent pushing away defenders, lifting things up, then putting them down.

Mackay came to life and rubbed his hands over his face. Massaging blood back into his cheeks and forehead. He looked at Malvin, who was staring at Cross, then tracked his eyes away from the red ant and lined them up with his younger brother. His face changed. Evolving from grey loss to the softened red of family familiarity. The edges of his cornea sharpened. His lower lip straightening from slack to horizontal. Even his chest rose and fell a little deeper. His hardened anguish was still there, battling behind recovery, but Malvin was intact. Alive. He wasn't down for the count yet.

Mackay's heart quickened. He shuffled his chair forward and placed a hand over Malvin's. Over the pulse-meter clipped to his fingertip. A big part of Mackay wanted to cry seeing him like that, but he couldn't. He needed to know things before his mind and body allowed him to shed any tears. That could come later.

'You're here,' Malvin whispered.

'I'm here,' said Mackay.

'Thank God.'

Mackay stood, leaned over his brother and touched his forehead with his own, then kissed it. Up close he could hear his lungs wheezing through the tubes. The sound unnatural and disturbed.

'Mackay,' began Malvin. 'Things have changed. Everything is different now.'

Mackay sat back down and pulled his chair in closer.

'I'm going to talk, Mackay,' Malvin said. 'It might take some time, but whatever happens, all I need from you are two things. Find Lincoln, and fix them.'

Malvin was a man of God. A steward of the holy cloth. It wasn't like him to talk about *fixing* something. But Mackay had a good idea as to what he meant. Plenty of corporals and sergeants who had run platoons and units had used the exact same words. Some during training. Some prior to going onto the battlefield.

Mackay spoke slowly.

'What do you mean by *fix*, Malvin?'

Malvin took a ragged breath, then looked Mackay straight in the face. Man to man. Brother to brother. An honest exchange.

'What do you mean, Malvin?' Mackay asked again.

'I need you to promise me you'll stop whatever they are doing. Because whatever it is, it is not acceptable. It is not of this world. It is not of God.'

'Who are *they*, Malvin?'

Malvin wasn't listening. He had his story to tell and needed to get it all out.

'I saw her body drop, Mackay,' he said. 'She died right in front of me. Her back burst open with two patches of red, then she just... dropped. Onto her knees, onto her face. She didn't move after that. I tried to grab her arm, but I couldn't. I couldn't move either. I fell over seconds after her. She was standing, then there were two loud shots, then she leaned forward and was gone. When I was hit, I prayed I would go too, but then I saw a man. He was shaking Angus, but Angus was still and floppy. I tried calling his name, but I couldn't.'

Tears pooled into the hollow of skin on Malvin's neck. He dry-retched and coughed, leaning forward as his body contracted into a fit. Mackay watched as the monitor opposite fluttered and bounced. The thin line hit a peak and quickened. Malvin stared up at the ceiling as he settled, his face in total loss.

'Lincoln was screaming,' he continued. 'It's all we could hear. Scream after scream. We rushed outside and followed his voice. Then we saw him and the blond man.'

'Where did this happen, Malvin?'

Malvin swallowed. He coughed again, five, six times. A flick of blood hit the white sheet at the end of the bed.

'You have to find them, Mackay,' he said. 'Promise me. Sometimes things need to be done. Sometimes we need to do what we don't like. When there's a greater good to be served.'

Mackay sat there, numb. His anger building.

Malvin looked deep into Mackay's eyes, then with whatever raw strength he had left, grabbed Mackay, and pulled him in close.

'Do what needs to be done, Mackay. For me, for Neve, for the boys, and may God be on your side. Whoever these men are. Find them. And whatever they're doing, stop it.'

'Where, Malvin? Where do I need to go?'

'Frans and Hoek Winery. Margaret River. Not too far from here. Something is wrong there, Mackay. There are people who want to try and cover it all up. So, I need to tell you as much as I can while I can. Do not trust the police. They won't do anything.'

'How do you know?'

'Ever get a sense of knowing, Mackay? Like someone or something is trying to tell you something? Maybe you felt it when you were out on deployment. Like something wasn't right. A sense from part of your consciousness, your spirit from within helping you put two and two together.'

Mackay was not a Godly man, but he took Malvin's words with humility. His brother had been a pastor for the best part of twenty years. Mackay knew what he meant.

Mackay said, 'I wish I could say yes, Malvin, but you know I've never believed the same way. The last time something went wrong in the desert, it came as a big surprise. I couldn't put two and two together then.'

Mackay looked over his shoulder at Cross. Listening. Taking it in.

'Malvin, be straight with me,' said Mackay. 'What do you mean by fix them? I want to hear you say it.'

'If God can make changes,' Malvin said, 'it's going to be through you. Fixing them is an act of kindness. It's best they don't live to be those kinds of people.'

Malvin painfully inched himself onto his side, as if to whisper a secret. Maybe something profane, out of character, or blasphemous. Something he'd never thought he'd say when standing and preaching at the altar.

'Jesus died for your sins,' Malvin said. 'And now, they have to die for theirs. Find them, Mackay and kill them. Kill them all.'

Mackay sat back and closed his eyes. Cross spoke next, taking over the heavy atmosphere.

'My name's Renee. I'm a friend of your brother.'

'Friends are special gifts,' said Malvin. 'Thank you for coming.'

'Could you see what these men were doing?' asked Cross. 'Before you were shot? Did you get a good look?'

Malvin rolled himself back, collapsing flat across the stretcher. His eyes went back to the ceiling. His chest rose and fell with short, shallow breaths. Like a child's.

'We were wine-tasting inside when we heard the screaming. Angus could never scream like that, but Lincoln could. He's autistic. Lincoln screamed a lot when he was younger. You got used to the type of sound. Each scream for a certain situation with a certain tone. We hadn't heard him scream like this before. It was more than just being scared. It was absolute fear and panic. He didn't stop. Neve and I ran out from the gallery following the sound. The blond one had hold of him, dragging him back inside a large building behind the main gallery. A modern-looking shed. I think where they press the wine.'

Mackay said, 'Can you think of any reason why they might have wanted Angus and Lincoln specifically?'

Malvin shook the picture of the incident away from his mind.

'I've been trying to figure that out, but I can't,' he said. 'Why would they want to take our two boys? It couldn't have been personal, I know that much. We'd never seen them before and I don't have any enemies. Not to my knowledge. The Protestants I knew from Belfast wouldn't do anything like this. This was a random act. But it seemed organised, like they'd done it all before. Like they were ready. They even approached us and asked if they could show them the wine press facility. Like it was part of a tour. The boys were so excited. Angus looked proud, like he knew his job was to look after his little brother. We were too trusting.'

'Any distinguishing features aside from the blond?' asked Cross.

'The man holding Angus had long hair. Brown and straight in a ponytail. There was also a rag, or some kind of cloth on the floor next to him. It looked wet, like it was saturated with a chemical. But there was no colour to it so it could have been anything. The other guy, the blond, was shaking Lincoln. Like a rag doll, trying to make him stop screaming. He had a syringe. The needle was long. Who knows what they were injecting them with, or why.'

Mackay shook his head, trying to make sense of it. Grasping the magnitude. He knew Malvin's information was credible. Didn't doubt him for a second. Didn't have to question it or check twice. His word was solid.

'Did you tell any of this to the police?' asked Cross.

Malvin shook his head.

'I couldn't let myself,' he said. 'I made a point of it to wait. For you, Mackay. For good reason. The same two cops I've seen here in the hospital were the same two first on the scene in the wine press. Which wasn't right. They arrived too early, before the paramedics. So, I kept my mouth shut and waited till I had the chance to request a phone and call you first.'

'What did these cops look like?' asked Mackay. The building tension and wrath was making him feel less jet-lagged and more alert. Like part of him had broken off and left him, giving way for a new sensation. A moving current of electricity.

'One of them was English-white. Heavier type with a buzz cut. Typical lawman. The other was European. Maybe Greek or Italian.'

'Big nose?' asked Mackay.

'Yes.'

'Like a Roman soldier?'

'Yes. He was kneeling down next to me, not long before the paramedics arrived, smoking a cigarette. He seemed calm, like it didn't faze him. He didn't do anything to help. Just squatted over me and watched. Like he was waiting for me to die in front of him.'

Mackay's stomach lurched, spitting a cocktail of adrenalin and bile into the back of his throat. His head suffocated as he recalled the same two men from earlier. Standing in the hall as they first walked through the ward. The same two who debated with the nurse whether he should be allowed inside to visit his dying brother. The numbness and apprehension he initially felt when walking in had subsided. Replaced by a quiet storm.

'Tell me more about Lincoln,' said Mackay.

Malvin knew the enormity of what he was asking his brother. He knew that being emotionally invested was the only way to fix this problem. He could see Mackay's rational sense of justification. He had already cut off his sense of duty and reverence for the cloth and had let go of the concept that every human being is precious. Because the lives of those men who took his wife and son were not precious at all. They weren't human beings. They did not deserve forgiveness. As a man of God, he was supposed to forgive, but there was a flipside to that ideal. For the forthcoming retribution he was requesting, he believed in a greater plan. One God would place into the hands of his brother. He was as sure of it as Mackay was blood. He knew, because while he was writhing on that hospital bed thinking he was about to die, God had given him the opportunity to call home. To call Mackay. And Mackay had listened.

> 0930hrs
> Tuesday December 18, 2012
> Royal Perth Hospital, Perth, Western Australia

'I saw Lincoln run,' said Malvin. 'I was on the ground, I couldn't move, but I saw him run outside. The blond one couldn't hold him. The screaming must've been too much. He let him go to stop the noise. He could be anywhere.'

Malvin closed his eyes.

'Your nephew needs you,' he said. 'You're the only one who can find him now.'

Mackay pictured the small boy alone. Hiding. Whether he was in the woods or holed up somewhere in the confines of the winery, the image of his six-year-old nephew roughing it alone put a dirty red fire in his belly.

'I'll find him,' said Mackay. 'Whatever it takes.'

'It was me who was supposed to look after him at the winery,' said Malvin. 'But I didn't. And I left him. He was frightened and scared and I couldn't help him. Like I couldn't help Angus.'

'You didn't know,' said Mackay. 'How could you? It's not your fault.'

'But it *is* my fault, Mackay.'

Malvin opened his eyes and turned to his brother.

'We brought him into this world, and I wasn't there for him,' he said. 'I will own that to the grave. There's nothing you can say or do to take that from me. If you ever have your own children, you will be so taken by their innocence you would do anything to protect them. If you fail that, no moral reasoning is enough to be at peace with that failure. Their whole world is bonded in your trust. That trust was lost.'

Malvin couldn't hold back the tears. He was tough enough. Where it counted. As a father. A family man. He contracted into another coughing fit, rocking back and forth. Mackay hated the sound. The phlegm. The struggle. Watching his older brother break down was a real kick in the guts. He could tell there wasn't much left in him. He'd seen it in other men back on deployment. Coming in from the desert covered in blood. Doing their best to hang on but ultimately losing the battle.

The ward went quiet. Malvin's wheezing and the quiet hive of electricity within the walls were all that could be heard. Occasionally a soft beep from the breathing machine next to them let the trio know it was still there, working, keeping Malvin alive.

'He can be strange sometimes,' said Malvin. 'The autism is obvious, but at the same time he sparks with bursts of brilliance. He doesn't always understand social cues or sarcasm, not even sympathy and compassion, which is awkward at first, but you get used to it. He is very literal. If he has a thought or opinion, he'll always give it to you in its literal sense every time.'

'The last time I saw him,' said Mackay, 'was after my first tour. We all met at your place down near Crawley. I remember how much he loved *Mary Poppins*. Didn't move from that couch. We had lunch, drank some, then had dinner. He watched it on a loop three times through. The whole afternoon.'

Cross smiled. Malvin's lips and the corners of his eyes tapered in. The slightest change. Like the beginnings of a smile, only it never quite made it through.

'He knows that film inside out,' Malvin said. 'Word for word. We all did, Angus too. That film was Lincoln's world for weeks.'

Malvin paused for breath. Let his feelings calm and his mind slow.

'There's a change in me, Mackay,' he said. 'I'm not the person I was. Not the pastor you used to know. Not anymore. I need you to find them, Mackay. I don't care how it's done. Will you fix this?'

Mackay didn't need to pause and think, or to contemplate. He didn't need to be asked twice.

'I will,' he said.

As a corporal, and with three tours under his belt, he already knew what it felt like to kill a man. Another human being. A few of them, actually.

Mackay said, 'From a pastor's perspective, is this murder, or revenge?'

'Neither, Mackay. This is killing, pure and simple. Call it a cleansing. There's a difference between killing and murder. Exodus twenty-three verse seven. God said, "Do not kill the innocent and righteous, for I will not acquit the wicked." These are bad people. They aren't innocent or righteous. You are a servant of God now. An avenger who carries out God's wrath on the wrongdoer. Roman's thirteen.'

'Do you want me to hurt them?' asked Mackay.

Malvin paused, then drew a long, broken breath of oxygen from the tubes.

'No. I can draw the line there.'

Still a man of the cloth.

'No need to make them suffer,' he said. 'Just deliver them from their own evil. Don't stop to think about it. Hesitation could get you killed. Just get it done. The authorities aren't looking into this. The police will likely have their own agenda to make it go away. Leave your anxieties and worries here. I'll take the burden with me when I go.'

Mackay leaned over, placed his head on Malvin's chest and held him firm and long. Malvin whispered into his brother's ear, 'I'm drowning, Mackay.'

'I know,' said Mackay. 'I can hear it.'

'They'll try operating on me again tomorrow. Today was a rest day, but they didn't seem hopeful. Said my lungs keep filling up with blood. Said the exit wound from the bullet was wide enough for a grown man's thumb. Even if I do make it, I was a witness to the whole mess. People may come for me, I want you to expect that. But please, promise me, find Lincoln first.'

Mackay pulled himself away. 'I promise,' he said.

He stood and took in Malvin's face, absorbing its features. Then he looked over the rest of him. Weak form and all. Bird's eye view. Head to toe. Memorising what would likely be the last time he would ever see him.

'Those people are bad news,' Malvin said. 'And bad news doesn't get better with age. Who knows what they'll do next, or how far they'll go. Take care of Lincoln. He is all I have left as a memory of me. Tell me you understand.'

Mackay swallowed hard. 'I understand,' he said.

'You are his safe place now.'

Mackay struggled for words. He focused on his breathing and looked deep into Malvin's face. His expression, his colour. Which was when he knew. After this encounter, he was sure he would never see his brother alive again.

'Whatever it takes,' said Mackay.

Nurse Moffat entered the room and drew back the curtains. With her was a table with juice, water, jelly, mashed fruit and pills. The two git cops stood at the entrance to the ward. Watching, leaning, holding up the foundations. The coffee cups were gone. Their hands rested casually inside their shady pockets. The bottom cut of their jackets were edged back, revealing their shiny authority, clipped front and centre for the world to see.

'You should go,' Malvin said. Then, 'May the road rise up to meet you. May the wind always be at your back, and may the sun shine warm upon your face.'

Mackay held him there. Took in everything Malvin ever was to him, then pushed it all down and let his final words beam an everlasting light inside him.

'How are you travelling, Malvin?' asked Moffat. 'You need to eat and rest before your surgery tomorrow. Your visitors will need to take a break now.' Then to Mackay and Cross, 'You'll be able to sign back in tomorrow.' Moffat had her nurse's hat on. And her nurse's voice. It was time for the pair to leave. She eyed them both politely and professionally. Her shoulders angled like a compass pointing away to the exit. No questions, queries or doubtful points permitted.

'What do those two want?' Cross said, jerking her head towards the entrance.

'The two detectives?' said Moffat. 'If I were to guess, I'd say they're hanging around to clarify more questions. Don't worry, I won't let them stay long. They can ask their questions later anyway, after he's rested. It's poor timing on their behalf. They were here for hours already this morning, as well two days ago when they initially brought him in.'

'Were they first on the scene?' Mackay asked.

'As far as I know. The persistent buggers won't leave. If you have any questions, by all means ask them. I could use the time to feed and administer Malvin's meds in peace.'

Mackay stood tall and threw Malvin a hard salute. Forty-five at the elbow. Fingers straight. Feet square. Backing up his final image of his brother. Malvin nodded once in return. As if to say it was okay. That there was work to be done, and they would meet again someday. On the other side. Wherever that may be.

Mackay waited a final second, then about-faced and walked away. Cross reeled and followed. As they reached the two detectives, Mackay slowed to a halt. One metre's distance from nose to nose. Close and confronting. One in front of two. Centred. A narrow triangulation. A ruler and pen would have made a perfectly neat geometrical configuration. Mackay absorbed their heights, their thicknesses, their posture. Memorised features and expressions. Filing it all away. He stood at ease. Tall in the torso, relaxed in the shoulders. Doing his best to hide the emotions in his face. Compressing it with a stiff jaw. Both the Italian and the Buzz Cut adjusted their stances. The proximity of a total stranger was too close. They both took one step back, feet square, clear of the wall with their hands out of their pockets. Just in case quick reactions and space was required. The Italian smiled. For a second it seemed genuine. A token show of professionalism. First impressions count on the force. Or perhaps it was a knowing smile. Ready for misleading answers to difficult questions. Arrogant responses to whatever information had been gathered from the wounded Englishman.

'Can I help you?' asked the heavier one. Buzz Cut. His chin was raised, but his cheeks and eyes were flat and tired. The coffee mustn't have helped.

Cross bit her tongue. She could feel Mackay's face stewing. Could see his thoughts racing. She tugged on Mackay's pants, then curled her hand over his bunched fist bulging from the inside of his pocket. A gentle *leave it be, let's go. There'll be time for this later.* Mackay swallowed the fire in his throat. He stared daggers, eyeballing the Italian. Eyeballing Buzz Cut. He gave it a three-count. One thousand, two thousand, three thousand. Then let it be. He had all the information he needed. The lines and colour in their faces, the dishonesty in their eyes, the corruptness in their body language.

'No, sir, I'm all good. Thank you.' Mackay rotated on his heels and angled for the exit. Cross followed as the two manoeuvred between the detectives and left the ward. Mackay didn't look back.

Before exiting the ground floor, they passed another two men in suits. Walking through the corridor in Santa costumes, leading a couple of therapy dogs. In one hand was the dog leash, the other held a bucket of candy canes. There to help make a patient's day that little less miserable. At least these two in suits were doing something good in the world.

> 1000hrs
> Tuesday December 18, 2012
> Royal Perth Hospital, Western Australia

Mackay and the red ant needed time to plan. Since Cross had made it to Sergeant, being one rank above Mackay at Corporal, she was used to planning. It came naturally. And between walking out of the hospital and figuring out which hotel they would sleep in, her mind was firing. It wasn't about having a completely buttoned-down strategy because that was implausible. People and circumstance always got in the way. She instead sought out a few basic steps with a best-outcome scenario. All of which involved breaking each step down to its simplest form: get from A to B first, then B to C, then C to D. Or wherever it might end.

Phase one's plan was basic. Book a nearby hotel or bed and breakfast, pay with cash. Buy a couple of pre-paid burner phones, pay with cash. Make a phone call, which was the first thing Cross would do the following morning. Mackay didn't ask too many questions about who Cross needed to call or why. He had complete trust in her. Like he did with his team back in the sandbox on tour. So, he left his questions to be answered in due course. He had his assumptions, but he followed the red ant's lead regardless. Sleep was also a priority, part of phase one's planning. Without sleep, decisions were skewed, and outcomes ended up FUBAR. Fucked Up Beyond All Recognition.

Following that would come phase two – pending on how said phone call would go. Phase two involved getting down south to Margaret River to scope out the winery, then deciding what they would do when they got there. Which at this point was a standard reconnaissance mission. How they got there also leaned on the phone call, which was still some hours away.

With sleep being first on the itinerary, they needed information for a good hotel. Ideally nearby, ideally with an above average rating. Nothing too expensive, or cheap and tacky. This was no holiday, and they weren't backpacking either. The best information for city sights, bars, restaurants, and accommodation usually came from cab drivers. And as luck would have it, one was arriving as soon as they exited the hospital. A cab turned into the drop-off zone at the forecourt as soon as they stepped out the doors. A maxi. Perfect timing and a total coincidence. The driver was dropping off an old couple. The bunch of flowers in the old man's hands seemed expensive. A select mix of seasonal reds, purples and whites encased in red cellophane and a light-blue ribbon. A beautiful choice for whoever was receiving them. The woman, presumably the man's wife, was exiting from the hydraulic lift in the rear, seated in a wheelchair. Mackay waited while the driver escorted the wife alongside her frail but upright husband.

'Excuse me, sir,' said Mackay to the driver. 'Wondering if I might ask you about nearby hotels. Something you might recommend in the blue-collar ballpark that isn't too expensive. I figured you might have some recommendations for me and my... friend, partner here.'

Cross raised a brow. Half impressed he'd used the word *friend* and *partner* in the same sentence. *If only he'd connected them together in a more proper manner*, she thought. *Or even in a more intimate way.*

'No problem, mate,' said the driver. 'Most of what's nearby would be in the white-collar ballpark though. Ritzy city hotels. There are plenty decent areas not too far from here. Just a stone's throw.'

'Perfect,' said Mackay.

'I know a few places. Nothing fancy. Quiet. Three stars. Some four. Not entirely el-cheapo though.'

'Sounds like our cup of tea,' said Cross. 'We don't want el-cheapo. If you're not booked for another immediate fare, would you be able to take us there? We need somewhere to wind down from the jetlag.'

'I assumed that all along, boss,' the driver said brightly.

It was good timing for both. An instant job for the cabbie and a quick ride out of the CBD for them. Easy come easy go. The driver, in his late forties, was basically a walking toad. Skinny legs with a keg laid on top. Obviously taking in the beers a little more eager than most, but he was still a long way off from needing a ratchet strap.

Cross wheeled herself over to the rear of the cab while the driver lowered the lift back to ground level. She let him take over as Mackay sat in the rear passenger seat. It was fast, efficient service done well.

'Victoria Park is just over the river,' said the driver. 'Five, ten minutes from the city, pending traffic. Good spot for food, coffee 'n' all that. Not too loud or busy either so you should be able to dust off the jetlag no problem.'

'Thanks for this, been a big couple of days,' Cross said.

'Not a worry. Don't mind helping you lot out. Got family in old England myself, in Sheffield. Though I haven't been to Ireland.'

'Nice to know you can decipher an accent,' said Mackay.

'I watched a lot of *Father Ted*.'

1000hrs
Tuesday December 18, 2012
Busselton, Margaret River, Western Australia

The first time news broke of the missing Perth art dealer eighteen months ago, Lydia Ferreira frothed over the pulpy juice like WD-40. Penetrating every facet. As a Margaret River local, no other story had ever been as big. Now, a second story was breaking within the same region, tied back to the same winery. This story, however, was tied to an international family: two dead, one missing, and one with gunshot wounds laying in ICU at Royal Perth Hospital. Lydia's fingers slammed down on her keyboard like hail. Her ears were hot and sweaty from the dozens of phone calls she'd been making between St John's ambulance, the coroner, the airline the family had flown in with, the state police department, neighbouring farmers and winemakers, even competing journalists. Some were helpful, some gave back nothing.

The five foot nothing, mocha brown thirty-year-old was a blunt piece of work. Her highly strung nature was outright annoying to some, inquisitive and fearless to others. She was both loved and loathed with her reputation for sticking her button nose in stories that preferred staying quiet. But nobody could say she didn't do a good job finding detail. Almost always she went above and beyond for the sake of a story, it was just a matter of how much detail came out in the wash which ruffled feathers. For her, detail was the job.

Lydia had a story she knew had merit. Knew had weight. Not because it would elevate her status as a journalist, but because it would expose the truth. She was a simple girl with traditional values: truth above all and expose injustice. Her story was propelled by her will to expose that same truth from eighteen months earlier. All of which was owed to the public. Not buried and forgotten under state corruption where government associations paid people off. Often leaving the families of the deceased in the dark. Left in the big ethereal world of questioning why. No rhyme, no reason. Keep things quiet, because quiet is good.

Not for Lydia.

Quiet meant something was wrong, and she was prepared to go to any length to shake it up nice and loud. Lydia's article, once published, would cement the same facts she'd presented months earlier, but with more gravitas. The internet had come, and for the future of her journalism, it had paved a wide road for truth. Her truth. Lydia's news was personal. She demanded front-line reporting, personal accounts, first-hand accounts. On all platforms: blogs, features, prime-time television. With two fatal incidences connected to the one and only Nicus Van Breeman, it would have to make the federal court stand and listen. They'd have no choice but to spread their investigations into the state's corruption. It couldn't go any other way. Some of her facts were loose, but through trusted sources, some of those loose facts were bona fide. She took every quote and statements on the missing Perth art dealer from eighteen months earlier and piled every new piece of knowledge of the family shooting on top of it. She matched every facet of information to the new case, and although the most recent details were a little open-ended, the coincidence of another incident in the same location with the same snakehead was too great. The parallels insurmountable. In half an hour, her report would be sent to her editor at the Margaret River local, as well as uploaded onto her personal blog in cyberspace.

At a quarter past ten, Lydia was done. No more online searches, no more phone calls. She didn't have everything fully fleshed out, but she had enough to raise plenty of eyebrows: an international family was gunned down, screams were heard, a medical evacuation chopper was phoned in. The two cops on the scene were also the same two cops involved with the Carice Hackforth case. And once again, all of it centred around the Frans & Hoek winery. Owned by infamous Perth millionaire, Nicus Van Breeman.

Lydia closed her laptop and finished her cream cheese and smoked salmon toasted bagel. She again phoned her immediate boss, also holed up in the main office, and gave her a rundown of the facts she'd ascertained. She was given the okay to send her story to her editor, which basically meant go for your life and open up a can of worms. She then rang her cameraman and told him to pick her up in ten minutes with all his gear. She washed her face, combed her hair, then brightened her complexion with various products. She walked outside to the gate at the front of her unit and waited. Her day was going to be a two-parter. First, a spot-news live report at Frans and Hoek winery. Second, a three-hour drive up north to check on the wounded victim at Royal Perth Hospital.

> 1015hrs
> Tuesday December 18, 2012
> Victoria Park, Bed and Breakfast, Perth, Western Australia

The driver pulled into a bed and breakfast. A lodge rated at four stars, not three, on the driver's recommendation. Away from major roads, businesses and noisy traffic flow. A reputation he assured was reasonably priced, clean, with friendly service and a quietness not found unless they ventured into the hills. The driver seemed genuine with his recommendation, and there was no I do for you, you do for me deal. He didn't prompt for a tip and didn't raise the cost of the fare. For a first option, it was solid. Mackay went inside while Cross and the driver waited for the approval.

Inside, the reception quarter imitated an open-plan art gallery bounded with sand-lime brick. The design flourishes were a mix of canvas paintings and panoramic photographs; ocean landscapes, coral paintings, and numerous aerial shots of dolphins and whales. A large-scale aquarium was built into the far wall behind the reception desk and a token bookshelf with tourist pamphlets ran adjacent to the entryway. The vibe was relaxed. Lounge jazz played from speakers in the corners while soft vanilla and lavender circulated the room. Compared to the hospital, the flight and the two cab rides, this was the place to be. Mackay stepped back outside and gave the cabbie the thumbs up. The driver nodded once, got out and lowered Cross from the rear lift while Mackay removed their bags and walked them up to reception.

The price was reasonable like the driver said. Free Wi-Fi, room service until ten, and housekeeping on request. Cross opted for the queen bed in a single room, which was cheaper than two singles in two separate rooms. Mackay didn't object. They were early for regular check-in, but the room was ready, and the chirpy receptionist took into account their travel time and jetlag. She booked them in for an initial starter of three nights, which Cross thought was ideal considering there was no surcharge to extend if they wanted. Happy days. Cash was paid.

They were shown to their room by the receptionist herself, a trim older lady in a fitted jacket with a never-ending smile. She moved like a dancer and spoke like she was the owner. Or at least part owner, obviously proud of the business she was providing. Mackay figured her closer to seventy but ballparked her in the sixties just to be safe. She had a conservative layer of red lipstick, of which some had made it to the front of her teeth, but it wasn't terribly visible, so neither Mackay nor Cross said anything. She cheerfully unlocked number twelve, handed over the keys and left them to it.

Inside the room, Cross opted to shower first. She rolled her chair to the corner of the room, locked the brake, leaned down and climbed out using her arms like stilts.

'Looks weird doesn't it,' said Cross.

'From an able-bodied point of view, it does. Only because I'm seeing it for the first time.'

'First time I had to try it, it felt stupid. For months. Now it's what I do. Breakfast routine, bedtime routine. You're the first normal person to ever see me do it.'

'Normal?'

'Aside from my parents and the rehab team back in Aldershot. You're still a weird-looking fucker, don't worry.'

'I feel privileged.'

'You should.'

Cross sashayed herself to the foot of the bed, reached up and took her carry-on backpack off the mattress. Mackay watched.

'I'm not sure what I should do to help you,' he said.

'Don't.'

The red ant dug into her backpack and collected an old toothbrush, an oversized T-shirt, a pair of shorts with a drawstring and a can of deodorant. All Mackay's old gear he'd left behind in Guildford. She picked them up and held the pile out to Mackay.

'You can take these into the bathroom and put them on the floor in the middle,' she said. 'Put a towel next to them and the bathmat where it normally goes.'

Mackay obliged while Cross hand-walked onto the bathroom tiles then turned and waited for Mackay to leave.

'You're sure?' Mackay asked, opting to be a gentleman one last time. 'I could get the hot water ready?'

'I'm an amputee, not a paraplegic. See.' Cross raised herself onto the ends of her limbs, reached up and grabbed the door handle on the inside.

'Impressive, not stupid,' said Mackay.

Cross flashed a brief smile and closed the door.

Mackay walked to the kitchenette, found a glass in one of the random cupboards, poured some water from the tap and took his daily hit of drugs. First the immunosuppressants, then the synthetic marrow stabiliser. Maintenance meds. He laid down on the queen bed and switched the television on. The mattress was a little springy in his opinion, for a four-star establishment. But it didn't sag and at least the springiness was evenly distributed. He'd slept on plenty worse.

ACCEPTANCE

There was not much happening in terms of news. It was too early for the evening broadcast, so instead he left it on some reality programme and tried to switch his brain off. A loud Greek-Australian family were bickering about who cooked the best moussaka, which version was best, and which of those versions would be served to their guests. After five minutes of nonsense, a news report cut in. A ten-thirty bulletin. It wasn't a national broadcast with a veteran anchor and a cityscape background, rather, a smaller, local channel. Still, the text that rolled across the screen noted an exclusive update. The reporter stood roadside in front of a long extravagant building with a tiled roof. Behind her was an extended wooden fence running left to right up to a gate alongside a huge signpost. In the far background were rows of grapevines. Mackay couldn't really make out the name on the signpost, as the focus was tight on the reporter.

The reporter, a short brunette with naturally tanned skin, began mentioning a few recently familiar names which made Mackay sit tall and lean forward. He turned the volume up with the bedside remote. She spoke directly about Malvin's incident. She mentioned three names specifically that, in the last few hours, were the exact reason why he and Cross had flown halfway across the world. The first name was *Margaret River*, where an ongoing police investigation was taking place. The second name was *Frans and Hoek Winery*, which was when the reporter moved, allowing the camera to focus on the signpost beyond her shoulder. It had the winery's name written on it in sharp blue and bronze font. The font was inscribed above a caricature of a half-eaten fish with prickly bones riding a stallion. The third name mentioned was *Van Breeman*. The same name their first cab driver from India had mentioned. The educated one with the Kufi cap. Fortunately, the reporter expanded that name to its fullest. Nicus Van Breeman. The reporter specifically stated that within a two-year period, this was the second, serious criminal investigation directly linked to the Perth millionaire. A forty-one-year-old South African native who'd made it big in the Perth social scene. The first investigation being Van Breeman's connection to his missing lover: art dealer and socialite, Carice Hackforth. Now a cold case wrapped under suspicious circumstances.

Along with these three names, the reporter mentioned the shooting of a woman, as well as suspicious circumstances surrounding the death of an eight-year-old boy which was apparently brought on by an asthma attack. She said it was unknown at the time whether the boy was the woman's son. She then stated that a man in his early forties had been flown to Royal Perth Hospital and was now recovering in ICU from a gunshot wound. Again, unknown whether the man was linked as the husband or father. She didn't mention the family was from the United Kingdom, or that there was, in fact, another boy missing. She'd obviously done her best with what limited information she could gather, but she did throw caution to the wind, saying this had the makings of another potential cover-up. The reporter finished her segment stating it was another serious blow to Margaret River's wine and tourism industry, and that a national inquiry to the truth behind both incidences would be paramount, and in the state's best interest.

'Someone has some good contacts,' said Cross, swaying out of the bathroom. She looked odd dressed in Malvin's baggy clothes, and although the men's deodorant didn't particularly suit, she looked brilliantly fresh, her skin radiating with post-shower warmth. She clinched one hand into the top sheet of the bed while the other hand grasped the bedhead. She pronged onto her limbs then hauled and twisted herself onto the bed. Like a horizontal pirouette. Her wet hair tickling his arm as she scuffled in next to him.

'We've got a bigger slice of the whole pie now,' said Mackay. 'We have names and a visual for the location.'

'Pie? I could easily murder a slice. I'm starving. I can't think.'

Mackay looked over at the digital clock on the bedside table next to the phone. 'How about ordering pizza?' he said. 'Surely there's a Domino's open at this hour getting ready for the lunch rush.'

'I'll call and order. Go shower.'

'Do you even know the number for Domino's here?'

'No, but the lovely old bird at reception might.'

Mackay took himself into the bathroom while Cross got on the phone. He turned the shower to hot. Hot as he could stand. The water pressure was excellent. He undressed, dunked his head under the jets and dragged his fingernails down his scalp. Hard. Left side, middle, right side. Front to back. Back to front. Opening the tiny blood vessels beneath the skin's surface. Releasing the tension, helping him feel that little more at ease. His own personal therapy. Near enough to what Swabinski had suggested, only at a physical level rather than mental. Short-term relief rather than long-term closure. He stayed under the scalding water for ten whole minutes. Probably the longest shower he'd ever had in his life.

Mackay walked out of the bathroom with a towel around his midsection. Cheese-grater skin in full view. Cross was sitting upright in the bed watching a train travel across eastern Europe on the television. Inside the train, an older man with a British accent spoke about the iconic Zagreb cathedral. A structure devastated by the Tartars in the mid-1200s in Croatia. Cross turned to look at him. Taking in his physique. Wide-capped shoulders, knotted abdominals, disfigured ribcage. Mackay wasn't sure whether to ask her to look away while he got changed or go back into the bathroom. He was also unsure if it was too early in their friendship to be sleeping next to each other. Thankfully, Cross spoke for him.

'Stop thinking about it,' she said. 'Close the curtains if you're that self-conscious.'

Mackay obliged and closed them, shutting out most of the daylight. Typical human nature in front of the opposite species. At least for a man who hadn't been seen by a woman for over a year. What light remained filled the room to a low amber, which was dark enough to sleep in considering the time of the day. Under the dancing luminosity of the television, he dropped his towel, picked out his shorts from his dive bag and put them on. Then came a knock at the door.

'Domino's,' stated a young voice. Mackay couldn't tell if it was male or female. If it was female, he figured she'd be somewhere in her mid-to-late twenties judging by the seasoned announcement. Maybe a university student, or maybe it was her full-time career, enjoying every minute of it. If it was male, he was most probably younger. Late teens, still growing into his adult self. Mackay opened the door. A female. Mid-twenties. Small and wiry. He paid the girl with enough of a tip for a couple of large coffees. Or a jug of premium beer. The girl smiled like someone had just done her tax return. He closed the door then sat down in bed next to Cross.

'She seemed excited,' said Mackay.

'They don't tip in Australia,' said Cross. 'Not customary. You made her day.'

They shared a large ham and pineapple, and a supreme, eating from the boxes on the bed while the man on the train exited Zagreb. He then travelled west into Slovenia and spoke about the proximity of Ljubljana, and how the Slovene language differed to Serbo-Croatian. Namely by its unique grammar, vocabulary and pronunciation.

Cross turned to look at Mackay. The flickering colours of the television drew spangled tones across his face, sketching the wrought outline of his jaw. She could see the muscles at the sides flexing. He was biting down, grinding his teeth. She sensed an unease. Whether it was because he was in bed with her, or because Malvin was lying in hospital with his life sapping away, she couldn't be sure. She traced the bristling hairs of stubble with her eyes and noted his subtle overbite. She noted how the tops of his ears were slightly blunted. Not in a bad way, they were still curved like normal only with a rounded edge. Like it'd been filed down or pinched inward like the crust of a pie. A result from all the knocks and scrums playing rugby.

Mackay turned to see her looking at him. In the there and then. He held her there. He liked the closeness. In that moment, he envied her. For a loudmouth extrovert, she looked totally serene. She had managed to get through her rage and inner turmoil since her own traumatic incident, and it emanated beautifully. Exuding a state of mind where Mackay wished he could be. At the same time, she made him feel calmer than he'd felt in a long time. He could feel his jaw start to loosen as Cross ran a hand down his ribcage. Feeling his uneven skin. The scar tissue, the abrasions, the rubbery texture. She caressed his side top to bottom. Hip to collarbone. Up and down, and back again. He let her feel his disfigurement. Mackay reached a hand around to Cross's own ribcage. It felt normal. Taught. Toned from years of boxing, her dimensions as good as perfect. He held her waist and pulled her closer, lifting her on top of him the gentlest way he knew. Up close she glowed. Her skin smooth as silk, bristling with measured restraint. With her free hand, Cross found the television remote from the bedside table and turned it off. She closed her mouth over his and curled into him, then onto him. Another physical release, this time mental as well.

> 1230hrs
> Tuesday December 18, 2012
> Frans and Hoek Winery, Margaret River, Western Australia

Nicus Van Breeman walked into the admin room of the main gallery to find Bryson, Kimbala and Wynand seated at a table, watching a news update on a small flat-screen television.

'Have you seen this, boss?' said Bryson.

Bryson had his feet up on the table, ankles crossed, leaning back. He was sipping coffee from a tall stainless-steel Thermos.

'Seen what?' said Van Breeman, pausing deliberately to look at Bryson's feet. Bryson didn't twig. Didn't take notice, or simply didn't see where Van Breeman was looking.

'Nice to see you making yourself at home,' Van Breeman said.

'What's that?' said Bryson.

'The retarded part of your brain seems to think you're in your lounge room.'

Bryson frowned with an *I don't understand* face.

Kimbala said, 'It's that same woman from last time. The reporter. Nosy bitch. The news has been running it since ten-thirty this morning. They're repeating it every half hour. With this amount of exposure, it's going to get bad. Twice as bad as last time. Or worse.'

Van Breeman exploded, 'Get your feet off the goddamn fucking table!' He grabbed Bryson's boots, heaved them up and kicked the chair's legs, knocking Bryson backwards onto the floor. He picked up the Thermos and threw it against the wall. Exploding the hot brown liquid like a Pollock painting. Bryson was taller than Van Breeman by a whole foot. Under any normal circumstances on the street, Bryson would have ripped Van Breeman's head off. It was only under employment obligations and monetary factors he stayed down, sprawled on his back.

Wynand and Kimbala stood. Van Breeman faced them.

'Have either of you found the boy?'

Neither spoke. Wynand stared at the floor. The television tweeted in the background. Spilt coffee filled the air. Van Breeman looked from Wynand to Kimbala, then back again. Bryson cautiously made it to his feet.

'I'll be another man down if I have to repeat that question,' said Van Breeman.

'No, sir,' said Kimbala. 'The boy's still missing.'

'Then why the fuck are you all in here watching television? And how is it nobody saw this bitch making a news report right in front of our establishment? Right in front of my brand? Where is my money going after it goes into your pocket?'

Nobody spoke. Van Breeman wasn't finished. 'She was right there on the front driveway. My own security, getting paid a bomb but can't even secure the premises. Tell me, who needs some fucking retraining here?' Van Breeman's eyes darted between his three men.

'To be fair, sir,' started Bryson, 'that report was made while we were out searching for the boy. Sometime between ten and ten-thirty. We'd been out searching on rotation since seven o'clock, and have only just come back in. And by the camera angle, she wasn't on our property. Even if we had seen her, why would we risk being filmed?'

Van Breeman stepped forward and grabbed the front of Bryson's collar with two hands. Bryson breathed and chewed thoughts. Slow thoughts at that. He considered his current reality, then calculated his options with realistic outcomes. He decided to stay still. The only person bigger than Bryson was Kimbala, who could easily have been a sideshow freak in a circus act. Still, if Bryson was on boil, he was plenty intimidating. His dopey-eyed stare and gentle giant appearance worked in his favour when taking children down to the wine press. But otherwise, he was an amalgamation of dense and psychotic. Which for the most part was why Van Breeman had him on the books.

'You don't ask me questions, Kefa,' Van Breeman said. 'You answer mine. Are we clear?'

After a long, drawn-out moment, Bryson nodded. 'We're clear, boss.'

Van Breeman let go.

'That reporter can do what she wants,' Van Breeman said. 'I don't care about her status as a journalist anymore. Women in front of cameras think they're invincible. She's our next target. She needs to go. Now get the fuck out of here and go look for the boy.'

Wynand, Bryson and Kimbala left. Then Van Breeman's phone rang. It was Taylor.

'Some good news I hope,' said Van Breeman.

'Not yet,' said Taylor. 'He's supposed to be admitted for surgery tomorrow, but it'll be done before then. We'll give the security guys a break.'

'Then he's out of the picture?'

'Easy done. One hundred per cent.'

*

Inside the hospital, on the same floor where Malvin lay drowning in his blood, Taylor and Derek waited. Waited on the clock. They were good at waiting. Part of their bread and butter. Biding their time for the right moment. They needed a quiet few minutes where security was lax. A time where back and forth texting was key to instigate a clean elimination of the British witness.

Taylor used his police powers and talked his way into gaining access inside the security control room. He needed to rewind some footage. The control room accessed all the CCTV footage and fed it back to the wall of screens. It picked up the halls, wards, and car parks in and around the hospital. Taylor had the rank, the badge, and the gun, all of which helped persuade the two familiar security personnel to let him inside. He told them he needed to revisit the morning's recordings from the ICU ward. Back to when a broad athletic man and a female in a wheelchair had arrived. A British couple who might have more information to help the shooting investigation. At least that's the story he went with and nobody questioned it. Rank, badge, gun. What he really wanted to do though, was completely different.

While Derek sat in the ICU's waiting room flicking through a year-old real estate magazine, Taylor sat in the security control room rewinding and scrolling. Wasting time, pretending to look busy.

'You guys been in here a while? Long shift?' asked Taylor.

'All morning. Nine hours and counting,' said one operator. Harrison. Written on his name badge.

'You guys must need a break,' said Taylor. 'Go grab a coffee. On me. Real coffee I mean, from the café on the ground floor.'

Taylor filtered through his wallet and peeled a twenty. He dropped the note on the bench and slid it across within easy reach of the guards. Neither of the two men responded. At first. Then Harrison raised an interested brow.

'I don't know about you, Steve,' Harrison said, 'but I was always taught never to refuse good hospitality.'

The second guy smiled and nodded. Steve. Written on his name badge. Obviously keen for a break. Maybe a trip to the bathroom as well to freshen up a little.

Harrison picked up the twenty. 'You want anything, Detective?' he said.

'No thanks, mate,' said Taylor. 'I got this to search through. Take your time. Finding the potential suspects involved in this breach might take a while. Hard to distinguish one person from another in the footage.'

'True, true,' said Harrison. 'Zoom in, zoom out, pause, play, repeat. We'll be back in five minutes. You all good here?'

'I'll be fine, cheers.'

Harrison and Steve left the control room with Taylor's twenty. Taylor pulled out his cell phone and texted Derek. *CLEAR NOW. 5 MINUTES.*

Derek felt his phone vibrate in his pocket. He checked the text then made his way over to the duty nurse on the ICU floor. Nurse Moffat. Derek went through the motions, like a good detective. He sought out her permission to see if he could go and see Malvin and clarify a few final questions. Taking the advantage. Poor Moffat had no idea of his agenda, so she wasn't to blame. As a show of good faith, Derek and Taylor had stayed clear of Malvin for most of the day. Intentionally. All part of the plan. It wasn't up to Moffat to refuse either, really. There'd been a serious incident. People had been shot. People had been killed. Questions needed to be asked and answered, which could only be done while Malvin was conscious and coherent.

'I'll give you your five minutes,' said Moffat. 'But no more. He needs to rest for his surgery tomorrow.'

'That's all I need, ma'am,' replied Derek.

Moffat escorted Derek into Malvin's ward. She pulled back his curtain and raised his bed with the controller hooked to the side of the bedframe. She pulled the sheets away from his chin and began rubbing his arms and hands, waking him gently. Malvin's eyes slowly began to open.

'I'll leave you two alone for a spell,' said Moffat. 'The detective here would like to ask you a few questions. It's his last chance before your surgery tomorrow. Then it's more rest. Okay?'

Moffat left. Derek pulled the curtain closed.

'You've come,' Malvin rasped slowly. Breathlessly. 'Do what you need to do.'

Derek paused momentarily. The weight of Malvin's words were almost enlightening. Nobody he'd ever killed had ever expected or anticipated their death quiet like the man lying in front of him. It was strangely difficult to absorb.

'Sorry, mate.'

'As am I. You'll see.'

Derek looked over Malvin's face and body. Malvin didn't move. Didn't scream or yell. He couldn't even if he wanted to. He didn't make any notion to react or retaliate at all. He simply looked his murderer in the face – watching as the detective switched off the monitor from the wall and unplugged his breathing support. No beeps, no alarming digital noises. Derek pulled the pillow from underneath Malvin's head and placed it over his face, pressing down on it with the bulk of his weight. Smothering him. Again, Malvin didn't move. Not at first anyway. Not until his brain began to shut down from a lack of oxygen and his body began twitching impulsively. Rocking and shuddering. Human evolution fighting back instinctively. Soon, the rocking slowed, the shuddering tapered out. Malvin's body relaxed and never moved again. Derek placed the pillow back underneath Malvin's head. He noticed Malvin's mouth and jaw were stretched wide open. Shock-blasted with the agony of suffocation. His eyes, however, were shut. Derek pressed the eyelids hard against the bottom of the sockets to make sure they stayed that way, then pushed Malvin's jaw closed. A strained, pleading expression fighting to live still there. Locked beneath the surface of the skin. Inside the muscles, lines, and contours of his face.

Derek turned the monitor and breathing apparatus back on. He opened the curtain and stepped out, leaving it drawn. Less suspicious that way. Then he left to go find Taylor in the security control room. He didn't see Moffat on the way out, which for him was a good thing. The less contact he had with her the better. She could have been anywhere. Checking other patients, running administration errands, speaking with other staff.

Who knew? Even if Moffat was back within her five-minute time frame, she would have been none the wiser to the silence. Malvin simply looked sound asleep. Moffat's first alarm signal for any patient was sound – beeps and blaring emitting from the monitors. Her second signal was movement – the patient's body convulsing. Neither was going to happen. Her third was the flatline on the screen. Derek had taken out two out of three. Whether Moffat took a look at the monitor immediately on her return was a chance Derek had to take. Part of the risks of the job. Prerequisites under Van Breeman's salary. If any fingers started pointing at him after the fact, he'd cross that bridge if and when it came.

On the way to the control room, Derek rang the head of the snake. Van Breeman picked up after the first ring.

'It's done,' said Derek.

'Good. Take the night off,' said Van Breeman. 'Have some time with the family. Tomorrow, I want you to collect the knobkerry and tucker telephone from my apartment, then drive back here. The others are kidnapping the reporter in the morning, so I need you back here by midday with the two implements.'

'Reporter? Hackforth?'

'Hackforth.'

'Okay.'

'We've still got a child to find as well. And bagging a reporter without witnesses is a tricky affair. It's going to be a big day.'

0430hrs
Wednesday December 19, 2012
Victoria Park, Bed and Breakfast, Perth, Western Australia

Mackay slept long and deep. Close to twelve hours. He woke to a long-forgotten sensation; a woman was in bed with him curled up against his shoulder. Cross was breathing deep and heavy. She was toasty warm and still very much asleep. A faint scent of motel shampoo still lingered in her hair. He liked it. He stretched his arm out slowly, rolled away from her, and stepped out of bed. He looked back at the red ant. Silent. Deep, heavy breaths. No change. He walked to the bathroom, closed the door and started the shower. He tried not to think on the night just gone. The sensations. The heaving of her breasts. The velvety skin. Her damp hair sticking to her chest and back. The lack of completeness in her limbs making her feel weightless on top of him.

Mackay turned the heat to normal. Not as hot as before, he didn't feel it necessary. He felt okay. Better than he had in a long time. Namely because of the sensual passing. The sex had taken a lot of the edge off. Worry and restlessness disappearing into the nether amidst the heated physical contact. But it wasn't all gone. He still had plenty of worries circulating. Deep and unnerving. The type where fingernails through the scalp, or drugs and alcohol, could only release so much. If Cross wasn't with him, if he were still sulking in his bedroom back in Guildford staring at walls, who knew what hole he would travel down. But time had passed. The sun had risen, and developments had surfaced. Malvin was lying in a hospital bed, dying. Possibly dead already. Mackay already had a sister-in-law and one nephew dead, with one other nephew missing. He was hurting, but he'd made a promise, and he had every intention of fulfilling it.

Sometime that morning, two phone calls would need to be made. Since Mackay was up first, the timing suggested his call should be first. Cross's contact, whoever that was, could come later. Mackay needed to phone the hospital. To clear the ticking bomb in his head. But it couldn't be done in the room. He needed to get out. The raw inkling of Malvin's fate kept poking him with a sharp stick. He needed to know whether his inkling was right or wrong, but he didn't want to bother Cross. She was deep asleep, and he wanted to leave her be. Let her catch up in her own time. Besides, he really wanted this next phone call to be private. No one but him and the voice at the end of the line. He slipped on a shirt, shorts, and shoes, and stepped outside.

The sun hadn't risen, but reception was fortunately open. Even though the sign on the front stated the office hours were 6am–10pm, there was a light on inside and the door was open. The same trim, older lady they'd met the previous day was behind the desk. She looked fresh as a daisy, now in a black and white top, matching skirt, this time with a darker shade of lipstick. Mackay thought she looked ready for a photoshoot for some corporate magazine. She was working at a computer. Probably part of her morning email routine. Sending, replying, filing, organising.

'You're up early,' she said. 'I just started my day. How can I help you?'

'Morning, ma'am, I know I have a phone in my room, but we have no directory. I was wondering if you had one in the reception here. Maybe a pen and spare paper? I was hoping to make a private call.'

'Certainly. We have a phone and a yellow pages directory over there in the corner. Underneath the Brett Whitely on the wall. Your pen and paper are free of charge.' She smiled. Wide and happy. Lipstick and teeth. Mackay looked to where she was pointing.

'Brett Whitely?' he said. Numerous artworks adorned the wall, none of which Mackay knew in any kind of artistic sense, only that the colours were vivid and mostly ocean related.

'Big Blue Lavender Bay. With the palm trees and long jetty. It's only a framed copy, not worth more than the frame itself but I just think it fills the space beautifully. I will have to charge the phone call to your room though if that's okay. Is it going to be international? I just assumed it might because of your accent. If it's a local call, it will only cost around fifty cents.'

'No, ma'am. By private I mean I'd just like the phone number, write it down then use a payphone outside.'

'Are you sure? I could leave the office if you like. No skin off my nose. I haven't had my coffee yet so it would give me an early break.'

'That's very kind of you, ma'am. But yes, I'm sure. I'll use a payphone.'

'Don't mean to push, but I have the internet open here, I can just search for the number on Google. If I'm being too nosy you just let me know.'

Mackay thought about it. Thought about the necessity of remaining totally anonymous if he were to fulfil Malvin's wishes. It wouldn't hurt if she simply got the number of the hospital for him. But then again, there was news breaking of a British man who had been shot, lying in intensive care in the city hospital. Mackay was British via Ireland, which would work in his favour, but Cross wasn't, and the lady seemed pretty switched on. Could easily put two and two together if people started asking questions. She could end up linked to a line of questioning down the track, which, for obvious reasons would follow straight back to them.

'That's fine, ma'am, really,' he said. 'I don't want to be a bother. I appreciate it all the same. I'll just take a look at the directory. And the pen and paper if that's still on the cards.'

'Of course. So polite, calling me "ma'am". Don't get to hear that too often. So refreshing. All I get is Mum, Nana, Lorinda, Mrs Hull.'

'Purely habit,' he said.

The lady handed Mackay a single sheet of paper and a pen and moved it across the reception desk. 'The closest payphone is less than a five-minute walk away,' she said. 'As you exit the driveway, turn left and follow the path. You'll pass a car dealership, then a line of restaurants and cafés. Stay on the left and it should appear opposite a Thai restaurant, close to a zebra crossing.'

'Thank you, ma'am.'

Mackay moved to the corner wall where a thick phone directory sat on a small shelf underneath the Brett Whitely painting. Next to it was a touch phone, and below that was a wooden stool with hand-woven Danish cord. Thick and sturdy to the touch. Mackay sat and flicked the phone directory to H, then ran through the pages. He'd called the Royal Perth Hospital only once before, back in Guildford. But he didn't have a cell phone and never copied the number down. Besides, remembering a sixteen-digit international number was near impossible. He needed the local version. There was one number. It would have to do. Even if he had to jump through the hoops again to get to Malvin's ward. Mackay wrote the number down, got off the stool and bid Lorinda a good day. Two minutes later, he was on a quiet sidewalk with minimal traffic.

The birth of the sun's rays had only just started peeping. He passed the car dealership with new-model banners, passed a closed pub, a waking independent café, a closed restaurant, and a closed franchise café. He spotted the phone booth with its aluminium frame sticking out from behind a telegraph post. It stood opposite a Thai restaurant, near an intersection with a zebra crossing. Mackay stepped in, inserted some coins, flattened out the paper with the number on it, dialled and waited. The line clicked and connected faster than he expected. He was put on hold by a female voice, but it wasn't Nurse Moffat. Different tone. Older. Harsher. A voice he'd heard plenty times before, in Afghanistan. Usually retained by old female sergeants and corporals stuck doing menial admin tasks. Living like they were two seconds shy of totally losing it.

The voice returned. 'Thanks for waiting, how can I help?'

'I'm calling regarding any updates on the state of my brother in ICU. Gunshot wound to the chest. My name is Mackay

Connolly, I'm the immediate next of kin. My details should be on file. I attended yesterday with Nurse Moffat. My brother's name is...'

'Malvin Connolly,' finished the nurse. 'We all know the patient. We were looking at how to contact you but there was no number registered. Are you available to come to the ward in person, sir?' Her tone was flat. Bleak and cheerless. Mackay knew the tone. Heard it plenty times before, also in Afghanistan. When the doctors spoke about fallen soldiers. He knew what it meant.

'Is he gone?' he said.

'I think it best if you come in. The doctor will explain.'

'Please, ma'am. I would really like to know that information now if you don't mind. The sooner the better. If he's gone, I can deal with some of that initial grief now rather than making a scene and breaking down in the ward. Never a pleasant sight. Not for you nurses, not for visitors. I can also begin letting our family know back in England and start the funeral arrangements, which will be quite a drawn-out process as I'm sure you understand.'

The nurse didn't reply.

'Is he gone?' Mackay said again.

'Yes. I am sorry,' said the voice. 'He was taken down to the morgue last night.'

The line was quiet for a spell. Nothing but hollow silence at each end.

'How late?' asked Mackay, bringing the conversation back.

'Pardon?'

'What time was he taken down to the morgue?'

'I'm not sure exactly.'

'Rough ballpark?'

'Well, I had just started my shift. Maybe half an hour in, so approximately eight-thirty. Why is that?'

Mackay hung up. He clenched his jaw and swallowed the pain. Did his best to stop himself from crying but the tears rose and spilled anyway. He stayed in the booth. One minute. Two minutes. He took a breath, then let his assumptions rise. Played the scenario over in his head. An undetectable lethal injection? Removal of his breathing apparatus? A knife? Suffocation? Switching off life support? All of the above? None of the above? Two detectives with badges inside a hospital didn't need to be supervised. They were trusted citizens. They could play the waiting game, find a moment, and do whatever necessary to silence a witness. It's what he would do, if he was a dirty cop. Walk in, walk out. No questions asked. Mackay needed a shower.

0515hrs
Wednesday December 19, 2012
Victoria Park Bed and Breakfast, Perth, Western Australia

Cross woke to the sound of water streaming from behind the bathroom door. She too tried not to think too much about the evening past. Her movements, entwined together with him, in a foreign country, had said everything she had wanted to say. Made things easier in the short term at least. Meant she didn't have to bring up feelings with words. Which were a nuisance at the best of times. Using real emotive words in a sincere manner wasn't her strong suit. Things were hopefully less awkward now. For the both of them. In the heat of the moment, she was certain she had felt Mackay relax. He seemed calmer. Looser. On all accounts, since coming to know him she'd felt a certain security with him she hadn't felt in a long time. Or maybe had never felt at all. There was an ease. Like she could just be herself. Loudmouth, stump legs, red hair, and all. And he accepted her. But she couldn't let emotions get in the way. Not now. Not yet. Maybe their evening affair would work in phase one's favour. Or maybe it would create tension. It was too soon to tell. Though it had felt right in the moment, and she had no regrets, they had work to do.

She quickly banked these thoughts to a reserved folder to ponder another time and instead retrieved a dormant phone number from a different memory file. A time preserved from a different life. As different as it could come. Before an IED had taken her legs and almost took her life. Before she learned to use a wheelchair or train soldiers at the boxing gym. Cross reached over to the bedside table with the in-room telephone. She located the dormant number in her head, hit zero to dial out of the hotel line, then pressed a series of buttons.

Mackay walked out of the bathroom, towel around the waist. The grisly skin glistening against the light streaming in from the bathroom window. He looked tense again. The muscles in his face a mix of lead and iron. His shoulders were raised, his eyes were narrowed. Like the weight which was removed the previous night had returned. Cross was sitting up in the bed, phone to her ear, speaking into the receiver with a slew of recurring answers: copy, wilco, understood. Mackay's initial reaction was apprehension and unease. Why was Cross calling from the room's phone? But from the tone of her voice and her responses, it was clear it was all business. This was her contact. No searching phone directories or asking Lorinda at reception for assistance. Anonymity maintained.

'Yes, he's here now,' said Cross into the phone. 'Tell him everything you just told me.'

Cross handed Mackay the receiver. As unexpected as it was, Mackay sat down next to her and went with it. There were no *good mornings, how did you sleep, want to order breakfast?* There was no fussing about. Mackay liked that about her. Work first, play later.

'Hello,' said Mackay.

'Hello. You don't know me, and I won't give my name over the phone, but I know your friend, Renee Cross.'

Mackay turned to Cross sitting next to him. She nodded. All business. Mackay placed one hand over the receiver and said,

'SAS.' Cross nodded again. All dots now connected. Cross had only briefly spoken about her time in Perth once, at the coffee shop, back at Madam's Apprentice Café next to the lake. She'd conducted pre-deployment training there before heading to Afghanistan to clear roads and minefields. She'd trained with Australia's best. Easily some of the world's best. The Special Air Service Regiment. Their main base was located in Perth, somewhere just outside the city. A beachside suburb. A strong part of him assumed he was speaking with an old flame of hers. Someone she'd spent time with. A month is a good amount of time to get to know somebody. Part of natural progression. Training environments often make way for blossoming relationships. Fit redhead, fit elite soldier. He tossed any emotional thoughts aside. The red ant's face looked positive. Like the source and the information was invaluable.

'I'm listening,' said Mackay.

'I'll keep it short and simple. We normally wouldn't allow this, and once the operation has been completed, it never happened. I don't know you, I don't trust you. But I trust your friend. So, you can consider me a friend of a friend.'

The male voice was casual, but to the point. Fluent and direct. The SAS in a nutshell. It sounded educated. Above average intelligence even for military standards.

'Because of your situation and circumstances in relation to the ex-sergeant, I've been informed you are moving in for a reconnaissance operation. So, I will make an exception here. For you, because of her. She's a blast from the past as they'd say. So, listen to her and look out for her. Being who she is and what she's gone through means I owe her a favour. A solid. It's the only reason I'm allowing this to go ahead. Copy?'

'Copy. What do we need to do?'

'Have you done any parachute jumping? Have you done a paratrooper's course?'

'Yes.'

'You comfortable with jumping?'

'Yes.'

'Good. At nineteen hundred hours tonight, there will be a C-17 Globemaster leaving RAAF Base Pearce. Bullsbrook. You'll want to be on it, so be there at eighteen fifteen. Once you arrive at the security gate, get out. I will meet you there and transport you through to supply stores. Acknowledge.'

'Acknowledged.'

'On arrival at supplies we'll fit you out in night operational gear. Full tactical, including a GPS, altimeter, Kevlar vest and a night-vision headset. You'll also get ration packs and water. Ideally, you'll want to pack light. I don't know how long you'll be out for, so whatever rations you do pack, you'll just need to make it last. Acknowledge.'

'Acknowledged.'

'The supply stores won't have this, but I will give you a bayonet, knuckle dusters, and a seal pup knife. Can't do any higher-grade gear than that. No ammunition, no handguns. That's out of my hands. Everything we have is accounted for. But if you acquire them yourself, then good for you. I won't ask, I won't tell. And Cross obviously won't be going with you, so no comms radio of any kind. You'll be too far away. She'll stay back on base. I recommend you buy a mobile phone for communication. Preferably a burner. Texting only. Acknowledge.'

'Acknowledged.'

'Over and out.'

And that was it. The voice on the line went silent.

Mackay turned to Cross.

'What did you say to him?'

'That we had a recon situation. That close family had been killed. Women and children. A likely cover-up from corrupt police, and a possible underground child kidnapping business.

Or worse. And that we weren't taking a taxi or hiring a car that far down south. And that he owes me.'

Mackay was stunned. And impressed.

'Malvin is dead,' he said.

Cross stayed quiet for a long moment, giving the gravity of the statement due respect.

'You looked different when you walked out of the bathroom,' she said.

'Different to what?'

'To last night.'

'Last night was nice.'

'It was,' said Cross. She went quiet again. Then, 'I'm sorry about Malvin.'

'I knew it was coming,' said Mackay. 'Even before we left the hospital. Malvin was prepared for it. Gives me more motivation to take care of all of this.'

'It still hurts when it comes. I'm here for you, okay?' Cross kissed him on the back of the shoulder. Mackay stared out to nowhere. Past the television, somewhere beyond the inner wall. A minute went by.

Mackay said, 'The guy on the phone. The soldier. You two were a thing when you came here for pre-deployment training.'

'Initially yes,' Cross said, being honest. 'To a degree. But it didn't last. Couldn't. Different lives and careers.'

'Why does he owe you? Taking a C-17 to do a parachute drop for a recon is a big favour.'

Cross didn't reply.

'You saved his life.'

Again silence, then, 'No.'

'Helped him out of rehab?'

'No. No more on the topic, okay?'

'You saved his dog.'

'Good guess. He had a dog, but no. He was a dog handler. That's enough for now, let it go. You have other things to focus on. We need get moving.'

Mackay let it go. Cross wasn't going to give. Not now. Possible bad memory. Possible complex relationship. Mackay didn't want to push. Besides, he had his own bad memories to deal with. Maybe he'd ask her about it later. Time and place.

The red ant flicked the covers off and got out of the bed. Mackay watched her bend from the hip and reach the floor with her hands. She shuffled over to her carry-bag and collected some clothes. Mackay's old gear. Baggy, but still fresh and folded. Shorts and a T-shirt. Comfort for the West Australian summer. Mackay watched her put the previous day's bra and pants on. She went without underwear. And fair enough. They'd left in a hurry and Mackay didn't own any female clothes, let alone female underwear. Mackay watched the lean contours of Cross's back as she did her thing on the floor and got dressed. Her spine flexed. The muscles flickered. He took in the outline of her glutes. The honed edges of her boxer's shoulders. He would have been happy to pick her up and move her back to the bed.

Cross said, 'We need to go to a shopping centre. First thing's first, I need underwear.'

'Roger,' said Mackay.

He collected a fresh assortment of clothes from his own bag and got dressed. Shirt, shorts, shoes. Loose and comfortable. Then he called reception and requested a maxi-cab.

0800hrs
Wednesday December 19, 2012
Westfield Shopping Mall, Perth, Western Australia

First stop before making their way to RAAF Base Pearce, was the mall. The red ant's needs needed to be met. Underwear was a basic human necessity. Start the day right. Nothing fancy. Cotton. A pack of three would do. On top of that basic-needs list was breakfast. It took around ten minutes for their taxi driver to collect them, then another ten to pull into a growing nest of traffic in the parking lot of the shopping mall. A Westfield. The driver parked at the rear of a short fleet of taxis then began sorting Cross onto the hydraulic platform. Mackay prepared the man a crisp twenty-dollar bill then bid him a good day.

They moved through a wide set of glass sliding doors into a blast of cool, air-conditioned goodness. The entrance opened immediately to a bountiful selection of retail outlets – eye-catching shopfronts first, then the rest. Spreading outward like a gigantic human body in wake-up mode. All the various moving parts at various states of readiness. Some parts good to go, others still limbering up for the day ahead.

Past the strip of retail outlets, the mall opened to a large food court. The massive semi-circle of shop space was flooded with commercial cafés, fast food, sandwich delicatessen's and Asian street food. Mackay and Cross aimed for one of the breakfast cafés and checked the menu. The options were listed on a board above a clear-glass cabinet: muffins, croissants, savoury quiches and bacon and egg wraps. Mackay ordered a chocolate chip muffin and a ham and cheese croissant. Cross ordered a spinach and asparagus quiche. Both ordered coffee. They found an empty table in the seating area and polished it all off.

At nine o'clock when all the retail outlets were opening, they checked in at the nearest information desk. Cross needed underwear, and direct advice on where to go was better than browsing around on the fly without a clue. A thin service consultant greeted them in a sharp suit – immaculately dressed and groomed. His name badge read Thomas underneath the mall's logo. He had a soft voice and a long fringe tucked neatly behind one ear. His booth was marked 'Concierge' and after their query for underwear, he pleasantly directed them to four options: a smaller clothing outlet on the ground floor, two larger department stores on level one, and a lingerie outlet on the second floor. The first outlet had what Cross needed just fine. BONDS. Iconic Australian cotton. No need to waste time seeking more options. The store specialised in men's, women's and children's underwear and apparel. Cross bought a three pack of cotton panties. Assorted colours. She paid cash. The next item on the list were burner phones. They went back and checked in with the same service consultant at the same booth. Thomas directed them to five options. Three of them on the ground floor, two on level one. Two were smaller, independent electronics stores, and three were big-name service providers. All with modern shopfronts run by trendy youths with lanyards.

They went with one of the independent stores and bought two phones. One each. They figured a big-name telecommunications provider would require personal details to sign up. Which meant a credit card, a license, a passport. They couldn't take the risk. Burner phones didn't require red-tape details and could be sold over the counter. Cash for goods. Nice and simple. There were three options for the burners. The cheapest and most basic, a mid-range with internet accessibility, and an expensive one with higher resolution, hotspot tethering, and an upgraded camera with night mode. They went with the most expensive. Mackay thought about the bigger picture. The end result at the winery could sway in their favour if Mackay took photos. Deliver a wider crackdown on police corruption or whatever was going on down there. Maybe stop a child paedophile ring. If there was evidence to be found, photos were ideal. Snap whatever evil was going on and hopefully make the world a better place.

*

With phase one complete and phase two prepped thanks to Cross's contact at the RAAF base, they had the capability to get to Margaret River. They just needed to discuss what was going to go down once Mackay landed. And there was still time enough for that. Time to massage phase two's development. The hour was moving close to ten in the morning, which meant they had about seven hours to kill before needing to leave, with at least an hour of travel time getting from the city to the Air Force base. Which Cross recalled was only about forty minutes – when she'd first flown into the country for clearance training back in the day. Travel times in cities always change, and they needed breathing space to allow for any potential traffic issues. A full hour was a better time frame. Being late was not an option.

They decided to find another café, order another coffee, sit down and make plans. Flesh out a running order of actions. Break down the details. Mackay and the red ant circled the ground floor, slow and causal. People watching. Window shopping. Perusing the modern warfare of contemporary retail. Gauging a sense of the West Australian materialistic culture. Beards, tattoos, plastic. Similar to the UK only less clothing and more skin thanks to the summer heat.

Before selecting a café, they passed a shoe shop. A sports footwear store. Runners and cross trainers. Mackay decided he required a pair. A personal necessity. His war experience combined with a primal gut feeling directed him to initiate the decision. If he was jumping out of a C-17 aircraft with a parachute, likely landing in a topography of earthy forest next to a winery, he was going to need appropriate footwear.

He passed on entering the sports footwear store. Most of it was garbage. He didn't need anything stylised or fashionable. He didn't need anything commercially made by poor young labourers in third-world countries. He needed something robust. Something with grip and toe protection. They went back to the same, long fringed service consultant at the same information booth. Thomas directed them to one option. Ground floor at the complete opposite end to where they were standing. For the third time, they set out in search of their given directive. The store specialised in hiking apparel, camping gear and trail running. Mackay spent fifteen minutes with an experienced staff member. He tried on four different pairs of shoes. Two were made for hiking, two were made for trail running. All four felt excellent. He didn't care about the looks, all were mostly black anyway. He went with a trail runner. The grip was exceptional. It had a Gore-Tex outer membrane to stay dry and breathable, and a protective rubber toecap. He paid cash.

Once at the café – a franchise establishment with about half the inside seats full – Mackay and Cross ordered, then sat and got busy with details. Phase two had some layers. Aside from straight-up reconnaissance and intel gathering, it was also about actions dependant on what situations would arise. That said, it could also potentially unfold into extreme scenarios. Essentially, Mackay was going in to eliminate targets from the list of names revealed by Malvin. There was no intent of capture and kill. It was kill only. But assessing that information was crucial. Figuring who was inside the corrupt chain of operations that needed removing was the main question. That was the recon. Mackay wasn't there to remove everyone. Maybe the winery had innocent members. Staff employed as part of the day-to-day duties. Cleaning house, gardening and maintenance, face-to-face customer sales at the front of house. Mackay realised he was down on odds for a preferred combat strategy; a three-to-one fighting capability. Normally, British forces would take out targets at an optimal fighting force of three-to-one. Three times the number of soldiers moving in on the enemy. That way victory was more likely. For Mackay, he was at the polar end of the odds. The inferior side of the ratio. The possibility of being captured, tortured and killed for Mackay was high – if the standing numbers from Malvin were anything to go by.

Priority one in phase two's objectives was to find Lincoln. Priority two was to take out the underground operations. Which included any attached personnel in the chain. Anyone part and parcel to the body of the snake. To what degree he would dismantle this, didn't really matter. Fix it, said Malvin. And Mackay would do his absolute best to oblige. Priority three was to eliminate Van Breeman. The head of the snake. The top dog headlining the corruption. The ultimate objective, however, was Lincoln. And if any of the planned measures in phase two were deemed inaccessible or impossible, with impending risk to Lincoln or to Mackay himself, they were to be aborted.

Communication of movements back to Cross were also crucial. Which would need to be established from the point of departure to the point of return once the mission was complete. Mackay had the point of departure, not the point of return. How he was going to get back to the base was the weakest link. A distance of over two hundred kilometres. They didn't have a time frame of how long Mackay might stay out in the field either, but what they did have was a burner phone. They could call and discuss those bridges when they came to them. Lincoln first. Everything else was secondary.

'We'll need a map of the area first,' said Mackay. 'Which means we need to find an internet café and a printer.'

'Most internet cafés should have printers,' said Cross. 'That'll be our next stop. Back to our friend at the service counter.'

Mackay ran his fingers behind his ears. Cross nodded.

'Phase two is a little complex,' she said. 'It will all depend on the actions in response to what might happen out there. Effectively, you jump, touch down, enter the winery and go into hiding.'

Their coffees arrived. A small biscuit was placed on the edge of each saucer. Cross took her biscuit from hers and placed it on Mackay's. They drank. Mackay ate both biscuits. They walked back to the service counter. Thomas with the soft voice and long fringe was still there, scribbling away with a pen in a diary or record book. Diligently doing his thing, like the good concierge he was. Or maybe he was just doodling, wasting time looking busy for the passing crowd. He looked up as Mackay and Cross approached.

'Welcome back,' he said.

'We were hoping to find an internet café,' said Mackay. 'One with a printer. What are the options here?'

Thomas bit his lip, turned his head in thought and tapped the pen on his chin.

'They're a niche commodity these days. I don't think the mall has one. Not inside anyway. If you venture back towards the city, Hay Street has a couple I believe. But that would be at least an hour's walk. What specifically do you need printed?'

Cross changed tact. 'We're actually planning on doing a Margaret River wine tour,' she said. 'I was wondering whether the mall might have maps of the region. Or if a travel agency like that might have them?'

Mackay turned to where Cross was pointing. Diagonally across the gallery from the service desk was a modern store with a line of desks and monitors. Staff wore headsets with little mics near their mouths. It reminded Mackay of the personal radios they would use while on convoy missions. He wondered why they hadn't thought of that earlier.

'Of course,' said Thomas. 'No need to find a printer for maps and waste your precious time. Most of the travel agencies here would have dozens, if not hundreds. Margaret River is our bread and butter for tourism. Perth is okay, but Margaret River gets all the praise.'

He pointed across the hall to the same agency Cross alluded to.

'We have Star Traveller over there, Flight Book near the main entrance, then Holiday Choice and Travel World on the second floor. There might even be one more on the third floor, but the name escapes me.'

Cross said, 'Anything specific to Margaret River would work fine.'

'Holiday Choice then, best one in my opinion. It's more oriented to interstate travellers too. I would start there.'

Thomas typed something on his keyboard and hit enter. 'Holiday Choice is on the second floor but in the opposite direction to where we are.' He motioned to a nearby set of lifts between a bookstore and a jeweller. 'If you take those lifts, it should pop you out near the cinemas, then keep walking down and it should be next to an R.M. Williams.'

Mackay looked confused.

Cross said, 'It's a leather store. Boots, belts, hats, jackets.'

*

Holiday Choice had pamphlets, magazines and maps for days. All lined across the inside wall. Cross put on the tourist vibe and asked for two detailed maps of Margaret River's wine region. She also asked for one which included the Frans & Hoek winery. Which they had, with a basic aerial view. The topography showed a clean enough layout of the roads coming in and out. It also showed a large parking yard in front of what was assumed as the wine-tasting gallery, and a large structure behind it which they assumed was the wine press. More buildings scattered the area in a wide arcing perimeter. All bordered with a fence line adjoining a large national park called the Jarrahwood State Forest. They were also handed a bunch of other maps and pamphlets detailing routes to a chocolatier, a cheese factory, local eateries and world-class restaurants. Some with chef-hat ratings. Cross happily took them all, maintaining fake interest as a wine enthusiast. Everything was free. No printing. Happy days. They left, dumped all the tourist advertising except for the Frans & Hoek aerial map and headed outside to wait for a maxi.

'Once you jump,' said Cross, scanning the aerial map, 'by grid reference it should put you at the north-eastern end of the forest. You can then make your way into the winery grounds from the forest edge. If you need to fuck off quickly, nip back in the forest and go to ground there. From the fence line perimeter, look for any possible security personnel or CCTV cameras first. The night vision may or may not pick them up. Depends how far away you are.'

Mackay said, 'Disarming the cameras will be pointless. As good as shouting a big hello. I'll make note of them and steer clear, then start searching the grounds for Lincoln.'

Cross said, 'Any photos you take, send them through to me. I'll store copies and keep as evidence. Keep the flash off the camera but try to get the best light source you can otherwise. Communication will be key. I'm going to want your location and status on the hour, every hour. Comms will have to be by text. Saves credit, plus it's quiet.'

Mackay said, 'No need for chatter if I don't have to. Sound carries in large spaces and vineyards have acres on acres. Water and food shouldn't be too much of a problem either. So said your contact. Said he'll have rations for me at the supply store.'

'Good. Same place as you'll get your parachute and tactical gear. Once you jump, I'll be notified from my guy. From there I'll give it ten minutes before I hear from you.'

'My descent won't take longer than five. Including another five to pack my shit and find a small clearing to get organised. After I land, I'll give you a sit-rep and loc-stat with a grid reference.'

Cross nodded. 'I don't know how good those burner phones are for GPS, I wouldn't even bother. Just use the military-grade one you'll get from the supply store.'

'What's his name?' asked Mackay.

'My contact?'

Mackay nodded.

'John. But even I don't know if that's legit. Whether it's his real name or not.'

'Special Forces are like that.'

'Once the sun starts to rise, you need to be tucked away. If you end up being tucked away inside one of the buildings, stay out of sight. At the same time, do your best to gather intel. Find out who is who, and who is doing what in the chain. You might have to filter out the innocent employees from the unsavoury.'

'Then take out the snake.'

'Head to tail.'

1030hrs
Wednesday December 19, 2012
Frans & Hoek Winery, Margaret River, Western Australia

They were all gathered inside the admin room. Van Breeman checked his watch. It was mid-morning. His pawns had been out doing the rounds for most of the night and most of the morning: the winery grounds, the state forest. No sign of the boy. They'd come back empty and annoyed. How could five adult men miss a six-year-old boy on their own turf? The boss wasn't happy. It had been forty-eight hours since the kid had run off. Forty-eight hours with no sign of life. Shameful.

'Wherever that kid is, he isn't doing too well,' said Kimbala. 'It's been two days since he vanished. A kid that age, the dingos and snakes would have a field day. I wouldn't be worried.'

Van Breeman didn't look convinced. He didn't look good at all. He was unshaven and unslept. A reduced representation of his normally groomed self. He sat in the admin room with the local newspaper open on a story and a close-up of Lydia Ferreira's face. The title read *Frans and Hoax*. Even if Kimbala was right and the kid met his maker with forest wildlife, there had been no body found. No body still meant the possibility of life.

'We'll leave it for now. Forget the kid. Let's move on to that reporter.' Van Breeman tapped his finger on Lydia's picture. 'Find out where she lives and bag her tonight. You three know what to do.' He lifted his eyes to meet Kimbala, Bryson, then Wynand, one by one. 'Now everyone fuck off. Kimbala, you stay.'

Bryson and Wynand left the room.

'Call Taylor and Derek. Tell them to go to my apartment and bring me the two black cases from the ivory trunk in the wardrobe. I want the tucker telephone and the rungu club.'

'The magneto and the knobkerry?'

'Yes. But we're not going to kill her. She just needs to be taught a lesson. Shake her up a bit.'

'Very old school, boss. A bit of homeland flavour.'

'I can't have any more disappearances connected to me. The magneto and knobkerry will shut her up. I've got a transaction this afternoon in Busselton. Inform me when Taylor and Derek arrive, and when you three have the reporter. I want her tied up in your hotbox.'

Kimbala stepped forward to leave, then paused and turned around.

'Wouldn't hand-cranking the electrical current through the phone kill a woman of her size?'

Van Breeman chewed on it. 'Only if it's maintained for extended periods. She seems like a tough bitch. I'm sure she can handle a few watts. Either way, if it does kill her, we'll deal with it.'

'And the club?'

'Heads, shoulders, knees and toes.'

> 1500hrs
> Wednesday December 19, 2012
> Victoria Park Bed and Breakfast, Perth, Western Australia

Back at the bed and breakfast, time elapsed slowly. They still had three hours to kill before required at the RAAF base gates. Mackay's head was swimming. Going through with the recon wasn't the problem. Killing those responsible for wiping out Malvin and his family wasn't the problem either. He felt there was a gap in their movements that needed to be secured. To stay ahead in their own game. Information that needed to be acquired.

'I need to know where Van Breeman's office is,' said Mackay. 'The driver from the airport, our first taxi, he mentioned Breeman was well known in this city. Said he probably lived or worked somewhere in the CBD. One of the main city streets.'

'Hay Street and Adelaide Terrace,' said Cross.

'It will enhance our chances of taking out the top dog if we find where he works. At least if he isn't at the winery in Margaret River.'

'Now we do need an internet café. Otherwise, it's a needle in a haystack. Dozens of buildings with thousands of apartments.'

'We'll have to go back to where Thomas suggested.'

'Thomas?'

'The mall concierge.'

Mackay sat on the edge of the bed lost in thought.

'I know you would like to see your brother,' said Cross. 'Say goodbye. You will, soon. Once this is done.' She wheeled herself over next to him. Grabbed his face and leaned in, kissing him against the side of the mouth.

'I'm okay,' said Mackay. 'My mind's occupied on taking out whatever fucked-up operation they've got going on down there.'

Cross turned Mackay's head with her hands, making him look at her.

'I won't ask this again, but are you ready to go through with this?'

Mackay nodded. No hesitation. 'I'm ready,' he said. 'Needs to be done. If not for Malvin, then for a wider benefit. They used kids. That's a no-go. For some reason I don't even feel scared, I just feel numb.'

'That's likely the grief kicking in. It'll come and go in waves. Once this is all over, let it wash over you. Now though, this mission is your backbone. Plus, you have an advantage.'

She ran her hands down his side. Over his ribs.

'Just don't become overconfident,' she said. 'Use the skills you know. Don't take on what you know you can't. Don't get into a situation you haven't trained for.'

'Quiet, slow, smooth. I'll be okay. There's a first time for everything.'

'I just don't want your first time to also be your last. Push through the shit, but at least for Malvin's sake, come out alive.'

Both didn't speak for a while. Minutes passed. Cross cut the silence.

'We should move,' she said. 'Grab those new shoes and pack your spare clothes. I'll order a taxi.'

Before exiting the cab on Hay Street, Cross queried the driver for the nearest internet café. The driver, a stout female, dropped them off in the best proximity of two she knew of. They paid cash and headed in what felt like a northerly direction. Cross's bearings were a little rusty to the way she remembered, but familiar sights kept popping up which kept her quietly confident.

Mackay stepped out in quick strides beside Cross as they worked their way through an open-air shopping mall. The lunchtime crowd was settling down. Most of the suits were gone, back in their office apartments trading shares, investing real estate, filing through complaints and grievances. That left the ground-floor crowd. Preened men and women reserved for the retail game, heading back into their designated shoeboxes.

After a set of lights near a T-junction they passed a row of stores with glass windows. Jewellery, apparel, specialty cakes, some were hole-in-the-wall cafés, some were sushi takeaways. The glass windows became tiled walls, the tile became brick, the brick became a combination of roller-doors and iron shutters. They were leaving the main hustle and bustle into an undefined boundary where the outskirts were a little quieter.

The cash-only internet café was sandwiched between a sushi takeaway and a Swedish coffee house where staff wore tiny aprons and headdresses. At the front desk, Mackay checked in with a tubby Asian guy with a poof of hair set in a man-bun. There were various options of payment for various time limits. They chose the half-hour option and handed over a five-dollar note. The guy punched a few keys and reserved them a computer in the back. They made their way to a row of desks lined with monitors, each made private with office partitions. Their monitor had a small black box in the top right corner with a numerical counter that read 29m:58s. Their time had started, the numbers decreasing by the second. A Google page was open as part of the default home screen. Mackay typed *VAN BREEMAN PERTH OFFICE*, then hit enter. The cyber channels processed the request and within seconds displayed a page with a multitude of options. Good broadband. Decent speed. They could have sat there a week and still not scrolled through every option. It took fifteen minutes into browsing before they found what they were looking for. It was a familiar story. The content basically the in-depth version of what their Indian driver had brushed over on their drive from the airport. A lengthy article written by a female journalist from Margaret River. Lydia Ferreira. Her headshot looked like the reporter Mackay had seen on the television in their hotel room. The one who stood roadside in front of Frans and Hoek winery. Her article was a conspiracy piece about the missing body of a Perth socialite romantically connected to Perth millionaire and wine producer, Nicus Van Breeman. The article went into elaborate detail of a potential murder and cover-up, connecting facts and figures, times, and dates. It exposed layers of evidence that was never admitted into court, expanding into corrupt Perth-based law enforcement connected to a wider body of organised crime.

The missing socialite was also an art dealer. Carice Hackforth. Her and Van Breeman had been the toast of the town at numerous charity events, balls, theatre productions and gallery openings. The article went on to mention how they launched the opening of a corporate high-rise building where they owned an apartment together. The Swan Quay Tower. A steel behemoth overlooking the Swan River. Once construction for the tower was finished, the couple hosted a red-carpet showcase. A huge event for pretentious couples in frocks and gowns. A real who's who in the zoo. Celebrities and athletes from across the country were invited, as well as barristers, the police commissioner, even a couple of A-List Hollywood stars were flown in. The party took up the whole of the tiered lobby on the ground floor. Then, a few weeks later, Carice was gone.

From the Google images, the Swan Quay Tower was mostly glass. The tinting navy-blue against the sky behind it. The rest of the exterior, including the lower foyer and tiered balconies, were white and silver. Evenly patterned. The building's name was in tall silver lettering above the ground floor's massive concourse. Two ornamental statues presided over the entrance leading to a huge revolving glass door. One of planet Earth with a wedge sliced out of it, the other a Greek goddess in a toga holding a smaller Earth above her head. Like a female

Atlas. Maybe his wife. The sidewalk in front had long sections of pruned hedges and three flagpoles: Australian, Aboriginal, and what Mackay presumed to be the West Australian state flag.

The rest of their five-dollar internet time was used to search for Van Breeman's specific apartment inside the building. They had no luck. They couldn't even find a floor. Nothing concrete had been reported on or written about. The clock ran down to zero and they ended their session. At least now they had the full name of the head of the snake, a visual of where he lived, and a map of the winery.

On their way out, Cross stopped for some question-answer time with tubby man-bun guy. 'Excuse me,' she said. 'Direction-wise, which way is the Swan Quay Tower on Adelaide Terrace?'

The guy hit the space bar on his keyboard then looked away from his monitor at Cross. He had a mouthful of half-chewed sushi. Most likely bought and delivered from next door. The guy chewed faster but Cross got bored and channelled her question a little more precisely.

'Is it towards the big park on the hill, or back this way towards the open mall on Hay Street? Or is it further back towards Victoria Park?'

Man-bun swallowed and motioned with his hand behind Cross's left shoulder. Fingers straight, palm flat, like he was chopping into the air.

'More towards the park side,' the guy said. 'King's Park. Directly behind the mall entrance on Adelaide terrace. Maybe, two hundred metres up.'

'Thank you,' said Cross as Mackay wheeled her out.

Walking along Perth's main street after lunch was more or less a hassle-free affair. It wasn't too busy. Nothing like London. At any time, day or night, London's CBD was crammed up. Everyone on their toes looking forward for space and access.

Perth's main strip allowed for an open street view. Front to back. Left to right. No dodging or weaving necessary, even during rush hour. The buildings were modern, gutters were clean, the pavement smooth. People moved along briskly and still gave plenty of room for Cross in her chair.

Mackay walked on Cross's right, closest to the stream of cars. His head and eyes were focused high, looking for silver lettering in tall bold font on a high-rise built with plenty of glass. His eyes dipped occasionally as they caught flashes of glare, reminding him both of Cross's misfortune and his own IED blast in the desert. He did his best to push them aside, but the fourth time he dipped his eyes away, he saw two familiar sights. Familiar figures getting out of what looked like an unmarked police car. Parked in a permit zone for special vehicles only. A four-door sedan with two big antennae installed – one on the bonnet, one on the boot. He'd seen the same two men before in the hospital while visiting Malvin. One, a hefty man with a buzz cut, the other a thinner man with a prominent nose. Both exuded police presence from a mile away. Both wore suits and aviator sunglasses. Detectives. Corrupt. They moved with purpose fifty yards ahead, walking in the same direction as Mackay and Cross. Cross slowed and looked up at Mackay.

'We're following,' Mackay said.

Cross stopped rolling, locked her brakes, and grabbed Mackay's hand.

'What are you doing?' said Mackay. 'We need to follow these two right now.'

'I can see that, I'm thinking ahead. Shut up and listen.' Cross's eyes darted between Mackay and something else ahead of them. 'There's a guy coming with a hat. A cap. Get your wallet out. You're going to offer him fifty dollars for it. I'll keep an eye on where those two are going. Cities have cameras everywhere, and you need to stay as anonymous as possible. If a hat is the only thing that can conceal your head and eyes, then it's better than nothing. Say whatever needs to be said.'

Mackay didn't question it. Good soldiers take orders from good soldiers. A younger guy of average height was walking towards them. Casually. Stepping slow, taking in the sights like he had no place to be and in no kind of hurry. He had a backpack slung behind both shoulders, earphones stuck in his head underneath a black and red sports cap. The emblem on the front like a big ocean wave.

'Excuse me, sir,' said Mackay, waving the guy down. Cross went rolling on ahead, maintaining distance with the two suits as best she could. The guy noticed Mackay, slowed down and moved one headphone to the side of his head.

'Hey, dude,' said the guy, waking himself out of whatever musical zone he was in. He stopped three feet in front of Mackay who simultaneously pinched a crisp fifty out of his wallet.

'That hat you're wearing, I can't seem to find one anywhere in town. It's the exact thing I'm looking for. I would love to buy it from you as a gift for my son. Would you take fifty for it? Right here and now?'

On closer inspection, the guy's eyes were round, lazy and red. Ready to pop out of his face.

'Shit, dude, you're Irish, man. That's so cool.'

'Aye, thanks.'

'Aye. That's cool as.'

'So, your hat for the fifty?'

'Dude this hat, man, is like, two years old.'

Mackay held out the note, inching it higher. 'I'm heading back to the UK today. Flight leaves soon. I'll be miffed if I go back without one. My son too.'

The guy brimmed with disbelief, finally realising Mackay had cash in hand.

'Shit, dude. I won't say no to that. You serious, man?'

'Like a shrimp on the barbie.'

The guy couldn't believe his luck.

'Sure thing, man. No strings?'

'No strings. Like I said, I'm off to catch my flight. A one-time opportunity. And I have nothing smaller to offer.'

'Damn. Well, your business is my pleasure. Happy to help my brother. Fifty bucks goes a long way in my world, man.' The guy took off his hat, handed it to Mackay and exchanged it for the flat yellowy-green.

Mackay moved on, picking up pace to catch up with Cross. Midway he adjusted the cap to fit and slipped it on his head. He could make out Cross's rolling shape a hundred yards ahead. Fifty yards beyond her were the two suits. Walking brisk with purpose, making Cross work to maintain speed and proximity. The suits suddenly turned left and were lost to sight, which was when Mackay lifted his eyes and saw the tinted glass edges of a high-rise. He also made out three flagpoles and a wide silver-grey concourse. He extended his stride and pushed faster. On closer approach, a white Greek goddess holding the Earth came into view, then he saw the enormous planet Earth with a big wedge removed. Cross slowed and waited for him next to the front hedge.

'Follow them in,' said Cross. 'Do what you can. Find out what they're doing or where they're going. Anything is good info.'

'Stay nearby,' said Mackay. He adjusted his new hat, pulling the brim slightly over his eyes for cover, then turned left. He walked past the flagpoles, the goddess, then past a wide driveway leading down to what Mackay assumed was basement parking, or a loading dock for delivery access. Or both. He then stepped onto a wide platform leading to a set of revolving doors and into a spacious lobby.

1630hrs
Wednesday December 19, 2012
Swan Quay Tower, Perth, Western Australia

Inside the lobby, Mackay briefly caught a side view of the two suits entering an elevator down a tiled corridor with remarkably high ceilings. He moved quick, but not too quick. Didn't want to be seen as rushing excessively so as to draw unwanted attention. Just fast enough to look appropriately busy. Give the impression he was late for a meeting after a rush-hour lunch. He moved swiftly between an assortment of office workers, a couple of delivery personnel and the ground-floor security. The elevators were just beyond a winding staircase leading to a tiered balcony jutting out above. Mackay reached the elevators late. They'd already closed, the yellow digits above the doors indicating the elevator was moving up. Fast. Mackay took a step back and watched the numbers flicker through increasing levels. He stayed put and watched the numbers rise as another five, six, seven corporate-looking employees wearing access tags milled around for the next available lift.

The floor numbers moved past ten, then twenty, then thirty. It slowed briefly and stopped at forty-seven. Mackay played it safe and left. Getting in the lift was not an option. He too would need an access card to get anywhere and didn't want to be the dumb loser stepping inside without a pass. He didn't have time to start breaking company protocol and be harassed and questioned by security in the process. As casual as he looked in his T-shirt, shorts, and surfer cap, he already stood out as a red flag. Instead, Mackay went in search of a stairwell. Every building had one.

Except this one. Not on the lobby floor at least, and he didn't want to hang about any longer raising corporate eyebrows. Mackay exited the revolving doors and headed back outside, where Cross was doing her best tourist impression admiring the statues.

'The elevator they stepped in stopped at forty-seven,' said Mackay. 'I'm going to head down to the basement and try and work my way up from there.' Mackay motioned to the wide driveway access to the far right of the building. 'I'm guessing that's all basement parking and delivery access.'

Mackay helped roll Cross down a steep driveway around the side of the tower. Down past the pruned hedges and flagpoles to a wider, curving section of concrete below the ground floor. A yellow boom gate with a swipe access was fixed in the middle of the path for vehicles but didn't entirely limit anyone from walking around it. The gap was plenty big enough for Cross in her chair, so they continued to circle the path and descend behind the building. As the driveway flattened at the bottom, they faced a huge concrete wall on their right, and the opening of the basement parking on their left. Like a bunker.

They kept moving into the basement following endless lines of parked cars. The cement flooring descended again, going even deeper underground into what felt like the central axis of the tower above. They stayed left along a row of reserved parking bays. Staff bays for various corporate bodies upstairs. Most of them filled with expensive vehicles. Most of them dark in colour and German in origin. They followed the reserved line looking for signage to a stairwell. A minute later, Mackay picked up a noise behind them. A van. The gurgling diesel bouncing its dirty exhaust tone off the basement walls. It slowed, stopped, idled, then began moving again – the driver obviously stopping momentarily to swipe an access card before continuing past the boom gate. The vehicle passed by on their right. A plumbing and gas van according to the signage. There was nothing Mackay and Cross could do to hide, so they simply kept moving forward, owning their space. Like they'd done it a hundred times before. What would the driver say anyway? He probably had an urgent job to attend to. If they were asked, either they were looking for their car, meeting a friend, or getting picked up. Plenty of options. They kept their pace steady and calm. No awkward movements or attempts to hide. Cross wouldn't be able to anyway. Their business was just as important as anyone else's.

The basement tapered out to level, then opened into a massive space the size of a football field. All one low ceiling filled with coloured columns designating more bays for more corporate bodies. The same as what would be found in a run-of-the-mill shopping mall: spaces for hundreds of yards across every direction. After a random right turn with an empty row of bays, Cross caught sight of a bright green sign hanging from the ceiling. It read, ELEVATORS B1, with an illuminated arrow underneath. They followed the arrow's direction around three sets of coloured columns to a triple set of lifts built into a far wall. Idling in a loading zone next to the elevators was the plumbing and gas van. Pumping out fumes. Smothering the oxygen. As Mackay and Cross got closer, they noticed two guys working together, pulling out hoses, gas tanks and random trade equipment from the rear doors. One was inside the van passing out gear to the other, who then stacked it into crates on a wide dolly in front of the lifts. Nothing in the entire vicinity of the basement stood out like a stairwell door leading into the tower.

'I got this,' said Cross, tapping Mackay's arm. She rolled forward, closing the gap between the workers and the elevators.

'Afternoon, gents,' said Cross.

They didn't seem too surprised. Likely because they'd already passed them on their drive down.

'G'day,' said the guy putting the gear on the dolly. He stood up, arched his back, and made the obligatory eye contact. 'You guys all right?'

'We parked our car near the stairwell, but forgot which corner, or coloured section, of the building it's near. All I remember is it's near the stairwell.'

The one who arched his back said nothing. He stared back blankly at Cross, then looked over at his co-worker.

'Yea that's easy, mate,' said the one inside the van. He stepped out and took five paces to his left towards a grey BMW sedan parked next to a green column.

'It's the other corner of the tower over there,' he said, pointing away, diagonally, above the BMW. 'The section with the sky-blue columns. You can pretty much make out the stairwell door from here. Should have no troubles.'

'Thank you very much,' said Cross. 'Sky-blue, that's right, now I remember. You feel so stupid forgetting something that is put there for that exact purpose, right?'

'Don't stress, mate,' the guy said. 'Has happened to me more than once. Some days you just need to get on with your day. You forget the coloured markers even exist.'

'I know that feeling,' said Cross. 'Definitely the way it went for us today.'

Mackay stepped over to where the guy had indicated, purposefully looking out across the layout of the basement. Like the query was genuine. The conversation had reached its end. It was time to go.

'Thank you, gentlemen, much appreciated,' said Mackay.

'Yes, thanks, guys,' said Cross. 'Have a good day.'

'Too easy. You too.'

The workers went straight back to it while Mackay and Cross beelined for the far corner. The stairwell was marginally concealed by the body of a big SUV. A black Toyota Landcruiser, which stood out from the rest of the mostly German vehicles. They were now at least two hundred yards from the workers at the lifts with no one else in sight. No security guards, no tradies, nobody collecting their vehicles. They were as good as tucked away and left to their own devices.

Mackay tested the stairwell's door handle. It gave, opening to a wide concrete chute. Zigzagging flights of stairs stacked over and over each other, shooting infinitely upwards into a never-ending abyss.

'Stay here,' said Mackay. 'I'll head up and check forty-seven, and if there's nothing there, I'll meet you back here. Give me twenty minutes. If I'm longer than that, get out of here and make your way to the Air Force base. I'll meet you there.'

'Fuck that, I'm staying here,' said Cross. 'In this basement. Who else is going to roll me back up that spiralling access ramp? I'll wait it out. I'm good at waiting. Basic military doctrine.'

Mackay breathed. He took her response and swallowed it. His level of care for her was growing, but at the same time he knew she wouldn't budge. She was a stubborn soul for her own independence – one of the first things he recognised about her. One of the first things he liked about her.

'What about a compromise?' said Mackay. 'Wait thirty minutes. If I'm not back by then, use the burner to call off your SAS contact. Tell him I won't make the C-17 in time. Make up an excuse. Then come find me.'

Cross thought on it. 'That's fair, but I'll compromise you one more.' Cross looked at her watch. 'You be back down here within twenty, then we leave for the airfield and get the rest of this plan rolling.'

Mackay nodded and checked his own watch. The time read three-forty in the afternoon.

'Twenty minutes. See you at sixteen hundred.'

Mackay paused and thought whether he should kiss her goodbye or not. Cross made the decision for him.

'Fuck off already,' she said. 'Get up there.'

No kiss.

Mackay turned into the stairwell and closed the door behind him. Metal and wood clanged shut, echoing up into the ether.

He took the stairs all the way to forty-seven. One floor at a time, counted by the numbers on the back of every floor's emergency exit. Mackay tested forty-seven's door handle. It gave. He checked his fifty-dollar surf cap, making sure the brim covered his eyes. He opened the door slowly, stepped through and closed it behind him. No alarms, no employees wandering about. Just a long, empty corridor with plush carpet.

> 1650hrs
> Wednesday December 19, 2012
> Swan Quay Tower, Perth, Western Australia

Of all the apartments on the forty-seventh floor, Van Breeman's suite was the most spacious. The cream of the crop. As it should be, considering the amount he'd paid for it. It overlooked the Swan River, and King's Park – Perth's most famous landmark. Formed alongside the Swan River, its views overlooked the entire landscape of the city's infrastructure.

Taylor and Derek entered suite number twelve with orders passed down the chain to retrieve two items from an ivory trunk inside. The trunk was a priceless antique box formed entirely of elephant ivory, made sometime during the turn of the nineteenth century in South Africa. It was kept in Van Breeman's wardrobe, sitting pretty on the carpet below his collection of suits. Inside were two black cases. One rectangular and boxy like a first aid kit. The other long and light, as if made for an instrument or sporting goods. A perfect fit for a bat or trombone. The rectangular one held the tucker telephone, also known as a magneto. The long one had the rungu club, also known as a knobkerry. The magneto was a straight-up torture device. A weighty implement designed with parts from an old-fashioned crank telephone, mostly used in American prisons during the 1960s. With an electric generator, the telephone was wired to two dry-cell batteries and, when cranked, the hot wires would be used to administer electric shocks. Often to the genitals. The knobkerry on the other hand was a wooden throwing club. Culturally significant to East African tribes. Traditionally used by Maasai men for warfare and hunting. Nowadays its popularity mostly circled around tourist souvenir stores. For Van Breeman, he preferred it in its traditional sense, warfare and hunting, and had it made with authenticity by a true Massai elder.

Taylor and Derek got on with the job, collecting the cases as instructed from Kimbala. Following that they were to drive the three hours back to the winery. Of the boss's last three directives, they'd completed two; they had the torture devices and had eliminated the British tourist from the ICU ward. The last witness to the messy debacle two days prior was now out of the picture. Things were looking up. Still, there were two matters that lay unresolved. Complications that continued to gnaw at the edge of Van Breeman's balance: the missing boy and one inconvenient reporter. The boy was as good as dead anyway. A six-year-old alone in the wilderness after forty-eight hours was basically a non-issue. And the reporter was about to get bagged.

SIX

BARGAINING

> 1700hrs
> Wednesday December 19, 2012
> Swan Quay Tower, Perth, Western Australia

Mackay walked forward along the plush carpet. It looked expensive and felt soft. No creaks or groans. Just silence. Just him and the opulence of a modern, multi-million-dollar high-rise. All the top-class furnishings were there: wall-mounted mirrors, armchairs, mini side tables with ornamental desk lamps, even decorative waste bins. The doors to each room throughout the corridor were wood and glass with thick stainless-steel handles, the glass tinted in syrupy amber and much too dark to see through. Halfway down the corridor was a second, cross-sectional hallway running horizontally, like an intersection at a set of lights. A junction. Mackay stopped short. He looked ahead, turned and peered left, turned and peered right. To his right, one of the doors opened inwards. Two men in suits stepped out, fifty feet away, each carrying a black case. One the size of a small carry-on suitcase, the other long and narrow. Both men looked up. Mackay had caught their attention. Maybe it was his hat. Maybe it was his silhouette against the white walls. Hard to miss a single individual standing upright down a long, dim corridor. Either way, Mackay decided to step forward and make himself known.

With fifty feet between them, it took maybe four whole seconds before Taylor recognised who it was wearing the hat. Those four seconds – counted in breaths – was practically a century in terms of what the mind can search through and narrow down. The height, the shape of the physique. Taylor had an excellent memory. Part of the fundamentals of being a detective. He'd stored every aspect of Mackay's image into his head while watching him and the wheelchair girl enter the ICU ward at Royal Perth. From watching their engagement with the British international, to sizing them up before leaving, he knew who it was standing in the middle of the corridor.

'*Can I help you?*' Derek had asked in the hospital.

'*No, sir, I'm all good. Thank you.*'

As the seconds passed, it was clear to Mackay he'd been recognised. The type of recognition that meant, *I know who you are, and I know why you're here*. Which also meant his choice was made for him. In the same space of time, Mackay knew how the two detectives would react. Their body language said it all. Mackay needed to go on the offensive immediately. Controlled logical momentum. The cops would drop the bags from their hands and reach for their weapons. A Glock .22 sidearm. Standard issue. He could see it in the way they stood – braced with one foot in front of the other. It was also in their expression, which was as good as a total confession. Full of wilful intent to harm followed by intent to silence and exterminate.

Mackay had no other choice but to strike first. Unless he wanted to meet the same fate as Malvin. He owed Malvin his promise, and Mackay was a man of his word. His decision was intuitive and made with good judgement. On the plus side, Mackay wasn't scared anymore, he was just angry. Ready to unwind the top of the bottle and relieve the pressure. Normally, under the threat of battle, he'd have some reservations. A fluttering nervousness was natural when it came to fighting, or even killing, another human being. Hand-to-hand real-life fights put people in difficult mental positions. Most find their mental state clouded. Somewhere between a rock and a hard place as they gulp back the fear. Following that, one of three things occur: fight, flight, or freeze. For some, like Mackay in his current situation, it poured out into murderous attack. He was bringing the fight to them. The hunters were now the hunted.

Mackay prepped a tackle. His heart skipped a beat. He aimed for a low scrum position and shot off. Between the time Taylor and Derek decided to drop the cases from each hand and reach for their Glocks, Mackay had already made forty feet. Their slow weapon readiness meant Mackay was within ten feet before their fingers even brushed their holsters. And Mackay was still building speed. His body a weapon in itself.

Out in the corridor, Derek stood on Taylor's left with a two-foot gap between them. Mackay wrapped them up, hitting both at the same time. Perfectly positioned. Chin low, arms wide, forty-five degrees at the waist. On impact, Mackay's head fitted snug right between that two-foot gap. Their hands had only just begun to swipe the lower cut of their jackets.

Mackay made contact just below their hips. His shoulders ploughing brutally high on the thigh, driving forward and upwards. He broke two femurs in one. Derek's right leg. Taylor's left. The upper end of both bones were torn completely away from the hip sockets. The three of them ended in a pile, flung five metres down the hallway. Mackay's tackle launched both detectives off their feet, arcing them into mid-air before landing back on the carpet. The shock of it all was overwhelming, which meant the pain would came later. But not before Mackay got to his feet and used every ounce of his rugby skills to kick them hard against the side of their heads, rendering them unconscious. He then dragged the bodies and two black cases back inside suite number twelve and locked the door from the inside.

What Mackay didn't realise initially, was how hard he had kicked the leaner detective in the head. Taylor was the first to take the kick which meant he probably took the heaviest blow. Unintentionally, Mackay killed the guy. Broke his neck and severed it from the spinal cord. The Italian died within seconds from a lack of oxygen to the brain. Mackay felt a little bad about it at first, but he had things to do. What he really wanted was to give the guy an opportunity for a discussion. For an I ask, you answer back and forth. That conversation was now down to Derek, who was still alive. With Taylor out, it meant he needed to be tactical in how he approached the questioning when the bigger guy woke. If Derek realised his partner was dead, his answers were likely to be untruthful out of spite.

Between leaving Cross, sprinting up the stairwell and taking out both cops, the time was just passing three minutes. On the fourth minute, Mackay locked the inside of suite twelve. On the fifth, he used a bunch of belts from a closet he'd found inside a bedroom to tie the men into chairs next to an ornately large desk. Which, Mackay noted, also had a bonsai tree set on the desk's edge. Also a ficus. Green oval leaves, thick gnarled trunk. Pruned a little neater and closer to the branches than Swibinski's back in Aldershot.

Although Taylor's body was limp with dead weight, there was a certain level of compliancy in his body. It was easier to move than Derek's, who smelled sour from sweat and took a whole extra minute to position. Mackay placed Derek in the biggest chair. An oiled mahogany piece with a leather-wrapped seat. The wooden backing and armrests helped keep his heft upright. He placed Taylor in the cheap one. A basic office swivel, which, for the size of the guy, was easy enough. He positioned them back to back and removed both their Glocks, mobile phones, and police badges. He tied Derek's ankles first, then his wrists. Then tied his ankles to his wrists, leaving limited movement and no chance of escape. Mackay left Taylor's ankles and wrists alone. No need to secure a dead guy. He just needed to strap him in, so it looked like he was sitting upright, and that if Derek woke and looked over, he wouldn't see his partner still and lifeless.

All that positioning and belt-tying took another five minutes, which put Mackay at ten minutes since leaving Cross. Which also left Mackay with ten minutes before he had to get back downstairs. And for any military sergeant, let alone Cross, timing was everything.

At the thirteen-minute mark, Derek began to wake. He came to with a howl somewhere deep within his vocal range. Part groan, part yelp. The pain flowing from the broken femur displaced from the ball and socket joint. Mackay had the two police-issued Glocks, the two badges, the knobkerry, the tucker telephone, and three pillows from Van Breeman's bedroom all laid out on the executive desk. He checked the magazines and working components of both weapons. Everything was as it should be. Fifteen rounds plus one in the chamber, the inner hardware lightly oiled. As expected for veteran officers of the law. All up Mackay had thirty-two rounds at his disposal. He took one Glock from the table and held it low at his side.

Derek didn't notice Mackay at first. Not until Mackay leaned over and tapped at his forehead with the tip of the barrel, forcing Derek to look up. Eventually, he adjusted and focused. His bleary eyes straining on Mackay's aggressive form standing in front of him.

'Can you hear me okay?' said Mackay.

Derek didn't answer. His face remained twisted in pain.

Mackay flicked Derek in the eye. Middle finger springing off the thumb.

'Fuck! Yes. I can hear you.'

'Two questions,' said Mackay. 'And be honest. Call it your last chance at redeeming yourself. Why did my brother's family die at the winery, and which one of you killed my brother in the hospital?'

'I'm a detective, you stupid asshole,' started Derek. 'You're fucked every which way till Sunday, no matter what happens in here.'

'Maybe. I'll deal with that later. But I'm not in the mood for your tone, or bullshit answers. I'm on a time limit. The redhead in the wheelchair needs me back ASAP.'

Mackay placed the gun on the table and took the knobkerry.

'I know what that telephone is,' Mackay said, pointing to the magneto. 'Had a lecture on it once in Afghanistan. Taliban are still using them. The Americans too, apparently. The CIA at least. But this,' Mackay raised the club over his shoulder like a baseball bat. 'I've no idea about this. Looks tribal.'

Derek watched Mackay swing the club, whipping the bulbous head inches from Derek's face.

'I'll have me a guess it's some type of African club,' said Mackay.

Derek said nothing.

'Looks traditional. Strange that two detectives would have this and a magneto in their possession. Strange also that neither of you have any paperwork justifying why you're taking stuff out of another man's apartment. And you guys obviously don't live here. Way out of your pay grade. This Van Breeman guy though, he is everywhere in here.'

Mackay pointed at the bronze nameplate on the desk with the words Van Breeman engraved on the front. He then pointed to the pictures of Van Breeman on the walls and shelves around the room. Some of them taken in his youth, some of them more recent. In some he stood alone, and in others, he stood with either family members or other rich cronies from similar rich-cronie circles.

Six minutes left.

Mackay said, 'Did you know this Van Breeman guy even has his name stitched into his bed sheets? And his pillowcases?' Mackay pointed to the golden embroidery on the edge of the pillows on the desk. 'I had a quick look around. The man's a tool. Must be a rich-guy thing. How long have you dodgy cops been working for him?'

Nothing from Derek. The weighty cop closed his eyes and rocked forward. Not that he didn't want to respond, he was just struggling. He couldn't. The pain in his femur and hip was at unbearable levels. It looked like he was about to vomit.

Mackay checked his watch. Five minutes left. He took a step closer and squatted down. Nice and close.

'I'll rephrase my first question, pig. What bullshit scheme is going on at the winery? The second question is still the same. Which one of you killed my brother in the hospital?'

Derek bided his time. Thinking. Mackay gave him ten seconds, counting it down in his head. He then placed the knobkerry on the floor and took the Glock and three pillows from the desk.

'There's no scheme,' puffed Derek. 'It was all an accident, you dumb son of a bitch.' Derek watched Mackay's hand on the Glock. His finger tapping the trigger. 'Taylor!' Derek yelled. 'Taylor, wake up!'

'He's out cold. I kicked him in the head, first. It was a good one. Who knows when he'll come round. Maybe he won't.'

'There's witnesses and statements,' Derek spat, wreathing in his chair. 'There was a deranged shooter. Some lone wolf with a gun. He came in and shot up the place, looking for money. They were unfortunates who got in his way. Wrong place at the wrong time. That's all.'

Derek forced air into his lungs. As best he could in his hunched form.

'No, I don't think so,' said Mackay. 'Let's say there was a deranged shooter. Where is he now?'

'We shot him.'

'Where's his body?'

'In the morgue.'

'Why were you two there so quickly after the incident? My brother, the one you guys finished off in hospital, said you and your friend here were there immediately. Like you had been there the whole time. Like you two were part of the action from the get-go. Is that right?'

'Wrong. We were notified from prison authorities about a mentally ill man. On parole, off medication. He was a red flag in our system, seen wandering around the area. Hyped up. Carrying a gun. A known felon who'd done numerous armed robberies in the region.'

'How does a man like that get all the way out to a country winery? During the day? Plain sight, sun shining, with a gun? Wineries aren't just gathered in suburban streets. They're miles away, where the soil is fertile. Where the grapes can grow uninterrupted. Where is his body?'

'I told you, at the morgue.'

'Which one?'

'Perth.'

'No news reports have stated anything of the sort.'

'That's why it's called an ongoing investigation, asshole. Limited details. The media only get portions until everything is cleared.'

'So why do you have this magneto telephone in your possession in an apartment that isn't yours?'

Derek didn't answer.

'Now back to that second question. Last time. Which one of you killed my brother? I know it was one of you two. You were the last two cunts I saw when I left my brother's hospital ward, and the first two cunts my brother saw after the shooting. I'm not the smartest guy in the world but I can put two and two together. And the coincidences in this scenario are just too big.'

Derek stayed quiet. Mackay counted to five in his head. Derek didn't budge. Mackay rolled Taylor's body around to face him.

'This is you in about thirty seconds,' said Mackay.

Derek looked at his partner. Slack jaw, unnatural angle of the neck, loose posture in the swivel.

'He's dead,' said Derek. A statement. Easy to make considering his partner's limp form.

'I told you it was a good kick,' said Mackay.

Mackay leaned Derek's big mahogany chair backwards and let him fall. Flat on his back, facing the ceiling. A bullet going through the floor was better than a bullet hitting a wall or window. Less noise, less mess. Mackay took the three pillows from the executive desk, placing one pillow behind the chair under Derek's back, and two over Derek's chest.

'I've heard the rumours about this Van Breeman guy,' said Mackay. Seems a bit off. Right now, I have nothing to lose. Once I leave that door, I'm heading down to Margaret River to find your boss myself. So, you can answer me or not, either way, you and your mate are done. Which brings me to one last question, if you're not answering the first two. How many men are with Van Breeman at the winery? I'd like to know what I'm dealing with.'

Derek inhaled then exhaled, long and shallow. 'You've got no chance, son. You set foot down there, you're finished.'

Mackay gave the man another ten seconds. Derek stared back. Stoic. A last resort at stubborn pride. Supreme arrogance in the face of death. He neither admitted nor denied anything. His silence confirmed it all. He was corrupt, and so was his partner. Which made Mackay feel okay about killing them.

Even though Mackay was trained to kill by the British military, he wasn't a trained killer. There was a difference. He was never part of any elite special force, and he was no paid assassin or hitman. He knew enough about himself that he was not a killer for the thrill of it. It wasn't who he was. Wasn't part of his natural being. What he did have though, was a sense of justice. For an occasion just like this, where an intent to kill was required.

Mackay checked his watch. Two minutes left. He pressed the Glock into the two pillows over Derek's chest and squeezed the trigger. Putting a single round through the fat cop's heart. The mildest touch. Hardly there. Like a heavy thud or stomp on the ground, or a book falling from a shelf. Nothing any apartment neighbour would think twice about. And the brass casing had nothing but carpet to bounce off. The round went straight through Derek and the back of the chair – the pillow and carpet left to soak up the draining lake of blood underneath him. Fifteen left in the magazine, thirty-one widow-makers in total.

Mackay picked up the shell casing then went around the apartment. Taking his final two minutes to wipe off any prints he may have left on the door handle, chairs, tables, and inside Van Breeman's bedroom. Another minute later he exited the stairwell on the basement floor with two black cases, two Glock .22s, two mobile phones and two police badges. He found Cross right where he left her. On guard behind the black Toyota Landcruiser.

Cross glared at Mackay, then at the suitcases and the Glock handles bulging from his pants.

'You're late,' she said.

'I'm assuming by late, you mean by one minute,' said Mackay.

Cross double-checked her watch. 'Late is late. How'd it go?'

'I have their Glocks, phones and badges.'

'Both dead?'

'Aye. Put the guns behind your back in your chair.'

'The excitement begins.'

Mackay put the cases with the tucker telephone and knobkerry down and gave Cross the Glocks. He grabbed the two phones, undid the backing plate, pressed out the SIM card and snapped it in two between his teeth. He went to the back of the Landcruiser and checked the exhaust pipe for size to dump the phones into. Too small. He checked two more SUVs – a Volvo then an Audi. The Audi's exhaust was a dual, one on the left, one on the right. It was a snug fit with just enough room to jam both phones in either side of the pipes. Sooner or later the owner would catch on. Or at least their mechanic would. The change in exhaust tone would be too significant not to notice.

'It should take a good while for someone to find them,' said Mackay. 'At least twenty-four hours. Probably more. Unless Van Breeman has a scheduled cleaner every day.'

'Are you okay?'

'Exceptional. They had it coming. You should see what's in this box-looking case. A tucker telephone.'

'A magneto torture device?'

'They were on their way out with it, taking it somewhere. We made contact in the hallway. And now I'm here.'

'Are you okay?' Cross said again.

Mackay paused and looked at her.

Cross said, 'I just want to be sure you're good with whatever happened up there. If you're okay with it, then I'm okay with it.'

'I'm okay.'

Mackay picked up the two cases. 'We need to hail a taxi. We've got a plane to catch.'

> 1720hrs
> Wednesday December 19, 2012
> Frans & Hoek Winery, Margaret River, Western Australia

Van Breeman rang Taylor and Derek's phones consecutively for a total of six times. Three rings per phone. Each time he rang there was dead air. Their numbers couldn't be reached. He then tried Kimbala who was sitting with Bryson and Wynand waiting inside a parked van. Parked on a verge eighty meters from Lydia Ferreira's front door. A late model grey Kia Carnival. Sliding door access, loads of space, anonymously bland in colour. Bought by Van Breeman for that exact purpose – to blend in and look ordinary.

Kimbala was put in charge, as usual. He was smarter than Bryson and less intimidating, which was very deceptive. Even at six-foot-four with his unruly beard, compared to Bryson he looked like a college principal, or a black Father Christmas. His soft, welcoming eyes could loll you into a false sense of security. But make no mistake, the man was a clear-cut sociopath.

Wynand on the other hand was completely different. Less carved out of wood or clay, he had boyish looks with long hair kept in a ponytail. Constantly slicking the fringe behind his ears. You could say he was your average Joe. Average in every way – height, weight, intelligence. Could potentially go unnoticed until the day he died.

Being dead-on knock-off hour for the regular working citizen, Kimbala's plan was to wait out Lydia's arrival. He first wanted to get a neighbourly sense of the street. Was it busy, quiet, or somewhere in between? Whatever the atmosphere was would dictate the modus operandi. He obviously preferred the street vibe to be clear and quiet, waiting out the most lulled point in time. And dark, which it wasn't. But Van Breeman wanted it done before nightfall, which made for tighter parameters. A daytime snatch-and-grab was dubious at the best of times. But it could be done, as long as it was done the right way. Inside the house.

Kimbala's phone rang with a mechanised chirp. A nominal ringtone unchanged from the box.

'You still parked?' Van Breeman asked.

'Still here.'

'Binoculars?'

'Man's best friend.'

'How long have you been sitting for now?'

'Two hours.'

'Not much longer then. Need to limit your visibility in public.'

'Understood. If she doesn't show within thirty minutes we'll leave.'

'I can't get hold of Taylor or Derek.'

'Since when?'

'Since four o'clock. I've been trying them both for the last ten minutes. Nothing.'

'I'll try them myself.'

'If you get through, tell them to call me ASAP. I want them back here by seven.'

'Could be a number of reasons why they haven't replied. Police life. Family life.'

'Irrelevant. They know the deal. If I have to call consecutively more than twice, they lose half their pay for the week. Same goes with you, and the two with you.'

'Understood.'

Van Breeman hung up.

Kimbala tried Derek first, then Taylor. No dial tone for either. Nothing received. It immediately went to an automated voice stating the number could not be connected.

'Boss will be pissed,' said Kimbala.

'They go AWOL?' said Bryson, holding the binoculars.

'They're not answering for some reason,' said Kimbala. 'Must be a good one. You two know anything?'

Bryson and Wynand shook their heads.

From where Bryson sat in the front passenger seat, he had a good observation point on the reporter's house. The road was completely flat and straight along the line of white-collar brick homes. He could see Lydia's front gate, front garden, garage door, and driveway with clarity through the lens. Waiting out during a stakeout was a learned skill, as was knowing what to bring to pass the time. Which for Van Breeman's top two associates, was usually in the form of greasy food and cheap caffeine. Aside from the microscopic elements of hair follicles, discarded fingernails, snot and skin grease, the car was littered with takeaway food wrappers and coffee cups. Wynand on the other hand was new to the game. Sitting in the back with little to do but watch and learn and occasionally observe on the binoculars. Wynand was bored. Restless and edgy like a restrained puppy. He'd messed up recently with the chloroform and the asthma attack. Given, the older kid's death wasn't really his fault. No one knew he would suffer a full-blown asthma attack, but still, he was part to blame for the lost kid and he desperately wanted to make up for it. Show Van Breeman he was capable. At least receive a pat on the back to validate his worth. After two hours of no action, a young guy like him with lots to prove was bound to get edgy. But then things changed. A vehicle entered the driveway.

'Perk up, boys,' said Bryson. 'We've got a car. A white Volkswagen Golf. One female driver inside. She looks cute. Long brown hair.'

'That's her,' said Wynand, leaning forward into the centre console. 'Has to be.'

'Relax, boy,' said Bryson. 'Keep your shit together.'

Wynand slipped his face covering on, then checked the stun gun in his pocket. It was long but light, like a big stapler with a pulse rate of fifty thousand volts. His job was to knock on the door, wrench it open once answered, then stun the reporter. Not that fifty thousand volts would kill her. Most of the voltage passing from the gun to the human body vanishes once it hits the skin. The end result means the victim only really takes about twelve hundred. If connection lasts for over three seconds, aside from intense pain comes loss of balance and muscle control, as well as disorientation and confusion. If Wynand did his job right, then Kimbala and Bryson would concurrently jimmy their way through the back door and grab the reporter from behind. Following that, they'd have her pass out for the long haul with a trio blend of liquid chemistry. A homemade anaesthesia kit. Telazol and ketamine in the neck. Chloroform rag over the mouth. Lastly, they'd tie her up with the zip ties and move her into the van, which was preferably parked in the driveway, or as close to the house as possible. Seven steps in total. All agreed upon prior to engagement.

'Take it easy, Wynand,' said Kimbala starting the van. 'Just sit there and keep your dick in your pants. We still need to give her another five minutes. Let her get inside and get cosy. And take that fucking mask off. You can put it on before you knock on the front door. You were here when we discussed the plan, weren't you?'

'Yes.'

Kimbala turned around and poked Wynand repeatedly in the chest with his finger. The digit as big as a rolling pin. 'Getting all pumped and frantic will only make things worse,' he said. 'You want to fuck everything up like you did back at the winery?'

'No.'

'If this goes sour because of you, you're going down. Like Snowy, but my way. Maybe I eat your heart while you watch.'

> 1730hrs
> Wednesday December 19, 2012
> Perth, Western Australia

Mackay threw the two cop badges into the hedges at the front of the tower, then followed Cross to an empty taxi zone next to a bus shelter. He set the cases down next to Cross's chair and waited. A free taxi amongst city traffic at five-thirty in the afternoon wasn't going to be a walk in the park. It was peak rush hour. Home time for more than half the city. The only silver lining was Cross seated in her wheelchair, which he hoped would provoke some level of sympathy amongst the cabbies. And it worked. A minor perk of being an amputee.

Within five minutes, a cab pulled up. An estate. In some parts of the world, they called it a wagon. It wasn't a maxi-cab, but there was room in the back for the red ant's chair and the two cases. No time to head back to the bed and breakfast and pack. They were on the run for murder now. Or at least Mackay was. A fugitive. Regardless of whether the deserving parties were corrupt, or who believed it. Their bodies would be found sooner or later, and the hunt would begin. Besides, they were on the clock. Cross's contact was expecting them within the hour, which meant they needed to head straight to RAAF Base Pearce along the most direct route. At this point, there was still enough buffer time between them and the law, but it would only get shorter and more unyielding once the bodies were found. They needed to use the time they currently had to its full potential: find Lincoln, find the head of the snake.

Mackay and Cross sat in the back. The driver obliged in the transaction of cash for transport and set the location of the airbase into his smartphone mounted on the dash. He slotted back into the steady stream of traffic, merged across two lanes, then exited onto an endless motorway. Five built-up lanes of rolling machinery heading home for the day.

'You took a hit for him, didn't you,' Mackay said. 'A charge. You spent time in jail for him. Some kind of fuck-up during an exercise. That's why he owes you. Why he's doing this massive favour.'

Cross went silent. She took a breath and made a face. She looked away from the passing faces in the cars, trucks, and work-cabs and turned to Mackay.

'We were engaged in a mine clearance drill. The SAS team were working with live fire. It was all planned and rehearsed. Orders were good. He accidentally shot one of my guys. A fire engagement gone wrong. My guy should have stayed down on his guts. Something was bothering him inside the back of his shirt, so he began taking his pack off. Went upright onto his knees and was shot in the back. High on the trapezius. Almost bled out. It wasn't even a negligent discharge on John's end. SAS don't make mistakes like that, but his boss was going to throw him in the can anyway. Make an example of him. Make him sweat it out for a week in the hole and miss out on a deployment he'd been training months for. I was our section leader and had the highest rank, so in the after-action report I told the MPs I gave orders for my guy to get up and remove his pack.'

'But you never did.'

'No. But it was the only thing that saved John. He got one night in the hole, then got deployed the next day.'

'And you?'

'A week.'

'How was it?'

'It was the long game that hurt. It ruined my career progression. Isolation at the barracks was fine. Food, clean bed, and television all provided. I just couldn't go anywhere, and the paperwork was bollocks.'

'That's big time, Renee. A huge call to make. More or less the definition of owing a favour.'

Cross raised a brow and stared at Mackay.

'What?' said Mackay.

'You called me Renee.'

'I did?'

'You did.'

'Is that good or bad?'

'I don't know yet. It's certainly new. Only my parents ever called me Renee.'

'Continue the story.'

'I wanted Warrant Officer, but it wasn't going to happen. I either told the truth and fucked two soldiers' lives and careers, or I told a lie and screwed one. It was the lesser of the two. My guy already had to deal with rehab and six months out of action. I thought taking a charge and waiting out career progression wasn't too bad. Sergeant was still a good rank.'

Cross stayed silent for a long moment, looking back out her window, remembering. Her eyes followed the flow of vehicles. Followed the line of palm trees and gum trees rising from red earth along the emergency lane. Vehicles exited and merged. Motorbikes cut and weaved. A train passed them parallel to the freeway. School buses full of children stared back. Some smiled and laughed, some waved, some just looked through the glass staring at nothing in particular.

'What was in your guy's shirt?' said Mackay, his voice cutting through the tyre roar and faint pop music on the radio.

Cross laughed. 'A scorpion.'

'Here? Australia?'

'Yes. Thing was hideous. Big as a fucking rat.'

*

BARGAINING

At 1815hrs the front entrance to RAAF Base Pearce appeared. A wide-gated compound enough to fit logistical trucks and heavy machinery hauling tonnes of loads. The main entry point was bordered with kilometres of high-set fencing with a central booth managed by security staff working two boom gates. One for coming in, one for coming out. The taxi slowed and turned into a small visitor parking lot fifty yards away. A drop-off zone. Mackay got out first and fixed the red ant's chair while she paid the driver with a generous tip for the extended drive. Phase two was about to begin.

As they waited on the verge for their escort, Cross stared out over the fence line at the horizon. Part nostalgic, part worried. Namely for Mackay and what he was about to do. The afternoon sun had started to dip, hinting at the sunset that was about to come.

'In about an hour that sunset is going to hit,' she said. 'Hopefully you'll get to see it from nice and high.'

'Would be nicer seeing it with you. While sitting on the beach with a few beers.'

'We can make it happen. You just make sure you come back in one piece.'

After a slew of nominal civilian vehicles, the boom gates opened for a G-Wagon. A Mercedes Benz off-roader. Bespoke for military operations. Once it exited, it made a hard right and headed straight for the drop-off zone. The afternoon was late and the windows were too dark to see who was inside, but it was clear to assume their contact had arrived. The G-Wagon pulled in and parked next to the verge. The driver's side door opened. A man stepped out dressed in standard army fatigues. Khaki, brown, olive drab. Barracks dress. A corporal's rank slide was attached to the front of his uniform. Two black stripes shaped like the letter 'v'. He stood somewhere around the six-foot mark, similar to Mackay. Only the guy was built for power rather than speed. His shoulders were about the width of a train carriage, his face narrow and unshaven, his eyes indifferent. Basically, a chiselled, modern-day Spartan made of balsa or maple.

'Cross. Nice to see you,' he said.

'Likewise,' said Cross.

Then stalemate. Neither spoke a word more. Hot air circulated. The Spartan stared at Cross. At her chair, her stump limbs. Mackay's eyes bounced between the red ant and the Spartan. There was no movement. No conversation. Mackay stepped forward with an outstretched hand.

'Mackay,' he said.

The Spartan paused, judging Mackay for all he was worth. His height, his width, leanness, facial features, body language. Mackay's entire value as a human being sorted in half a second. Then he gripped Mackay's hand in return. Covering each digit like a baseball mitt. Firm and welcoming, no ego, no arrogance. War-dog to war-dog.

'Irish,' said the Spartan. A statement, not a question. A travelled man.

'Aye,' said Mackay.

'John Nuttall. Call me Nutty.'

Nutty stepped back to match eyes with Cross again. As big and intimidating as he was, he could not respond to Cross and why she was sitting in the chair in front of him. So, she helped him out.

'You can bend down and hug me, you big cockhead,' she said.

And he did.

Nutty dropped a knee, leaned forward, and threw his arms around her. Around her whole chair. She hugged him back. Lost friends found again. They stayed low and connected like that for ten long seconds.

'I never knew you got hit,' said Nutty, letting go. 'It's hard to see you like this.'

'This one's not your fault,' said Cross. 'You didn't know, and I wouldn't have told you anyway. We lost touch.'

'I wish we didn't.'

Cross looked away, somewhere over Nutty's shoulder. Nutty stared at the ground. Mackay watched Nutty exhale and slump. Like a gladiator ready to give his head.

'Some guys I know look similar. Just not any women,' said Nutty.

'I do okay,' said Cross.

'I bet you do,' said Nutty. 'Probably better than most women, even those who can stand with two feet. IED?'

Cross nodded.

'When did it happen?'

'After I left Perth. After our training stint went to shit. I eventually ended up on my third rotation in the sandbox.'

'I'll never forget what you did for me. I'll probably never be able to repay that day.'

'Maybe today's the day.'

'I would have done this favour even if I didn't owe you. Taking a charge and a week in the big house is ten times the gratuity compared to me shooting your guy. You more or less gave up your career.'

'I liked Sergeant. Less paperwork than a warrant officer, and more action. Getting out, getting dirty. Fighting the good fight. Maybe it was a good thing you shot my guy.'

'Said nobody ever.'

Cross smiled. 'Getting shot is no good for nobody,' she said. 'Unless it's a cave-Nazi weighed down with enough steel to give them a haemorrhoid.'

Mackay smiled.

'Let's crack on,' said Nutty. 'There's a C-17 being prepped.' Nutty turned to Mackay. 'And according to our conversation, you need to be on it.'

Mackay helped Cross monkey into the G-Wagon, then stowed her chair in the back next to him. Nutty got in, turned the key, and steered the vehicle back towards the boom gates. Nutty waved at the guard, the guard waved back and the gate went up.

'There's a few stop-offs we need to make before we get to the airfield,' said Nutty as they drove through the base's quiet streets. Everything was neat, clean, and tidy. The sidewalks were meticulous. Every grassed edge trimmed, every bush and hedge clipped. A detailed standard found only on military bases.

Nutty said, 'We'll make way to supplies first. They know I'm coming. The bayonet, knuckle dusters, and seal pup knife are in that black backpack on the floor at your feet. The pack is yours.'

'Appreciated,' said Mackay.

'I've done what I can. There's room in the pack for your rations, and room for those two Glocks Cross had stashed behind her arse in her chair. And when you jump, make sure you take it all with you. Make sure your pack is tied to your front.'

Cross turned and looked at Nutty with a wry smile.

'So, it wasn't my fat arse you noticed?' she said.

'I could feel the cold weight when I hugged you,' Nutty said. 'Not that I was intentionally reaching for your fat arse. I bet that's a good story, having those guns on you.'

'Don't ask,' said Cross.

'Whatever gets you over the line to live another day is what I say.'

Nutty pulled into a parking bay in front of a long brick building. Plastered to the front wall in bold blue capitals, read RAAF PEARCE SUPPLIES.

'Your tac gear and rations are in there,' said Nutty, turning back to Mackay. 'Your chute is on the aircraft.'

> 1830hrs
> Wednesday December 19, 2012
> RAAF Base Pearce, Western Australia

Inside the supply store, Mackay was introduced to a clerk sitting at a desk in front of a shed full of equipment. A warehouse with shelves full of Air Force gear. Lots of blues, whites, and blacks. Fatigue uniforms, standard dress, and every accessory that went with it. The clerk was an older guy. Had probably started there not long after the prehistoric age. Narrow reading glasses pinched the bridge of his nose under a tidy wipe of thin greying hair. Age, experience, and rank had seen him get nice and comfortable as the years went by.

The clerk placed the magazine he was reading onto his desk next to a half-filled mug of coffee. He stood, put his hand out and gave his name. Andy. The hand was firm. He shook Cross's. He didn't shake Nutty's.

'Time to get on with it then,' said Andy. His accent was British. A little Newcastle, a little country. His tone was well rounded and clear enough, though a little dusty and flat. Pitched from the back of the throat like he was speaking from his chin. He ushered the visitors around his desk, into the furthest recesses of the warehouse. Like a gateway into an entirely new world.

'Sounds like you're from Newcastle,' said Mackay.

'I am, son,' said Andy. 'Born and bred, until the wife got sick of the rain and fog. Been here thirty years now. Strange how people keep their home-grown accents. Like yourself. Mostly Irish, part British.'

Another travelled man.

He took Mackay to a corner section with six rows of shelves, all of which contained black-coloured materials. Some plastic, some metallic. Much of it light and easily stored on a person. Mainly accoutrements for inside webbing, satchels, pockets, and concealed compartments. Some items were thick, some were thin, some were woven and seamed.

'This is your section apparently,' said Andy. 'And that broad ox standing next to you has requested that I give you, free of charge by the way, my best night operational tactical kit. And some extra goodies. A right bollocks request for starters, this is not a charity. But apparently what the broad man says, goes.'

He looked straight at Mackay. His forehead was creased but not much else was given in his expression. He was old-school British. Somewhere from the baby boomer generation, used to a class system.

'And don't worry,' Andy continued. 'I won't throw in any of the tall man's beard oil. Unless you really want it. It's usually on special request, but there's no point in looking good when you're out field, yea?'

Mackay smiled. Nutty didn't.

Only Mackay could tell Andy was being sarcastic. Nutty saw it different. The human cinder block stood stiff and rigid. Somewhere between high alert and simmer. The kind of body language that said cinder blocks didn't do games or banter. The same body language that said things should be moving faster.

Andy reached low into a blue tub on the bottom shelf stacked with black chest rigs. Kevlar vests. Bullet resistant, not bulletproof. Not completely. He handed it out to Mackay. The item was moderately weighted even without a chest plate. It was fitted with Velcro and seamed with straps.

Nutty turned to Mackay. 'Are you going to need a chest plate for this op?'

'Better to take full protection every time,' said Mackay. 'Hope for the best, prepare for the worst. Orders are that I come back in one piece.'

'Fucking oath you'll take a plate,' said Cross. 'That's not even a question.'

'Had to ask,' said Nutty. 'If it's just a recon, sometimes the guys prefer to travel light. I get the sense it may be more.'

Nutty eyed Mackay up and down. Top to bottom. Noting the stretched material around his thighs and glutes. The bulging slab of quadriceps inside almost as visible as his face.

Andy said, 'Of course he bloody well wants full protection. The full beans at all times. The full French letter. You get a vest, you get a plate. Anyway, who's this Cross you spoke of giving orders? Never heard of him.' Andy threw a wink at Renee.

Nutty rolled his eyes. 'Her,' he said. 'This is her right here. A sergeant by the way.'

'Ex-sergeant,' said Cross.

Andy pulled a ballistic plate from a second tub and handed it to Mackay.

'Of course, of course, I remember her story,' Andy said. 'Sergeant Renee Cross.' Andy stepped over to a second shelf lined with lunchbox-sized cubes; lightweight foam cases bearing night-vision headsets. NVG.

'British engineering unit,' said Andy. 'Got put in the hole after a negligent discharge blunder. Some big fuck-up that was all hush-hush. A little ways back. You took the heat from a certain special forces soldier. I wonder who that be?'

Andy winked again, this time at Mackay. 'And some say I haven't got a scooby doo.'

Nutty's posture sharpened even further. His spine rose an inch, his back expanding like a canvass.

'How the fuck do you know about that?' said Nutty.

'Thirty years in the military, son. It's a wonderful world here. Like little teenagers we are, matey, the top ranks love gobbing off. Good news, bad news, it all circulates and finds its way down here. Keeps my job interesting. Keeps me livelihood prickly.'

Nutty took a long breath in, held it, released it. Didn't reply.

'It's alright, son,' continued Andy. 'Got the utmost respect for the SAS. Any good soldier who fucks up once never fucks up again. Don't stress, even you lot are human.'

'Appreciate that, sir,' said Nutty. 'But if I may, there's an aircraft waiting for us. We need to be on it. Like yesterday. Can we hurry this up?'

'Alright, then, let's hurry along, shall we. The broad man has spoken.'

Andy moved a few steps across the shelf lines and pulled a GPS tracker from a storage cupboard.

'There's a pocket in the front of your vest for this,' he said. 'Normally for thirty-round mags, but it should fit there nicely. You have a watch?'

'Yes.' Mackay raised his left wrist.

'G-Shock. Like the rest of us. Standard military gubbins the world over. Good man.'

Andy continued his way around a corner where the walls merged and finished into a small corridor. The business end. A niche section where soldiers of the field were robed for battle. Where the strategic protection of a war-dog began. An arsenal of accessories camouflaged for day or night in the field. All warbled in pattern with their own special names like 'desert sand' and 'foliage green'.

Andy stepped aside and ushered Mackay into the hall of shelves.

'All my stock here is in inspection order,' he said. 'Don't go rummaging around willy-nilly mucking things about. You've got combat trousers, belts, socks and boots on the left. Jackets, shirts and hats on the right. Camo face paint cases on the bottom. Go for gold. The mirror's there in front of the jackets.'

'Thanks,' said Mackay. 'I'll sort myself out. I'm good for boots, though. Took care of those already.'

Nutty looked down at Mackay's feet noting the Gore-Tex footwear. Hardened rubber sole with a protective toecap.

'Good choice,' Nutty said. 'If I were to have a guess, I'd say you're planning on moving around a bit with that kind of footwear. Like you need to stay light on your feet.'

'I'll hunker down for a beat, if necessary, as long as it takes. But I do need to move. There's a kid I need to find, the last in the Connolly line.'

Mackay started with the cargo trousers until he found the optimal widths and lengths. He worked his way around, taking one size up than usual for both undershirt and overshirt to cater for his barrel chest, then checked and double-checked for fitting and adjustment. He checked off all straps, zips and buttons, pocketed a small case of camouflage paint then slung the Kevlar vest with ballistic plate over his shoulder. Good to go.

Nutty turned his attention to Andy. 'Sir, last item, can we grab a couple of ration packs? Assuming you've still got them.'

'I never run out of anything,' said Andy. 'It's why they still keep me on the books.'

On the opposite end of Andy's desk, the warehouse floor opened to a wide section of space crowded with wooden pallets. Most were laid with olive-green trunks of various sizes. Some filled with leather gloves and bungee cords, some filled with green water canteens. Two were stockpiled with cartons of beer, wine and spirits. Obviously ready for Air Force downtime. Andy navigated through a maze of six or seven pallets and came to a stop at one filled with large aluminium tins resembling rubbish bins.

'Wet or freeze-dried?' asked Andy.

'Dried,' said Mackay. 'Lighter and easier for eating on the go. I'm not banking on taking time out to cook. I'll just take one.'

'Each to their own,' said Andy, handing Mackay an oblong packet the size of a lamb roast. 'And you'll want a bottle of water too, I'm sure.'

'An essential. I won't say no.'

Andy grabbed a green canteen from the trunk next to the spirits, walked over to a nearby tap, filled it, and handed it to Mackay.

'Appreciate your time, sir,' said Nutty. 'Mackay, it's time to go.'

Nutty turned on his heels and began striding back through the pallets. Mackay offered his hand to Andy. He shook it.

'Whatever you're in for, keep your wits about you,' said Andy. 'Use what you've been taught, and don't fucking die. Maybe someday you'll be back in here with beers and a good jackanory for me.'

'Jackanory?' said Mackay.

'A story,' said Cross. 'Cockney rhyming slang.'

'That's the one,' said Andy. 'Keep up, Irish.'

'Is he invited?' said Mackay, nodding at Nutty's imposing figure marching away.

'Certainly. The more the merrier. And if he doesn't like me humour, he can piss off just like everybody else.'

```
1830hrs
Wednesday December 19, 2012
Frans & Hoek Winery, Western Australia
```

Van Breeman watched Lydia breathe and whimper and strain. He didn't like her. Not since what she'd written about him eighteen months ago when Carice went missing. Lydia was fixed to a wooden stool bolted to a cement floor in the middle of the room. The hotbox. Part of the old dairy farm's original brick cabin down the far end of the winery. Even though the sun was setting, and the afternoon was overlapping into evening, the room always retained the heat of the day. Summer or winter, the chamber was always hot and humid.

Lydia was awake with a black cloth bag over her head. She was breathing okay but was groggy and confused from the liquid combination: telazol, ketamine and chloroform. Not to mention the volts from the stun gun. And being on a stool meant she sat without armrests or a back support, and in her condition, that was hard going. Her legs were roped together in two sections: calves and thighs. Her thighs were tied to the seat of the stool and her hands were zip-tied behind her back. Because the stool's legs were bolted into the floor, no matter how much leaning, pulling or swaying Lydia tried, she wasn't going anywhere. She could arch backwards – to a point – but arching backwards past ninety degrees was not an ideal position to be in. It was unsupported for her spine, and she was no contortionist or gymnast. It was either upright or forward with her chest on her thighs. Shallow breathing. Sweating it out in the heat.

Lydia's feet were immersed in a large tub filled with a mix of blood and hair. The blood was part animal, part her own. Taken with a large syringe they'd normally use on cattle. The hair was all hers. A lengthy portion taken from the back. The ponytail end. After she'd been dragged in, seated, and strapped to the stool, Kimbala held her down and lopped off a chunk. A straight cut with large gardening clippers. Steel handle, double bowed with an eight-inch blade. Shears mostly used for pruning hedges and small branches. Sometimes used for splitting bones and removing hoofs from goats and sheep.

On the floor behind her was a shrine. Set with a line of lit candles along the edge of the wall, flickering a muted light throughout the room. Above the candles displayed high on the brick wall was a large figure made of bone, leather and yarn. A relic. A fixed sculpture of a face trapped in a scream, and not entirely human. An ancient African idol representing the god of the dead. The keeper of souls. There were features of a white skull, but the teeth were hollowed out and blackened with ash, the eyes marked with crosses made of sticks. The hair sprawled upwards with twigs and puffs of fur, while the neck was a winding mass of bristly fibre made from corn husks. The idol loomed over Lydia's body like it was preparing to inhale her. Sucking her soul into its hollow black mouth.

Van Breeman didn't like that particular room, and never went in. Something about the dank heat and the thing on the wall. Walking around inside was like moving through a swamp. He stood outside the door with his phone to his ear as he dialled Derek one last time. The door to the room was ajar and he could see Lydia tied to the stool. That was enough. The faint air that drafted into the room, did however make Lydia feel better. It circled around her legs, over her knees and underneath her dress. With the bag over her head, she couldn't tell who was in the room. Or what. All she could feel was the draft, and a presence. One person for sure. Maybe two.

Both Bryson and Wynand were back at the front of house manning security and completing wine orders. Or at least that was where they were supposed to be. And since Derek and Taylor hadn't returned with the rungu club and magneto, Van Breeman had given Kimbala the go-ahead. It was now up to his main man to deliver the consequences to the journalist. Van Breeman preferred the more traditional methods with old-school African military torture, but this time he had to make an exception. He had to make do with Kimbala's dark practice. Both men's tactics had their strengths and weaknesses. Both reserved a time and place in Van Breeman's moral balance. But by default, without the club and hand-cranked telephone, the penalties submitted onto the petite brunette fell back to plan B: Kimbala. Which in the long term was quite possibly the worse option. All Van Breeman really wanted was to deliver a message. Put her in her place. Maybe leave a few scars while at it.

*

Kimbala stood inside the room, just a few feet from Lydia's sagged form in the centre. One hand was clasped around a thick clay pot. Inside it was a pestle grinder. One of those heavy pounding tools with a rounded end – like a small rolling pin used to crush herbs, spices, and drugs. His other hand held a blowtorch. Trigger operated with an adjustable flame control, fuelled with a can of butane. On the floor were two other items he'd recently used: gardening clippers and a large tranquilising needle.

Kimbala took the clay pot and scooped up a portion of hair and blood from the tub at Lydia's feet. He took the blowtorch and heated the contents until it boiled and smoked up a consistent haze, creating a wafting stench of burnt rubber and off meat. Then he started with the chants. His voice thrummed along, rhythmic and incoherent, reciting strange verses in dialogue that could only be described as blabber. Van Breeman wanted to stay and supervise but once Kimbala began burning the hair and blood in the pestle, he had to leave. The stench was too much. The fumes too toxic for anyone not accustomed to the craft. Besides, he had things to do. Derek still wasn't answering his phone. As he headed for the door, behind him, Kimbala closed in on Lydia. Toe to toe. Wafting the smoky fumes of hair and blood over her body. Fanning it on repeat, all while increasing his chanting volume. His thrumming tones cast from the pit of his stomach.

Before Van Breeman left, Lydia's body shot up straight like it had been yanked vertically by an invisible force. Her head tilted back as she stretched her mouth open like a fish out of water. She drew in a breath and screamed, just once, long and piercing, then flopped back onto her chest and began moaning. Expelling a lamenting wave of pained air. The sounds unnatural for her size and gender, but eerily matching Kimbala's rhythm. Their vocals rolled around the room like they were in a duet. One in melody, one in harmony. Van Breeman closed the door and pocketed his phone.

SEVEN

CONVICTION

1845hrs
Wednesday December 19, 2012
RAAF Base Pearce, Perth, Western Australia

The C-17 Globemaster sat warming up on the tarmac. Four Pratt and Whitney turbofan engines sucked air and reached all the right temperatures. Live flight tracker engaged, engine management systems cleared to go, fuel systems full and operational. The hulking construction was one of the biggest military aircrafts in the world, capable of fitting over a hundred soldiers, tanks, and other combat vehicles. For this particular evening the steel bird was reserved for a small section of elite war-dogs. A team of eight soldiers all cut from the same cloth. All had clustered around the rear of the empty cargo hold to play hacky sack with a small soccer ball. Passing the time while they waited out Nutty and his special guest. They could have been playing full court basketball the cavernous space was that big.

Once Nutty arrived, it was game on. A static-line parachute jump. A standard airborne exercise which basically ticked another box in their training. Each soldier needed a certain number of jumps throughout the year to maintain qualifications. Training privileges like this didn't get much better. The men were half kitted up. Their body armour and webbing kits were strapped and rigged to their chests. On the front of those rigs were black unit patches. Hard-earned insignia. A dagger with wings and a banner that read *Who Dares Wins*. The Australian SAS. The other half of their gear – the parachute packs – laid on the fold-down seats across the fuselage wall. Port side. A static-line jump was different to skydiving. As the soldier left the aircraft the parachute would deploy immediately, rather than freefalling before pulling the cord yourself.

Nutty boarded the craft first, checking in on the boys. He counted heads, counted seats, counted packs. There were eight heads, nine seats and nine packs. One spare waiting for Mackay. Things were in order, timing was okay. It had just hit 1832 hours. Two minutes late. Poor by soldiering standards, but not too bad considering the extra effort in organising their guest.

The enormity of the space inside the metallic construction made the boys look small and insignificant. Like midgets. Or special forces hobbits. Nutty turned and looked back down the boarding stairs to see Mackay and Cross waiting on the tarmac. He nodded once and gave the thumbs up. Good to board. Mackay turned to Cross. The rushing wind forced into the engines drew a trickle of water from her eye. She wiped it away.

'I'm not fucking crying don't you worry, Horse Killer,' Cross yelled above the jet whine.

Mackay half smiled. 'You know about that one?'

'It's the Army. Everybody talks.'

'I still feel bad for that horse.'

'So you should. Everyone loves horses. But a war story is what makes our lives memorable. I like Tin Man better.'

The sun sank further, sitting just above the horizon, dimming the sky to a light shade of marigold. Mackay considered bending down and kissing her. Cross couldn't stand, so it would be up to him if he was going to reach her lips. But then, Cross made his mind up for him. She grabbed him softly between the pants. Underhand. Palms up. Squeezing gingerly. Forcing Mackay to bend down.

'You stay alive and keep me posted,' she said. 'Ten minutes after your jump, then on the hour, every hour.' She held her lips against his. A moment passed. She let him go.

Mackay slung Nutty's backpack on one shoulder, complete with two jacked Glocks, knuckle dusters, bayonet, seal knife and all the rest from Andy's supply store. He slung the Kevlar vest with the ballistics plate on the other shoulder and boarded the plane.

Nutty met Mackay at the top of the stairs. 'You're jumping first,' he said. 'The rest of the guys are off to Albany. Or somefucking-where, I'm not a hundred per cent sure. I've notified the pilots and jumpmaster of your grid reference for Frans & Hoek winery. The jumpmaster will tell you when you're up. Just be ready. Once you jump, I'll get notified by the pilot. Nobody knows why you're jumping, they just know you're out the door first. But your landing won't be exact. Never is, so here…'

Nutty handed Mackay a folded sheet of paper with a set of coordinates.

'Once you land, wherever you land, punch this into the GPS tracker. It'll get you within a hundred metres of the winery. We'll be back here to support, but once you're in the air, you're on your own.'

'On me tod. Thanks, Corporal.' Mackay stashed the coordinates into his pocket.

Nutty said, 'Cross will stay in the air-route control centre. There are beds in there, plus a kitchen and television for guys who stay during long-haul exercises. She'll be comfortable. I'll be hanging about part-time, checking in. You have three days before I start to sweat and send a search party. Seventy-two hours.'

Nutty put his hand out, Mackay shook it. Mackay turned to look outside at Cross waiting on the tarmac. She gave him one final nod.

'She really seems to like you,' said Nutty. 'All the best.'

Once Nutty exited the craft, the jumpmaster drew the boarding stairs up and sealed the entry. Mackay looked over at the rear cargo space noting the eight soldiers. He then noted nine seats folded along the port side and nine parachute deployment packs. One of the men walked forward to greet him.

'You need a hand getting rigged up?' said the soldier. Mackay couldn't see a name badge on his uniform, or any rank. Anonymity for special forces was everything. At a fingernail below Mackay's eye level, he was the shortest member of the team. A great fighting height for hand-to-hand combat.

'That'd be great,' said Mackay.

'Irish?'

'Aye.'

'We look after our own.'

'I'm not SAS. And I haven't jumped for years.'

'No one gives half a fuck. If you're jumping out this shell with us, then you're one of us. Simple. Like Forrest fucking Gump.'

Mackay smiled. Mostly on the inside. Some soldiers had a way with words. At the same time, some soldiers also got leery if you smiled at them the wrong way. The soldier got to strapping in Mackay's vest and plate – front, back and sides. Mackay removed the night vision from his backpack, then fixed the backpack to his front. The soldier checked and double-checked every strap and harness point, then grabbed Mackay's wrists.

'Your altimeter, where is it?' he asked.

Mackay opened the top zipper of the backpack, took out the altimeter and fastened it to his right wrist.

'Buttoned up and sorted,' said the soldier, and whacked Mackay across the shoulder. 'Don't say we mutts never do anything for you.'

'Wouldn't dream of it,' said Mackay.

'Let's put your D-bag on.'

They walked over to the furthest grey deployment pack waiting first in line to the exit door. More straps were tightened and secured, checked, then double-checked. Being fully kitted out in tactical felt good. Made Mackay feel like part of the team again, which was something he hadn't felt in almost a year. Not since the explosion. The finishing touch to the whole get-up was face paint. Should cameras or patrolling security be watching him, as a milky-white Irishman he'd stand out like a stripper in a monastery. Especially in the moonlight. Mackay patted his pants till he felt the small flat box in his pocket from the supply store. He opened the pack, dug three fingers into the green, black, and brown, then lathered up. From neck to ears to the top of the hairline. Hands and eyelids too. The whole nine yards.

A voice came through an invisible speaker somewhere inside the aircraft.

'Take your seats, chaps, this is your captain speaking. Airborne op with a chalk of nine. Evening exercise for Operation Sand Digger. We're out of here.'

The Globemaster moved, slow and steady like a giant glob of molasses. Taxiing along the curving runway towards the main straight. The eight others began checking each other's gear, fitting and adjusting their own deployment packs, tightening straps, checking and double-checking. The raucous drone of the engines increased, this time pushing the aircraft with pace and thrust. The fat tyres pressed deep into the tarmac for almost two and a half kilometres as the giant bird hustled on. Then the nose spiked upwards, and the wings hooked the air – two hundred tonnes of steel resisting gravity like it was nothing.

> 1845hrs
> Wednesday December 19, 2012
> Frans & Hoek Winery, Western Australia

Van Breeman made his way across the winery grounds to look for Wynand at the main gallery. Hoping he was inside the admin room waiting for orders like a good dog. Which was where Bryson was. He needed Wynand to run a few errands. Derek and Taylor were uncontactable, which meant he had to bite the bullet and send Wynand to look for them. He couldn't send Bryson or Kimbala as both were already engaged: Kimbala in the hotbox terrifying the journalist, Bryson looking after the CCTV.

He needed to send Wynand back to Perth to check on the three places he figured Taylor and Derek would most logically be. The police station, their family home, and floor forty-seven of the Swan Quay Tower. Which was the first place Wynand needed to look.

Failing that, if the men weren't found, Wynand would return immediately to help Bryson with vineyard security. If Wynand did end up finding the two cops, Van Breeman was considering giving him the night off in Perth. Let him off the leash in the city. Hit the pubs and clubs. A small token of thanks for his efforts. Acknowledgement for not hampering the kidnap of the journalist and doing his job properly.

Wynand was not at the main gallery. His phone however, was. Left on the long wine-tasting bench next to a can of Fanta he'd just consumed. Because it was hot. Because it was a West Australian summer. Which now meant he was in a lot of trouble.

With Wynand uncontactable, the job had to be given to Bryson: drive to Perth, find Taylor and Derek, retrieve the two torture devices. Which also meant Bryson was unhappy and would have it in for Wynand when he returned.

Wynand, for dumb reasons regarding potential accolades from the boss, was in the main wine cellar. Doing a job of his own initiative. The wine cellar was the underground storage room, about halfway down the property line between the hotbox and the front of house. He figured his boss was under a high level of stress, which he was, which was also a dangerous position to be in as an employee. He knew Van Breeman needed all cogs and chains to be in place, turning, working, getting things done. So Wynand took it upon himself to get busy. Something he thought the boss would appreciate. Raise his standing in the food chain. He figured he'd take care of the empty wine barrels. Transfer them down to the lower end of the winery into the maintenance cabin. But it wasn't a priority task. The job wasn't necessary. He'd already proved himself competent with the kidnapping, and this would effectively bring that job back down to irrelevant. Now, he couldn't be contacted. Leaving his mobile phone back in the gallery was an amateur move. Possibly fatal.

Irrespective of his title as a vineyard operator, Wynand was basically a lowly, entry-level farmhand. A run-around. There to perform rudimentary labouring tasks. Part of his duties, however, did involve moving empty wine barrels from the cellar to the maintenance cabin, and from the wine-press facility to the cellar. Both of which he considered himself quite good at. Using a tractor and trailer, he would regularly move the empty casks to the maintenance cabin's rear wall – where all the wooden barrels went to die. Stacked in two rows, one on top of the other. Waiting for an ashen death. Or maybe reused as ottomans, wall art or bar tables. The maintenance cabin was a large structure built fifty metres in front of the hotbox and horse stables with a wide dusty courtyard separating them in the middle. The cabin was built specifically for property maintenance, laid with a huge patch of concrete worn smooth and spoiled with stains of oil. Namely used for storage. Barrels, tractors, gardening equipment. It might only have been fifty metres from where Lydia sat fighting for her soul, but it was exactly where Lincoln was hiding.

> 1920hrs
> Wednesday December 19, 2012
> Somewhere over Margaret River, Western Australia

It took about fifteen minutes before the captain was on his comms, informing Mackay of their location. They were approaching Margaret River, and in two minutes would be flying over his grid reference. His jump was coming up. The jumpmaster motioned to him with hand signals he'd seen before: stand, walk over, gear check, ready to jump.

The jumpmaster moved to the side exit where a red light was illuminated on a panel above the door. Red for 'hold'. He hooked himself up to a safety line then hauled the side door open. A whistling rush of wind blew in, then vanished. Mackay stood steady on his feet. Relaxed, and ready. No need to anchor himself into the moment by psyching up with self-talk or taking deep breaths. His only wish was to be out the door and on the ground. Hunting. He looked out the exit to the world beyond. The horizon was lit with birthing tones of pinks, purples, and oranges. The colours materialising from nowhere, like an invisible artist sweeping a watery brush across the sky. Minute by minute the sun disappeared against the edge of the Earth and the colours became deeper and more vivid. Filtered gloriously between scattered clouds wisping by like soft lazy sheep. In the moment, he wished Cross could see it with him.

The soldier who'd helped Mackay check his straps also stood. He motioned a twirl figuration with his finger, gesturing for Mackay to turn around. He looked him over with a final visual sweep and gave a thumbs up. For the second time he slapped Mackay hard across the shoulder.

'You got this shit,' he said. 'See you when I'm looking at you.'

Mackay strapped the night-vision goggles over his head, leaving it switched off with the lens above his eyes. No use draining the battery yet, there was nothing much to see jumping from ten thousand feet. He pulled the folded sheet of paper with the winery coordinates Nutty had given him, set the numbers into his GPS and placed it back in his front vest pocket. The jumpmaster checked in with the captain through his headset and ushered Mackay forward to the exit. Both men stood waiting, staring at nothing, saying nothing. The jumpmaster didn't move. Five seconds passed, then ten. Mackay watched and listened to the wind push its way inside and play around with the chains and tie-downs. Finally, the jumpmaster raised an arm as the red light flicked on above the exit. He held out three fingers, then two, then one. The red light switched off, the green light switched on. The jumpmaster pointed out the door.

Mackay jumped and left the craft.

Ten thousand feet.

The wind screamed and ripped Mackay backwards while gravity sucked him down. He fell twenty feet before the static line snatched straight and detached, spitting him out at forty-five degrees past the aircraft's tail. The last of the evening's fiery orange vanished, slowly drawing the infinite space outside into shadows of cool grey. The land below was set for a mild, dry night. No chance of showers. Maybe some scattered clouds and dusting of stars, and the beam from a half-lit moon if he was lucky.

Once the parachute exploded it was steady sailing. Over the darkening land below, Mackay was still able to make out the basic forms and undulations in the terrain. Most of which was farmland, forest, and estates with wineries. Roads and houses spread and scattered in every direction. Street and building lights were minimal. Occasionally blinking here and there, but mostly it was indistinct.

Eight thousand feet.

Mackay's memory of parachute training at Aldershot was partly blurred. A three-week block of training going years back. Short days that were fun and easy: deploying the parachute, exiting the craft, safe landing techniques. The nights were half filled with rugby training while the other half was filled with booze. Basically, a holiday camp. From the training, the most difficult aspect was controlling the steering toggles for a safe landing. Adjustment and alignment was everything. And if winds were high, you'd really want to be paying attention, or your legs and back were gone.

Five thousand feet.

Mackay now had a clearer picture of what was a safe landing area and what wasn't. The dusky patterns of land below varied in formation and size. As gravity pulled him closer, a clearing between the dark forest head became obvious. He chartered his course towards it, adjusting the chute's steering lines to a lighter patch of land next to a perimeter of forest growth. Nothing else was prominently visible. Landing along the forest perimeter meant he was more likely to touch down with ideal concealment. If the landing was satisfactory, he could easily go to ground and hunker down unnoticed. Mackay checked his altimeter.

Three thousand feet.

Mackay could still make out the horizon in the darkness, which would add greater reference on his height when slowing his descent rate. Guiding the canopy to the landing zone meant constantly adjusting the toggles. A small pull here, a hard tug there. Finesse was key, as was continuously controlled movement. And experience. Which Mackay didn't have much of.

Two thousand feet.

The swirling breeze grew stronger the faster the ground leapt up at him. Bad news. The fluttering gusts pulling at his clothes, hooked under the canopy briefly, then died. Strengthening for a moment then tapering away. On repeat. Mackay needed to modify his flight path in order to reach his landing zone: a field of wild grass further up the forest perimeter. He pulled gently on the left toggle for a flat turn and angled parallel along an outer edging of trees.

One thousand feet.

Mackay was able to slow the canopy's drag through the air – pulling evenly on both toggles to ready his alignment next to the tree line. Then a second current of breeze broke his line of descent. More bad news. The surge of air lifted and pulled him away from the open field and above the forest instead. The clearing was too far. If he didn't whip his canopy back to the clearing, he'd be caught up in a tonne of branches. Ripping through his legs and torso. Slashing and scarring his body worse than it already was. At worst, he'd hit a branch or trunk thick enough to finish him for good. Instantly.

Five hundred feet.

Mackay pulled a hard left on the toggle, tipping him back towards the open field. But gravity rules, and he was descending faster than expected. A flash of forgotten memory jolted in his head. Something from his training course. The lower you are to Earth, the faster everything accelerates at you. Let nothing hinder your landing or the ground will end you. The field was too far away and Mackay was too low. It would be a tidy miracle if he cleared the expanse of trees in time. By a wing and a prayer. Otherwise, the vastness of looming forest would swallow him like a volcanic mouth.

Mackay maintained a strong pull on the left toggle, but it wasn't enough. The trees kept rushing. He kept drifting over, and at three hundred feet, he began hitting leaves. Then branches. Reaching and mauling at his legs. There was nothing he could do. He tucked his legs up and flared the canopy, pulling both toggles down as hard as he could. One last attempt at gliding towards the clearing. His body kept dropping. Coursing through the thick growth.

Mackay let go of the toggles and covered his face with his arms. If he was to make it, even if his body was broken, he still wanted to be able to see. Suddenly he felt a passage of air around his legs. No leaves, no branches. Nothing but breeze. His body jerked hard. Once, then twice. His canopy had stopped. Caught and tangled somewhere in the growth above. Good news. His body bounced around a couple times, then slowed to a gentle bob and sway, dancing in mid-air like a marionet. He did a quick mental check for any injuries. Legs, feet, and vitals. All intact. Nothing sliced open, just a few bruises. Easily managed. He breathed deep with an exhaled sigh of relief then looked down. He was closer to the ground than he thought. A two-metre drop at best. Three metres at worst. He double-checked the height with his night vision. Better than using the altimeter, which was useless this close to the ground.

Mackay fitted the night vision which had enough clarity to pick up individual strands of wild grass below. Which made him feel better in terms of his height. A clean drop without injury. He opened the top of the backpack, grabbed the seal pup knife and sliced himself free from the tangled mess of cords. As he dropped, he immediately fell sideways to distribute the landing blow evenly. Another tip for amateurs he'd learned. Better to let the body take an impact horizontally than sending jarring shockwaves through bone, joints and ligaments.

The landing was soft enough, namely due to the abundance of wild grass cushioning Mackay's body. And the ground consistency was firm, not marshy, which was a plus. The thirsty heat and lack of rain had kept everything nice and dry. Mackay stood, refocused his night vision and rotated three-sixty degrees. A slow pirouette, taking in observations and sound. He noted a wide-open clearing only a few paces away, and as for sound, it was quiet as a church. Whatever nocturnal animals were about were either taking it easy or waiting to start their night-time routine: hunting food, discussing ambush plans or finishing off their basic housekeeping. The only sound came from a small crew of cicadas doing their thing, but other than that, everything was at camping volume.

Mackay took out the GPS and stepped off. According to the coordinates, the clearing he could see through the trees was in a north-westerly direction. After twenty-two paces, just before the forest's edge, two large, dark boulders began to shape-shift and elongate in front of him. Hulking figures rising to over six-feet tall. They ran straight at him. Moving fast. Bounding and weaving through the shrubbery. Mackay had no weapon in hand, so he went to ground. Leopard-crawling on his guts back behind the closest tree. He rummaged in his backpack for one of the Glocks, found it, then slowly raised on his elbows to aim and observe. The figures kept coming. Without warning, the figures changed course. Dodged right and cut away. As they faded, the moon's silver glimmer lit up their true form. Mackay let out a chestful of humiliated air. Two kangaroos. Nothing overly threatening. Big ones. Likely male, having a feed. Night-time routine. Or maybe they were male and female, mating. Either way they were probably annoyed. Disturbed in their natural habitat, doing their thing.

Mackay regained his composure.

'Fucking kangaroos,' he said.

He stood and walked back to the clearing. At that point, Mackay thought humans might just be easier to deal with.

1920hrs
Wednesday December 19, 2012
Frans & Hoek Winery, Western Australia

Kimbala bunched a second wad of Lydia's hair in his fist and hacked at the lengths with the shears. Nice and close to the base of her neck. He expected her to cower and scream, but she just let him do it. Which bothered him. Every other woman he'd ever played with either retaliated, or cowered, sobbed and wailed. Which he liked. The show he was currently putting on was lacking in excitement. He couldn't continue the proceedings this quiet. He wanted a response. His inner sadist needed some kind of reaction, which would also help in the sexual gratification he got out of it. Otherwise, there was no point. And the ultimate effect of his voodoo wouldn't work. Without the screams and wailing, the restless spirits Kimbala attempted to summon would remain distant and passive – passing over her body unnoticed and ignored. In order to possess a body, a demonic entity needed a show of fear. The unseen thrived off their host's terror.

Kimbala took the pestle and poured the remaining ashen liquid of burnt hair and blood into his mouth. He swallowed part of it, then walked over to the rear wall and stood in front of the relic. With outstretched arms he sprayed what was in his mouth over its entire face: the whites of the skull, the hollowed teeth, the sprawling hair of leather and yarn. Misting it all in red. The contrast of ash, blood and bone above the flickering candles almost brought the face to life. Enticing its host to release her spirit and permit her body to die.

Kimbala stood behind Lydia and resumed the chanting. Incoherent words, low, mumbled and deep. Gibberish to any listening ear. Words he himself probably didn't understand. He then raised his voice and called out to the relic: Damballa. Repeating its name. His vocal pace quickening, his volume amplifying. He stretched out his arms above Lydia's body, bouncing rhythmically on his heels to his own dolorous beat. Lydia remained silent. Kimbala wasn't reaching the full demands of the craft. The voodoo demon would remain idle without a display of terror from its conduit. Kimbala had to up his method to a physical level.

He moved around to face Lydia at her front. He knelt at her feet and scooped up more liquid filth from the tub. He trickled it over Lydia's head, then through her sweaty, mangled mop of hair. It ran down the base of her neck and spine, her collarbone and cleavage, then seeped into the back of her dress in a widening blotch. Then he wiped the remaining burnt crimson down her pale white face. For the final show – his last resort to gain the spirits' attention – he picked up the grinder from the floor in one hand, grabbed Lydia's jaw in the other, lifted her face and slogged it. Lydia's head snapped across her shoulders then flopped lazily back onto her thighs. She coughed and moaned, then eventually began lifting her head. The hit had woken her up, bringing her back to some level of obscure consciousness. Her upper body was loose and sagged, but her lower body was strapped to the stool which made the rebound to her spine brutal. Stretching and tearing at her abdomen and lower back as her torso whipped about. All part of the method. Van Breeman's idea. Old-school African POW tactics.

Kimbala hit her again, and again. Knocking nothing but air and guttural sounds from her lungs. There was nothing vocal. No screams. No wails. Lydia took it all. Took the beating without reaction, internally shutting down her pain responses and bottling it. Nothing escaped her lips but carbon dioxide. Either she was messed up from the burnt toxic vapours, or her internal genetics were hardwired for extreme resilience. Whatever the reason, Lydia was unwavering, angering Kimbala even further.

1930hrs
Wednesday December 19, 2012
Jarrahwood State Forest, outskirts of Frans & Hoek Winery, Western Australia

Out in the clearing, the dome of moonlight over the fields helped Mackay set himself up. He took the backpack from his chest, knelt down and unzipped it wide open. He grabbed the knuckle dusters and slid it inside his pants' pocket, then sheathed the bayonet and seal pup knife inside a belt attachment either side of his waist. One of the Glocks went in the front holster of the vest, the other went inside the rear. He took the altimeter from his wrist, dropped it in the bag and took out the GPS. He found the pocket normally allocated for a thirty-round magazine and slipped it in. A perfect fit. Thanks, Andy.

The next thing he saw glinting inside were three foil medication packets sandwiched with the map of Frans & Hoek winery from the travel centre. All were bundled and tied with a woman's hairband. Two were immunosuppressants, one was his Phragazom bone marrow preserver. Mackay shook his head in disbelief. *Good work, Renee*, he thought. He popped one of each into his mouth, waited for the saliva to build, then swallowed them down.

The time had just clicked over 1900hrs. Phase two was now well underway, which also meant productivity needed to remain on point with little wasted time. An intelligent approach with intelligent responses, all left on Mackay's shoulders. Something he had to bear whichever way the cookie crumbled. He took out the burner phone, switched it on, dialled in the number for Cross's burner and sent her a text:

TOUCHED DOWN. PERFECT LANDING. PREPARING TO MOVE. THANKS FOR THE MEDS.

Mackay slid the phone into a side pocket on the bag then secured the pack to his back. A more comfortable position now the deployment bag was obsolete. Mackay's final detail was his night vision. He positioned the lens back over his eyes, adjusted the focus and double-checked the headwear mounting straps. He pulled the GPS from the front pouch, punched in the coordinates for Frans & Hoek winery, then set sail for a three-kilometre hike.

The terrain was easy to begin with. From the open field flanking the bordering forest, Mackay scaled back in a southern direction for six hundred metres. The topography was flat, and the vegetation was the same wild grass he dropped into when falling out of the parachute. After six hundred metres he took a quarter turn to the left. Directly east for four hundred metres. The vegetation stayed the same, but the land began to rise slightly. Then came a vast change. Instead of wild grass he met a wall of dense forest. Acres of prehistoric timber and undergrowth. According to the GPS, he had approximately nineteen hundred metres of it to work through before getting to the winery. Good thing he was wearing night vision.

The canopy of branches and leaves in the forest crowded over, eliminating any light to peek in from the moon above. Forcing the image inside the night vision to darken to a deep clover. Thousands of behemoth trunks hugged together tightly, doing their best to keep out anything or anyone who didn't belong. Good for hiding, not good for moving.

Mackay trundled slow and steady. The shallow depth of field inside the night vision meant he constantly needed to scan his head; left to right, right to left, picking up as much of his surroundings as he could so he didn't trip or bump into anything. There were tonnes of debris all over the ground. Fallen logs, prickly shrubs, decaying bones. At head and chest height, there were low-lying branches and metres of sprawling spiderwebs, not to mention jagged ends of snapped wood everywhere. Like walking through a land of spears. Beyond the trees and scrub there was nothing to see, only inky blackness. Mackay crept on. Goose-stepping, sidestepping, ducking and weaving all things pointy, all things sticky. He didn't cross any more kangaroos which was a bonus, and the crickets and cicadas continued to perform which helped reference his position. On numerous occasions bats flew and clipped around his head, possums crawled and observed him curiously, while sugar gliders jumped from branch to branch keeping tabs on his movements. The occasional owl swooped and hooted, claiming territory and alerting the night crew of an alien form wandering about like a lost sheep. Beware, friends, this strange species knows not what it does.

Mackay ascended the land for nearly two kilometres until the infrared vision picked up lighter tones breaching out towards an open space. To another clearing. He'd reached the end of the forest density and was about to exit. Escaping what seemed like a never-ending loop of the same sequence of trees, through the same thickets of shrubbery. The dense Australian bushland finally releasing its grasp and granting Mackay his freedom.

> 2000hrs
> Wednesday December 19, 2012
> Jarrahwood State Forest, Western Australia

At the eastern edge of the forest perimeter, Mackay stopped. His GPS had him pinned two hundred metres short of Frans & Hoek winery. He checked his watch. 2000hrs. It'd been a hard-going thirty minutes through slow-rising terrain of broken, Jurassic vegetation untouched for the last millennia. The lay of the land in front continued at a steady incline, only the trees were less crowded, and there wasn't much variation in undulation. It sloped upwards to a point, reached its pinnacle, then flattened out to open ground a hundred metres ahead. He used the GPS to note which direction he was facing. Whether the winery was due east, north-east or south-east. The only options. Anything further north, west or south was back inside the minefield of trees. Where gangs of bats and owls had already given him a pass. A second time through would mean he'd really have to explain himself.

Mackay sidled up against the last tree at the forest's edge and took out the travel centre's map. He peered out into the dark, scanning the distance, looking for any distinguishable structures resembling the map's bird's-eye view of two large buildings. Which, according to his position, should be the first features to appear. And appear they did. The infrared picked up two barn-like structures lit with sharp rows of light like lightsaber beams along the front facades. The light shone out towards the front of the winery, rather than back towards the forest. There were no signboards, advertisements or logos stating the vineyard's name. Which made sense, really. Advertising should be exclusively seen by the masses, out front where visitors travel by car and tour bus on the road. Not out back with the wildlife. He knew he was in the right place.

Mackay had only been to a handful of wineries in his lifetime, and the only area he'd ever set foot in was the front gallery. To him, all other vineyard constructions, for all intents and purposes, looked the same: large storage constructions made of brick, wood and steel. Any extra buildings probably existed as part of a wider, universal winery package: managed gardens, rolling hills, random machinery, random livestock, as well as water tanks and water bodies. All commonplace, all complementing each other.

Mackay moved up the gentle rise of the embankment, visually taking in what he could. The grass and shrubs petered out as he closed in on an approaching fence line. The buildings now one hundred metres away. His peripherals constantly monitored movement. Animal or human. Taking special note of whether he could identify possible security cameras fixed to either of the two cabins. The long, snaking border of wire and pickets shot off for hundreds of metres left and right, then enclosed around acres of grapevines and fields. Beyond the fence, the land revealed a property as big as the day is long. Another four buildings came into view further off in the distance. Six buildings in total scattered the acreage. The growing sheen of a three-quarter moon making them reasonably visible through the night vision.

Mackay removed the lens and head wear, stuffed them into his backpack and allowed his eyes a few moments to adjust to the darkness. He walked thirty paces closer and stopped. The colour illuminating from the two buildings was a dull yellow. Incandescent. Hot light. Yellow like egg yolk, arcing around the edges of the walls in a semi-circle out front. The buildings were old single-storey brick. Built during a time of British growth and rural prosperity after the colonisation of Perth. Sometime in the mid-1800s. On closer inspection, the nearest two cabins seemed to be part of one plot of land, separated with a wide space in the middle. A clearing of sorts, or a courtyard or paddock. Both were warehouse in size, or mini mansion. Both similar in length and width, only that the one in front was built to a taller scale and had a single chimney sticking out the top. Like it was built for a farming family's cottage back in the day. The structure at the back was pitched lower and built with a long extension. A possible storage facility for feed, or a stable for horses considering the scatterings of hay on the ground. Aside from differences in height, the two were built to the same exact dimensions in length and width. In the very centre was a small, gated prism which looked like a hand-operated water pump inside. Old school. Self-supply from the earth.

Mackay dropped to his guts on the rise just outside the forest. From where he lay, the yellow light pooling around the building helped expose the old family cottage for what it was: a wide-open shed with huge storage space. Tailor-made for parking ploughing machinery and modern vineyard tools. All the hardware needed for maintaining a winery to its opportune best. The shed had no doors or gates or securing fittings of any kind. It was simply an open space built into the structure of the cabin. No other buildings were lit on the property. There was no movement anywhere from what he could tell, but he needed to get even closer for a clearer assessment. The casting light had to be either work lights, security lights or motion sensors. And as caution goes, if they were on, they were on for a reason. Mackay had to assume something, or someone, was moving or operating in the area. Animal or human.

Mackay duck-walked fifty metres to the edge of a knoll where the land levelled horizontally along the fence line. Far enough away not to be picked up by any motion sensors, close enough to better gauge any movement around both buildings, front and rear. A minute passed. No movement. Nothing observed, nothing heard. He got back on his guts and leopard-crawled another fifteen metres, tracing the arcing curve of the fence line towards the rear building's side wall. Still concealed, now with a clearer view of the horse stable and the open space between the two structures: the dirt courtyard. He waited behind a thicket of shrubs and grass for ten whole minutes. Nice and low, pressed into the ground. Invisible. Observing on an angle, propped on his forearms. Assessing as much information as he could on the vineyard's security. Patience was key for any recon, an effort in itself. Nobody is born with the natural ability, or tempered care, to wait. Babies, children, even adults, throw tantrums simply because they cannot wait for their next feed, new toy, or computer program to load. It takes practice and nobody learns it better than the military. Hurry-up-and-wait was part of the job. From where he lay in the thicket, Mackay was committed to the evening's activities for the long game. People were relying on him, which meant nothing needed to be rushed. Rushed actions often ended an operation. In the middle of summer in the West Australian heat, lying low and waiting was a breeze.

Scanning his sights to the furthest left and right of the fence line, Mackay passed another five minutes on his guts.

Still no movement. Nothing doing except for the local insects and wildlife. Crickets and cicadas chirped away. A few lonely frogs croaked near a pool or dam singing in their froggy choirs, and then there were the bats. Hundreds of them. Flying low. Screeching, fighting. After another minute, Mackay deemed his observation satisfactory. He got up and traced the fence line for twenty more paces to a position directly behind the closest building. Ten metres from the back wall on the forest side. Twelve at most. He dropped back to his stomach, obscured by darkness, away from the cabin's pool of light.

Part of the cabin's illumination lit up a small security camera fixed into the top of the corner awning. From Mackay's position it was only just noticeable. Like a small triangular smudge, angled diagonally to pick up a wide field of vision. A basic closed-circuit set-up. It was the only one he could spot. Time to get even closer. Mackay got up and scanned the wiring to see if it was electrified. It wasn't. He bent, squatted and twisted his way through, got back on his guts and leopard-crawled ten more metres to the corner edge of the rear wall. Close enough that his left shoulder was touching the brick. A position where the camera's range couldn't pick him up. He poked his head around the corner like a snake, examining and checking for threats. So far so good. He needed another portion of time to evaluate why the lights were on. Whether someone was inside working, whether there were animals about setting off the sensors, or whether they were on as part of night-time protocol. He waited, watched and listened. Two minutes. Still nothing. No movement.

But there was sound.

A low murmur. Like a baby calf calling its mother. Only softer. Faint, like whatever it was, was in pain. Mackay couldn't tell whether it came from his left or right, but he was certain he hadn't seen any cows on the property. A large animal like a cow would have stood out. Easily picked up by his night vision regardless of colour. A thing that big and warm would emit a tonne of heat, the thermal imaging picking it up like blobs of lava. Mackay stood, rounded the corner and paced silently to the cabin's front edge. He tilted his head and listened. The sound came again. Low and long. This time ending in more of a grizzled cry. It came from his left. The wall side. The sound was no animal. It was human, and it was hurting. As much as he wanted to identify the sound and release it from its pain, he couldn't. No good soldier rushes about in a frenzy. There were numerous things to consider. Was the noise some kind of trap? A beckoning call made to throw him into an ambush? Was there more than one person in trouble, or in pain? How many? Would there be innocent bystanders? Was someone inducing the pain? Did they have weapons? Could he take them on? The British military operate at a three-to-one ratio for an attack on an enemy. Mackay was only one man. His best odds for a fight were a one-to-one ratio as a minimum. Lots to think about and even less time to think about it.

2010hrs
Outside the Hotbox

None of it mattered in the end. Any and all considerations were lost in a flicker. Before Mackay took another step he was met by a fast-moving shadowy mass. A large black form ascended upon him from out of nowhere. All he saw coming were the whites of two large ovals: pearl-white eyes, rushing at him like synced fireflies dive-bombing for his face. No time for a considered response. Zero time to pull a weapon. Mackay's senses were abruptly assaulted with a toxic odour. A smoky haze clouded him, penetrating his eyes and lungs. A smell like an overcooked desert carcass. Whatever it was restricted his vision and made him feel sick immediately. Curdling a torrent of bile from his gut, up into his mouth. Before he had time to think or clear his vision, two massive hands attached themselves around his throat, crushing his windpipe. One of the most basic, coldest ways to kill a man. All Mackay could do was resort to instinct, grabbing at the wrists to try and wrench them away. He went to peel at the fingers but all he could think about was air, which he needed immediately. The oxygen supply to his brain was slowing down. Panic was weaselling its way into his system, taking hold. This was it. A bigger, stronger force had him. It was taking him down and there was nothing he could do about it.

Mackay's internal fight responses finally responded. He tried lifting his legs, knees to chest to try and kick himself away. But whatever, or whoever, it was that had him was too close. All over him like a squid, and devastatingly strong. The fingers around his neck sunk in deeper, shutting off every artery and vein. He could feel himself choking out, his lungs fading, everything getting colder inside. His head pounded under immense pressurised blood. He tried kicking out again. No use. The mass was in too close, its hot breath all over Mackay's face. The same awful scent of decay annihilating his senses.

Mackay lifted his body and raised his legs around the mass's waist. He tried moving his hips higher, shuffling his thighs over the mass's shoulders. If he could get one leg in front of its face, he might be able to pry the arms and hands from his throat with his body length. Like a lever. That was no use either. Another failed attempt. The mass lifted, then dropped Mackay into the ground, expelling more wind from his lungs. Mackay started to pulse and shake and kick. Involuntarily. He was convulsing. Shutting down because of lack of blood and oxygen to the brain. Properly going under. Everything he and Cross had planned was now in vain. He had maybe ten, twenty seconds left at the most. If he was to remain in this position, he would certainly die. Lincoln would die. Malvin, Neve, Angus and who knows how many others also dead, all for nothing.

Mackay could do one thing only. He went for the eyes. Pressing both his thumbs in as hard as possible into those pearl-white balls. The mass's eyelids closed immediately. Unfortunately, Mackay's thumbnail was short and couldn't cut into the skin, but his right thumb had wiggled into the cornea enough to dig behind the eyeball and try and pop it from its socket. Which he succeeded with. The left eyeball left the mass's skull. Which was when he let go of Mackay's throat and cried out.

The mass stood, growling like a wild dog. The end of the eyeball hung from inside his head and dangled at the cheek. Mackay sucked air like a newborn. Like he'd never had oxygen in his life. His diaphragm struggled to take it at first, then like a backdraft it flooded in. The rush of air, however, brought his sense of taste back, which made him convulse. He had to stop, keel over, retch and empty his bowels. Ejecting the lingering burnt rubber so he could gather himself and reset. Ready for round two. His round.

Mackay got back on his feet to reclaim some sense of stability. He took a moment, forcing himself to think and reset. Some dizziness remained, but it didn't hinder his thought processes. He knew he had a Glock at the front and rear of his vest, and that he needed to use one immediately. He pulled the one from the front and got a shot off, targeting the mass's upper body before it rushed in again, knocking the weapon out of his hand with a meaty swipe. The mass didn't go down. Didn't change his forward assault one bit, he just kept swiping. Luckily Mackay had enough returned blood and oxygen to gauge his peripheral judgement. He stepped away, dodging the blows, drawing the mass further into the light to see what he was really up against. On clearer inspection, the hulk of the thing was immense. Not the biggest Mackay had ever seen, but a good head taller and a barn door wider than he was. Thick with fat and muscle, and skin so dark he was near invisible in the night. A genetic colour inherited from African tribes going back thousands of years. His shirt, pants and beard were black too which didn't help. The only thing that made him stand out were his partially white sneakers and the whites of his eyes, which was now down to one, staring hellishly at Mackay.

The mass was at a disadvantage. One eye hanging from its socket and a bullet hole somewhere in his chest or stomach. Mackay had the upper hand. He was still breathing, had no bullet holes, and both eyes were intact. Plus, he had a second Glock holstered on his back. He tried to draw it but fumbled – a second failed attempt. He hadn't rehearsed the movement well enough for a smooth reach, draw, fire. The mass kept at him with good form. Closing distance. He rocketed forward with double hooks at Mackay's head. One fist connected, cracking the bridge of Mackay's nose. A single knuckle splitting the skin and breaking cartilage. Mackay kept his ground, but the hulk's huge black paws just kept swiping. He never slowed and never stopped. The big guy had to work hard though, shuffling his weight to match Mackay's change in direction as he dodged the blows. Defence and stepping were all Mackay really learned back at the red ant's gym, and not much in terms of punching as an attacking tool. With the size difference between them, even if he was a skilled boxer, Mackay would still fare poorly. Not that he couldn't give it a red-hot go. He never had much technical mastery, but he usually got the job done. His Irish fists, if well timed, could do plenty of damage even if it didn't look pretty. Against this heavyweight though, even if contact was good, it would most likely bounce off his sheer bulk like a blowfly hitting glass. The fight would go on and on. Mackay could easily get gone and hide, but it wouldn't help. Wherever he ran to, the mass would still be out there. Mackay *had* to fight. So, he kept fending the blows, dodging and waiting for the right time. For a split-second opening to react.

Mackay's hands stayed high with his legs bent, like the red ant had taught him. Toed on the balls of his feet. If an opening arose, he needed to be ready. In and out in an instant. The swiping motion from the black mass, though fast, wasn't lightning quick. Wasn't practised. Aggression without control. His weight transfer was his weak point, which Mackay needed to use to his full advantage. Use his agility to feign the mass toward one direction, then deliver his blow in another, while he was off balance. After two consecutive swipes, Mackay went in for a fake hook to the left jaw. It didn't work. The hulk didn't take the bait, he just kept swinging. Seething with tunnel vision. Mackay changed tactics. He needed to physically move the mountain, which he was quite sure he was capable of. The mass was big, but not the biggest human he'd ever seen. He'd lifted and tackled men twice as big on the rugby field. All of them props. Gargantuan men used to prevent the opposition from breaking through the defence. And most of the time those men were literally running at him, not dancing in circles.

After four more swipes Mackay ducked a right hook, sidestepped and moved under the blow, missing the fist within an inch of his life. Just enough to find himself facing the mass's backside – right where he needed to be. The man's blockhead and frayed beard were aimed directly at the side wall of the building. Mackay moved immediately. He gave one hard shove against the back of the mass's arm, just below the shoulder, putting the crazed animal off balance into a perfect tackle position.

Mackay went for it.

Nice and Low. Shoulder up under the mass's backside, both arms wrapped around the upper thighs. Mackay lifted the man then ran at the wall with the hulk's head leading in front. All up it took ten strides. A moderate jog was the best Mackay could do for the distance, but even at jogging pace, the mass's head hit the wall hard enough to shake the foundations. The noise clearly audible like a boot slugging a football. Even the horses next door kicked up a whinny. Any normal man would have been killed on impact. Or put into a deep concussion. That said, the mass just got back on his feet and turned around.

The turn, however, was slow. The impact to the wall obviously shook the guy up, triggering a lack of gait control which allowed Mackay time to realise two things: it would either take a lot of bullets to put this guy down, or he would have to repeat the tackle into the wall. Maybe a second or even third time if it was going to do any proper damage.

Before the hulk rotated enough to face Mackay, Mackay went instinctive. Reacting with a third option. A dogged primeval attack aimed right for the cervical spine. The soft tissue at the back of the neck. The impact needed to be strong enough to penetrate the mass's neck fat. A protective layer, rubbery and dense like a walrus. From feet to fist, the well-timed strike needed to happen immediately. It was the only thing Mackay could think of that might drop the guy.

With the mass half turned and the back of his neck exposed, Mackay drove home the blow. A hook from the soles of his shoes to the knuckles of his fist. The elasticity in his new ribs aiding the kinetic rotation like a loaded spring. Complete range of motion into the base of the skull. Mackay broke through the mass's spine.

Not much was heard as his fist connected. A single whap was all it was. A dull clap of the hand. It took two seconds before the mass began to stumble. His feet hobbled, trying to maintain balance but he failed. His legs turned to jelly, then he dropped. Vertically to the knees first like he was praying, then slumping horizontally to the ground. His legs twitched, jerking the knees and flapping the feet with a weak pulsating spasm. Normal considering the kinetic impact of Mackay's fist displacing the vertebrae. The twitching lasted maybe five or ten seconds, then he stopped moving altogether.

'May the cat eat you,' Mackay said aloud. 'And may the devil eat the cat.'

Mackay watched the body for a whole minute. Just to be sure before checking for any rise and fall in the chest. There was nothing. All clear. Bish bash bosh.

2020hrs
Inside the Hotbox

Satisfied the mass was down and out, Mackay went and collected his Glock from the dirt. The one from the front pouch. He checked the working parts, holstered it, then moved towards the door of the cabin. The first door leading into the big square room on the left. The hotbox. No longer a guest house or bedroom from the good old farming days. The door was light, like it breathed open all on its own. As if it was being pulled inward by an invisible force. Inside, Mackay first noticed the sickening odour. The same musky stench the black mass had sprayed into his face, showering his senses with flavours of burnt rubber and rotting meat. Next, he noticed an ugly, maniacal image on the back wall. A relic of some type. An idol made to look like a face. And from what Mackay could tell, African tribal. The image was of a large demonic skull looming over the entirety of the room, taking up the top half of the rear wall. It had bone, leather and thick twisted thread with an open mouth and teeth black as ash. The hair on the skull's head sprawled out in tufts of twig and fur. No matter where you stood, it was as if its malevolent focus was always on you.

Something was seriously wrong inside. Once again, the toxicity of the smell constricted Mackay's breathing. And he was sweating profusely like in a sauna. All of his senses communicated the need to leave immediately. His focus was already drifting, dizziness and confusion shutting down the clarity of his spatial awareness. Mackay pulled up his undershirt and covered his mouth and nose as best he could. Even then, the smell was so powerful it was a struggle to stop retreating to clean, fresh air, but he had to stay. The sight of a slumped shape in the centre of the room required attention.

Beneath the relic, a line of candles lit up a shape seated on a stool, strapped at the legs. As Mackay stepped further inside the shape's form became clearer, evolving into the petite structure of a woman. Alive and breathing. The finer, smaller features of her neck, back and arms rose and fell ever so slightly as she breathed the dank musk. Her head hung low over her knees, her hair short, chopped not cut – the straggly ends sticking together in wet tufts at the base of her neck. Her feet were immersed in a large tub filled with liquid and a black head bag lay on the floor behind her. Mackay knelt down. The stench near the tub was at its worst. On closer inspection, the liquid from the tub had spilled out onto the floor. It was thick. A mixture of blood and ashy chunks of what seemed to be the remains of her once well-managed locks. Bile covered the woman's shirt and pants. Heaved out of her system and forced in only one direction.

Mackay placed a hand under her chin and rotated her head towards him. There was a small air of familiarity about her, like he'd seen her somewhere before, but he couldn't place where. Not then and there. The woman was breathing, but he still needed to check her face. Observe her mouth and eyes, feel the pulse underneath her jaw, then assess her body for any major wounds. All part of basic battle first aid. Mackay peeled her eyelids back.

There was no pupil. Nothing but the whites. But the white wasn't normal. It was murky. Dirty-yellow and bloodshot to hell. He'd never seen anything like it. Made her look like an empty vessel. A blank canvass of a human stuck somewhere in time, leaving her diminished and stonewashed.

As he lowered her head back down, she let out a long, low groan. Discordant and hateful. Her primal pain responses wanting whoever had done this to her to stop. It was the same wounded sound he'd heard outside the cabin. The cry was reactive, the pain expressed vocally from a subconscious state. Most of her face was plump with blood. Like she'd been hit, and not just once. Mackay checked her pulse. It was fast, like she was in the midst of running a marathon. Fear had taken her senses for a ride and wasn't letting go. The horrid scent invading her body had taken its toll. Mackay needed to move her outside into fresh air immediately. Getting her away from the toxic smell was the first best thing he could do for her.

Mackay checked the stool. It was bolted to the floor not going anywhere. So, he took his seal pup knife and cut through the four zip-ties keeping her legs together. He undid a leather belt keeping her lower half fastened to the stool, then raised her chest and stomach and did a vital organ check for any lacerations or punctures. He checked her back, limbs and neck. All okay. There was however, one big track mark on the inside of her arm. The soft inner side of the elbow. A hole made by a big syringe, drawing out her blood and then emptied into the tub. Or by a needle meant for wound irrigation, shooting medical adrenalin or kick-starting hearts. Why the woman's feet were in a tub of her own blood was beyond Mackay. Although, from what he could piece together looking around the room, it was obvious. All part of a dark arts practice – the smell, the relic, the genetics of the dead mass. The setting and situation pointed to one thing. Voodoo. Why out here on a winery on the coast of

Western Australia was anyone's guess. From Mackay's end, he wasn't there to find out. There were higher priorities on his list.

Mackay cut through a fifth zip-tie binding the woman's hands behind her back. Before her body slackened, Mackay wrapped one arm around her legs, the other around her back. He lifted her into his arms and walked outside. As her bloody face sheened in the night it suddenly came to him, he remembered where he'd seen her before. On the television in the bed and breakfast. The reporter, first on the scene. Breaking the news of the slaying.

With the stable only a few metres next door along the cabin, Mackay took it as the best and only option as a safe place. Lie her down, get her rested. He wasn't experienced in farms or equine establishments, his knowledge base was limited to the basics learned in school; horses, horse accessories and hay were usually linked together. And hay was soft. At least if it was laid out in a spread. He could leave the woman inside the stable until an emergency response team arrived. Although unconscious and with no clear responses, her main concerns were satisfied. She was breathing and had no major wounds. Her blood loss, though substantial, wasn't at dangerous levels. She wasn't suffering because of blood loss, her symptoms had come about from something else entirely. Mackay had to move on. There was another urgent task he needed to attend to. He also needed to communicate back to Cross. On the hour, every hour. Or she might resolve to thinking there was a problem, and who knew what chain of events that would lead to.

2030hrs
The Stable

At the entrance to the stable was a wooden gate, built chest high for stable-hands, trainers and owners to easily peer in. It kept the interior space open, allowing the horses to see out without becoming claustrophobic, which horses tended to be naturally. There was an accessible spring-latch on the right, permitting the door to swing inwards. As Mackay carried the woman inside, he noted four individual horse stalls, but only two horses. One in each of the front stalls facing opposite each other, watching a stranger carry a woman into their quarters. As to what kind of horses they were, Mackay couldn't tell. Both looked black in the dull security lights. They weren't ponies or Clydesdales, that much he could ascertain. Even with what dingy light was available, Mackay could tell the place was low rent. Everything was basic and old with upkeep kept to a minimum. The bulk of the owner's cash obviously spent elsewhere, which narrowed down Mackay's final assessment: the beasts were ex-racehorses. Bought after their golden bookmaking years, now kept purely for sport and leisure.

They both started up as soon as Mackay's hand flicked the latch, expressing their disapproval. Like the possums, owls and sugar gliders. They didn't become overly dramatic though, Mackay guessed because they were a little older and wiser. Just a couple of old-timers who'd seen plenty of life. Been there, done that. Mostly they just stirred and shuffled their hoofs, with some added low-level snorting for good measure. All very understandable.

Mackay eyed the two empty stalls in the far back for mounds of hay, which were loaded with them. All in rectangular prisms in stacks of six, built up around the walls somewhere between seven and eight feet high. Whoever stacked them had to have done it by hand, which wasn't an easy task, and likely achieved by a big, capable human. No machinery would have been small enough to fit inside to do it. Mackay wanted to assume it was the dead mass whose spine he snapped, but if it wasn't him, then whoever loaded them in was probably even bigger. Mackay had dealt with some of the world's biggest humans on the rugby field, but if he had to deal with another monstrosity, he wasn't sure what the outcome would be a second time round.

Inside the rear stalls was enough hay to sleep a whole platoon on. Obviously, the central hub for storing the roughage. Mackay eased the woman against the inner stall wall for a moment, then tossed up a cushy bed of straw in the back corner. Furthest from any prying eyes. Concealed even from the two stroppy steeds at the front. He then laid her down on the spread in recovery position: head turned over an outstretched arm, mouth angled down, one leg bent to stop the body from rolling. First aid standard the world over. Same as for a soldier on the battlefield.

Mackay sat down next to her, unzipped his backpack and took out his water bottle. He took a small mouthful, swallowed, then opened the woman's mouth just enough to tip a drizzle in. No response. If anything, she'd absorbed a few drops on the inside of the mouth. Two or three mills at best. At least she was in fresh air, albeit with the mixed aroma of tangy manure and earthy hay. Typical odours found in stables, but it wasn't too bad considering where she'd come from.

Mackay took a second mouthful of water, capped it, then pulled out his night vision. He made one final check of the woman's breathing and pulse, then exited the stable – leaving her with the two steeds for company. He moved twenty paces out past the yolky-yellow light of the cabin, past the hand-operated water pump, and stepped into shadow. Somewhere between the two buildings in an empty, dusty void.

The brick building in front was a hundred yards ahead. Dark at the rear, light at the front. He checked his immediate surrounds and noticed he was standing on a dirt courtyard with blooming patches of weeds as thick as tent pegs. Which was when he realised what he was standing on. Or at least what it used to be: an old horse paddock. A training field. It wasn't big enough for racing by any stretch of the imagination. Rather, it was for breaking them in. Readying them to plough the fields back in the day. Only it wasn't fenced off anymore and looked like it hadn't been for a very long time. Before Mackay refocused his lens, or even thought about which direction of the darkness he'd move to next, the sound of a vehicle started up. Something slow, likely fuelled by diesel and propelled with big tyres. Ten seconds after that, from a two o'clock position, a set of headlights swung into view.

> 2045hrs
> Wednesday December 19, 2012
> Frans & Hoek Winery, Western Australia

Once the wine barrels were emptied, either decanted into bottles or transferred to new barrels, they were moved to the maintenance cabin for storage. Placed along the rear wall of the large shed behind all the machinery. If the barrels were in good condition, they were cleaned and taken apart, refabricated into tables, stools and artwork. If they were spoiled or broken, they were used as firewood. The shed was essentially set up as a parking bay for the forklifts, trailers, lawnmowers and tractors – all to help till the earth and haul large bits and pieces like the barrels or forest debris. And on the odd occasion, a dead animal or person.

As a vineyard operator, Wynand was usually tasked the menial jobs. The run-around stuff. The underground cellar where he'd been for the last twenty minutes – initiating his own menial task – had two empty hogshead barrels that needed to be moved. Transported down to the maintenance cabin. Which was far from a priority job, but Wynand wanted to prove himself. Show the boss he was self-motivated with a sense of pride in his employment. The two barrels Wynand was moving were of the larger oak variety. Three-hundred litre capacities. Normally Wynand would have Snowy helping him, but Snowy had been sent through the woodchipper and was now part of the compost fertilising the grapes. Moving the massive barrels from the cellar to the cabin would usually take about forty-five minutes – if there were two people on the job. But since Wynand was on his own, that time frame would easily stretch out closer to two hours. Both barrels had to be loaded onto a trailer with a pallet jack, winched out of the cellar with a tractor, and finally towed down to the machinery shed. The one with huge storage space built in front of the horse stables and hotbox. Where only minutes before Kimbala was beating their female hostage's face in with a pestle grinder.

Wynand did well, completing the job in only an hour and a half. He'd reversed the trailer efficiently into the empty shed's floor space, moving it fore and aft with minimal gear changes. One of his few skills. Once parked, he rolled the two barrels off, then danced them up and down like a seesaw until the kinetic motion tipped the edge of the barrel onto its flat bottom. Which was three-quarters of the job done. All he had to do then was raise the barrels with the forklift and stack them along the back wall with the rest of the spares. With the job done, there were now twenty-two empty barrels in total. A row of eleven on the bottom, eleven on the top.

What Wynand didn't know, was that halfway along the two rows there was an old, concealed firepit in the brickwork. A hollow edifice built into the cabin's wall, likely during its original construction back in the 1800s. Tucked away by the bottom row of barrels long before Wynand had been given a job there. As Wynand manoeuvred the forklift to place the second barrel on top of the first, he overshot the forklift's motion, rolling a couple inches further than needed, ramming the barrel into the brickwork. The impact between wood and brick wasn't especially loud, but considering the spacious flooring, the collision sent an echoing shockwave through the wall. The crunch of wood against brick splintered the side of the barrel, shuddering the walls enough for them to move. Still, it was loud enough to scare Van Breeman's old racehorses into a whinny back in the stables, as well as a small boy curled up inside the obscured firepit.

At first, Wynand thought the separate shriek to the horse's whinny was part of the oak scraping against brick. Or creaking from the metal bands that tie the wooden slats around the cask. The bilge loop. Metal, wood and brick together in a forced impact could potentially make all sorts of sounds. Except, that singular shriek lasted a fraction of a second longer than everything else. Which made Wynand second guess whether the sound had anything to do with the oak barrel at all, and whether there was some local wildlife stuck behind the bottom row of casks. The direction of the sound was unmistakeable – arising low from behind the middle of the two rows.

Wynand shut the forklift off, paused and listened. Then stepped out to take a look. He moved to the centre of the row where he figured the noise had come from. He could see the gapped fissure where the structure of the bricks hollowed inwards into a wide recess. Different from the uniform structure of the wall. There was a cubicle large enough to fit an office desk and a filing cabinet. An unmistakeable fireplace. The cabin's centrepiece. Made grand and opulent back in the day when the cold nights brought the family together for warmth. To play cards, drink whiskey and smoke tobacco. A section of space Wynand had never seen before.

To climb over, Wynand needed to reach the top edge of the barrelhead for grip, then jam his feet inside the nooks between the stack for balance. The barrels still weighed a solid number even without the liquid grape, so clambering over was a non-issue. Before looking into the recess, Wynand braced in anticipation for a wild animal – a dingo, possum, goanna, or at worst a king brown or tiger snake, coiled up ready to attack. Take his face off. Maybe they were all in there, crouched, hiding out, teamed up. Planning a takeover. Weirder things have happened.

As he steadied himself and leaned over the top, Wynand's hesitancy in shielding himself vanished. There was no motley crew of animals staging a guerrilla attack. There was nothing there. What he did notice though, was that the recess was deceptively wider in its breach. Wide enough to slide down into it himself, so he figured he'd drop in to take a proper look. Wynand reversed his clambering process, scrubbing his boots down the wall for support, then dropped inside the mouth of the hearth. Which was when he heard a shuffling noise from inside. A shimmying sound. Nice and close. Steadied with rubber and cloth. Wynand stepped back so his feet were flush with the main wall. Just in case whatever was inside did strike. He knelt down, tightly squeezed between brick and oak, then leaned in for a look inside the void. The light from the ceiling didn't project very deep inside – creeping in only about a metre then cutting straight to black. Wynand squinted. To his best ability he could just make out the vague shape of a small pair of shoes. Emerging from the shoes were two small legs sprouting upwards to a pair of knees. He couldn't make out anything else.

For Wynand's intelligence, or lack thereof, he still had some fundamental wiring capacity in his head. It took a few moments before the synapses in the back of his brain clicked, concluding that those shoes and legs were of a small boy. The missing, runaway six-year-old from three days prior. A child who had holed himself inside an old, concealed fireplace for safety. In fear of his life. After three days he was certainly starved and dehydrated. Traumatised and in need of his mother and father, longing desperately for safety and comfort. Wynand smiled and reached in. The child cried out a second time.

EIGHT

REDEMPTION

> 2100hrs
> Wednesday December 19, 2012
> Frans & Hoek Winery, Western Australia

Mackay had been watching Wynand work for about ten minutes before he heard the cry. He had moved around the back of the building, forty yards out behind a sloping drop in the landscape. Low and flat on his stomach. Blending into the darkness. Over the course of those ten minutes, Mackay took the phone from his backpack and sent off a text. Completing his second communication back to Cross. On the hour, every hour. Which he hadn't done since crash-landing into the forest canopy.

ALL GOOD. OBSERVING A WORKER ON THE GROUNDS. ENGAGEMENT TBC.

Brief and concise. Let her know he was still in the game, completing the mission as planned. Which almost didn't happen, thanks to the unhinged witch doctor. All other details could come out in the wash later.

Mackay bided his time. He observed the skinny worker in the shed and regrouped his thoughts. He watched the man do a decent job of reversing the trailer. He watched him roll two massive oak barrels from the trailer to the shed floor, then watched him jump into a forklift and manoeuvre the barrels onto a second row of casks along the rear wall. Then the man made an error of judgement – driving the forklift too far forward and cracking the second barrel against the brickwork. A horse from the back stable let out a stark neigh. Following that the man shut the engine down and paused. He went still, as if listening intently, head cocked to the side. The human version of what a dog or kangaroo does when pricking up its ears. After ten seconds, he got out of the forklift and began climbing the barrels, disappearing over the top. Thirty seconds later, Mackay heard a scream. Clear as day.

A cry like that, for an angry man listening in the dark, sent fast, immediate messages into his auditory cortex. It rang out into the night, prickled across Mackay's hair cells and created a picture in his mind's eye. Deep inside the temporal lobe. In that moment, at that exact time and location, Mackay knew it was the scream of a scared little boy. A boy who, without a doubt, was family. Part of his blood. A scream that belonged to Lincoln. A switch flicked inside him. No matter what kind of human being you were – good or bad – a child's distressing cry can yield inconceivable things deep within. Heartache, rage, compassion, hatred. Mackay's fight response kicked in. His immediate impulse. Honed from years of combat training and on-field rugby experience. The only other instinct that went hand in hand alongside it, was to save.

Mackay tossed up various options for his approach. With force? Violence first, questions later? Or reccy elsewhere to save his strength? The guy wasn't a boss or a high-level operator, that was a no-brainer. He was obviously an underling. A lacky chump doing a lacky chump's job. A farmhand. However, anyone working on the grounds this late was no innocent front-of-house staff either. Coming off the back of dealing with the witch doctor, finding the beaten woman, and now hearing Lincoln cry out, Mackay was under no illusion the man was part of the wider operation. A skinny cog in a big machine. Either he was a groundsman with information, or he was an ignorant groundsman who needed a wake-up call. With all things considered, on this night, ignorance was not an excuse.

Mackay narrowed down two methods of engagement. He could run straight inside the cabin with force. Complete shock and awe. Eliminate the threat, grab the boy and get the hell out of there. Retreat by way of the forest and communicate a pick-up reference point with Cross. Dark and unseen amongst his nocturnal friends. Or he could take a slower approach: eliminate the threat, leave the boy where he was, take out any remaining parties, come back for the boy afterwards. This was the safest choice, but it wouldn't be very kind to a lost, distressed child. Some recons were better suited to be drawn out – waiting days for the right moment, then crawl in and neutralise. Slow, cold and merciless. This wasn't that moment. Lincoln's cry was serious, dictating an immediate problem requiring an immediate response. He needed someone familiar, someone who could tell him everything would be okay, even if it was just a simple warm hug. Hearing that shriek meant Mackay's time limit had been shortened to a very narrow margin. Lincoln's scream meant bad news. And bad news doesn't get better with age.

Mackay went with a combination of the two options. He was making good time and would use that advantage to get to Lincoln first, then clear all buildings of any personnel involved with the operation. Pick them off one by one. He rolled to his side and ran his hand over his thigh, confirming he still had the knuckle dusters. The hardened, knobbly steel hadn't moved.

He then tapped the Glocks fitted to both front and rear holsters of his vest. All intact. Mackay was satisfied. He stood up and moved. Speed and precision. Whether the security camera picked him up, he didn't care at that point. More important things were at stake. Mackay strode ten quick paces, pulling the front Glock from the vest, paced another quick ten and made it to the edge of the cabin wall. He rounded it with the weapon pressed out front. Two hands snug over the grip. One firm, one easy. Safety off. The faint yellow glow from the cabin's lights turned to sunshine as Mackay entered the wide-open floor. There was no one there. No immediate threat. From wall to wall the space inside was big enough for five tractors parked side by side plus wiggle room. The left wall was filled with star pickets and gardening tools, while the right was stacked with the smaller stuff: spindles of wiring, rope, plant pots, faded gnomes and ornamental bird feeders. Immediately, parked to his left, was a ride-on lawnmower. To his right was the tractor, trailer and forklift transported by the skinny worker. Beyond that was the rear wall. Full of empty, double-stacked oak barrels.

Mackay moved slowly across the floor between the lawnmower and tractor. One foot after the other, heels rolling silently to the toes. He heard something scuttling down the back, clambering behind the stacked barrels. Cloth and rubber scraping across the brick wall. The casks obscured whatever was making the sound, so Mackay kept the Glock steady out front. Chest level. He passed the tractor, the key was still in the ignition. He passed the trailer, its rear gate was down. He passed the forklift. He was ten metres deep when he saw the thin man start a reverse descent from the top row of barrels. Swinging his legs down with his back towards Mackay. He had no idea a man in tactical uniform with an ominous painted face was standing less than a metre beneath him. Holding a Glock with fifteen rounds.

Instead of a straightforward kill, Mackay changed tact. It was better to face the guy if he was going to take his life. Showed character. Not a good trait shooting a man in the back. Robert Ford made that example clear when he shot Jesse James. Mackay wanted to give the guy a chance to explain, just in case. Just in case he wasn't party to killing his brother's family. Or potentially keeping a six-year-old autistic boy captive inside a brick wall. On the whole, Mackay figured he'd still need some information regardless, and maybe this was just the guy to give it.

Mackay silently holstered the Glock. At that point Wynand's feet were right in front of his face, levelled with his shoulder. Gripping the small nooks between the casks for support. Perfect height. Mackay dug his right hand into his pocket, fitted the knuckle dusters then slugged Wynand in the ankle. Hard and sharp. Snapping it against the curve of the cask. Metal into bone, bone into wood. A short hook. Just like Cross had taught him. Full hip rotation, power from feet, to shoulder, to fist. The metal-on-bone made a loud crack – the sound of the steel edge separating the skin and softening the bone underneath to a paste.

Wynand lost his footing, swung sideways and dropped flat on his side on the concrete. The wind was knocked out of him immediately. Mackay leaned over and whacked him twice more in the chest anyway. *Crunch. Crunch.* Right in the middle, cracking the sternum. For insurance. Better than losing both sides of your ribcage in an IED explosion.

Wynand's mouth and eyes opened like a tuna fish. Like the catch of the day pulled onto the deck. He couldn't speak or yell out in pain. His mouth opened and closed as it searched for breath. For air that wasn't coming. Nothing was filling his lungs. Seconds passed. Mackay exchanged his knuckle dusters for the seal pup knife. He removed it from his hip and pressed the tip firmly into the hollow socket of skin just above the man's collarbone. Below the trachea. Just in case he needed to slice it open for the guy to breathe. Maybe he'd hit the sternum too hard and punctured a lung, making him drown within from his own blood, like Malvin.

Mackay watched, waited and let him struggle. At the thirty second mark, Wynand began taking small, shallow pockets of air, bringing life back into his cheeks. Mackay kept the point of the knife where it was.

'About how old is the child you got back there?' said Mackay.

Wynand couldn't answer, he didn't have the capacity to speak yet. Either from falling to the floor having the wind knocked out of him, or getting his sternum punched in. Probably both.

'Maybe I help you breathe a little easier,' Mackay said, pressing the point of the knife in.

Wynand sucked his throat inwards and shook his head. Spittle ran down his chin. Mackay looked into his eyes for a second, ascertaining the man had a low-level IQ. Part of the young man's genetic make-up wasn't all there, which couldn't be helped. Mackay almost felt sorry for him.

'Wait, wait. Stop,' Wynand managed. He swallowed, sucked air and gasped.

'How old?' Mackay said again.

Wynand blinked and refocused.

'Maybe five or six.'

'Boy or girl?'

'Boy.'

Good enough for Mackay. He needed nothing else from the man, so he took him out. Unconscious, not dead. Same right fist, same knuckle dusters. A right hook across the jaw, which put Wynand to sleep. And maybe tore the jawbone from the meaty attachment point on the side. Mackay stood and walked up to the stacked barrels, looked between the little gaps, saw the wall, then saw an even larger gap in the foundations at the bottom. A wide, hollow edifice. A fireplace. He started climbing, made it to the top, braced against the wall and dropped over the other side. He scanned the tight fissure against the fireplace then leaned into the hearth. He saw a pair of small white shoes with little legs protruding out. The shoes had Velcro straps. Mackay remembered wearing the same design when he was a boy. Easier fitment for small hands, made for children who hated the hassle of tying laces.

The rest of the child's body was pressed all the way back into the firepit's wall, obscured by darkness. Mackay still had the night vision lens attached to his head, so he pulled the optical over his eyes and twisted the iris to focus. It was Lincoln. Same as he ever was, only thinner, malnourished and soiled. The firepit stunk of excrement, soot and oak. Lincoln hadn't moved for at least two, maybe three days. He was curled into a ball, arms around his legs, as far from the winery's savages as he could manage. His face was between his knees, covered over with the same mop of hair Mackay had always remembered. Curled over his ears, eyes and collar like ivy tendrils. The boy had held on the only way he knew how. Retreating within himself, mentally wishing he was elsewhere, in a better place far and away somewhere in his imagination.

Mackay now needed to coax him out. But he didn't want to frighten the poor thing. Or create alarm or give reason for him to scream and draw attention. He needed to ease the distress slowly, which required a calm approach. The type of approach that said, *I am family, I'm here to protect you and take you away from this bad place. Away from this dark, god-awful hellhole.*

Mackay removed his night vision and began rubbing the painted camouflage off his face. If and when Lincoln eventually came out, he'd want to see the familiarity of his uncle rather than the nefarious warmonger he currently resembled.

'Lincoln. Your name is Lincoln,' Mackay whispered. 'I know it's you because I am your uncle. It's Mackay, Uncle Mackay. I'm here to get you out of here. To a safe place.'

Lincoln didn't move.

'I am your father's brother. Your father's name is Malvin. Your mother's name is Neve. Do you remember me?'

Still no answer. Maybe it was because Mackay was whispering, so he tried using his voice. Flat and soft. The same Irish brogue as the boy's father's.

'In Aldershot, we used to watch Disney movies on that ugly grey couch in the spare room. Downstairs in the games room. With the bike you said was stupid because it never went anywhere, and the plastic plant with the leaves you used to chew on, then get in trouble for it with your mother.'

Still nothing.

Mackay thought harder, talking wasn't working. A silent moment passed before it came to him. Mackay needed to sing. A song he knew Lincoln knew. One of the many from Lincoln's favourite film. If Mackay could work the words and the tune with some form of tone and melody, maybe it would connect. It was worth a shot. Mackay gave it his best, his voice as good as a droning microwave but at least he had some modulation. He only knew a few bars of 'Chim Chim Cher-ee' from Mary Poppins, which was enough, and ironic, considering Lincoln was more or less holed up inside one. He went through as many of the lines as he could remember. His tone low, hushed and quiet. Lulling and soothing. He repeated the verses over and over. On the fifth reprise Mackay heard movement. A slow shuffling of the Velcro shoes, edging out closer towards him. Out of the pit, into the light.

'Mary Poppins,' said Lincoln, hoarse and cracked. Then, 'Ugly grey couch.'

2100hrs
Wednesday December 19, 2012
Admin Room, Front of House, Frans & Hoek Winery, Western Australia

After Van Breeman ordered Bryson to find Taylor and Derek, he took a moment. Excluding the murdered family and the reporter tied down in the hotbox, he had two missing cops on his payroll. That was the kicker. Taylor and Derek were solid, and had never faltered once. They were always contactable. Always picked up their phone. He paid them well to make sure of it. And even if they didn't, they'd always call back within the hour at the latest. They were cops after all, both with mortgages and families. And being detectives, Van Breeman was aware of the nature of their work. He knew they had high-end jobs that needed attending to. Homicide, kidnapping, rape, the works. Was it a coincidence they were out of the picture? He didn't think so. Something was wrong. With Taylor and Derek silent, the coincidence was too big to ignore.

The best Van Breeman could do was to stay put and watch the security feeds. Just in case something came up. He had two monitors set up: one in the admin room where he stood, the other inside the strongbox next to the main gallery, where his personal investments lay. Van Breeman didn't like coincidences, and with the two detectives currently out of the picture, it was necessary to keep things under full control. Under lock and key with eyes on. His eyes. All night if he had to. Tomorrow was a new day, bringing new decisions and plans, but for now, he would use the remaining hours of the night to mind his goods. Like the good paranoid businessman he was. And when Wynand, the useless prat, finally showed, he'd have him help. Two eyes were better than one. Van Breeman monitoring from the strongbox, Wynand from the supply room. Possibly with a bullet in his leg or shoulder for not being contactable.

Van Breeman rang Wynand one more time. It rang immediately, the chirping call imitating an old rotary phone which belled and vibrated somewhere close, but it wasn't the admin room. The sound came from the gallery next door. He followed the twittering to find the phone at the end of the wine-tasting bench opposite the drinks fridge. Next to a can of Fanta. Recently consumed too as it had a small wet ring under it. Condensation from a change in the drink's temperature. He put Wynand's negligence to the front of his consequence list in his head then left the room.

He exited the front of house and walked along the balcony to the strongbox at the end of the building. He punched the code into the keypad, then sat in the middle of the room to watch the security monitors. He observed the twelve panels on the screen for five minutes before he found Wynand – driving a tractor, hauling two oak barrels out of the cellar loaded on a trailer. He watched him tow the barrels down to the maintenance cabin, then reverse the trailer into the floor space and park it. At least Wynand was working, Van Breeman thought. He then thought about lowering the level of consequence he'd planned for him, just a little. But he knew Wynand better. He knew he was passing the time doing a low-priority job just to look busy, keeping out of his way. The kicker was that Wynand was without his phone, which was a non-negotiable. Van Breeman decided to keep the consequence as it was. A bullet. Somewhere that wasn't life-threatening. Leg or shoulder, which he thought was fair, especially at a time like this. With a young boy still missing and two detectives unreachable. Being inaccessible under these circumstances was poor form.

At ten minutes into watching Wynand, he observed him get into the forklift and raise the second barrel to the top row of casks along the wall. Which was when he heard his horses whinny, all the way from the bottom of the vineyard. Which also meant – though he couldn't really tell from the black-and-white image – Wynand had stuffed up the manoeuvre. Likely jamming or crushing the barrels, which had spooked the horses. Another act of incompetence and another mental note for the back burner. At eleven minutes into watching Wynand, he observed him get out of the forklift and begin to climb the double stack of barrels. Hands and feet grappling over the casks then disappearing behind them, which made Van Breeman curious. Made him lean forward a little, take a little more notice. Between the twelve- and fourteen-minute mark, nothing happened. There was no movement. He couldn't see Wynand at all. Then, at the fifteen-minute mark, a dark figure appeared, walking onto the floor space of the shed. Not some lost wild animal from the state forest. It walked upright on two legs, and it wasn't Kimbala. It moved slow and measured towards the rear wall. Arms raised at chest level, hands out front holding something. Likely a handgun. It was a presence Van Breeman was more or less expecting. The loss of contact from Taylor and Derek started to make sense.

Whoever the newcomer was, he, or she, was fitted in what appeared to be some form of tactical get-up. In the black-and-white picture on the feed – fitted to a nearby tree – Van Breeman could only make out a few key features. For the money he spent, the camera's picture was decently clear, but it wasn't close enough to pick up any high-clarity definition. He could make out a backpack and a set of night-vision goggles. As the figure moved further inside the cabin, the angle on the monitor's grid switched from a rear observation point to a front observation point. The view now high above the barrels on the rear wall. The image closer and clearer. In quick succession, Van Breeman realised three things. Firstly, even though the figure's face was concealed with some kind of dark coating, he could tell it was a man. The lean shape of the face, the broad shoulders and thick torso were unmistakeable. Secondly, he knew the type of weapon in the man's hands. The way it was held: two hands wrapped snug over the grip with the slide protruding above the knuckles. He knew it was a Glock. The same pistol Australian police officers were issued. The very same Taylor and Derek used. The third thing Van Breeman realised was that the newcomer was no amateur. The way he moved and the way he was dressed meant he was either military or police.

On a single rectangular grid on the monitor, the dark entity moved past the tractor, past the trailer, past the forklift. The next thing he saw was Wynand climbing out from behind the double stack of barrels. The figure stopped dead and watched on. Waiting there while Wynand awkwardly clambered down, controlling his footing between the barrel's grooves and arches. Waiting for Wynand to descend closer.

Van Breeman couldn't help but watch. If nothing else, it was out of total intrigue. For a moment or two, he wanted to see what was about to play out. Like the big reveal or twist at the end of a movie. Whatever was going to happen next was as enthralling as real life could get. As Wynand lowered himself from the top row of casks, the dark figure holstered the Glock then, as cool as a southerly breeze, placed a hand into his pocket, dug it back out and pivoted with a right hook into Wynand's foot. His right ankle, just as he placed it on the edge of a lower barrel. The figure knocked Wynand clean from his grasp, dropping him to the concrete floor below.

That was enough of a finale. Van Breeman stood and left the strongbox in a hurry, leaving the front door wide open in his wake. It wasn't on account of Wynand's welfare, he couldn't care less. There were bigger things at stake. If all he did was continue to watch the security monitor, who knew where the tactically dressed man would end up. Or what secrets he might uncover. The gravity of problems he could potentially stir wasn't something Van Breeman wanted to comprehend. The dark figure was a spanner in the works, and he had a very good idea as to why he had arrived. He needed to be removed immediately.

Van Breeman ran back across the veranda, through the gallery into the admin room. He opened the wooden cabinet tailor-made for his vineyard-select weaponry and removed the shotgun. A Lanber 2097. Pre-loaded with two shells. Good to go. Single trigger action, twenty-six-inch barrel, twelve gauge. A proper mess-maker with immense power. Solid and reassuring. The best option for the evening's situation. He would have preferred a pump action with a five-shell load, but in Australia, semi-automatics and pump actions were banned. For close-range kills, the spray from the Lanber could easily wipe out a horse or camel. Taking down a human would be a cinch. He pocketed two extra shells from an open box then hurried out into the darkness. He passed the wine press, the underground cellar, then continued down the worn dirt path toward the back of the property. As he closed in on the old colonial lodge, he slowed to a walk, taking a wide birth silently around the maintenance shed at the hotbox end. He wasn't heading for the tactically dressed man straight away. Not just yet. First, he wanted to stop in at the stables. As he continued, he kept an ear out for Kimbala. Or hopefully a cry from the journalist, but it was completely silent. Nothing but crickets. Instead, he found Kimbala perched against the wall of the hotbox like it was mid-morning break – ready for coffee and cigarettes. Only Kimbala was motionless with his head facing into the bricks. Van Breeman was impressed. The stranger had taken out one of his best. Credit where credit was due. The big witch doctor was down. No more chanting. No more dark arts.

There was no need to muse on his losses, so Van Breeman moved on. Treading quietly toward the central stable where his two ex-racehorses nodded and snorted in familiarity. Approving their owner's presence. As he arrived at the two long faces behind the gate, he reached in and took the coil of rope hanging from an inside hook. A lariat. Horse rope used to lead and tie the animals. Made from quality nylon for superior strength. The rope was part of his bread and butter growing up on his father's farm in Franshoek. A modest, yet unique item he could use, and use well. The boss had a plan. It might work, or it might not.

Next, Van Breeman opened the stall to his fastest horse, Rye. The thoroughbred. Chocolate brown with a sliver of white on the forehead. Too old for racing, young enough to live a full life working on a winery. He reeled Rye out of the stall and ambled him up the old training ground towards the maintenance shed. Towards Wynand and the tactically dressed man. Closing in on his prey silently, like a crocodile. The yellow glow from the aged colonial cabin brightening at every step.

> 2300hrs
> Wednesday December 19, 2012
> Maintenance Shed, Frans & Hoek Winery, Western Australia

Mackay needed to move Lincoln out of the hearth and over the double stack of casks to safety. But where was that safety? Having Lincoln in his grasp was a new phase he wasn't prepared for. This was a new development in unknown territory in an unprepared point in time. He couldn't take him back to a police station as he was surely a wanted man by now. If he knew for certain he would find Lincoln, he would have planned three, four steps ahead, making sure the boy's protection wasn't jeopardised. But Mackay could only move one step at a time now. His priority was Lincoln's safety, and regardless of what steps or course of action came, he could not leave him to scope the rest of the vineyard for further threats. That was not an option. Lincoln was finally reunited with someone of familiarity. He was with family, and after a hard slog of surviving on his own, Mackay could not leave him again. Not for anything. Not for any sums of money, bargaining or compromise. From here on, he would be at his side until his last breath. Till every last drop of energy was drained dry from his system.

'We need to get you out of here,' said Mackay. 'Back over those barrels.'

Lincoln didn't respond. His weakness was obvious. Days without food and water bodes worse for a child. Mackay took his backpack off, found the water bottle, unscrewed the cap and offered it.

'Small sips,' said Mackay. 'Take it easy.'

Lincoln drank. Three small sips, then a breath, then another three, this time in gulps. The boy was thirsty. He handed the bottle back to Mackay. 'Enough,' he said.

'Okay, let's move.' Mackay held Lincoln's hands and pulled him to a shaky stance, waiting a second or two to let his gait and balance settle. With his hands around his waist, Mackay pushed him up to the second tier of casks, jamming his little feet into the grooves between the barrels for stability.

'Hold the rim, tight as you can,' said Mackay, then climbed up next to him. He pulled and twisted Lincoln's body onto the very top then followed suit.

Halfway there.

Mackay lowered himself down backwards to the concrete floor with Lincoln bear-hugged in his arms. Which, considering the way Lincoln was facing, made for a well-timed coincidence. Lincoln was facing toward the mouth of the shed looking out, Mackay wasn't. He was facing the barrels. Lincoln immediately noticed a man in jeans and a collared shirt moving into the shed's yellow glow. He wore a coil of looped rope around one shoulder and a twenty-six-inch shotgun raised and braced against the other.

'Gun!' screamed Lincoln.

Mackay didn't drop quick enough. All he could do was anticipate the shot. Experience and training evaluated the tone of Lincoln's scream measured against the options in the space of the shed. He had no idea what type of shot he was about to be hit with so the best he could do in the moment was to go defensive. Keep Lincoln safe. Hold ground with his back toward the enemy. Allow the ballistic plate to absorb whatever round was coming.

Mackay shielded Lincoln inside his arms and ducked his head. The first shot hit him square in the back like a wet slap, the spray from the cartridge ripping through the backpack. The force was incredible. Enough to send the two of them flying into the bottom row of barrels as the blast echoed around them. Lincoln screamed out. Mackay recognised the sound: a shotgun shell. Distinct all to its own. Not like a crack from a rifle, more of a boom, amplified inside the confines of the cabin. Coming from a shotgun meant it would take a moment before the next round, or two, were cocked and triggered.

Mackay's back ached hot immediately but he stayed covered over Lincoln. In the two seconds between hitting the barrels and dropping to the floor he was able to turn and glance at the assailant: a man in jeans and a collared shirt with a coil of rope around his shoulder. And he was reloading. Jacking a round inside a twenty-six-inch barrel ready to go again. That second round came faster than expected.

*

Van Breeman knew what he was doing. He was on his home turf using his own weapons. His first round knocked the tactically dressed man down as expected. There was however, one major issue: he should have had a kill shot. A head shot at the least. Especially considering the mere ten metres he stood from the man at the shed's entrance. It should have been a given. He had no other excuse for missing his prey, except one. In the milliseconds leading up to squeezing the Lanber's trigger, he noticed something he was not expecting: a small boy, aged between five or six, held in the man's arms. The same young child he and his men had been searching for over the last seventy-two hours. The boy had seen his approach – just a glimpse – but it was enough. Allowing the man time to cover up and take the impact of the round in the back. Against a ballistic vest made of Kevlar with a ballistic plate. He couldn't leave the two of them alive, not now. Another non-negotiable. If planning to use a weapon, use it to its full effect. Neutralise them completely. Especially if said enemy would expose him and interrupt his booming black-market sales. Van Breeman released the second round immediately, bouncing the Lanber's butt off the ground to engage the recoil, then firing the second pin.

*

The two seconds between the first and second shot allowed Mackay enough time to identify the shooter's aim and move out of the way. He used the grippy, hardened rubber of his Gore-Tex shoes to press into the floor and thrust himself backwards. Sliding his and Lincoln's body across the concrete. The second spray hit the oak cask just above Mackay's knees, splintering the barrel into a cloud of wood chips. A miss. All vital organs still safe and intact. All bones accounted for. Lincoln screamed out again, which was when Mackay released him, scuttled to his feet, took a chance and ran at the shooter.

*

On all accounts, Van Breeman was a resourceful man. He'd been toting guns, riding horses and tying hundreds of ropes and knots since he was a nipper. All drilled and berated into him by his father on the Franshoek estate. He was ready for the intruder. Plan A and B were shells one and two from the shotgun – both expelled. Which meant he was down to plan C, his backup: the coil of rope. Between moving from the stables to the shed, Van Breeman had tied a honda-knot at each end of the rope, essentially forming two lassos. An old cowboy cinch used as a noose for hanging men back in the day. He coiled one end of the rope around his left shoulder and left the other end slack over the horse's neck.

The tactically dressed man let go of the boy, rose to his feet and began steaming forward. Nicus Van Breeman dropped the Lanber, took the lasso from his shoulder and threw it. All in one slick, well-contrived motion. It took him a single swing to get the momentum going before flicking it long and high toward the rapidly approaching form. The diameter of the lasso was slipped to a length normally sized for a horse, but it also suited the physical movement of a running man perfectly. The loop of the lasso arced, swelled wide and hooked around the man's torso. Van Breeman zipped it tight immediately.

*

Mackay didn't see it coming till it was too late. He didn't even get close. The rope was already in the air before Mackay was on his feet – dropping over his head and shoulders before his first four strides. Before he'd reached any form of acceleration. All Van Breeman needed to do now was drop the rope, step towards Rye concealed behind the wall and give him a hard giddy-up. Across his rump. Which he did.

The thoroughbred bolted, wrenching Mackay into the darkness of the vineyard. Once the horse moved, physics demanded both loop ends of the rope to snap shut, tight as a weld. With the business end at over four hundred kilograms, Mackay had no chance. The beast took him like a featherweight. Like discarded trash ready for the heap. It yanked him off balance, face first onto the concrete floor, ripping the night-vision goggles from his head. Snorting and braying as it dragged him into the night.

The mountain of muscle did what mother nature intended it to do: run. Like it was still on the green of the track. The race machine hit almost forty miles per hour, then maintained it for half a mile, dragging Mackay's useless body behind it. Through the fields. The tilled earth. The rows of grapevines. Mackay tried but couldn't grasp the seal knife at his hip to cut the rope. The pounding and scraping of the earth underneath him dislodged any attempt from his hand. All he could do was bounce, twist and spin across the dirt.

Reaching the farthest boundaries of the vineyard's fence line, the charging beast tired and slowed. Mackay had a window of opportunity to steady his hand, fold some fingers around the knife's handle and cut the rope. The glow of the moon helped, making the jerking lariat an easier target to slash. The knife was sharp. Well done, Nutty. With one stiff controlled swipe, he was free. The instant release from the pace of the animal threw Mackay into a meticulously aligned row of vines – the knobbly trunks and arms beating his momentum into submission. He slowed to a roll and stopped. All he could do was lay still, reset his breathing and check for injuries. The dizziness was next level, stirring another cloudy cocktail inside his head. He had no idea where he was, and his brain was a thousand miles from anywhere being remotely focused. Dirt and grass caked his lips, teeth and ears, and his face felt pulpy and sore. The bony parts across the sides of his head were pulsating and swelling already. All of which were small scale for the injuries list, and wasn't too bad, considering.

As his mental clarity slowly returned, his neural pathways gave the all-clear. Nothing twisted, no bleeding, no broken bones. Bruises and lacerations only. Good news. Mackay rolled to his front and took a knee, inhaled a few litres of clean air, exhaled just as much dust. He resheathed the seal pup knife then instinctively went for his weapon holstered at his front. Good soldiering skills: one weapon away, another at the ready. But there was nothing there. Just an empty pouch. The Glock had likely dislodged during his rollercoaster ride with the earth and could literally be anywhere between him and the cabin. An easy three-hundred metre stretch of long, orchard grounds. An area of between seven and eight hundred square metres. He considered it lost for good. One weapon down.

Mackay still had his backpack on, which was lucky considering the amount of earth-beating he'd taken. He dipped a shoulder, removed the pack and patted the back of the vest. The second Glock was still there. He took it out and checked the working mechanisms. The magazine didn't release and neither did the slide. He double-, then triple-, checked it. It was finished. Rendered useless. Two weapons down. Bad news. The buckshot from the shooter had hit him square in the back where the vital organs live, and the Glock was holstered right in the middle of the rear ballistic plate. The silver lining: the plate did its thing and protected him. Thank you, Andy. He was alive because of it. The metal pellets inside the cartridge had passed through the contents of the backpack, cracking the slide and handle. Likely fragmenting the firing pin, barrel, recoil assembly and magazine tube. Mackay checked over the pack. It was tattered up and full of holes. Basically a strainer now. And it was wet. He emptied the contents and spread it on the ground. The water bottle had cracked through and leaked everywhere. The ration pack was torn apart and crumbled. The burner phone's screen was shattered, and the number pad had slivers of buckshot embedded into it. As did the altimeter. With both firearms down, his defence capabilities were limited. It wasn't the end of the world though; he still had the two blades and knuckle dusters. And even though the ration pack was a mess of morsels, it could still be useful, crumbled or not. Food was food, so he stuffed it back inside the pack, zipped it up and threw everything else away in random directions. He took the broken Glock, wiped it down with his sleeve and threw it away as well.

Mackay looked around to gather his bearings and rubbed away the layers of earth encrusted in his face and ears. He found himself on a slight decline at the bottom of a hill. Behind him was the bordering fence extending in an arc around the property. A divide between the vineyard and forest from where he'd entered. The dark mass of woodland silent and still, sinking low into the lay of the land extending no level of welcome whatsoever. Not wanting any part of whatever was about to play out. In front of him, the grapevines lined up in one long parallel row, planted in perfect arrangement all the way up the hill where the horse broke away and dragged him. Where he'd found Lincoln inside the old cabin. The machinery shed. Where he needed to return to immediately.

Mackay propped himself up and kneeled between the rows of vines. Like the head pin at a bowling alley with the grapevines set left and right like gutter guards. Mackay raised his head and looked up the rise. At the top of the hill, a hundred yards away was a silhouette. The outline of a man on a horse with a gun. The same guy who took two buckshots at him only moments ago. Who used a coil of rope as a lariat, lassoing him like a pro. The silvery light of the moon illuminated the image directly overhead, casting a halo effect around the horse and its master. Staged picture perfect for some geographic, farming or equine magazine. The head of the snake in all his glory.

Mackay heard a voice, barely audible from his position at

the bottom of the slope. The rider had yelled out. All Mackay could make of it were words to the effect of, 'Here I come, motherfucker.' Or maybe it was, 'Yeehaa, motherfucker.' Either way, 'motherfucker' was the word of choice. If he had in fact yelled 'yeehaa', Mackay figured the rider was more crazed cowboy than criminal architect. A real whack-job entrepreneur. Which didn't make much sense, considering the overall picture he was getting of the guy. Either way, he couldn't really shout back and ask the rider to repeat what he'd said. That would just be awkward.

Mackay couldn't match the rider with a shooting weapon anymore, and he had no throwing skills with a blade. His options were to either run back into the forest, leaving Lincoln stranded, or stand and fight. Mackay would rather take a point-blank to the head than go with the first option, so, *fuck this guy*, Mackay thought. Whoever the man was on the horse, it would be fight first, and figure his name out later. Maybe it was the boss, maybe it was a lackey. Time would soon tell.

Mackay grabbed a fistful of earth. Soil and grass. Trickling the grainy textures between his fingers. It was moist. In the early stages of going dewy in the cooling humidity of the night. Not the best for traction, but good enough for easing slips and falls. Which would be a benefit for his next proposal. His next plan of attack – something completely separate from phases one and two. Or three, if he ever made it back to Cross alive. This was a stand-alone plan. Which would one hundred per cent involve falling hard between the stretches of grapevines. On the rugby field, Mackay often thought about why he enjoyed tackling. When the blood was pumping and the adrenalin was high, it was exhilarating. Drawing out primitive elements of his hunter-gatherer psyche. On occasion he'd been able to put two grown men onto their backs in one hit, such was the power in his legs and core. This, however, was different. This was going to hurt.

A hundred yards of ground lay before him and the rider.

Mackay just didn't know the guy's name. Didn't know it was the ringmaster himself. At this point it didn't matter. He would do what he could – what he had trained his body for. In one sense, this was his only option. In another sense, it was going to be the biggest test of what his new body was now capable of. How much his thermoplastic bone structure could take. The reality of what he was about to do filtered in and out of his mind. Taking on a horse was suicide to any normal man, but in the heat of the moment, those thoughts didn't bother him. He had confidence. Part of which was fuelled by adrenalin and anger, but considering his body's recent capabilities, he might just stand a chance. What he was about to do was only achievable if he wasn't shot in the face, and the rest was best wishes and best of luck. Could he realistically take on a horse? He wasn't going to overthink it.

Mackay checked his vest and tightened every strap. Abdomen and shoulders. He squatted and grabbed a handful of grass to steady his launch. Hunkering low like a sprinter: chin down, shoulders forward. His core, quads and ankles bracing and quivering as he coiled low into the earth. Mackay raised his head and looked up at the rider. The rider looked back over the horse's mane. Both man and beast sniffing the night-time air for a sense of what was to come. Two men. A hundred yards between them. No discussions. *Better aim for my head*, Mackay thought. *But you'll miss, and then I'll bury you.*

The rider went first, kicking his heels into the beast, shotgun held out front like a lance.

Ninety yards between them.

Mackay went second. His anger rising for a three-count before unleashing. One thousand, two thousand, three thousand. His heart drawing in all the hurt within, then storming off the line like a tormented bull.

Seventy yards. *You can do this.*

Van Breeman yelled out again. 'You're a dead man!'

Mackay didn't hear a thing. The only sound was the rushing wind over his ears and the pumping of his blood.

Forty yards. *You can do this.*

A shot rang out. The pellets hitting nothing but air. Mackay didn't slow – the slabs of meat over his legs kept on. The forward propulsion for a mere human being was immense. His lungs inhaled and exhaled while his arms and fists pumped like jackhammers. He hit the same thirty-mile-an-hour mark he'd reached back in Aldershot. This time though, he was moving uphill. It didn't matter, he was doing just as well. Who knew the potential if it was a decline.

Twenty yards. *You can do this.*

Mackay eyed the glinting barrel in the moon's glow. He zigzagged unpredictably. Left, right. Right, right, left, disrupting the shooter's windage. A second shot rang out. Both shells done. Nothing but an empty stick.

Fifteen yards. *You got this.*

At this range, Van Breeman had a clear picture of the rapidly approaching man's face. With most of the face paint scrubbed away, he could make out the basics: white, male, early thirties, sunken eyes, a prominent brow, angry beyond comprehension.

Ten yards. *Time to shine.*

Mackay figured if he threw himself front and centre at the horse, it would kill him. So, it had to be the leg. Shoulder shot, just above the right knee. A leg can ultimately heal, even if the horse does go lame. He thought one last word, *scrum*, then timed his strides and aimed low. Mackay leaped into the horse with his entire being like he'd been pronged with an iron rod. Right shoulder into the front leg, colliding just above the beast's right knee. Execution with precision. All bodies hit the ground.

NINE

DISCOVERY

> 2330hrs
> Wednesday December 19, 2012
> Vineyard Plantation, Frans & Hoek Winery, Western Australia

Mackay wasn't sure how long he was out before he came to. Minutes or hours could have passed. Whatever the time, it was still dark, and he was still breathing. His head, chest and collarbone hurt, but overall, he deemed himself okay. Another tick in the box for the thermoplastic. He dragged his knees up and propped himself onto his hands. Once again having to scrape clotted dirt and grass from his mouth, as well as pick out grapes, leaves and shoots from his shirt. He must've been flung through a section of grapevine because when he stood, he wasn't in the same row as before. As he looked around the expanse of the property, there was no horse and there was no rider. He did, however, hear a combination of heavy laboured breathing mixed with a strange gargling snort: the horse, just a few metres away, lying on its side one row over. Back where the collision initially occurred. Where he'd played chicken with the beast, with his body. Mackay could just see the height of its rump and flank as he peered over the grapevine's hedge.

Mackay crawled through a tight section of vines and came through the other side of the row. From where he stood, he could only see the horse. Rye. Lying still on the ground, struggling to breathe, coated in a thick layer of dust. Its front leg where Mackay made impact was bent backwards. Pulled awkwardly underneath its belly – torn from the genetic assembly of the meaty front shoulder. Its head was also angled somewhat unnaturally away from its neck. Out of alignment from what Mackay deemed normal. The beast must have rolled and flipped, smashing the ground headfirst and breaking its neck in the process.

The rider was nowhere to be seen. Not until Mackay stepped a few paces closer. The toe end of a boot came into view first as Mackay reached the horse's tail. Just one boot, reflecting a dull sheen beneath the beast's massive belly. Sticking out diagonally above the horse was the rider. Chest, arms and head. Most of the saddle was rotated underneath the mess. The stirrup must have caught the rider's foot during the tumble, locking him in then wrenching the saddle underneath itself.

The man's eyes were wide open, staring up into the night. The gargling sound wasn't coming from the horse. On second inspection, the animal was dead. Mackay shook his head. He had killed another horse. That made it two for two, he thought.

The gargling was the man's attempt to suck air and stay alive. His stomach and chest were being crushed by the animal's dead weight. A dark smear coloured the man's lips and leaked from the side of his mouth. He too was covered in dust and grass, so Mackay couldn't really tell what he looked like. He didn't care. To him, it was a guy who was part of the vineyard's sick operation. Boss or not, he was down. All part of his plan. Happy days.

'Can you hear me?' Mackay said, peering down at the man.

Van Breeman blinked. His eyes shifted slowly towards the figure standing above him. More blood exited the side of his mouth. Instinctively, he raised his arms and grappled the ground around him, searching for something that wasn't there. A weapon. The shotgun. Mackay watched him reach and flail and search, desperate for one final shot at victory. His last chance for a win before he was done. There was nothing there. Whatever weapon he thought he had was gone. Lost somewhere on the grounds within a twenty-yard radius. Like the Glock. There was nothing he could do.

Mackay took a step closer, standing on the dead horse's body. On that big ribcage. Placing a further eighty kilograms of pressure down on Van Breeman's vital organs.

'What's your name?' Mackay asked, giving the man reasonable time to respond. Van Breeman either couldn't or refused. Mackay continued the one-sided conversation.

'My name isn't relevant, but you and whoever you work with here killed my brother, the Irishman in hospital. He was shot somewhere on these grounds. Then someone had him finished off in hospital. The bent cops given the dirty work are both dead. Someone here also killed my brother's wife and one of his sons. That'd be my sister-in-law and my older nephew. Funny thing, a news reporter I saw on television, the same one I found in your god-awful cabin beaten half to death said my nephew died from an apparent asthma attack. The boy wasn't asthmatic. Now what do you make of all that?'

'You're Irish.'

'For fuck's sake.'

'I hit you… with my horse,' Van Breeman said, gravelly from the back of his throat. He gurgled again then choked back the blood from his mouth. Mackay could see the cogs turning slowly, unsure what to make of the man standing over him. Alive.

'You did,' Mackay said.

'How…?'

'That's a long story, and you're not going to be alive long enough to hear it.'

Mackay knelt down for a clearer picture of the man's shadowed face, using what light he could to take in his features: the forehead, the cheeks, the jawline, the chin. Great bone structure all round. Everything was well proportioned and aesthetically pronounced. Cut from wealthy lineage, unlike the voodoo mass and dweeb cowboy he'd encountered earlier. Even through the layer of dirt covering his face Mackay could tell the man was clean-shaven. A disciplined trait. His hair was thick and lush and shiny in the moonlight, probably never went a day without its essential oils. His body, from what Mackay could see, was lean and athletic. Not sculpted from years in the gym, rather refined from years of working the lands. Labouring on farms and vineyards. With all angles and perspectives considered, Mackay concluded that the man, slowly suffocating beneath him, was the boss. The head of the snake. All the little pieces made sense.

'You're Van Breeman,' Mackay said.

'Yes,' Van Breeman exhaled. 'The boy was an accident.'

'And that makes all the difference, does it? No point trying to justify it now. Man up. Own your fuck-ups. Show some character before you die. The other son, the one who's back at that storage building, you left him to die. That's unacceptable, me feiner. I'm here to bring him home. And while you die here, I'm going to go and get him, then I'm going to make a phone call. Soon after that I'll leave. Like I was never here.'

'We tried looking for him,' Van Breeman said, hushed and coarse.

'You did a sheit job of it.'

'We would have fed him, looked after him, given him to child protection. We don't kill kids here. Not my style. And we're no paedophile ring.'

'So, what then? What have you got going on in this place? I didn't get a chance to poke around. You should save me the time. One final good deed.'

'I almost had you,' Van Breeman said, avoiding the question.

'Almost? Like you almost killed me with your horse? Yet here I am, and there you are. I'll ask again, what business have you got going on here?'

Mackay again gave the man due time to respond. Van Breeman swallowed air and blood, then started to smile. A small crack at first, then it spread wider. He started to laugh, which – under the weight – came out as a raspy hiss.

Mackay said, 'Whatever it is has something to do with that girl tied up in that toxic room. Am I right?'

The raspy hiss continued.

'Don't bother then, I'll poke around myself. Whatever else may come can come.'

'Do what you want,' said Van Breeman. 'Finishing me off won't help stop this. I've got people lined up for miles ready to take on my legacy. We're like lizard tails. Cut one off, another takes its place. Those who come after me, will come after you too. Picking off everyone in your bloodline. Burning them all to the ground. My empire will thrive with or without me. Guaranteed.'

'Good story,' said Mackay. 'Once again, me feiner, what are you running here?'

Van Breeman stared long and glassy at Mackay. 'Second time you said that,' he gurgled.

Mackay paused, then it clicked. 'Me feiner? Means you're a selfish cunt. Thinking only of yourself and your bags of money. Taking lives for some such reason and trying to get away with it.

Last chance, what are you playing at down here? Open up and share, it'll feel right. Might save your soul.'

Van Breeman let his lids peel up to the stars. 'Good luck, Irish.'

Mackay nodded with acceptance. 'Aye. Stalemate. Was genuinely hoping for a little more from you. Good luck it is then.'

Mackay got off the horse, took a step back and contemplated its position.

'My brother, the one you ordered to be killed, he sounded similar to you right now. Choking from a big hole in his lungs. That's either irony or coincidence, I'm not sure. Anyway, how are we going to do this? What would a right cunt like you prefer? A quick death or a slow one? You want me to leave you be or would you like it done and dusted?'

Van Breeman breathed short, small puffs in and out.

'Someone will come for you,' he said, the liquid over his eyes glassy. His pupils dilating like dinner plates. He was scared.

'Like those two cops on your payroll? Let them come. I took Laurel and Hardy out inside your office. Right near your little bonsai tree.'

Van Breeman blinked, taking it in.

'Some say bonsai trees are a symbol of harmony and balance. In your case I'd say it's power and domination, and a control of fear.'

Mackay left the conversation open for a moment, hoping for a response. It didn't come. Van Breeman probably expected a bullet, or maybe a knife across the throat. Mackay could have used a knife, but not a gun. One Glock was busted and ineffective, and the other was out there, lost in the dark. A knife was too easy. Instead, Mackay went with a third option. He wanted to be true to his word and bury him. Under his horse.

Mackay tucked his shoulders and arms under Rye and packed a one-man scrum. Crouch, bind, set. He pushed low into the ground and slowly began to roll the horse upwards. Lumbering the beast over Van Breeman's chest and face. He'd been involved in some big scrimmages and heavy lifting in the gym, but a dead horse was different. He hooked his left arm around its hind legs and used as much leverage as he could to begin the rotation, taking every ounce of strength he had to move the beast onto its back. From there, gravity and momentum did the rest. The last thing he saw of Van Breeman were his eyes bulging from his skull with the horse halfway over him. Then came the cracking of his chest – the weight of the beast pressing the man deeper into the earth. With a final shove, Rye flopped over with a quiet thud. The boss was covered head to stomach. Only his legs were left exposed, one of which was still attached to the stirrup. All twisted up and mangled. Like the wicked witch of the east.

On his way back to Lincoln, Mackay found the Lanber in the dirt. Just by chance. Almost mistaking it for a crooked branch. He eased it under his arm and double-checked the barrel, confirming it was empty. Good habits. He released the two empty shells – Van Breeman's wasted double shot – then wiped it down with his sleeve and left it on the ground. He had no use for it. He also accepted that the second Glock, the one flung from his vest while he was dragged by the horse, was gone for good. He wasn't going to waste time searching for it either. Lincoln was priority. Second priority was the reporter in the stable. Third priority was getting out of there unnoticed.

As he approached the maintenance shed, thankfully Lincoln was still there. He'd moved away from the thin, unconscious man and sat himself at the mouth of the entrance. Under the safety of the dim yellow glow, looking out into the night. Rocking back and forth awaiting his uncle's return. As Mackay neared, Lincoln tracked his form until he sat down in front of him. Lincoln looked into uncle's face and touched it. He stopped rocking. He ran a finger across Mackay's nose, down his lips and chin.

'Bleeding,' he said.

'I'm okay,' said Mackay.

Mackay opened his backpack and took out the mushed-up rations. He ripped off the plastic wrapping and removed the gutted contents covered in gooey liquid – some kind of jam. He then filtered out the best three options still decently intact: an apple fruit pocket, a tube of condensed milk and a tin of peaches.

'I don't have any more water for you,' Mackay said. 'We'll go look for some soon, but this stuff looks alright for now. I want you to try. You need some energy back.'

Mackay opened the condensed milk and squeezed some into his own mouth first to show it was okay. He then offered it to Lincoln. His first taste brightened his expression immediately, drawing a touch of colour to his cheeks. More than what he'd had in days. The sugary sweetness almost made him smile. Mackay did the same with the rest of what was still reasonably edible, taking a little first, then giving the rest to the boy. Under the glow, Lincoln's first meal in days was as good as a seaside banquet, or a five-star buffet.

0100hrs
Thursday December 20, 2012
Frans & Hoek Winery, Western Australia

Mackay carried Lincoln like a koala across the vineyard to find a bathroom and some water. And hopefully an undamaged water bottle for the journey back home. Lincoln needed more fluids, a good wash down and a fresh set of clothes. The clothes were a long shot, but two out of three was better than nothing.

Mackay moved steadily up the rise towards the front of house at the top of the hill. Slow, like a shark. Circling the lay of the land in a wide radius. Sometimes doubling back, sometimes making figure eights just to be safe. As he skirted around the underground cellar, he did eventually trip a motion sensor light, but the place stayed quiet and still. Nothing happened. He took a quick peek inside, but all there was to see were lines of casks. Nothing stuck out worthy of a second look. He did the same with a bigger, more modern building halfway up the rise. The wine press facility. A wider stream of security lights lit up the grounds as he neared closer, but again there was nothing but crickets. He walked inside the open doors to another flood of trip-lighting and checked every structure and space for movement and personnel. Silent as a tomb. Nothing but four massive, stainless-steel wine presses. Two on either side of the wall. Bladder presses. Horizontal drums with drainage ducts housed in steel shafts. Built to hold huge loads of grapes. Only one old-school wooden press remained. A big antique thing set in front of what seemed to be an inbuilt extension. A gyprock wall. Painted to match the same wooden colour of the press. An afterthought erected to showcase the antique structure. It had a huge wooden basket in the middle with heavy-duty beams raised either side. The basket had thick rotating capstans, constructed to multiply the squeezing force as it pressed out the grape juice. A sturdy artefact of the times kept as a tourist attraction.

Aside from the occasional low-flying bat, there was nothing doing on the property. Lincoln clung to Mackay's chest, asleep, all the way to the back entrance of the gallery. It was completely clear. No kangaroos. No sugar gliders. No possums. Mackay waited a whole two minutes at the rear of the building before entering. Halted with his shoulder against the far wall's edge. Listening for any sound or movement that could potentially be hostile. Again, nothing. Just the sound of Lincoln's warm breath against his neck. He was out cold. Nestled in. After the timer was done in his head, Mackay checked the back door, found it open, then moved into a moderate space he could only describe as some type of common room or administration room. There was a television, a desktop computer, stacks of wine cartons, a dining table, a fridge and a tea and coffee station. It also had a large flat-screen security monitor against a side wall marked with a huge brown coffee stain. Somebody must've been having a bad day. There were no immediate toilets or bathrooms, but there was a sink at the tea and coffee station. As well as cups. Mackay sat Lincoln down on a chair and rubbed his back, waking him gently. He then filled a cup of water and offered it.

'Drink this, nice and slow.'

Lincoln guzzled it in seconds. He then had two more cups before rejecting a third.

'Do you think you'd be able to walk, Lincoln? We need to find you a bathroom and clean you up a little.'

Lincoln nodded. Mackay picked Lincoln off the chair, stood him to his feet and reached out his hand. Lincoln held it. Mackay walked him through a door into the next room, twice as big as the first. The main gallery. The front of house. Against the wall next to the doorframe were a panel of light switches. Mackay flicked them on one by one, lighting up the gallery in a series of warm-white fixtures across the ceiling and walls. The first thing he noticed was that the front door was left open. Which pricked up Mackay's sense of caution again. Waking his fight and flight senses and slowing down his movements. But the alarm was not warranted. Nothing but a steady flow of air came through. Mackay assumed, and hoped, it had been left open by one of the three he'd left spread on the winery's grounds.

The second thing Mackay noticed was that the gallery was well presented. Regal even. High ceilings, lavish furnishings. A lot of money had been spent in making the room appealing for the tourists and connoisseurs. In front of them, a long, polished granite bench with curls of white marble reached halfway across the room, standing as the front counter. The wine-tasting bench. Behind it, a stockpile of wine bottles were neatly arranged on a criss-crossing fixture of shelves along the wall. Whites and reds filled up the spaces. Shiraz, Merlot, Chardonnay and Verdelho, as well as a Frans & Hoek signature Cabernet Sauvignon. Scattered around the other walls were large, framed artworks. Most of them photographic. Some appeared to be of the Margret River region and the local surf boroughs. Some were of the winery land itself – when it was an old dairy farm with a grain mill.

There were no toilets inside the gallery either, so Mackay needed to explore a little further. Before he walked outside, he caught sight of a bright orange drink can at the far end of the granite counter, recently consumed. A Fanta, with a small ring of water pooled underneath it. Next to the can was a mobile phone. And behind the counter was a clear glass fridge nestled against the far wall. It seemed both Fanta and phone had been left out either because someone was in a big hurry, or someone was just plain forgetful. The fridge was lined with various flavoured cool drinks. For the consuming traveller who wanted something other than wine. Something sweet without alcohol to stay hydrated in the hot climate. At the bottom of the fridge were stacks of plastic water bottles. All half a litre in volume. Mackay walked over and helped himself to two, stacking them inside his backpack. He grabbed a third, necked half, gave the rest to Lincoln, then pocketed the phone from the bench. Which was the common-sense thing to do, seeing as he was down any means of personal communication back to Cross.

Mackay took Lincoln's hand again and walked outside. Lincoln held close, walking languidly beside him, his exhausted body still trying to recover. They moved onto a long veranda out the front, stretching equal lengths to the left and right of the gallery. Conveniently, right in front of them was a universal toilet symbol, attached to a wooden beam built into the staircase leading to the entrance. The symbol was of two black stick figures: one with a narrow torso, the other wider at the hips in a triangle. Male and female. Plain as they come. An arrow underneath the symbol pointed to a set of doors on the far left. On the far right of the veranda at the opposite end, was another door, left wide open. The timing for an ambush or a sudden rush of violence was long overdue. Over the last half hour since burying the snakehead under his horse, there'd been no noise or movement. Not a creak, odour or breath. Nothing but the flutter of warm air through distant leaves. Like the phone and can of Fanta, Mackay was certain it had been left open either because someone was in a hurry, or someone was just plain forgetful. *Lincoln first*, he thought.

The doors to the toilets were locked, but that wasn't an issue. Mackay chose the female door and kicked it in. He opted for the female because of comfort factors male toilets almost never provided. Sure, bad smells run both ways, but eight times out of ten the world over, the female bathroom was more pleasant. Inside, the vanity mirror was a narrow, shoulder-width piece in portrait orientation. Below that was a deep porcelain sink in the middle of a bench with room enough either side to prop Lincoln on for a wash.

'You okay if I take your pants and underwear off? We need to clean you up.'

Lincoln didn't reply. He didn't protest either, which Mackay took as an agreeable response all the same. He was stained and filthy, and a good wash-down needed to happen. Mackay undressed Lincoln's lower half then stood him on the bench. With warm running water and paper towels stacked underneath a fire extinguisher on the wall, Mackay got it done. Bringing him back to some level of dignity he hadn't felt in days. He threw Lincoln's underwear in the toilet and flushed the soiled thing away. Being without underwear was a minor issue most boys were okay with, and it was better lost through the pipes than left behind as evidence. Mackay removed

Lincoln's shirt, wiped him front to back, then refitted his shirt and shorts. Good to go.

Mackay washed his own face in the basin, then headed back out to the other end of the veranda. To the wide-open door. To close any paranoid feelings of unaccounted personnel. He kept Lincoln behind him, hand held, and walked inside. He found a single light switch on the inner wall and discovered a sizeable room. Around six metres by three. About the size of an average sports bar. Cooled to a light chill with air-conditioning. Four big freezers lined the walls, the chest kind. The reach-in design with the lid on the top. Two freezers sat across the back wall with a single freezer on the left and right. All the same make and model. Long, silver and modern. Big storage capacities with a couple hundred litres each at least. All positioned over a large set of digitised platform scales with a digital reader located at the front. Mackay figured the air conditioning was installed to allow for a cooler setting, so the freezers didn't have to work overtime in summer.

There was a table in the middle of the room set up with a desktop computer and a large flat-screen monitor. On the screen were twelve security panels in grid formation. Mackay could see a number of the locations he'd moved through on the property: the first building where he'd tussled with the black mass, the noxious room where he'd found the reporter, the horse stables, maintenance shed, underground cellar and wine press. Some of the images looked out to the winery and some overlooked the driveway entrance and car park. He could just make out the lifeless body of the black giant in the corner of one of the panels, as well as the unconscious skinny cowboy in another. He couldn't tell whether the skinny guy's chest was rising or falling, nor did he care. Otherwise, from what he could see across the grid, there was no movement. Animal or human.

0200hrs
Thursday December 20, 2012
Frans & Hoek Winery, Western Australia

Out of pure curiosity, Mackay moved over to the closest freezer against the right wall and lifted it open. It was filled with grapes. Frozen of course. Many still on the vine in bunches. Probably harvested and kept when there were harsh seasons and poor yields. A plan B. A backup when crops were low and export demands needed to be met. Lincoln also peered in. Then, for normal reasons relating to the enticement of a cold, juicy grape on a hot day, Lincoln picked one and popped it into his mouth. He chewed on it a little, then spat it out and made a face. Vineyard grapes aren't always great for snacking. Often high in acidity, thick-skinned and riddled with seeds. Mackay hadn't a clue what variety of grapes were in there, but he thought he'd try one, nonetheless. Not that he felt like it, it was more to get alongside Lincoln and humour him. Besides, icy fruit in the heat of the night would feel nice in the mouth, maybe a little sour, but it was still edible. How bad could it be, really? Mackay pinched one off a vine and crunched into it. Almost immediately, he too spat it to the floor. Something was off. Sour was the wrong word to use. He was no grape specialist, but he did know the difference between a vineyard grape and the grocery-shelf variety. And these grapes were neither. The aftertaste was punchy and awful. Icy, coppery and metallic. Exactly like blood.

Mackay grabbed a bunch and took a closer look. All the little bulbs on the vine had a tiny little pockmark on their skin. A tiny puncture. Like a track mark on a drug addict. He moved to the back wall, opening the next two freezers. Visually inspecting, tasting a grape from each horde, then spitting it out. All the grapes were the same. Bloody. Literally. Its original juice extracted, then replaced. Injected with blood by someone, or a working crew with fine fingers and lots of finesse. Probably female. Delicate work undertaken by Van Breeman's other staff. Possibly the friendly faces from the front of house who serve the tourists. Mackay moved to the far left and opened the fourth freezer. It was empty. Nothing more to test. He then wiped his tongue back and forth across his shirt and scrubbed off as much of the bloody extract as possible. He took a water bottle from his backpack, filled his mouth, gargled and spat, then gargled and spat again. He offered the water to Lincoln who did the same.

Mackay hadn't a clue whether the blood was animal or human, though he erred on the human side considering what Malvin had seen when he stumbled into the wine press. Not to mention the voodoo situation earlier. He knew less than squat about voodoo practices, but he knew enough from reading the British newspapers over the last decade. Many reporting on the hundreds of African children abducted and trafficked into the UK for blood rituals in underground communities.

Mackay stepped back to observe the room. On the front of each freezer was a label with a series of Roman numerals written in black marker. Likely to keep the details inside discreet. The numerals were number ranges. The freezer he stood in front of had the numbers marked IV–XII with two specified columns underneath: one marked M, one marked F. The two along the back wall both had the number XVIII+, also with two columns M and F. The last freezer on the right wall had the numbers XIII–XVIII, same columns, M and F. In English digits the numbers equated as 4–12, 18-plus and 13–18. To anybody else walking in, seeing the numerals and the frozen grapes would simply assume a date range or a grape vintage. Maybe even a weight or a volume. And the M and F columns could have stood for Month and Fruit. Mackay knew better, though. He'd switched on. Pieced it together. The number ranges were human years for children, adults and teens. The M and F columns were the gender split for male and female.

Below the labels, attached with a white fridge magnet, was paperwork. Which resembled an itemised checklist for quantity and quality. He didn't know what the specifics were, and he wasn't going to read them to find out either. Blood had been forcefully, or in some way involuntarily, taken from tourists and their children. Injected into the fruit then distributed. Sold on the black market as a pricey commodity through the Dark Web. Van Breeman's moneymaker. Marketed to rich elitists with a disregard for human decency, and probably exported to African countries still practising voodoo. In any case it was a vile product for a vile customer. Hidden in plain sight. Part of the front of house where guests and tourists spent their money. Lincoln, fortunately, had alluded to the venture by accident. For the bigger picture, Mackay thought, it wasn't completely realistic to have that much blood taken from winery tourists alone. Those four freezers held almost a thousand litres of volume in total. The frozen grapes inside, taking into account how much each bunch could hold, needed more than just a couple of tourists' blood a day to be extracted. There was a greater operation at play. Van Breeman would have to have more connections through blood banks, paramedics, pathology clinics or phlebotomists to fill that many bulbs. Someone out there was offering patient samples in exchange for cash. Or special services. Malvin and his family just happened to be the ones passing through at the wrong time. Tourists doing tourist things when illegal demands needed to be met. Judging by the empty freezer labelled IV–XII, Mackay gathered Van Breeman had no more children's blood and needed a fresh sample ASAP. A snap-decision leaving a horrific mess, seeing an entire family wiped out.

Mackay needed to leave. He wanted nothing more to do with the place. He didn't know how far or how wide Van Breeman's connections went, and he didn't want to know. Wasn't his problem. It was a clean-up project for someone else. For real cops with the right conscience. He knew they existed, he just wasn't sure they existed locally. He'd found his nephew and made a dent in the ring of employment. That was enough. Above all things, his priority was to get Lincoln back to the only place he would be safe. Where both of them would be safe. Even from law enforcement, good or bad. Only back at the airbase would he and the boy have some form of refuge from the litter of bodies he'd left behind. He could potentially make it back to the UK even, if Cross's contacts held up. Which meant he and the boy needed to make exit moves straight away – if Mackay wanted to remain a free man. Sure, he had a phone, but it wasn't the burner he had originally purchased. The phone he had didn't have Cross's number logged in its software. He didn't know her number from memory and hadn't made the time or effort to write it down. Nonetheless, the phone he did have provided an opportunity. If played right, it would hopefully supply him with a vehicle to get him and Lincoln back to the Air Force base, and at the same time create an even bigger dent in Van Breeman's operation.

> 0230hrs
> Thursday December 20, 2012
> Frans & Hoek Winery, Western Australia

Mackay walked Lincoln back inside the main gallery into the admin room. He found the remote control for the television and turned it on. He needed something to occupy the boy while making his way out to the maintenance shed to pick up a few supplies. The television options were quite boring at half-three in the morning: international news, a handful of home shopping channels, low-budget cooking shows and music videos. He opted for the cooking shows. Easy on the brain, not too exciting.

DISCOVERY

Mackay sat Lincoln on one of the pleather armchairs. 'Ten minutes, then we're out of here.' Lincoln nodded once, tucked his knees up and looked at the screen with heavy eyes.

In the machinery shed Mackay found both things he was looking for quickly and easily. The first was a jerry can, the second was a lighter. The jerry can he found on a tiered shelving unit next to the ride-on lawnmower. It was half full and more than enough to start a blaze. The lighter was inside the skinny cowboy's front jeans pocket. As Mackay searched his pockets, the cowboy began to wake. Starting with light moaning first, then slowly building to an annoying bleat. Like a hungry young calf looking for its mother. The pain signals shooting up from his ankle, sternum and jaw into his nervous system, then back down again. For good measure, and to keep him out of the picture, Mackay cracked him in the face. Twice. Right fist, middle of the forehead. Enough to put him back to sleep and prolong the headache he was about to have. No knuckle dusters this time, the poor lackey had suffered enough.

Next, Mackay went back to the stable for the woman. As he entered the swinging gate, the lone horse left inside started up, just like last time. Braying and snorting. Backing away from the gate and kicking up a fuss. Mackay felt a little bad for the poor thing. It didn't have a clue about what had happened to its friend: a broken neck, dead, lying out there in the vineyard on top of its master. Mackay didn't intend it that way, the beast was basically collateral damage. Maybe the animal welfare groups would call it manslaughter, or whatever terminology was used in that context. He could never live down that moniker now though. Horse-killer. Two in one lifetime was a solid effort.

The woman was where he had left her. Still breathing, still bruised and swollen. She hadn't moved. Mackay picked her up and placed her over his shoulder. He held her there with one hand and carried the jerry can with the other. He threaded back through the property, left the jerry can out the front of the wine-press facility, then continued with the woman all the way up to the main gallery. The cooking show was still playing in the admin room, lighting Lincoln's face with a cool blue. Some frumpy woman with grey hair and glasses was pulling a cheesy dish from an oven. Lincoln was asleep. Out cold with exhaustion. His chest rose and fell steadily which was comforting. Mackay wished his brother was there to see him. See his son lying there, alive and comfortable. If there really was a spiritual place to go to after death, he hoped Malvin was there and knew Lincoln was safe. Watching over him from above, or perhaps standing somewhere nearby.

Mackay moved quickly outside to the front veranda. He didn't want Lincoln to wake and see the sunken, bloodied form of the woman on his shoulder. He then moved toward the open room with all the freezers, but he didn't go inside. He laid the woman down, just outside the door on the veranda floor. Recovery position. Head turned sideways over an outstretched arm. The soft hay would have been more comfortable, but he wanted her there. The emergency responders needed to see her body first.

Before getting to the main theatrics, Mackay stepped inside the room and walked over to the freezer on the right wall. The one numbered XIII–XVIII. He moved around behind it, found its power connection and ripped out the lead. He shuffled the bulky prism away from the wall, opened the lid, reached underneath and lifted – pouring all the fruit bulbs of blood onto the floor. It was as if a massive gumball machine had exploded, scattering millions of frozen purple and green balls everywhere.

Mackay moved onto the two freezers lining the back wall numbered XVIII+. He performed the same four-step process. The first of the two was an exact repeat: power lead out, shuffle it from the wall, open the lid, lift and tip. More grapes everywhere. The second of the two was slightly different. It was heavier. Mackay went through the same motions, only when he got to lift and tip, he had to readjust his hand position underneath, clamping down harder and lifting with more effort. This time there weren't just grapes being emptied from the inside compartment, a body toppled out with it. A frozen female. Folded in half to fit. Naked and dead and purple. Like the grapes. She had needles fixed with tubes attached to various sections of her see-through skin. Whoever the woman was, she was now shrivelled, dehydrated and ultimately sucked dry of all her blood. Part of Van Breeman's 18+ catalogue. Her face was a gaunt outline of bone. Her prominent features reduced to a film as thin as food wrap. Her hair, strangely, was tied up away from her face, wrapped in a neat bun. Her eyes, once wide and pretty, were now hardened to glass. She had high cheekbones with even features at all angles. Probably a looker back in her day. How long she had been crammed at the bottom of the freezer only Van Breeman would know. Now a dead man's guess. No rhyme or reason. *Another tick in the box for humanity*, thought Mackay, *and someone else's problem very shortly.*

Mackay didn't need to empty the last freezer. The one numbered IV–XII was bare anyway, so there was no point. He left the room and worked his way down to the wine press, moving inside with the jerry can to the most flammable object in the facility. The antique wooden structure. The old basket press he'd come across earlier. All wood, all old, all ready to burn. Luckily Van Breeman liked to keep some forms of tradition alive, which for this job was a good thing. Mackay felt a little bad about destroying it, as it was rather beautiful considering its age and craftsmanship, but it was owned by a dead guy with shameful ethics. In the end, Mackay figured burning the old press was serving a purpose for the greater good. Like a martyr.

The two vertical beams were tall enough to almost reach the wooden ceiling joists. Another good thing. Especially when the flames started licking at the top. Mackay doused the press with fuel from the jerry, splashing evenly at the front, then pouring a nice little pool inside the central basket to get the heat going. He then moved around to the back of the structure, tight up against the gyprock wall behind it. Using what fuel remained, he doused it along the back of the beams and rotating capstans. Suddenly, Mackay stumbled sideways into the gyprock with his shoulder – falling inward through a door cut into it. Seeing as the wall itself remained erect, Mackay figured he'd fallen through a concealed partition. A false door. Opening to an entirely new room completely separate from the main facility. As he looked around, the first thing he noticed was the long wooden table in front of him, extending left to right. Two tables aligned together end to end, stained with shades of purple and red. Grape juice. Or blood. Most likely both.

Set at the table closest to him were six chairs: three chairs per table. On the other side were four surgical trolleys, all lined with stainless steel trays. The two trays on the left were neatly laid out with laboratory equipment, as if prepped for a high school science experiment. Each tray had an open box of surgical gloves, pathology syringes, a vial rack filled with a dozen vials, two small strainers, a box of paper filters, beakers, and a set of everyday kitchen scissors. The two trays on the right were lined with cutting implements. Some were surgical like scalpels, forceps and scissors – same as what you'd find during an autopsy. Some were more industrial like what you'd find at a butcher: cleavers, boning knives, chef's knives, clam knives and scimitars. A fully fleshed-out blood-grape operation. It was worse than Mackay originally thought. They weren't just acquiring blood volumes through pathology clinics or blood banks; they were also taking their quantities by force. Victims captured and killed. Taken down like slabs of meat at an abattoir. The wall on the left had a set of black aprons on hooks. Shiny waterproof ones made with rubber and vinyl. The wall opposite had a big stainless-steel wash basin. The floor was laid with smooth tiles and a small drainage grill fixed in the middle. There was also a retractable winding hose reel set in the corner, which Mackay assumed was used to pressure clean the floor with, and regularly too. There wasn't a hint of leftover residue or debris to be seen, everything was immaculately kept. No flies and no smell either. Someone somewhere had been running the place to inspection order.

The room was obviously set up for blood injections. Employees who were probably shuffled around in alternating shifts to inject grapes, then serve customers at the front of house. Six chairs for six workers, though could easily allocate for more considering the space. Workers who would soon find themselves unemployed wherever they were. This was the real daily grind of the winery. Working bees diligently slicing, dicing, draining then infusing. Who knew what they did with the remains, or whose the remains were or where they came from. The list of possibilities was a wide-open source: locals, tourists, refugees, illegal immigrants, even international cadaver shipments. A matter for a higher power. Not Mackay's problem. He'd be long gone before anybody came looking for him, and he was about to burn the place to the ground anyway. Better that way. There'd still be plenty of evidence left over for an open-and-shut case, but at least the most crucial elements would be taken down in the blaze.

Mackay stepped back through the gyprock wall and lit up the old wooden press with the cowboy's lighter. The theatrics started slow, creeping from a smoulder to a flame, to a blaze to a bonfire. The final dent in Van Breeman's enterprise. He then made his way back to Lincoln who was still sound asleep in the chair basking in the warmth of pulled pork sliders on the television. He could see Lincoln's eyes moving underneath the lids. Dreaming. Hopefully about chocolates and *Mary Poppins* and not of the brick fireplace or whatever else he'd been through over the last three days.

Mackay left the room again, letting Lincoln sleep. Safe and comfortable. There was still a little time, and Lincoln had earned a bit of shut-eye. Somebody needed to be notified of the situation: the beaten woman, the blood in the grapes and the hollowed, defrosting body from the freezer. And that somebody was not going to be any individual paramedic or police officer. Or anyone with any connections to the local emergency services in the area. He needed to call everyone. Because chances were, if all emergency departments were there, accountability to manage the truth was at a much higher percentage. The more members dealing with the bodies, fire, and Van Breeman's exports, the higher the likelihood it would be handled through correct processes. The more the merrier.

Mackay took out the mobile phone he'd found on the wine-tasting bench and stepped onto the veranda. Which was when he encountered a problem. He didn't know Australia's emergency number, which he recognised put him in the complete-idiot category, pure and simple. Then and there, his greatest dumb-arse moment of his entire life. Cross would never let him live it down if she ever found out. He was a world-traveller. A soldier. A corporal for goodness' sake. Yet he hadn't the foggiest idea. Europe was all 112, and the whole world knew 911 was for the United States and Canada. He even knew the secondary 999 number of Ireland, but Australia? He'd never visited before. Never needed to know. Foreign number, foreign country. His mind was blank.

'Fuck. What the fuck is the emergency number?' he said out loud, hating himself every passing second. Spoiling the momentum right when things were swimming along. In that same flash of disappointment, Mackay heard a small set of feet shuffling through the gallery behind him. Tiny tiptoeing steps, slow and light. Mackay turned. Lincoln's malnourished form hobbled over next to him. Mackay knelt down as Lincoln wrapped his arms around his neck and hugged him, like it came naturally.

'Zero, zero, zero,' Lincoln said in Mackay's ear. His voice dry and automated.

Mackay paused, blinking away his confusion. He shuffled back and faced his nephew.

'What's that, Lincoln?' said Mackay.

'You told me.'

'What did I tell you?'

'After your accident we visited. You said soldiers don't say oh. They say zero. That's the emergency number here. Zero, zero, zero.'

The little autistic boy knew it.

'How did you figure that out?' said Mackay. 'Who told you that was the emergency number here?'

'I read it.'

'Where?'

Lincoln pointed to the female toilets at the other end of the veranda. 'A sticker on the big red bottle.'

From where they stood, Mackay could just make out the fire extinguisher fixed to the wall through the female bathroom's vacant doorframe. Above the paper towels he used to wipe Lincoln down with.

'You're incredible,' said Mackay.

'You could still dial one, one, two,' said Lincoln, 'it wouldn't matter. It would still go to an Australian emergency line.'

'How do you know that?'

Lincoln shrugged.

Lincoln's spectrum quirks made Mackay feel even more stupid.

'I'm tired,' said Lincoln, and nestled his head on Mackay's shoulder. Gently, comfortably. 'You should call right away,' he said. 'There's a fire out there.' Lincoln turned and pointed. 'Behind us. I saw it. It's far away so we're okay now, but it's big. You're supposed to call the fire department if you see a fire.'

Mackay's sense of stupidity vanished, immediately replaced with endearment for the boy. An uncle's love. A family tie that would never break. In that moment Mackay had found his new purpose in life: to look after Lincoln until he was a grown man. Until he was able to manage the world on his own.

Mackay dialled 000. A recorded message began:

"You have dialled emergency triple zero. Your call is being connected. An operator will answer your call and ask whether you need police, fire and rescue, or ambulance."

An operator came on the line.

'Do you require Police, Fire or Ambulance?'

Mackay gave his best Australian accent.

'All of them. Frans and Hoek Winery in Margaret River is on fire, and there are bodies everywhere. Some are alive, some are not.'

That was it. Mackay hung up, wiped the phone down with his sleeve then stomped it to pieces. He had no further use for it and being traced was not an option. He had no idea what Cross's number was, or any other contact in Australia for that matter, so he couldn't make any calls regardless. Even if he wanted to source military aid from his old contacts back in the UK, it would leave a trail. Which meant from that point on, he was completely on his own.

0430hrs
Thursday December 20, 2012
Frans & Hoek Winery, Western Australia

Day was breaking. Black was slowly morphing to a muted grey. Which, against the contrast of the bristling fire behind the gallery, made for a bleak morning. Unfortunately, it made the morning feel worse than the world could give credit for. Really, it was just another day. The planet had turned. As it would the next day and the day after that. People had died. But Mackay was alive, and Lincoln had been found.

After destroying the phone, Mackay carried Lincoln across the winery car park, over the road into a litter of trees behind a single wired fence line. Into more forest growth, like most of the land surrounding the vineyard, only it wasn't as densely populated. After thirty paces Mackay found two wide jarrah trees living next to each other, providing enough cover from either direction of the road. He sat down with Lincoln asleep in his arms, his face pleasantly contrasting the dusk's gloom. He propped his back against the thicker of the two trees, closed his eyes and waited. Resting and thinking. He tried clearing his mind, but he was too wired. Attacking brain waves of self-awareness kept slipping through. All noise and chatter. The events of the evening playing over and over, along with the doubt of getting out of the situation without the authorities catching up with him. His head was like a scream-fest blaring incoherent thrash metal somewhere in the background. He ran his fingernails hard through his hair. Around the ears, the temple, the crown, down the nape. Drawing blood into the scalp. Painful and relaxing at the same time. For a long moment he wished he was back in Afghanistan. Slinging banter with the boys, prepping for an operation. Mostly, he thought of Cross. Back at the airbase, waiting for information to come through. A loc-stat or sit-rep report. Which he couldn't give because he had nothing to communicate with. He knew nothing could be done, but he was still fuming about not knowing Cross's number. Or having any contact written or digitally keyed in somewhere for that matter. He and Lincoln were surviving purely on the concept of luck and soldier experience, which had served well so far. To a point at least. The only reason he had come out on top was an insolent will to survive, as well as the fortuitous addition of some enhanced technology imbedded inside him.

At ten minutes into dozing with Lincoln's sooty hair brushing his neck, a distant wail hit the air. It travelled across the valley, starting low in the hilly range, rising steadily, then shrieking into life as a big red fire truck, pulling into the vineyard's entrance. The driver quickly established a manoeuvring point then beelined down behind the front of house where a monstrous orange blaze licked the dawn clean out of the atmosphere. Mackay could feel the warmth of the fire even from behind the thick jarrah. He was a little annoyed though, as he had hoped the paramedics or police would arrive first. Namely so he could hijack their vehicle and start making tracks. Taking a firefighting truck would be slow and cumbersome on the roads, and much too visible. Even at this hour of the morning.

Three minutes later, this time without the noise and theatrics, the paramedics arrived. Which made sense. The cops would arrive third, seeing as Mackay had not stated whether the bodies were in immediate danger. He mentioned a fire in progress first, with bodies everywhere second. The order of arrival may have differed if he said it the other way around. Either way, Mackay was happy with an ambulance as a mode of transport.

From between the two jarrah trees Mackay watched the ambulance park in front of the gallery. He then watched a second ambulance arrive, which gave him even better odds of scoring a vehicle. Having two vehicles arrive made sense, given his open-ended description of bodies everywhere. Typically, one ambulance catered for one critical patient, but with two, they'd be able to assess the situation and possibly request a third, or a fourth. For the numbers, five ambulances were required: the reporter, Van Breeman, the cowboy, the black mass, the frozen woman. Though, Mackay wasn't sure what they'd do with her.

She was undoubtedly a cold case. Literally and figuratively. Dead and frozen for a good long while. A missing person from way back. Whether she was a police concern or a paramedic concern was a debate he wasn't going to have. He needed to steal one of the two ambulance vehicles as soon as possible.

In the fiery light, Mackay watched both sets of paramedics exit their vehicles – each in tow with a detailed heavy-duty response kit. The four of them gathered on the veranda around their first casualty as expected: the beaten woman. The petite brunette he'd laid at the open door with the tipped freezers and blood-grapes. All of which were thawing out on the floor. Easy evidence which Mackay hoped would already be releasing its coppery blood stink as they rose to temperature. He then watched them mediate and discuss things, looking at the signs of mayhem. Nodding and pointing back and forth, finalising decisions on who was doing what. After a few seconds, one paramedic from the first ambulance slowly entered the room while his partner opened the response kit and began tending to the woman. The second pair from the second ambulance then left the veranda and disappeared behind the gallery. Either to collaborate with the fire department or to look around to find the initial caller. Or maybe they went searching for more potential casualties. Whatever they were doing was irrelevant. Mackay picked Lincoln up and dashed back across the road toward the car park. To the closest ambulance with its driver's side door open. Staying silent at this point was also irrelevant. Any sound made crunching across the gravel was dampened by the sound of a building being reduced to kindling over a hundred yards away. Not to mention the hundreds of pounds of pressurised water smothering the woofing inferno.

Mackay checked the keys were still in the ignition then hopped into the front seat. He slid Lincoln's sleeping form over the console into the passenger side and closed the door. So far so good. He'd gone by completely unnoticed. Mackay reclined Lincoln's seat back a little for comfort, strapped him in, then secured his own seat belt. He selected reverse on the gear lever, backed out of the parking bay, then shifted into drive – creeping out of the winery towards the road. Before leaving the grounds, he made a final left-right sweep across the side-view mirrors. In the driver's-side mirror, he could see the rear end of the fire truck with two guys operating a hose on a raised ladder. In the passenger's mirror, he saw the first two responding paramedics spring from the veranda and start running towards him.

Mackay exited the gravel driveway and turned left. He got no more than a couple hundred metres down the warming blacktop before a van appeared over a crest in front of him, moving with purpose. A second after it passed, it pulled up hard. Its tyres shrieking painfully as they bawled to a halt twenty metres behind Mackay in a cloud of smoke. Through his rear-view mirror Mackay watched the van back up and work a fast three-point turn. Lock-to-lock, one-eighty degrees. Changing direction to the same as Mackay's line of travel. The van accelerated furiously up beside him on the right and then swung into his lane. Cutting him off completely and pulling to an immediate stop. Forcing Mackay to bed into the brake and hold the vehicle steady, halting inches from the van's tailgate.

The light of the dawning sun hadn't completely split the horizon yet, so Mackay wasn't sure of the exact colour of the vehicle. From where he sat, it looked silver-grey, however the make and model were distinct: a Kia Carnival. The chrome badge and lettering gleamed from the soft red of the brake lights. The van moved, veering to the farthest edge of the road on the left before backing up and swinging around again. The full process: three-point turn, lock-to-lock, one-eighty degrees, blocking Mackay the entire time. Then it crawled forward. Aligning its driver's-side door right alongside Mackay's. Each vehicle facing the opposite direction in the middle of the road, one metre apart from handle to handle. The driver, a man, powered his window down and leaned out, taking in the clearest observation possible through the dark-grey tint of Mackay's window. His eyes were searching and agitated. He had a thick neck and a blockhead with a ballpark age of around forty. It did not seem like he had stopped to ask for directions. Rather, he was assessing the occupants: Mackay, wearing a military-grade tactical uniform, and the small passenger reclining next to him. A young boy, asleep, aged around five or six.

Over a surge of milliseconds, Mackay processed a number of deductions linking the driver and the vehicle. This included the time of day, the frenzied approach, the screeching tyres and lack of driver etiquette; not having his low beams on in the dimness of the morning. Even though Mackay couldn't clearly see the driver's features through his window, he could tell he wore a dark collared shirt and that the man was tall – considering how close his blockhead was to the roof lining. All calculations boiled down to the theory that the driver did not want to be seen, yet needed to move with speed and purpose. The man was pressured to reach a specific location with utmost urgency. Which quashed Mackay's first three proposals: either he was a concerned neighbour, an unmarked police vehicle or another emergency responder out of uniform. Neither proposal felt right. In the end, tying it all together was the driver's expression. Which brought Mackay to his fourth and final conclusion: the driver was one of Van Breeman's men.

At the same time all the little pieces connected, the driver also joined his own dots as to who Mackay was. Or at least who he suspected he was, because without a flinch, word or gesture, once he locked eyes on Mackay, he dipped his shoulder below the doorframe, raised it, then extended his arm out the window holding a weapon. A big one. Blue steel frame with distinct cylindrical chambers. A revolver. The guy's paws were big, wrapping comfortably around the handle, but the weight of the piece was obvious. His wrist wasn't flush and the barrel angled slightly lower than level. Which meant the chambers were full of lead. Beefy .357 rounds. All of which indicated something powerful, most likely a Magnum. A Dirty Harry. Sure-fire single burst, no safety, would not jam. One hell of a gun. Not something any regular Joe could just walk into a gun store and purchase. At least not in Australia.

Mackay hit the gas pedal in the nick of time, right before two cracking blows punched into the side of the ambulance. The first round shattered the window next to Mackay's head. The hydrostatic pressure from the slug exploding the glass like silver confetti, embedding the chips into his hair and face. The second round drove through the B-pillar next to the headrest. None hit flesh or bone which was a positive, but a shard of glass split Mackay's left eyelid, making the landscape a little pink and blurry.

Mackay had no idea where he was going, he just knew he was on a country road leading away from the winery. Luckily where vehicles drove on the same side as back in the UK. He had a marginal head start which was somewhat advantageous, thanks to the direction he was already facing. Whereas the other guy had to drop the Magnum, sit back in his chair and work the transmission again. Third time lucky: three-point turn, one-eighty rotation, then pile on the gas. Enough time for Mackay to extend his lead by about seven or eight seconds. Enough to get ahead, but not enough to be out of sight. And the daylight was only getting brighter which made everything more conspicuous. Especially an ambulance.

Mackay drove fast but steady. Big vehicle, unfamiliar roads. He did his best to drive to the conditions and gain as much distance as possible, but at the same time had to keep in mind there was a small boy curled up in the seat next to him. Which also meant Mackay needed to think. Think about how he was going to eliminate the encroaching enemy without a weapon or a secondary aid. He had no spotter to help give directions, divert attention, or blanket the van's windscreen with a spray from a machine gun. There was nobody sitting next to him who could hold a rifle and take head shots or blow tyres out. Mackay was on his own.

After four minutes of long sweeping bends, hills and dives, the West Australian sky cracked a sliver of orange, opening the landscape with good visibility. And with regular glances into the rear-view mirror, it was obvious the ambulance was the heavier vehicle. The silver van behind them slowly but surely kept creeping closer. The driver familiar with his vehicle and the roads. Time was running out and Mackay had to think harder. There was only one road snaking through the terrain, so he couldn't divert onto any alternate routes or forks or bush tracks. The fence lines either side holding back the wildlife made veering off the road impossible, as were the road shoulders which were deeply gravelled for drainage. When a break from the fence line did intermittently open, the scattered trees, ditches and thickets of bushland were too dense. The vehicle was not an off-roader, so it wouldn't be able to take it. Even if a diverging track did miraculously appear, careening across the red earth would make his position too obvious. The mammoth plumes of burgundy dust billowing into the air would pinpoint his location like a beacon. Bad idea. As was turning the vehicle around to try and veer the driver off the road. Playing chicken on a reckless impulse with Lincoln in the vehicle was not an option.

Mackay needed to wait for the road to rise into a tall ascent, tapering to a blind hill at the top. A peak with nothing to see over the crest other than the horizon. Which came a few short kilometres later as the route twisted around the land. As the slower vehicle, what Mackay was about to do, he had to do rapidly. The van was less than a kilometre behind him, literally only a few hundred metres. Every passing second, the driver was increasing speed and cutting his distance. Mackay had one chance to get this done, and get it done right. Which was a big ask in that pressure-cooker moment. The last time things got hairy whilst operating a vehicle he had made mistakes. He had reacted without thinking, without applying standard operating procedures. Drills he'd practised hundreds of times had gone out the window. He had failed his training. Team members were killed. That could not happen again. All steps in this next strategy needed to be applied aggressively. Slow and smooth would not work.

Once the vehicle started climbing the crest, Mackay reached over Lincoln and grabbed his seat belt, holding his forearm firm against Lincoln's chest. Once the vehicle hit the peak of the rise Mackay held his line and began braking steadily. Not hard enough to activate ABS, but heavy enough to pull to a stop without burning rubber. Consistent, modulated pressure. Burned rubber and smoke was as good as giving away his intentions.

The ambulance twitched and skimmed until the top of the vehicle dipped beyond the peak then slowed to a stop. Invisible from the rise behind them, dead centre of his lane where the road continued into the horizon. Narrow as a blade of grass. Lincoln's eyes flicked over to his uncle, watching as he undid both seat belts in frenzied succession, crawled across the centre console, pulled him into his arms, opened the passenger door and leaped out. With Lincoln cradled against his chest, Mackay dove at a low angle, ensuring he hit the roadside shoulder first – his momentum sending them tumbling into the red earth.

Three seconds later a chrome grill rose into view as the silver van appeared over the crest. It didn't slow until it was too late, ploughing headfirst into the back of the ambulance, doing well over a hundred kilometres an hour. Metres from Mackay and Lincoln huddled in the dirt. The ambulance bucked forward and exploded. Not into a cloudy inferno with fire and smoke, but into pieces. Chunks and sections of body panels, seats, engine components, first aid equipment and an ocean of glass. The stretcher flew up vertically, wafted like a kite and landed off into the shrub.

The front end of the van crumpled like an accordion before bouncing away, careening sideways onto two wheels then rotating over and over up the road ahead. Like a spit roast over a flame, it just kept turning. Flipping and breaking apart before settling against a pod of grasstrees and sedimentary rock.

Mackay stood immediately and carried Lincoln over to the silver wreckage. He remembered the words of an old sergeant. A warrior's battle code: if your enemy is down, make sure he stays down. After a hundred paces Mackay peered into the mouth of the carnage – where the front windscreen, bonnet, headlights and grill should have been. The trashed machine lay upside down, the make and model now completely unidentifiable. The whole front was a blended mesh of steel and plastic. He left Lincoln on the roadside then stooped down to look under the crumpled bonnet. There was no body in the driver's seat. Which was only half true as the body that was there just wasn't complete, and wasn't breathing, which was all Mackay needed to know. The driver's torso had dropped onto the road, fallen out of the windscreen with his legs and buttocks still partially attached to the seat. Courtesy of the fastened seat belt. At some point during the impact and subsequent flipping, glass and steel had cut him open. The man's trunk was agape. The separation between upper and lower body like the open jaws of a shark. Fleshy slabs of red and white were crusted over with glass. Gravity and positioning had done its thing and spilled his innards. Spread like a tray of butcher's sausages. Plenty enough for a family barbecue. All in a neat little mound on the blacktop underneath him, which Lincoln didn't need to see. Flies had already gathered for the feasting, crawling around and sucking on his blood.

TEN

UNRAVELLING

> 0500hrs
> Thursday December 20, 2012
> Somewhere between Perth and Margaret River, Western Australia

With the sun-baked land heating up, Mackay knew he had to get moving. There was no shelter, no farms or houses of any description in any direction. There was literally nowhere to hide unless he dug himself a bunker and ate off the land's provision. Which he had no idea how to do. He may have been a qualified corporal back in the day, but the British military didn't teach how to survive in outback landscapes. On the crest of that blind hill, it was all trees and shrubbery, red earth and fence lines. Three hundred and sixty degrees all around. And important people with badges and uniforms were certainly looking for him, considering what he'd left in his wake. Local law enforcement, if not the federal police would already be working on tracking him down. Even the paramedics might have called a secondary crew to try and triangulate his position based on the direction he left the winery. After all, it was their own local backyard. How far could a foreigner in an ambulance really go? To keep from getting caught he would need to take his chances in the bush. Completely off-road away from all forms of vehicles and transport. Anything with a fast-moving set of tyres was a potential witness. If the law requested an aerial search, he would deal with that bridge if and when he heard it coming. Which he gathered would only happen in about two or three hours once the road searches lucked out.

The temperature was rising by the second and Mackay's biggest concern wasn't Lincoln at that point. It was himself. He was thirsty, and somewhere inside, a strange sense of fatigue was emerging. A feeling he'd felt before, back in Aldershot. After chasing down the two thieves, then later waking up kicking and screaming in hospital. He was down to one bottle of water in his backpack, which at half a litre wasn't going to be enough for the both of them. Not for a full day under the sun. A native ant would need more. If he couldn't look after himself, Lincoln wouldn't survive either. Which meant things were down to a very fine point.

Mackay checked his front breast pocket. He still had the GPS tracker, a military-grade tool which should give him bearings to his location. He took it out. The screen had a single crack, etched like a hairline fracture across the top third of the screen. Most likely from the tumble dryer treatment he endured through the vineyard with the horse. But it was working. His saving grace, and another credit to Andy. It put him at an inland position from the coastline. Thirty-three degrees latitude, one hundred and sixteen degrees longitude. As a geographical reference it put him two hundred and five kilometres south of RAAF Base Pearce, which made it one hundred and eighty kilometres south of Perth.

Fair judgment combined with his newly acquired thermoplastic capabilities, Mackay figured he could reasonably aim for the city. On foot. At running speed. If he could hold out that is. In any case he had no other choice. They were both dead or caught if they stayed in the bushland or took the road. Then, once they got close enough to civilisation, they could hopefully hitchhike the last fifty or so kilometres to the airbase. Managing Lincoln for the journey was going to be Mackay's greatest physical test. Even greater than taking on the horse, which, at the thought of it, sent a few shots of panic spasming through his head. If he was going on foot with Lincoln on his back, he needed to figure out a way to secure him. And fast. The sunbeams flaring off the earth were intensifying by the second.

*

Mackay removed his backpack, the Kevlar vest and ballistic plate. He gulped down half his last bottle of water and handed the rest to Lincoln. He pulled his belt from around his waist and removed the bayonet and seal pup knife. He left the vest in the dirt, pocketed the seal knife, then skewed the bayonet through the first waist-loop at the front of his pants – using it as a makeshift belt. A replacement for his actual belt which would need to be used to secure Lincoln. He worked the blade and the cross-guard through the buttonhole to stop his pants from falling down, which was tight, but unless he wanted to run with his pants down it was his best option. He then took his field shirt off and tore it in two, wrapping one half around his head and the other around Lincoln's, like a bandana. For sun protection. Lincoln, who sat half asleep on the ground, looked a little more hydrated than when Mackay first saw him inside the hearth, but his expression was still nowhere near normal. Mackay dropped a knee and faced him.

'We need to get moving,' said Mackay. 'I'm going to carry you on my back using this belt to strap your legs tight around my stomach. It'll stop you from falling off.'

Lincoln said nothing. Mackay couldn't tell if he understood, his doughy eyes were too red and glazed to gauge any acuity or feedback. After a moment, Lincoln stood, then walked behind Mackay and started climbing onto his back. Mackay curled over, allowing Lincoln to step and straddle, then adjusted the boy's slender arms over his shoulders.

'I need you to clasp tight around me,' said Mackay, standing upright. 'I'm going to start running. Fast. I can't have you bouncing off.'

Mackay rocked on his toes to get Lincoln shimmied into the best position. With his belt, he hooked the strap behind Lincoln's left leg, then the right, then threaded the tip through the buckle. Keeping Lincoln's knees just below Mackay's chest. Snug enough to keep them from rubbing or bouncing while he ran. He checked and adjusted one last time. Everything felt taut. Good enough to run, but not too restrictive to cut off the breathing capacity of his diaphragm.

'That okay for you? Not too tight?'

'Okay,' said Lincoln.

'I want you to fold your arms around my neck, just don't choke my throat.'

'No choke. Run and breathe.'

Regardless of the water he'd just had, Mackay's thirst continued to swell. Like the heat of the morning. His body wanted more. And worse, that deep-set uneasy fatigue felt like it was growing. Numbing his insides. He had no immunosuppressants and no synthetic marrow medication to settle his condition. How long he would last was now down to luck and determination. All big negatives. And he had no real idea where he was going either, just that he had to head north towards the city. On the positive side, at least his footwear was good, and he and Lincoln were together. The two things that counted the most right now. Though whatever gel technology was inside his shoes was about to take a beating. The pounding under the extra weight of Lincoln, at Mackay's pace, would start to wear inside an hour. The situation was all sides awful. On one hand he could give up, hand himself to the authorities, in turn putting Lincoln into institutional care, or he could take his chances in the scrub. Which he did, stepping away from the road and into the arid landscape. Lincoln pinned to his back.

'We're good to go,' said Mackay.

Mackay shot off. He didn't know how long he had, he just knew he had to get going with as much pace as his body could handle. No heat, nor thirst, nor fatigue was going to get in his way if he could help it. The back of his legs flexed like rods of thickened bamboo – the bulky strands of fibre picking up speed, then more speed again, generating a human motor Mackay didn't yet know the limits of. Even with Lincoln's slight, thirty-five kilograms strapped in like a jockey, Mackay moved with agility. Light and completely fluid, his muscles rippling like a bag of walnuts.

His feet moved across the land with soft levity like they were barely touching the earth. Once his breathing increased and his body temperature rose, his circulatory system engaged to maximal capacity. The Phragazom compound doing its job to allow copious amounts of air in and efficiently remove toxins and carbon dioxide. His oxygen debt was cleared in seconds. The normal build-up of lactic acid and shortened breath didn't even surface. His adrenalin and noradrenalin increased only minimally compared to any Olympic-level runner. His increased lung capacity from his wider chest cavity allowed him the space to push on with ease. His pace kicked up in gears stride after stride, bounding, dodging and hurtling in one direction. North.

Creating a whistling wind tunnel and pressing the hair over his head like an invisible cap.

In 1996 in Atlanta, US Olympian Michael Johnson was clocked running his record-breaking two-hundred metre sprint at an average speed of thirty-seven kilometres per hour. Taking just a smidge over nineteen seconds. One of the fittest men to have ever lived. For a seriously trained athlete, that time could only be kept up for short bursts. At thirty-seven kilometres per hour, Mackay was working hard, but he was only just warming up. His body was even more capable. His legs and arms increasing in rhythm and tempo, enabling him to peak at a little under Australia's suburban road limit: forty-nine kilometres per hour. Thirty miles an hour in the old British imperial system. Three miles an hour faster than what he'd reached back in Aldershot. Mathematically, if Mackay maintained his current pace, with distance equal to speed multiplied by time, it predicted just over a three-hour journey to Perth. Whether Mackay's body could take that kind of abuse was a different story.

Mackay held that pace for an hour, his synthetic system working effortlessly. Then, the dry desiccant wind picked up behind him. Assisting his rolling stride. Adding a few extra kilometres per hour to his cadence, helping him range somewhere between fifty and sixty kilometres an hour. Mackay oscillated over stone and earth, shrubs and logs, passing through hordes of humming insects and scurrying animals like an automaton. Kilometres disappeared under long, ground-gaining strides, the gravel and dirt rattling and pluming on every step.

Running with Lincoln on his back was a feeling of being alive like no other. The morning sun beat down on his head and shoulders like a hammer, but Mackay took no notice. His mind was on autopilot. A trance-like state wired to his physical systems on a loop – extending, compressing, springing forward. Cutting through the air like a hot knife. His long, gapped footprints the only sign he was ever there. Time and energy lapsed on that lonesome terrain while Mackay made good ground. And Lincoln loved every minute – tucked in tight behind his uncle, eyes closed from the teary wind. He began to hum effusively. Keeping his little world occupied while the human train created enough G-force to alter Lincoln's spatial awareness. Mackay's speed against the earth's gravitational acceleration stimulating his senses with exhilaration.

Then the wind died, and Mackay started feeling awful. Physically, everything started to hurt. Rough as guts. All forms of atomical matter inside felt doughy and hot. There was no water at hand, no creek or waterhole, but there was no way he was going to stop. He pressed on, still the master of his body. As focused as the first day he marched onto the desert battlefield.

Mackay, however, was still a mortal man. And deep, disgusting exhaustion eventually showed its dirty face. His strength began to wane. His incredible pace dampening to an illusion, enticing him to quit. Even the shadows among the trees were tempting. Calling him to cool off in their shade. Despite gritting it through, Mackay's tortured body slowed. After two and a half hours of working overtime, he was bordering on useless. Any normal man would have hit a wall over a hundred kilometres ago. Exhaustion was an understatement. Something was wrong. His thirst was insatiable and there was nothing cooling his engine. He dropped down to twenty kilometres per hour. To fifteen, ten, then finally to a slow walk. Stiff and rigid like a drunkard. Inside his skin, things quickly became unbearable. With only fifty kilometres left, the real-world pain had started shouting murderously in his face. Screaming from every facet and fibre, bone and joint. His insides were cooking him alive, overheating way past red line. The taste of bile and blood flushed his mouth. His bones wished for death.

Mackay stumbled, then stopped. Though quivering like an ocean, he still managed to raise his eyes and look ahead, but there was nothing to see. It was all the same reddish, steampunk landscape he'd been travelling since he started. Now it was even more hazy. Unsure what was real and what wasn't. He dropped vertically to his knees like an anchor, then fell like a tree. Biting the dirt and throwing Lincoln off to his side. Summoning any amount of energy felt like pushing grass through concrete. All he could manage was to undo the belt buckle and loosen Lincoln from his waist. Before he passed out, he thought of his parched throat and the endless terrain – concluding his mission was futile and that he and Lincoln were going to die. And there was nothing he could do about it.

Lincoln shuffled himself off Mackay's back then watched his uncle struggle for breath in strained, wheezy rasps. Before his eyes glazed over, Mackay looked into his nephew's face as he slipped away. He had no words. Couldn't speak. Couldn't tell him things were going to be okay, because they weren't. He couldn't reach up and give him a hug or shelter him from the sun. His eyes blurred in and out as he searched Lincoln's face, trying to apologise. Desperately wanting to tell him how sorry he was. How hard he tried. His vision petered out beyond the trees where the hot air shimmered like vapour. In his final seconds, he noticed something beyond the leaves and branches. Some hundred metres away his faltering state was still able to pick out a man-made object. Dull and faint, raised high off the ground. A contrasting difference from the surrounding colours of dry crimson. An old, rusted signpost poked through the trees like an imaginary oasis. Weathered white, yellow and red. A symbol in the shape of a clam. An abandoned fuel station. Before oblivion took over, Mackay raised a finger and pointed to it.

> 0800hrs
> Thursday December 20, 2012
> Somewhere between Perth and Margaret River, Western Australia

Caged with a surrounding barrier of fencing, the fuel station looked set to be demolished. At one point. A job long forgotten. Left in an ignored landscape that would never see completion. The decayed walls were clapboard with only the thinnest hint of its original paint. The scorched construction was now a grotty piece of battered history, as if erected only a few days after the colonial years ended. The roof had fallen in, its windowpanes were shattered, crispy insect shells and cobwebs clung to the walls along with animal nests and their excrement. Most of the rest of the insides were covered in ash and soot, as if a fire had licked it up long before the crew arrived.

Lincoln clambered through the fencing barrier which was easy enough. There were no cutting barbs or sharp points to deal with. He slid between two barrier posts and walked inside the compound, moving beneath the rusted overhang which covered three old bowsers. Prehistoric fuel pumps. One diesel, and two 91 unleaded. He stepped up the concrete platform in front of reception and walked through what used to be the front door. Inside, he was greeted by a collection of grimy gas cylinders, all empty and useless. Next to them in the corner was a melted Coca-Cola refrigerator, and next to that was the burnt-out counter crumpled in a heap. Adjacent to that was an ashen walkway to a back room, likely the rear entrance. There were no taps, sinks or signs of water anywhere. Lincoln walked on through to the back and pried open a charcoal door.

A hundred metres beyond the petrol station nestled below a rise of olive-green hills was what looked to be an abandoned shed. Perhaps a garage or barn. Possibly belonging to the old owners of the very fuel station he'd just exited. Lincoln walked towards it.

After a number of monumental ant mounds and a series of trees sprouting needle-like fronds, he arrived. It was not a shed, garage or barn. It was a home. At least once upon a time. Half corrugated iron and half brick. Scoured, but not decaying. Made to stand the test of time. A stripped-out tractor with flat tyres stood guard out front of a waist-high fence circling its front yard. Full of dead weeds and wild spreads of wheat and chaff. The metal gate at the front groaned in protest as Lincoln pushed and entered. Its front porch was a dirty concrete slab leading to a narrow, flaking yellow door. Two grimy windows were set in the wall on the left, and the collapsing remains of a barbecue from the First World War stood on the right. Clearly the kind of place where you'd only ever use the back door. The rear of the building stretched back at least twenty metres, opening into a massive backyard where the fencing turned into star-pickets and wiring with no visual end. It just expanded backwards into the landscape. Into farming property hundreds and hundreds of metres up into the hills. Possibly used as an old cattle farm or sheep station. Whether it worked for livestock or horticultural purposes was anyone's guess.

Lincoln stood at the peeling front door, knocked, then waited. A common neighbourly courtesy. He listened for movement, heard nothing, waited a few seconds more, then repeated. Knock and wait. A social politeness he'd learned. The decent thing to do, rather than walking up to the door and opening it, which he tried next, but the door was locked. Or jammed from hard weathering. Or both. Lincoln stepped off and walked around the side of the house. There were no windows, just a path lined with more weeds, broken pallets and old paint buckets filled with dirt. He continued to the rear of the building where the backyard opened like the parting of the red sea. Where the mountains in the distance grew out to an expanding property large enough to house a city.

At the rear of the building, a large, corroded water tank as old as the land behind it stood against the back wall. A hundred metres further was a lonely windmill, its rusted fans still grinding over its pyramid assembly. The water tank had a single piece of rope attached between the tank's flow pipe and the gutter jutting from the roof of the house. A makeshift clothesline. One pair of faded dark jeans was pegged on it – a possible sign of life. Next to the flow pipe near the bottom of the tank was a tap. Even at six years of age with diagnosed autism, Lincoln could run the numbers: a tap, a water tank, a dying uncle. He twisted the tap. On his first attempt he managed a quarter turn. With two hands buckled over the handle he managed half a turn more. The tap squealed and the pipe shuddered. A single drop of water emerged. He tried again. More squealing and shuddering, then a trickle. Lincoln ran back to the side of the house, tipped over one of the paint buckets filled with dirt and ran back to the tap. Which was when a door flung open behind him. A thin, dark-skinned man in a navy-blue singlet ran out holding a shotgun aimed head high. Lincoln turned.

'Water,' said Lincoln, hoarse and soft. 'Uncle. Water.' Lincoln raised a hand and pointed back beyond the house.

The man, older than sixty, younger than eighty, squinted at the boy in disbelief. Not that he'd never met a small boy before, but standing there alone looking for water in his backyard was a first. Not what he was expecting. The man lowered the gun and walked over. 'You need water?'

Lincoln shook his head. 'My uncle. He looks bad.'

'He's out there?'

Lincoln nodded.

'You know where to find him?'

Lincoln nodded again.

'Come along,' said the man, and grabbed Lincoln by the hand. He discarded the paint bucket and walked him inside the house. He collected a large water bottle from a cupboard, filled it from the kitchen tap then ran back outside with Lincoln leading the way.

Mackay was still there. Deteriorating in a clearing of rubble. Cooking in the sun and breathing dirt, but at least he was breathing. A group of crows – a murder – as well as two wedge-tailed eagles had gathered around to watch, staring at his body. Waiting for his chest to stop rising and falling. Patiently killing time before their next meal. They even stayed put when Lincoln and the man arrived. Staunch and stoic. Unflinching to the strangers on their turf; our soil, our backyard. Optimistic they'd still get a chance to feast on him later.

The man grabbed a fistful of Mackay's shirt and dragged his body to a shady patch under a hulking eucalyptus tree. He sat down, pulled Mackay into his lap and opened his lips – trickling droplets of water into his mouth from the bottle. There was no response. The man repeated the process. Minutes passed. Mackay remained unconscious.

Suddenly, a merciless roar pierced the sky above them. Like a choir of dinosaurs gargling hand grenades. A shadow the size of an island covered their position, blocking the sun for three whole seconds before opening the world again. The man ducked instinctively, scrambled over to Lincoln and pulled him close. A colossal chunk of flying metal passed over. The span of its body almost low enough to jump up and grab hold. The ground shook as the behemoth dipped low and adjusted its arrival in the old man's backyard. A C-17 Globemaster had just touched down in the field behind the crumbling iron-brick home.

> 0830hrs
> Thursday December 20, 2012
> Somewhere between Perth and Margaret River, Western Australia

The man noted Mackay's tactical dress then looked back towards his home.

'Somebody's special,' he said. 'Looks like you got friends in high places, son. If that bird's for me, either I've done something really bad, or really good.' He turned to Lincoln, sitting next to him with one hand on Mackay's chest, willing it to keep rising and falling.

'Suppose you're a bit young and small to give me a hand carrying him?'

Lincoln said nothing.

The man stood and hauled Mackay over his shoulder, which, for a man his age was impressive. Obviously, a farmer or rancher of some description. Decades of experience working the land and grappling livestock. Wrangling and tossing them on the backs of trucks and pickups.

'But you can carry the water bottle,' he said. 'Maybe we'll meet them halfway.'

Lincoln grabbed the bottle and followed his uncle's lifeless body hanging over the dark farmer's shoulder, moving back towards the abandoned fuel station. At the same time, a unit of six soldiers were moving their way towards their position from the other side. From where the Globemaster had landed. All wore a uniform of colours. Multi-terrain field patterns: khaki, brown, olive drab. Military garb. Australian Army. Of the six, only one soldier was armed: the one out front. The scout. A tough, Asian-looking guy with the face of an assassin. He held an F88 Austeyr rifle, standard Australian issue. His name badge wasn't visible, but from appearance alone he was of either Korean or Japanese origin.

A scout position with a rifle in front of a moving team was a standard manoeuvre, namely for precautionary reasons. The enemy situation amid an outback environment was low, but when you don't know your terrain, be prepared. The four soldiers behind him worked together carrying a stretcher, while the soldier at the rear moved without restrictions. Freely mobile.

A familiar face, if only Mackay was conscious enough to see it. A Special Forces operator. A friend of a friend. Corporal Nuttal.

Once they met up and the stretcher was grounded, Mackay's body was lowered and secured. Nutty hauled Lincoln into his arms and ordered everyone to double back to the aircraft – including the old man. The team, working quickly and efficiently, hustled Mackay's body up the lowered cargo ramp and into the idling monolith.

'How is he?' asked another familiar voice, rolling her wheelchair alongside the men as they rushed Mackay inside.

'Alive, but barely,' said one soldier. Another Asian. Tall and wiry. Same height as Nutty, only a quarter of the width. The name Kitano was stitched above his breast pocket. Japanese origin. He had two diamonds etched on his epaulette – a lieutenant. Obviously, the medic in charge.

'He's breathing, but he's burning,' Kitano said. 'Never felt any soldier this hot.'

'Holy shit, he found the boy,' said Cross, turning to see Nutty enter from the ramp with Lincoln curled tight against his chest. Nutty nodded back. The reality of the situation was unprecedented. Lincoln's presence alongside Mackay in the West Australian outback exposed yet another layer to Mackay's abilities.

The soldiers – all medics – started cutting at Mackay's shirt and stripping him down. They worked fast, like a well-oiled machine, transferring Mackay's body onto a large operating stretcher raised on a trolley, kitted with all the bells and whistles of hospital-grade care.

'Sir,' shouted Cross from the cargo ramp. She wheeled herself toward the dark-skinned man walking in behind Nutty. The man seemed awkwardly out of place. Unsure where to be or what to do, only that he was there as Mackay's first responder. Staying out of a personal respect. Seeing through his service for the casualty to full safety and care.

'You were with my guy on the ground as we flew over,' said Cross, upping her volume over the whining engines kicking back in.

'Yes, miss,' said the man. 'The boy there turned up to my home, looking for water. Took me to the man's body, unconscious, hot as an oven. I started giving him water but then this flew over.'

'Was there any abandoned vehicle nearby?' said Cross.

'No, miss, just the boy.'

'Any tyre tracks?'

'Not that I could see. Didn't do a wide enough search. Just some clumsy footprints. Nobody comes out this way unless by helicopter, camel or four-wheel-drive. It was as if the earth had spat him out.'

Cross turned back to Nutty. 'You saw it,' she said. 'Tracking his GPS. Moving and winding off-road like a dune buggy. But he wasn't driving anything. We tracked him at over fifty kilometres an hour for over two hours. Carrying the boy. What the fuck else is he capable of?'

Nutty couldn't respond.

'Was he wearing a backpack?' Cross asked the man.

'No, ma'am.'

Cross turned to Nutty. 'Means his meds only lasted him two or so hours, or they'd emptied from his system beforehand.'

Half angry, half terrified, Cross wheeled herself next to Mackay's perishing form as the medics began inserting half a dozen needles into his arms, neck and stomach. The nest of tubes were all connected to IV bags pegged on hangars either side of his body, transferring clear saline. Two more needles flowing from turquoise and honey-coloured bags were also jammed between the thermoplastic ridges of his enlarged ribcage.

The Japanese lieutenant took a syringe the size of a Thermos, filled the barrel from a blue vile and stabbed it down with force, just off-centre of Mackay's sternum.

Cross shot him a hard glance.

Mackay didn't flinch. His body contracted, stiffened for a moment, then relaxed again. Aside from the tubes in his nose and throat, he looked sound asleep.

'Don't worry,' said Kitano. 'This will settle him, not wake him. A heart reset if you will. Cools everything down and slows his vitals. I've never seen a temperature that high on any human in my life. I'm surprised he made it this far.'

Cross looked over at a temperature monitor on the screen behind Mackay's head. It read fifty-four degrees Celsius. The highest core temperature ever recorded on a human body was forty-six. Willie Jones, a middle-aged guy suffering heatstroke in 1980. The human body can barely withstand anything over forty degrees before cardiac arrest starts shutting things down. Mackay was still holding on at eight degrees higher than the record limit. The only two questions were, would he wake up, and if he did, would his brain be affected? Had his brain coped with the excessive heat stress, or was it fried off like liver in a pan?

'The more he moves, the worse he'll become,' said Kitano. 'Captain Andersen's orders are for complete sedation.'

'How long will he stay unconscious?' asked Nutty.

'Hard to know. At this stage I'm not even sure he'll wake up. Never worked on a patient with his... unique condition. Or anyone in this particular state either. His body and vitals look worse than what we've learned from any Holocaust survivor or Vietnam POW. He looks like he's been tortured for weeks.'

Cross looked over Mackay's body, at the tubes pouring out everywhere. A large part of her simply thankful his chest was still rising and falling. She wheeled in close to him and ran her fingers down his arm and knuckles, then folded them in between his.

'His brain, it's surely cooked,' Cross lamented. 'Is there nothing else we can do?' She turned to the lieutenant.

Kitano shook his head. 'We don't have the right treatment for whatever's inside him here. Realistically, nobody can survive what he put himself through. But if he's survived this far, based on what Captain Andersen has informed me of, who knows. It's out of my control. Pray the worst has passed and hope for the best. Keeping his body going is the priority.'

'Captain Andersen is in Aldershot,' said Nutty. 'That's over eighteen hours of flight time. Without the right treatment how can you be sure he'll even last that long? His body is one thing, but his mind is more important in my opinion.'

'Your rank has no opinion, Corporal,' said Kitano firmly. 'And we're not going to Aldershot. Andersen's been relocated to Tokyo, which is where we're going. Ten hours flight time. Better than eighteen.'

0900hrs
Thursday December 20, 2012
Somewhere between Perth and Margaret River, Western Australia

Lieutenant Kitano took a step back, as did another soldier, the lead scout from the initial rescue. Still holding the F88 Austeyr. Thirty in the clip, one in the chamber. Plenty to go around for everyone. He raised it at the group working on Mackay and lined himself up next to the lieutenant. The mood turned. The medics all made numerous sideways glances, first at each other, then at Cross, then at Nutty. Nutty, still holding Lincoln, went for his sidearm with his free right hand, but the lieutenant was ahead of him. A Browning Hi-Power 9mm appeared from under his shirt. He aimed high first, shooting Nutty in the shoulder, then dropped the barrel low and blew one through his thigh, the slugs tearing through the right deltoid and meaty flesh of the upper leg. Tearing away sections of rotator cuff, meniscus, tendons and bone. All key functional constructs of the body, eliminating any desire Nutty might have to draw again and retaliate.

Lincoln screamed in fright as Nutty dropped in a heap. His cry accentuating the initial clap of the gun, both sounds rebounding off the aircraft's internal skeleton. The team of medics all lifted their hands and stepped away in a wide semicircle, arcing around the machines and IV stands around Mackay.

'You stupid little cunt,' said Cross, reeling herself forward at the officer. Her instinct to fight splitting like an atom. 'He's still holding the boy for fuck's sake!'

'Easy there, stumps,' said Kitano, reversing his aim back at Cross, still keeping his full attention on Nutty. Cross pulled herself up just out of arm's reach of the Browning.

'You, Renee, I actually don't need. So, I've got no issue with putting you down if it comes to it. If you feel like being reckless. A cripple without any qualified aircraft skills is of no use to me. You're basically a waste of time here.'

The lieutenant switched aim and position, directing the barrel at Nutty's head. He then stepped behind him and Lincoln for a better view of everyone. For a wider arc of vision across the fuselage; Mackay and the team of medics on his left, the dark-skinned man near the cargo ramp on his right.

'As for him,' said the lieutenant waving his gun at Nutty, 'he is useful. And don't worry, a bit of metal in the shoulder and leg never hurt anybody. I'm sure he's had worse. I just needed him out of the picture. You know how it works, most competent soldier down first.'

Nobody said a word. Hands were raised and pulses were high. It was stalemate for everyone.

'And, Corporal,' Kitano continued, eyeing Nutty's hand for any sudden movement, 'I'd like that sidearm too, thanks. Slow and smooth. Two fingers.'

Nutty eased Lincoln to the floor beside him, Lincoln however, didn't release his grip. He kept clawing his fingers into Nutty's jacket, burying his head into his torso for security and comfort.

With two fingers, Nutty slowly removed his own Browning attached to the holster on his leg. He tossed it over to the lieutenant who picked it up with his spare hand, then swung its aim across the fuselage – locating their guest standing at the rear of the bay. With a gun in each fist, one steady at Nutty's head, the other at the old man's chest, the lieutenant had a strong case as the man in charge.

'You're in this too,' said Kitano, directing his attention to the visitor. 'What you've seen and been part of here, is unfortunately highly classified and very, very expensive. Can't have you running around out there telling any of your clansmen, which means you're staying. I need you over there with the cripple.'

The lieutenant waved his gun, ushering the man to move towards Cross and the rest of the group.

'Hear no evil see no evil,' said the man. 'All my people moved off long ago. It's just me, the trees and the wildlife. I'll tell nobody. Be gone like a breeze.'

'Wrong place and wrong time for you,' said Kitano, raising his aim at the man's head. 'You're in a difficult, unfair position, and I'm sorry. Nothing personal. We appreciate your help, but the situation on that stretcher is of bigger concern and interest than any of us here. With all things considered, if you don't play by the rules, it's your life, so move.'

The man didn't budge. He eyed the ramp's edge and angle, his thought processes considering whether to chance a bullet or run back and jump out. His lack of response was too long for Kitano, so the lieutenant made his decision for him, letting off two rounds near his head. Warning shots. Hitting air, or a tree or a giant ant hill beyond the rear of the craft. Enough to scare the man to take three steps forward and join the rest of the group.

The soldier with the rifle, the one without a name and obviously second in command, pulled a two-way transceiver radio from his pocket. 'Raise the ramp, we're good to go,' he said. And they did. Whoever was in the cockpit was on the same team.

'Let's just say the man on the stretcher is the cat we let out of the bag,' said Kitano. 'Deliberately let loose but constantly monitored. Curious to see how he'd perform. A test of new technology if you will.'

'A test?' said Cross. 'For the fucking Japanese military?'

The aircraft started to move.

'We're working to a different scale now,' Kitano went on. 'He's worth a lot of money to some very important people. There's a turning point coming for the Japanese soldier. For our new military machine. The bureaucratic powers want to get back to their pre-World War Two roots. Back to being a dominant force.'

'They want super-soldiers,' said Nutty sitting down holding Lincoln, his left hand pressed hard into his right shoulder.

'Correct,' said Kitano. 'If this gets out it would be an international circus. A nightmare for both military and civilian sectors the world over. We can't let that happen. Your boy needs to be locked down without any leaks. He's a prized subject for one country alone. For decades we have lost our pride and given away our honour. All for materialism and commercialism. Cowering from the likes of America, China and Russia. Our strength and ability to perform on a global scale is weak. We must return Japan to its former strength, then exceed it.'

The lieutenant pointed his weapon at Mackay as the aircraft aligned itself on the flat strip of land.

'With what that man has demonstrated, we can provide a new capability for our forces. Outperform any other military power and bring Japan back to being a real, prevailing world leader.'

'The leaks are already out,' said Cross. 'He was witnessed by dozens running at suburban road speeds back in England.'

The air flowing through the engines hit another gear. The whine intensifying like a thousand musicians playing the same note. The mechanical thrusters from the engine pulled in tonnes of litres of air and pushed the colossal structure across the outback at increasing speed.

'That's been taken care of,' said Kitano. 'All eyewitnesses to that incident have already been brought in for questioning and silenced. Now go take a seat, we're about to take off.'

'Relocated or abducted?' said Cross, studying him indignantly.

'What's that?' said Kitano.

'Captain Andersen, you fucking retard. You said he's been relocated to Tokyo. Or was he taken by force?'

Kitano smiled, lingering on Cross's hungry silence for answers.

'Neither,' he said. 'He's running this show.'

ACKNOWLEDGEMENTS

Thank you to those who have made this book possible: Darryn Swaby and my father, John, who helped with character improvements and finding any inconsistencies in the story.

To the friendships created at both Greenbank and Bullecourt Barracks, training with you truly helped this story come alive.

Derek Austin, your enthusiasm for the narrative really pushed me to keep writing.

Dominique Hourez, for helping me with continuity errors and making valuable editorial amendments.

Daniel Jurin, your efforts and thoughtfulness played a big part in the finished product.

And to my wife, Lisa. For giving me the time to write through our busyness in parenting. We make a good team.